# HELL *or* HIGH WATER

## BETH BOLDEN

Earl Gray Publishing LLC

www.bethbolden.com

beth@bethbolden.com

Publisher's Note: This is a work of fiction. Names, characters, places, and incidents are a product of the author's imagination. Locales and public names are sometimes used for atmospheric purposes. Any resemblance to actual people, living or dead, or to businesses, companies, events, institutions, or locales is completely coincidental.

Book Layout © 2025 Beth Bolden

Book Cover © 2025 Ozark Witch Cover Design

Photography © J. Ashley Converse Photography

Model Joel Ros

The people in the images are models and should not be connected to the characters in the book. Any resemblance is incidental.

Ordering Information:

Quantity sales. Special discounts are available on quantity purchases by corporations, associations, and others. For details, contact Beth Bolden at the address above.

Hell or High Water/ Beth Bolden. -- 1st ed.

# AUTHOR NOTE

*Hell or High Water* and the Toronto Thunder series take place in the wider Beth Bolden universe: a universe that is more inclusive and welcoming than our own.

In Beth-world, the first professional athlete to come out of the closet was Colin O'Connor (*The Rainbow Clause)*, and after this happened, approximately ten years ago, there have been numerous players, coaches, and even owners who are living their best queer lives freely.

# CHAPTER 1



*June*

The guy was hot.

He moved through the crowd at the bar with a confidence that said he knew it too. Knew everyone was watching him and he'd long since made his peace with that fact.

Nate hadn't come out to the bar looking for a hookup, and even if he was into the hottest guy he might've ever seen, he had a feeling there'd be a line out the door for a shot in his bed.

Nate wasn't into sharing. Might've at some point been into the casual hookup scene, but he was tired of putting guys into his phone as "big dick" and "even bigger dick" with no names to be found.

He wasn't sure the whole marriage-white picket fence-happily-ever-after thing was for him either, but he thought maybe this year he could find some sort of happy medium. Something straddling the line between "big dick" and "monogrammed towels."

And yeah, this guy, he was definitely more the former than the latter. Slid through the crowd like a hot knife through butter, gaze assessing even as he kept his expression blank, like he was allergic to giving himself away.

A guy who'd never give a thing away.

Nate would never even get his number to put in his phone as "hottest guy with the biggest dick."

But even if he didn't, that didn't mean Nate couldn't look.

Lane, a tight end and one of Nate's best friends on the Thunder, had said he was coming out too, but then he'd bailed at the last minute, even when Nate had gone out of his way to mention that Trevor, Lane's younger stepbrother, new to Toronto and to the team, would be welcome.

Lane had ended up blowing him off, claiming he had a hookup, but Nate had a feeling if he headed over to the apartment he was now sharing with Trev, he'd catch them drinking beer and playing *Call of Duty*, badly.

Nate had nothing else going on, so he sipped his beer and watched as the bartender flirted with the hot guy. Then poured him a drink.

Hot Guy just shrugged, casually, easily blowing him off. Doing it in such a way that Nate was fascinated, because he was pretty sure the bartender hadn't even realized it had happened.

A girl approached him next, and she barely got a second glance.

The bar wasn't full despite it being a Thursday. After Nate finished his beer, he didn't worry about losing his table when he went to take a piss.

Sure enough, when he returned from the bathroom, his table was unoccupied.

Well. No. That wasn't quite true either.

There was a fresh beer there, right at the spot where Nate had been sitting and a man in the barstool across. Not just any guy. *The* guy.

Nate hesitated. Maybe he was reading the situation wrong.

But then hot guy glanced up, meeting Nate's eyes, and tilted his head towards the beer.

Nate hadn't even realized that Hot Guy had noticed him.

He swallowed hard, reminded himself that he wasn't really interested, even as his heart beat a little faster, and made his way over to the table.

"Hey," the guy said. "I got you a beer." He waved over towards the bar casually. "Nicky said this was what you were drinking."

Nate didn't know which part of this whole thing was taking him out more—that this guy had come over here, clearly planning it, and yet acting like it was all just casually accidental, or that, up close, he wasn't hot after all.

He was beautiful.

Blond curls, tousled all over his head. Eyes that turned out to be an unearthly light blue. A face that wouldn't have been out of place in one of those ridiculous perfume commercials he'd tried not to get off to when he was a pimply thirteen-year-old. And the body? He had broad shoulders, filling out his plain white T-shirt, and a narrow waist. Tanned biceps and forearms that made it clear he knew his way around a weight room.

Nate reached out for the beer and took a sip, despite that he almost never took drinks from strangers.

"Yeah," Nate agreed, mouth suddenly very dry despite the beer. He *had* game. Hardly a slouch himself, plus he was fairly well known in this town, even though this was only his second year on the Thunder.

Had this guy come over because he thought Nate was an easy mark? Rich and famous?

Beautiful guy smiled, even white teeth flashing in his mouth. He was a little less startlingly gorgeous when he flashed them. It made him look more real, less like an underwear model on a gigantic billboard.

"I'm Ramsey," he said. He didn't extend his hand, and Nate didn't go to shake it.

"Nate," he returned, though he was about eighty percent sure the guy had clocked him and had come over here with a free beer only because he was Nate Bishop, defensive end and captain of the Toronto Thunder.

That was annoying, for sure, but Nate would be lying if he said he wasn't used to it.

"You don't sound very Canadian," Ramsey said, who didn't sound very Canadian either.

Nate didn't do a double take, but he wanted to. Was it possible . . .was it *possible* this guy hadn't recognized him?

"You don't either," Nate countered.

He *was* sure guys probably saw Ramsey sauntering over in their direction and fell to their knees, slobbering all over themselves for even a chance to touch his hand.

But that wasn't Nate's style. Never had been. Hot was great and all, but he liked a guy with a little substance to him. Even if all that substance ended up being was saved as "big dick" in his phone.

"Nope," Ramsey said. "From all over, really. Spent some time in the Pacific Northwest. Now I'm in Buffalo."

"This isn't Buffalo."

"Hot *and* smart," Ramsey said with a smirk.

Nate shot him a look full of disbelief. He was good-looking, sure, but there were far more attractive people at this bar, Ramsey included.

Ramsey just shrugged, like he knew all of what had just flashed through Nate's mind. "You've got a nice face."

"Okay, sure," Nate said, laughing now. "You gonna tell me what you're doing in Toronto?"

"You actually want me to?" Ramsey asked.

Nate also hated the pointless exercise of small talk. He'd never been good at it. Probably one of the reasons he was done with the hookup lifestyle. Going through the motions of looking interested in something more than a guy's dick when he wasn't, at all, seemed pointless. Like a waste of everyone's time.

"Not really, actually," Nate admitted.

The smirk on Ramsey's face deepened, like he enjoyed catching Nate in that little morsel of tasty honesty.

"I wasn't going to tell you anyway," Ramsey said.

"What lie were you going to tell me?" Nate wondered.

Ramsey's eyes lit up, genuine interest there now. Before, he'd been at least a little honest, but maybe more playing a part than anything else.

Nate's heart quickened. He shouldn't care if this was more than just two bodies in the dark, especially when one of the bodies looked like that, but he *did*.

"Hmm, that's an interesting question. Businessman up here for work?" Ramsey suggested, and Nate shook his head.

"You can do better than that," Nate challenged.

"Maybe I'm up here to cheat on my wife," Ramsey offered.

"Your wife?" Nate asked in disbelief. "You barely noticed that girl who tried to hit on you. Am I supposed to buy the story that you cared enough about a woman to marry her?" He paused, glancing down at Ramsey's hands. They were bare, but well-formed. Ghosts of callouses visible in the dim light of the bar. "Plus, no ring line."

"Caught me again."

"I sure did."

"How about, I'm in the city to do research?"

"For what?"

"Thinking about buying a business here," Ramsey said.

"What kind of business? You want me to buy your story, you gotta offer a few details."

"He's a tough critic," Ramsey observed, grinning. He sounded delighted. Nate was trying to feel less delighted by this fact.

This guy wasn't anyone's happily-ever-after.

But Nate was having a good time. And there was the added bonus of getting to look at him a little longer.

"You're telling me you're not capable of doing any better?" Nate wondered. But he knew the answer to his question before he even asked it. Undoubtedly Ramsey was used to getting by on his drop-dead looks. But he was smart too. That much was obvious, if you were paying any attention at all.

And Nate sure was.

"A bar. Considering buying into a bar. Cool place."

"Not this bar then," Nate joked.

"Nope. Not this bar. Maybe I'm doing some research, scoping out the competition."

"Trying to lure the bartender away?"

Ramsey chuckled deeply and it pulled, sickly sweet, at the feeling at the base of Nate's stomach. This guy was trouble.

Nate should walk away.

"You assume I could. Maybe Nicky likes working here, working the crowd, a bit."

"He tried to work you," Nate said.

Ramsey didn't look even the tiniest bit sorry about this. There was only frank acceptance in his expression. "Yeah."

"So are you gonna invest in this bar?" Nate asked.

"Jury's still out," Ramsey said. "I like the concept. It's solid. Business plan's good. But I wanna be a little more hands-on, and I'm not sure ownership would be into that."

"Why?"

"Why are they against it?"

"Why do you want to be?" Nate shouldn't find Ramsey fascinating. Or, maybe he *should*. Maybe he'd have to be dead not to find this guy fascinating. The problem was more extricating himself before fascination was all he felt.

Before he built a castle in the sky he'd be alone in once morning hit.

"Ah, well. Kind of at a loose end at the moment." Ramsey fluttered his eyelashes. "How was that?"

"Pretty good. Decent enough."

Ramsey pouted, which shouldn't have been attractive, but with his face and his lips and his eyes, he could do anything he wanted and still make it attractive.

Nate wondered if that was ever a curse, or Ramsey only saw it as a blessing.

"How about this one?" Ramsey said. "I'm a professional athlete."

Nate tensed. Maybe Ramsey knew what he was, after all. But he forced the tension out of his shoulders. "Yeah? Which sport? Professional eyelash batting?"

"Hey," Ramsey retorted without much heat.

"Which sport?" Nate asked again.

If Ramsey said football, then he knew.

But Ramsey didn't say football. "Hockey," he said instead. "I'm a hockey player. Up here for summer training. With uh . . .McDavid. And um. Auston Matthews."

Nate shot him a pitying look. "Auston Matthews? He doesn't train here, you idiot. He's from Arizona." He wasn't going to tell Ramsey this, but he'd met the captain of the Toronto Maple Leafs a handful of times. Once on the sideline at a game. Another time at a club. Once, in passing, at a restaurant. He was a solid dude, and most definitely did not train here in the summers.

If he told Ramsey that, though, he'd reveal his own lies.

"Right, okay." Ramsey looked bashful. It didn't sit right on him. "Not Auston Matthews. Uh, how about Elliott Jones?"

"Their new forward? You're training with him?"

"Gotta keep up with the new blood."

"Yes, and you're Willy Nylander's dog sitter, too."

"Guess the hockey player wasn't very convincing either," Ramsey admitted, shrugging.

"Neither of them were very good," Nate said. "But I'll give you credit for trying, at least."

It wasn't surprising when Ramsey challenged him back. Nate hadn't sensed he was the kind of guy who took a loss for very long. "Well, what are *you* doing in Toronto?" Ramsey asked.

Obviously, Nate couldn't tell him the truth, but he'd never wanted to be anything else, other than what he was. Even worse, he was a shitty liar, with a distinct lack of creative flair.

He went with the very first thing his mind grasped. "I'm a manager at Tim Horton's."

Ramsey shot him a look. His eyes lingered, up and down Nate's clearly athletic form. "Seriously?"

"I don't eat very many of the donuts?"

"They must pay Tim Horton's employees more than I expect." Ramsey's gaze drifted down, to the watch on Nate's wrist. And yeah, it was a Rolex. Whoops.

If Ramsey had noticed that, maybe he really *was* over here because he'd scoped Nate out as an easy, rich mark.

"Uh, I manage a whole bunch of Tim Horton's?"

Ramsey laughed. "Committed to the role. I like it."

"Yeah?" Nate leaned in. "What else do you like?"

An alarm bell was clanking noisily in the back of his mind, but Ramsey looked even better up close. Flecks of gray and darker blue in his eyes. The faintest hint of blond stubble along his flawless jawline. His hair looked impossibly soft, and Nate's fingers itched to bury themselves in it.

"Thought that was pretty fucking obvious," Ramsey teased.

"Still wondering what your angle is." It was the most honest Nate had been, but he couldn't keep the confession in.

"Maybe I'm just, what was it you said? A professional eyelash-batter."

Nate didn't know much, but he knew that Ramsey wasn't. He was too smart for something as simple as grift. Relieving grateful marks of their valuables would be tedious for him.

Of course, that didn't mean he was willing to hand his Rolex over either.

"Nah," Nate said. "You'd get bored in a minute."

"That's it, right there." Ramsey said it casually, but there was the ring of truth there, lingering between his words and in his intent blue eyes.

"What?"

"Why I'm over here. I saw you watching me, and saw you look right through me."

"Doesn't happen very often?"

"Almost never." Ramsey paused. "Happened only once, actually."

"How come you're not with him then?" It was a guess, but Nate figured it was a pretty good one.

Ramsey hummed under his breath. Took a long sip of his drink. "Who says it's a he?"

"Come on," Nate said, rolling his eyes. "Again, you barely noticed that girl."

"Fair. But that doesn't mean I'm into whoever it was."

Nate flicked his eyes up and down Ramsey's delectable form in the most obvious way since he'd first spotted him. "You're joking, right? You're the type who absolutely wants to fuck what he can't understand."

Ramsey didn't answer immediately. Traced the edge of his glass with a fingertip. Nate was pretty sure that was calculated too, to drag his attention from what he'd asked to the way Ramsey's hands looked. Ramsey was probably hoping he'd get distracted, thinking about those hands on him, later, in some dark room, and forget what he'd said.

It was damn tempting.

But what Ramsey hadn't counted on was that figuring out what was going on behind those gorgeous eyes was just as intriguing to Nate as the eyes themselves.

"It wasn't just one guy—it was two. A couple. And no, I didn't fuck them." He made a face. "I did try though."

"Ouch," Nate said, and Ramsey shot him a hot look.

"It gonna end the same way tonight?" Ramsey asked.

"I don't know," Nate said. More honesty. Maybe that was Ramsey's real superpower—not the eyelash batting, but being a particularly heady dose of truth serum.

"You don't know?" Ramsey raised an eyebrow, like he could barely believe it. And that was probably true. Nate could assume that rejections came few and far between for this guy, especially when he put the effort in.

But Nate still wasn't sure he wanted to know what Ramsey's naked skin felt like against his, especially when it was obvious it was going to be a one-and-done type of situation. He didn't need to be haunted for weeks or months or years after by someone he couldn't have.

Someone who wouldn't even be in his phone as a nuclear option to hit when the longing got too out of hand.

"I don't know," Nate repeated.

Ramsey sighed. "Let me guess, you're the kind of guy looking for someone who sticks around. Who calls two days later. Who goes on dates. Who you can take home to meet your parents."

"At least one of those," Nate admitted. He wasn't going to apologize for wanting more. Not necessarily out of Ramsey, but out of *anyone*.

"I'll tell you, when I clocked you checking me out, I didn't imagine you were the type to have a meet-the-parents kink."

Nate chuckled. "It's kind of unfair, don't you think?"

"What's unfair? You wanting to drag me behind your white picket fence? It absolutely is."

Part of him didn't want to give Ramsey the satisfaction, but it was impossible to stifle his laughter. He didn't even *want* to.

"No, you looking like that, and then being smart *and* funny. You ever think about using your powers for evil?"

"All the fucking time, baby," Ramsey joked.

"Not surprising."

"Not doing it now, unless trying to convince you to leave with me is evil." Ramsey stared at him, like he *did* have mind control powers.

Nate could feel his heartbeat in the tips of his fingers. The energy between them crackled, not just with sex, but with a hazy kind of possibility. Possibilities that wouldn't ever come to fruition, but then the chemistry between them didn't know that.

He could always start his search for his boyfriend tomorrow. Enjoy one last night of what promised to be really great sex.

Ramsey leaned in more. "Come on," he murmured, his pink tongue peeking out from between even pinker lips. It was unfair. Even playing dirty. Nate should feel gratified that Ramsey was pulling out all the stops to convince him, but he wasn't.

He was only frustrated.

Because Ramsey wasn't a normal kind of hookup. He was that kind of guy you talked about years later, when you'd had one too many beers and you got maudlin and sentimental. *Wish I could've had more than one night,* he could imagine saying. Could imagine, too, the memory ruining him for anyone else.

"To be clear, you're not going to want me to call you tomorrow."

"Baby, you're not even going to be able to call me tomorrow." Ramsey actually smiled, like he knew what a boon that was. Like Nate was like all the other guys who were looking for hot anonymous sex and not for any kind of strings.

It was the first thing Ramsey had fucked up since he'd appropriated Nate's table and brought him a beer.

"Sorry, then, no."

Ramsey's smile didn't waver. Not exactly. It just got more forced. More artificially charming. Nate wondered, before he cut the thought off hard and fast, if that was the kind of smile the *other* guys got. If this was Ramsey's normal mask, and maybe Nate had seen behind it. If he'd been one of a very select few. The exception that proved the rule.

But if he thought like that, then Nate might change his mind, and he wasn't going to.

"You're serious," Ramsey said flatly.

"Yeah," Nate said.

"You already have a boyfriend," Ramsey guessed.

Nate shook his head.

"Ah, you *want* a boyfriend. And I'm . . ." Ramsey waved up and down his body. "I'm going to fuck that up."

"Something like that."

Ramsey sighed. "What if I told you a boyfriend was overrated?"

"Like you know anything about that," Nate said. He wasn't going to say it—that might be more honesty than Ramsey deserved—but it came out anyway, thanks to the frustration, sexual and otherwise, curdling in the base of his stomach.

"Not me, but . . .yeah. It is. Boyfriends fuck you up." Ramsey had the nerve to look sincere about this confession.

"And you wouldn't?"

"But the trip would be so good." Ramsey slid around the table, and Nate stupidly didn't take a step back. Couldn't get his feet to move. "We'd have so much fun. All night long. I want to pull you apart. See what makes you tick. Turn you inside out."

There wasn't anything particularly interesting in Nate's innards. But he didn't say that. Instead he said something much stupider. "Would you let me see, too?"

Ramsey tilted his head. "What makes you think you don't already see?"

"I'd want to see it all."

Nate could imagine them lying next to each other, Ramsey's head pillowed on his chest, blue eyes sleepy and languorous, all his truths laid bare. It was the most appealing image yet, and Ramsey had been nearly irresistible from the first moment.

*Nearly.*

Ramsey drummed his fingers on the table. Looked away. Like he was afraid Nate already saw. "I don't do that," he said quietly.

"I know," Nate said. He'd never be able to parse the truth from the lies. Not all of them, and he'd drive himself crazy trying to untangle them.

"I don't like this," Ramsey said, a little bitterly.

"You could always go back to the bartender." But Nate would leave, before he had to witness that.

"He was *easy*." Ramsey was scornful.

"That what I am, a challenge?"

Ramsey touched him for the first time. Curled his fingers around Nate's forearm. He felt the crackle spark. Couldn't not imagine what it would be like, if they were naked and pressed together. "Something like that," he murmured.

Maybe if Nate was challenging enough, Ramsey would stick around for a second night. A third. A fourth.

But Nate knew he wasn't that challenging, underneath. When Ramsey excavated him, he wouldn't find anything special. Nothing particularly unique worth sticking around for. Ramsey just wasn't used to being seen through. Didn't like being told no.

"Ramsey," Nate said quietly.

Ramsey let go of him.

"Gonna think about that for awhile," he said. Paused. "You saying my name, like that." There was heat in his eyes when he lifted them to meet Nate's. Nate knew exactly what circumstances he'd be thinking about it under.

Every inch of Nate's body throbbed. He wanted to give in. Wanted to tell Ramsey that he'd changed his mind—but that was exactly what Ramsey was after. He was scrappy. Desperate.

Nate wondered what else Ramsey would try, just before Ramsey slid even closer, right under his guard, his palms landing on Nate's chest.

Letting out a shaky exhale, Nate almost pushed him off, but truthfully that was the last thing he wanted. Ramsey felt like pure fucking heaven pressed against him.

Then he tilted his head, all the warning Nate got, before Ramsey murmured, "Gonna be thinking about this, too."

Ramsey kissed him.

If Nate had guessed how Ramsey might go in, it would be slow and seductive. Calculated. A kiss designed to wear down Nate's barriers. To make him wild about it, all while staying removed and in total control of the situation.

But he would've been wrong, because Ramsey threw himself into it. It wasn't smooth or sweet. It was wild and uninhibited. Like Ramsey believed this was his last chance to find out how Nate tasted.

Ramsey's tongue in his mouth didn't feel like a tactic, it felt like a plea.

And it was easy, so fucking easy, to give in to it. To give Ramsey what he wanted, and to take it back.

Ramsey's mouth lush against his own, their bodies pressed together.

It was an even better kiss for all those reasons. The kind of kiss Nate *would* think of later, and even later, and far later still.

Ramsey groaned at the back of his throat, tilting his head to get even deeper, fingers digging into Nate's shoulders. There was an unexpected strength in him, a well of determination that belied his pretty boy looks, and Nate, who already liked him too much, liked him even more because of it.

Tearing his mouth away from Nate's, Ramsey looked away, chest rising and falling with his ragged breaths.

Nate couldn't catch his either.

His grip tightened on Ramsey's waist. Ramsey might be strong, but Nate had a feeling he was stronger.

Except in this moment, when every part of him had gone weak.

"I shouldn't have done that," Ramsey said, over Nate's shoulder.

That was all the warning Nate had before he shucked Nate's embrace and took off.

Not even looking back.

Nate's mouth dropped, the taste of Ramsey still thick on his tongue, and he stared at his blond head as it disappeared out the door.

There was only a handful of seconds to rethink. To rethink *and* to decide.

But was it even a decision? Nate was beginning to think it wasn't.

That the chess match between them hadn't even started until *after* the kiss.

He abandoned his half-finished beer on the table and took off. He was out the front door in seconds and glanced wildly back and forth on the street. It was a warm summer evening, the sidewalk full of people. But he spotted Ramsey's blond head, halfway down the block.

Ramsey couldn't catch his breath.

It came in short fits and pants as he strode down the street. He didn't even think this was the right way to Wes' building, but it didn't matter. He just needed to get away. To try to gain his normal composure.

He shouldn't have kissed Nate. And he definitely shouldn't have fucking *admitted* to Nate that it had been a mistake. That was exposing, in a way that Ramsey hadn't been in ages.

He should've stayed away.

The last time this had happened should have been a cautionary tale.

But Ramsey had been bored, and boredom was always the enemy.

Out of nowhere, a hand gripped his shoulder and he whirled around, ready to tell whoever had just grabbed him to fuck off, when he realized, a second before a softer touch cupped his cheek, it wasn't a stranger.

It was Nate.

He hadn't wanted Nate to come after him. That hadn't been why he'd run away. He'd run away because . . .well, for a lot of complicated reasons.

But Nate had come after him, anyway.

That was all the thought Ramsey got before Nate was kissing him.

People flowed around them, but Ramsey barely registered them. It was just Nate, his big body, warm and real, pressed against him. Mouth on his, like the deeper he kissed Ramsey, the deeper he could insert himself into Ramsey's world.

Ramsey was rarely interested in letting anyone even try. Rarely interested beyond a cursory and often ultimately unsatisfying exploration in the other direction.

But Nate intrigued.

They broke apart.

Ramsey's breath came in shuddering pants.

It was the kiss. It was something else too, a feeling he'd only brushed up against a handful of times in the last ten years. It was terrifying, but it made him feel alive, too, and that was hard to resist, especially these days.

"I changed my mind," Nate said quietly, the seriousness in his dark eyes making that very clear.

Ramsey considered telling Nate that he hadn't. Because he didn't think Nate really had. Nate was just hoping, despite everything they'd said to each other, that Ramsey didn't really mean it. That with more time, with a whole night, he might be able to change Ramsey's mind.

Ramsey could call him on it. Could tell him the truth that Ramsey could see so clearly lurking in his expression. All that painfully earnest hope.

By this point, Ramsey should have found it unappealing. He normally would. But he didn't. Not today.

"I didn't change mine," Ramsey said steadily. He didn't add, *and I'm not going to*, because he thought that was pretty damn clear.

But Nate only nodded in agreement, accepting, at least at face value, what Ramsey was offering. "My place is only a few blocks away," he said.

It was definitely not the first time he'd gone over to a guy's place, and it wouldn't be the last. No question—Ramsey knew how to do this. How to be normal about it.

But his pulse was beating faster as Nate took them to one of the apartment buildings dotting the waterfront. It was one of the nicer buildings, and after seeing the Rolex on Nate's wrist, Ramsey wasn't particularly surprised when he hit the button for the second highest floor.

The guy wasn't managing Tim Horton's, that was for sure.

But when they got to Nate's door, he didn't turn any lights on, let Ramsey see just what kind of view several million bucks bought him.

Ramsey opened his mouth to lightly bitch about that, but before he could, Nate was on him, pressing him to the nearest wall, tongue in his mouth and hands tangled in his hair.

Someone groaned—Ramsey thought it might have been Nate, but it also could've been him. He was wound up—wound *tight,* in fact, too many nights spent hanging out with Wes at his place. Maybe that was why Nate had appealed so much that Ramsey had broken one of his personal guidelines and had approached *him*, not even bothering to wait to see if Nate would come up to him.

But then Nate slid a hand down, over his ass, and lifted him up, with what seemed like barely any effort.

Yeah, that was *also* why Ramsey had gone up to him. The guy was built like a brick house—big and hot. So big and so hot Ramsey couldn't wait to get his clothes off. See exactly what he was working with.

Nate's mouth moved to his neck, and Ramsey had the fleeting thought that he was *damn* good at this. He'd known from the first kiss that Nate knew what the fuck he was doing, but it was one thing to think it and it was another to experience it.

"Bedroom?" Ramsey murmured. Aware of how rough edged his voice had gotten. How desperate he sounded.

"I got you."

They were only words. Sexy, dirty talk. Nate didn't really mean it. He didn't know Ramsey. Ramsey didn't even *want* to let it all go, let someone else catch it all. But feeling Nate's broad shoulders, Ramsey thought that if he wanted to play for a night, to imagine that if he was ever tempted, Nate might be a decent choice.

The bedroom was dark too, only a dim light on in the corner.

Nate deposited him on the end of the big bed, reaching down and tugging Ramsey's shirt off. His chain got tangled and Nate made an appreciative noise as he let it fall back against his skin, his touch more gentle than Ramsey had expected.

It wasn't particularly surprising that Nate wanted his clothes off. In his experience, most men did, but it was surprising that Ramsey, who was used to being the director of most sexual encounters, let him.

He also didn't protest when Nate, still kissing him like he couldn't figure out a way to stop, sank to his knees, the warm calloused pads of his fingers sliding down his chest. Unfastening his jeans, he tugged them down, leaning in as Ramsey's heart rate accelerated.

"God, you feel so good," Nate murmured, mouthing at where his cock throbbed, caught in his briefs.

He should be *doing* something. Flipping them, taking his normal control back. But Ramsey didn't.

For once, would it be so bad if he just leaned back and let himself enjoy it? Let Nate lavish him with all the attention?

He'd not been tempted by even the possibility in so long, but then he couldn't remember the last time someone had seen so much of him, so easily. Everyone else was usually fooled by the shiny, pretty exterior and the deft way Ramsey always turned the tables.

But Nate hadn't been, and he wasn't looking for Ramsey to do anything right now either.

His fingers tightened around Ramsey's upper thigh, the muscle flexing before Ramsey could stop it.

"Let me," Nate asked, glancing up. He was beautiful too, in this light. Dark eyes, dark hair, scruff edging the intriguing planes of his face.

Ramsey nodded.

Nate pulled his briefs off, and Ramsey tried to bury the shocked gasp as his mouth closed over him, hot and wet and perfect.

Over the years, he'd had a lot of exceptional and even wild sex.

A simple blowjob shouldn't unwind him like this, but there was something about the way Nate sucked him tenderly but insistently. The curl of his hand around his thigh. His touch soft but sure. Like he wasn't trying to prove anything, he just wanted to give Ramsey pleasure.

Most guys tried to overdo it. Tried to win the sex Olympics. But Nate kept it simple and Ramsey found himself sinking into the comfortable mattress, his mind unraveling from its normal machinations. Able to just relax and *enjoy* it.

"So good," he murmured, reaching down, keeping his touch equally soft. Tangling his fingers in Nate's short hair.

Nate pulled off, the head of Ramsey's cock still leaking against his tongue. "You want more?"

Not, *I want more.* Not, *I'm gonna take more.* But, asking, *you want more?* Like whatever answer Ramsey gave would be enough for him.

Men always grasped at him with claws. Like they could outthink and outmaneuver him into staying trapped in their cage. But Ramsey already knew that wasn't Nate.

He offered his hand and didn't snap it closed the moment Ramsey sighed and said, "Yeah."

He just gave him more. More of that soft drugging pleasure, fizzing along his nerve endings. The callouses on his fingertips teasing his balls. A slick finger sliding back, pressing into his hole.

It wasn't a new act, but it felt so different.

Before, it was always him on the receiving end of the begging pleas, but tonight, Ramsey barely even noticed that it was him doing it.

Not until Nate laughed roughly. "You sound so good. As good as I imagined."

Ramsey hadn't even realized he'd said anything. Had only been conscious of two fingers deep inside, stretching him out, Nate's tongue teasing his cock.

"Did you?"

"Imagine? Oh yeah."

Ramsey gasped as Nate's fingers hit a particularly good spot and then he kept them there, not grinding but caressing. Soft, but inexorable. He squeezed his eyes shut, wanting more, but suddenly, inexplicably afraid of it.

Maybe when Nate finally slid inside him, his dick wet for the first time tonight, everything would change.

He'd become like everyone else.

"Thought about you just like this. Knew you'd feel this good, look this good."

"Not on your dick?" Ramsey choked on his next breath.

"Oh, we're getting there," Nate said.

Burying his head into his bicep, Ramsey squeezed his eyes. Trying to get ahold of himself. He couldn't remember the last time he'd been this pulled apart during sex.

Even the first time he'd been fucked, he'd been in control the whole time. The guy hadn't even known it was Ramsey's first time, because he'd made damn sure that he didn't.

Sometimes guys wanted control. Ramsey gave it to them, but made sure they knew, too, every step of the way, that it was Ramsey choosing to concede it. And none of those guys ever treated the control as carefully as Nate did.

Not like Ramsey would break without the softness, but like he deserved something tender.

Nate fit a third finger inside of him, his movements deliberate and slow, but purposeful.

Ramsey panted into his bare arm. "I'm good, I'm good," he muttered. Closer to the edge than he wanted to admit to.

Nate still took his time. Didn't rush. Didn't push. Stripped his clothes off, and even though Ramsey could see his fingers weren't steady, didn't immediately go for the condom. Stronger men hadn't been able to resist Ramsey practically mewling to be fucked *now*.

Instead, he leaned in and kissed him again. It was hot—a kiss with this guy couldn't be anything but, and Ramsey was going a little insane with how much he craved him inside—but it was more too.

Something else, pressing up against the inevitable arousal.

Ramsey pushed it aside, digging his fingertips into Nate's shoulders and pulling him in with the strength of his legs. "Get in me," he begged against Nate's lips.

"Want you," Nate echoed, despite that Ramsey hadn't put that thought into words. Not exactly. Not the way Nate had.

Ramsey didn't care. He just wanted it. Wanted Nate closer, even if it fucked him up later.

*But it won't. You won't let it. You never let it.*

That was true. Even now, there was a part, shining diamond hard, inside of him, that no matter how deeply Nate buried his cock, he'd never reach.

Ramsey held on to it, even as Nate slid inside.

He was big and hard, and it felt like he kept coming and coming, gentle but unyielding.

"Fuck," Ramsey muttered. It had been too long. That was the reason why his throat kept closing every time Nate leaned in to kiss him.

He'd been a little afraid that when it came down to the moment, Nate would be too sweet about it. When Ramsey wanted fucked, he wanted to *feel* it, and to Ramsey's surprise, he didn't have to say a word.

Nate set a brisk pace, grinding into him, fingers clenched tightly around Ramsey's thigh, fucking him deep and sure. Hitting all the good spots, his abs rubbing up against the head of Ramsey's cock.

He'd been close before Nate even got in him—not that he'd have ever confessed that. It felt like exposing himself, like he couldn't control himself the way he'd expect. But it didn't take long for Nate to peel away the rest of his self-control, even as Ramsey tried desperately to dig his nails into it.

"Fuck, fuck," Ramsey panted as Nate hit a particularly exquisite angle. "God—right there."

"Oh yeah, I wanna feel you," Nate groaned.

Nate's thrusts were beginning to get more erratic, his breathing labored, and Ramsey decided he should come soon, too.

But before he could push himself over the edge, Nate leaned in, thrusting harder right on that angle, and Ramsey fell apart, the orgasm practically dragged out of him.

Nate's head collapsed onto his shoulder, mouthing at the bare skin there, and Ramsey felt rather than heard the moan deep in his chest as he followed.

For a breathlessly long moment, Ramsey just lay there. God, he'd done this before. He *knew* how to do this. Gently push Nate off. Get up. Clean up. Get out.

But he was so tired. He didn't want to. Nate was a heavy and warm but ultimately reassuring weight on top of him. Normally that would make Ramsey feel hemmed in. Controlled in a way he hated. In a way he always tried to avoid.

But not right now.

Now, he didn't feel caged, but cherished.

"Better than I imagined," Nate murmured into his ear. "Good for you too?"

There was a sudden urge for Ramsey to laugh hysterically. To ask, actually out loud, if maybe it would have felt like this if he'd ever gotten Wes and Marcus into bed.

But he hadn't, and so he hadn't known sex *could* feel like this.

He didn't feel *that* different. He was still Ramsey Andresen. Still a professional hockey player, even if he wasn't getting on the ice. Still had the headaches. Still knew how to weave a better web than anyone else he'd ever met. But Nate made him feel softer, too.

Something had eased inside Ramsey that had always felt tight before now.

"Yeah," Ramsey agreed.

This was probably the moment Nate was going to get up. Clean him up. Want to cuddle. Hope, despite everything that Ramsey had said before he'd gone home with him, that Ramsey might be amenable to another night. To putting his phone number in Nate's phone.

There was still that diamond bright, hard as nails center to him. He could reach for that. Use it to get him out of here. He'd done it so many times before in a way that had always felt natural and as easy as breathing.

But he didn't *want* to. Not tonight.

"You want something to drink? A shower?"

Ramsey's mouth was dry. He wasn't sure he could tolerate a shower—because undoubtedly Nate would want to be up in his space, and *that* felt like a step too far—but he wouldn't mind a drink.

Sharing a drink in Nate's kitchen or his living room wasn't cuddling, but it wasn't leaving either.

It occurred to Ramsey then that part of Nate seeing through him so well was *this*. Nate anticipating Ramsey's moves and circumventing them.

And even more interestingly, Ramsey not instantly feeling the need to counter.

"Yeah, a drink," Ramsey said.

Nate pressed one last kiss to Ramsey's shoulder and pulled away.

Ramsey got his first good look at Nate's body then, and it was every bit as incredible and powerful as he'd hoped. He'd spent a lot of time in locker rooms and wasn't a stranger to built guys, but this was different.

When Nate returned a moment later, he had a damp washcloth in his hand and he handed it over to Ramsey. Like he knew that too was a step too far.

Ramsey cleaned up, and pulled on his briefs and jeans again, but didn't bother fastening them or putting his shirt back on.

He didn't miss Nate's approving glance either as he tugged on a pair of sweatpants from a drawer in the dresser opposite the bed and then led him into the kitchen.

"Beer? Water? Gatorade? Something stronger?" Nate asked, flicking the kitchen light on as he headed towards the fridge.

If Ramsey's mouth had been dry before, it turned into the fucking Sahara Desert now.

Because the kitchen and the living room were really one big space, taking up the lion's share of the apartment and now that the light was on, Ramsey could see why he owned this place. Why he wore the Rolex on his wrist.

Opposite the massive flat screen TV, there was a whole row of framed jerseys.

Not hockey, but football.

Even worse, Ramsey recognized the colors on the last one on the right—the blue and white that matched his friend Wes' team—and the last name.

*Bishop.*

Wes had mentioned a Nate Bishop more than once. *Great defensive player. Leader on the team.* Even, once, in a damning memory Ramsey wished he could exorcise from his brain, *a nice guy. You'd probably even like him.*

Yeah, he sure fucking had. At least until Ramsey had discovered all of this.

His heart rate picked up.

"Ramsey?" Nate asked, poking his head out of the fridge.

When Nate had been nobody, when Nate hadn't been someone this close to his circle, to something that mattered, it had felt . . .well, not *okay* to relax his rules, but safe enough.

Nobody would ever know.

And Ramsey could control it.

"Ramsey?" Nate was suddenly right there. Looking at him, while Ramsey stared at the jerseys. The truth of his identity laid bare. But Nate had never lied. Or he had, but not well.

Nate, the hot guy from the bar who'd looked into Ramsey's eyes like he *knew* him, was one thing. Nate, who claimed he managed Tim Horton's for a living and didn't even eat their donuts.

Nate Bishop, the defensive end for the Toronto Thunder, was something else entirely.

An entity that Ramsey couldn't control. Smashing into his life. Except no, he was already fucking there, because Wes knew him, and probably if Ramsey was still around Toronto in the fall—a nightmare that Ramsey couldn't even put into thoughts, nevermind words—Wes would probably want him to come around the team with him. He'd expect it. He'd be confused if Ramsey refused.

Panic streaked through him in a nauseating wave.

He'd never be able to keep this guy contained. Not easily. Probably not at all.

"Oh. Well. Yeah. By the way, yeah, I do play football," Nate said, shrugging awkwardly and then having the nerve to look worried, like this changed something.

He was fucking crazy. It changed *everything*.

Ramsey knew he should say something. Something easy, breezy. Make his exit. He'd done it a hundred times before. Wes was always marveling at how effortlessly he could extricate himself from a hookup's place.

But his normal skills seemed to have deserted him, and Ramsey wasn't sure why. Had it been the unsettling and extraordinary sex? Or the unexpected reveal of who Nate really was?

"Don't tell me this is fucking you up." Nate looked like it was half a joke, half a serious concern.

*Be easy, be easy, be easy.*

"Had a good laugh at my expense, huh?" was what came out instead. *Fuck*. It was one thing to be affected and it was another to reveal it.

Nate looked surprised. No, *shocked*. "Uh, no?"

"I should go." It wasn't the easy, charming exit he was known for, but at least it was an exit.

"Are you serious? Because I didn't tell you I'm a football player?" Nate frowned.

Ramsey wasn't cruel; he'd learned early, so early he couldn't even tell you when, that you caught so many more flies with honey than with vinegar. But he found himself saying, "I was going to leave anyway."

He'd never made a secret of it, but no doubt Nate had expected he'd get a chance to change his mind. And maybe if Nate hadn't been Nate Bishop, he'd have gotten it. Maybe he'd have even conjured a miracle and convinced Ramsey to give him his phone number.

But that wasn't happening now. The best Ramsey could hope for was that the next time they met—because with Wes in both of their circles it was probably inevitable—they could both pretend casual ignorance.

"I know you said it—" Nate started to say hesitantly.

"I never made any secret of it," Ramsey retorted. He left the kitchen, going into the bedroom to grab his T-shirt. Find his shoes and socks.

But then the sex had been like *that*. And when normally Ramsey might have extricated himself from the situation—grabbed a quick shower alone and then left—he'd stayed. He'd agreed to a drink. Would have maybe even acquiesced to a cuddle, a second round, maybe even a sleepover.

Nate trailed after him. Clearly not getting the memo that everything had changed.

"No, but I thought . . ." Nate looked at him, all wounded dark eyes, and Ramsey wanted to yell at him.

Something he never did because what was the fucking point of losing his temper? It never changed anything. Hadn't changed his shitty childhood. Or what had happened last year.

"You thought, what, you'd fuck me really good and then I'd change my mind?"

Nate reared back.

Ramsey wanted to snatch the words out of the air, because *again*, what were they going to change? They weren't going to change those jerseys on the wall of the living room, and they weren't going to change Nate's last name.

Finding his T-shirt in the clothing next to the bed, Ramsey pulled it on. Made sure he had his phone and his wallet in his jeans still.

"Is any part of you real? Or is it all just some charming front you turn on and turn off?" Nate asked, so seriously it was like he really wanted an answer. But he didn't, because he wasn't going to like it.

Why had he not just played his regular part? Why had he gotten angry? Why had he gotten nasty? Making an enemy was always pointless.

"Oh, baby," Ramsey said, because he couldn't stop himself now, "I'm whoever you want me to be."

Nate frowned. "That's such bullshit."

It *was* bullshit. Total, complete bullshit. Nate had seen further into the real Ramsey than anyone else in a long time, but he couldn't tell him that. If Ramsey gave Nate an inch, he would want to take a mile.

Ramsey had to get out of here before he was tempted to let him.

"Believe it or not, it doesn't matter to me." Ramsey flashed a smile. His patented *devil may care* smile. The one that always brought all the boys to the yard.

The moment he did, he knew it was the wrong kind of smile, because hurt flared over Nate's face.

"You're right." The last thing Ramsey had actually expected was to be believed. Nate had seen through him from the first. But not now, apparently. "You'd better go if that's how it is."

Protests and denials crawled up Ramsey's throat like heartburn but he swallowed them back down. Gave Nate one more of those smiles, like he didn't care after all, and walked out.

It wasn't ridiculously late, and Ramsey felt like he needed a minute to get his shit together as he walked back to Wes' building. It wasn't far, and he'd genuinely believed he'd marshaled his wits about him by the time he made it back to his friend's apartment.

But the moment he let himself in and Wes looked over at him from his spot on the couch, it was obvious he hadn't. Wes was watching one of those trashy reality TV shows that he loved and Ramsey couldn't stand. *The Bachelor* or *Love is Blind* or *Love Island*. They were all the same to Ramsey. A dozen or so people all pretending to be someone they weren't.

"Hey, you okay?" Wes asked, actually pausing the show. Which said it all.

Ramsey wanted to escape to the guest room. Get away from his friend. Go back to Buffalo, maybe, but Buffalo was awful. He'd *left* Buffalo because it was awful.

He just looked at his friend and didn't say anything. Sometimes saying nothing was better than a lie. It was usually better than the truth.

Wes sighed and patted the couch next to him. "Come 'ere. You have a headache?"

For a second, Ramsey considered arguing, but then he went. "No," he said.

Wes put his arm around him and Ramsey let himself be pulled in. "You wanna tell me about it?" Wes asked.

Wes *would* want to talk about it. "No."

Humming under his breath, Wes tugged him closer.

"You know how I usually complain you're pathetic?" Ramsey asked. He felt guilty. He'd felt guilty all the way back to Wes' building. So guilty that half a dozen times he'd nearly gone back to Nate's place and told him the whole truth. Something he was never tempted to do.

Wes had the nerve to laugh about that. "Oh, yeah."

"Maybe it's not just you."

Same as getting angry, there never seemed to be any benefit to feeling sorry for himself, so Ramsey just didn't do that. He always just kept pushing forward. It wasn't relentless optimism, more like Ramsey betting that something better *had* to be on the horizon and if it didn't happen naturally, then he'd figure out a way to *make* it happen.

"You really don't want to tell me about it? I didn't think you had hookups go bad." Wes said it easily. Too easily. He wasn't even half the actor Ramsey was, despite all the times Ramsey had attempted to coach him.

The problem was Wes didn't have any good reasons to hide, so he was never motivated to pretend.

Ramsey didn't want to talk about Nate. Okay—that was also a lie. He desperately wanted to tell Wes all about Nate, but he couldn't. He *wouldn't*. So he changed the subject instead.

"You ever think about what would've happened if you and Marcus had actually slept with me that night?"

Wes tensed.

Ramsey almost never said Marcus' name, if he could help it. Same as Wes, these days. If Wes was more like Ramsey, he'd have already figured out that Ramsey had done it to distract him. But Wes *wasn't* like Ramsey, which was probably a blessing all around.

"No," Wes lied, unconvincingly.

"Come on," Ramsey wheedled. "You do. I know you do."

But Wes' eyes were clear when he looked over at Ramsey. Maybe he *was* telling the truth. "I don't, actually. It would've been a garbage fire, and then we wouldn't be friends still, because you'd have ghosted us, like you always do."

Ramsey wasn't sure if it hurt more because it *was* honest. Maybe the lie would've been easier for him to swallow.

"And don't even say you don't," Wes continued. "I know you, remember? You're my best friend."

Ramsey let himself settle back into the couch. Into the comfort of Wes' arm around him. "Yeah," he agreed.

"You're really not going to tell me how it went bad? Did you actually fail at charmingly making your exit?"

"Something like that," Ramsey said.

"Huh." Wes looked over at him. "What else?"

"He wasn't who I thought he was," Ramsey said, and, of course, Wes laughed.

"Oh, that must've been fun. Two of you lying to each other. Was it weird sex, too?"

Except that Ramsey hadn't lied. Not really. Nate hadn't believed him, of course, because the shit he'd said *had* been unbelievable. But it had still been true.

"No," Ramsey admitted.

"Good sex, then?"

Ramsey was genuinely worried if he started, he'd just word vomit the whole evening up. So he just said, "Why are you always trying to get me to give you the deets, Matthews?"

"Maybe because only one of us is actually having sex," Wes said wryly.

"You could be having it if you wanted to," Ramsey reminded him.

But Wes only smacked him on the arm. "For the millionth time, I don't want to sleep with you. You're my best friend."

"Dumbass. Who wouldn't want to sleep with me?" Ramsey retorted, though by this point, they both knew there was no way they could ever sleep together. Wes wasn't the *last* person on earth that Ramsey would ever have sex with—that honor went to Wes' ex-boyfriend, Marcus, who was undeniably attractive, but Wes would kill him slowly with a dull, rusty knife if he ever went there—but still solidly in the top three.

It was because Wes knew him so well. Better than anyone else. Better even than his other best friend, Brody.

Maybe that should've been a hint that he should've listened to the concerned voice in the back of his mind and not gone there with Nate tonight. Just walked away.

"I'd say you're an egomaniac," Wes said, glancing over at him, "but I know better."

"Ugh, I hate you."

"You don't." Wes was smug. Knowing. "You like that I actually *know* you. 'Cause if it wasn't for me and Brody, you'd be even more pathetic than you are now."

"Maybe I hate that you know that," Ramsey suggested. There'd been a time that he had hated it. Been equally horrified and fascinated by Wes' knowledge. With Wes, he'd learned to live with it.

He wasn't sure he could've ever dealt with Nate.

Maybe what had happened was for the best.

"You don't," Wes said loyally, squeezing him harder. Wes was too good. Probably too good for a friend like Ramsey, but he'd attached himself like a barnacle, and now that Marcus was gone, the chances of Ramsey dislodging him were close to zero.

He was more than okay with that—at least *used* to it—if only his proximity to Wes didn't automatically mean proximity to Nate.

Maybe fate would actually do him a solid and he'd be recovered from his concussion and back in Buffalo by September, playing hockey again. If that happened, Ramsey could put this whole thing behind him—his interminable stint on injured reserve and Nate, both.

He wouldn't even be in Toronto, and so it wouldn't matter if Nate was around.

That was the solution: get better and then none of this would matter.

# CHAPTER 2



*August*

"This better be worth all the theatrics," Nate muttered under his breath as they walked down the dark alley towards God knew what bar. Wes had insisted that he knew the best place to take the group to, and Nate had gone along with it because that was what he was doing these days.

Not just floating along, not necessarily, but all summer Nate had felt one step removed from the world around him. Like the only thing that had been real had been the blond man he'd met at the bar. Ramsey had turned out to be exactly like he'd thought he was, but even having his initial suspicions justified hadn't stopped Nate from thinking about him.

From replaying that night over and over in his mind, even when he shouldn't.

Sterling, the other defensive captain, had pulled him aside more than once during camp, making sure he was okay. Making sure his head was on straight.

Well, it wasn't on straight.

"It's worth it," Wes reassured him. "It's just down here."

Nate supposed he shouldn't be all that surprised when Wes led their group further into the alley and then down a set of stained concrete steps set into the ground.

"It's like we're descending into hell," Lane said, sounding delighted.

"Only you," Trevor, the other demon twin, muttered.

There was a black wooden door at the bottom of the stairs, its surface unexpectedly shiny and new. A key, outlined in gold, shone to the right of the door.

That was apparently the only sign they were going to get.

"We're gonna get killed," Cam complained behind him. "Our organs harvested. That happens in big cities, right?"

Nate chuckled under his breath.

Heard Dawson murmur, "Rook, I promise you, I'm gonna personally make sure your organs stay unharvested."

Wes knocked on the door, and a hidden window in the door opened.

"Holy shit," Lane exclaimed.

Nate was intrigued, in spite of himself, as they stepped into the main bar. It was like the whole room had been transformed—from the huge oval-shaped wooden bar to the couches and the walls upholstered in richly luxurious fabrics and colors.

"Holy shit," Lane said again, hushed and reverent again, and yeah, it was pretty damn cool.

And then Nate glanced over towards the bar, and everything inside him froze.

Leaning against the bar, like a daydream and a nightmare rolled into one, was Ramsey.

Nate told himself not to react, even as his insides liquified into a nauseating combination of terror and regret.

How many times had he regretted the way that night had ended? He'd lain awake too many times over the summer, wishing that instead of making up that stupid as fuck Tim Horton's lie he'd just told the goddamn truth. Said, "Hi, I'm Nate Bishop, and I play defensive end for the Toronto Thunder. That's football, in case you didn't realize."

But he hadn't, and Ramsey had apparently gotten freaked out about it. Because up until that point, it had been going even better than Nate had hoped. Ramsey hadn't immediately left after sex. He'd seemed like he wanted to stay. But then they'd walked into the kitchen of Nate's place, gotten a glimpse of those jerseys on the wall, and everything had changed.

"Oh hey, there he is," Wes said, and it took Nate—still stupefied that Ramsey was *here*—a beat too long to realize that Wes was gesturing in his direction. Like they knew each other.

Ramsey pushed off the bar and sauntered towards them, looking every bit as gorgeous and untouchable as he had that night in June.

That Ramsey merged with the one Nate tried not to remember. The one who'd lain beneath him and that he'd kissed and who had squeezed his eyes closed against the something that had bloomed, unexpectedly, between them.

"This," Wes said, waving towards Ramsey, "is Ramsey Andresen. He's a hockey player for the Buffalo Wolves."

If Nate had thought the way his organs curdled was bad before, it was nothing compared to how they felt now. Shrinking up into a wrinkled package. Churning away. Nate thought he might go over to the bar and puke into one of their shiny glasses.

*"Hockey," Ramsey had said, "I'm a hockey player. Up here for summer training."*

Nate hadn't believed him. He'd *laughed* at him. And the whole time, he'd been telling the truth.

He'd even called him Willy Nylander's fucking *dog walker,* for God's sake.

It was actually fucking amazing that Ramsey had been willing to go home with him after that, honestly.

But maybe it explained some of why Ramsey had panicked at a glimpse of who Nate really was.

Maybe, anyway. He wasn't sure how much credit he was willing to give Ramsey just yet.

"Hey," Ramsey said. "Welcome to Vault."

Nate was trying not to have a whole dissociative episode as the Ramsey in his mind and the Ramsey in front of him melded together into one person.

That was the way his voice had sounded, that night. It had been cocky, then surprisingly soft, and then cruel.

Now it just sounded neutral. Nate might've been fooled, but there was a reason Ramsey wasn't looking at him. Was looking anywhere *but* at him.

"This place is so sick, isn't it?" Wes said excitedly. He pulled Ramsey into a hug. For a split second, over Wes' back, his gaze found Nate's, and then it slid away, like they were the opposite ends of a magnet.

Well, Nate wasn't about to say anything about what had happened. Wasn't about to go over to Ramsey, pound him on the back and say, "how about that fuck we had in June? You ever think about that night?"

Nate would rather walk over hot coals than ever admit to anyone, nevermind Ramsey himself, that he remembered him.

That he was still thinking about him.

"Here," Wes said, "let me introduce you to the team."

Nate had a feeling if he hung back, Aidan would do the Aidan thing where he took over, and not surprisingly, he did, stepping forward. Offering his hand and introducing himself.

"You're the QB, huh? Mentoring Wes here?" Ramsey asked.

But Nate had a feeling that if Ramsey was as close to Wes as it seemed, Ramsey knew exactly who Aidan was. This was just another part of the act. Another facet of the shiny, hard surface that he worked so hard to maintain.

Aidan nodded. "Hockey, huh?" he said to Ramsey.

Nate felt a little more justified then that he'd missed it too. But then Ramsey was so gorgeous, he'd never have expected a hockey player to look like him. Maybe that was stupid or short-sighted, but it was still true.

Dawson approached next, and Nate wasn't surprised by that either. Dawson was single, and while he and the rookie punter hung around each other some, anyone with eyes was going to make a move on Ramsey.

Speaking of the rookie punter, he added a flustered, "Oh my God, you're hot."

Ramsey didn't look even the tiniest bit shocked by that outburst. How many times a day must he hear that? Nate wondered if he got tired of it. If he ever wanted to walk around with a paper bag over his head.

But Ramsey did surprise Nate because he didn't shoot Cam that cool and careful put-down, the way he had the bartender back in June. He just smiled, a glimpse into the Ramsey behind the mask, and teased back, "Hey, so are you, kid."

Nate was still smarting over how their one night together had ended. Ramsey had the capability to be cruel, even if he hadn't been cruel to the kid, now.

The demon twins approached next.

Wes listed them all off. "That's Cameron, we like to call him Cam. Then there's Levi. Lane. Trevor. And Nate."

Nate was pretty sure Wes wasn't aware they knew each other. Instead, his final inclusion on the list was because he was hanging back. Maybe he didn't want a night out after all. Maybe he actually wanted to escape this bar and go far away, somewhere Ramsey wasn't.

Ramsey greeted everyone smoothly, with the kind of charm Nate expected of him. He hoped that by the time Ramsey got to him, there wouldn't be much left. But of course that wasn't true.

When Ramsey looked over at him, meeting his eyes for what felt like the first time since that night—since they'd walked into the kitchen and Nate had stupidly flicked the lights on—he smiled, and even though nothing Nate had said to any of the other guys had even registered, Nate absorbed every word Ramsey said to him.

"Nate, yeah? It's good to meet you."

It was only seven words, but every single one *hit*.

He should say something but all he could do was nod, stupidly. Relieved when Ramsey moved on, like it hadn't really mattered what Nate did or didn't do.

"I got us one of the private rooms," Ramsey said, the whole group clustering around him like he was starting a cult. Nate *hated it*.

Nate had known Ramsey was going to play it like they hadn't ever met. That they'd never kissed. That he hadn't ever been inside of him. But it was one thing to be sure of it, in his own mind, and it was another entirely to hear Ramsey perform the lie.

He'd expected it, but it still felt like shit.

Like he'd been just another guy, despite that he'd been telling himself the whole summer that he'd, in fact, been *just another guy*.

Was he hurt? Was he angry? An ugly, toxic blend of both?

"There's different private rooms?" Dawson asked as they headed to the bar.

Nate had spent the last minute debating whether he'd turn around and leave, but if he did that, even if he figured out a half-assed excuse, it would look weird to his teammates. But even more than that, Ramsey would *know*. He'd know he was bothered by his presence, and Nate refused to give him the satisfaction.

"Oh yeah. Several different gaming rooms. Pool tables and darts. A poker room. A library. And the vault," Ramsey said, his voice weaving around the group like he was the Pied Piper in that children's fairy tale.

"There's an actual vault? Holy shit. That's so fucking cool," Lane said.

Lane hit on everything that moved; it was inevitable he'd end up sleeping with Ramsey. Nate just hoped that he wouldn't have to witness it, because he liked Lane a lot. And he didn't want Ramsey to poison their friendship.

"Next time we'll try that one out," Ramsey said, winking.

It felt like a performance. Pitched perfectly to the group he was with. But then of course he knew how to deal with professional athletes—he *was* one.

Just another one of those truths he'd cloaked in lies.

Nate stepped up to the bar, not even glancing at the menu, thick midnight blue paper embossed with gold lettering. It was fancy, a reflection of the surroundings they were in, but Nate didn't need any of that classy shit. He just needed a drink, a useless attempt to forget the way Ramsey had tasted.

The bartender looked at him, and he just tapped the shiny wood finish of the bar. "Rum," he said. "And keep it coming."

He took one shot and then another, but the ugly knot in his stomach refused to loosen.

Lane leaned against the bar next to him. "He's damn hot, isn't he?" he murmured under his breath.

Nate didn't have to ask who Lane was talking about. "I don't know," he said, because that was safer than either being honest—*he's the hottest guy I've ever seen, and that's not even why I want him so bad*—or lying and claiming that he wasn't. Lane would tell him he was blind, and then despite his own stupidity, probably guess why Nate refused to admit what was so fucking obvious.

"Oh come on, dude, he's *hot*. And interested. He keeps looking over here. Maybe time to break your dry streak?"

Nate didn't know which was worse: that Lane had decided that Ramsey was interested in *him* or that he wasn't aware that Ramsey was entirely, one-hundred-percent, to blame for kicking off Nate's spell in the first place.

"Nah," Nate said, picking up the beer he'd asked the bartender for. If he took as many shots as he wanted, he'd probably end up saying, or *doing*, something he shouldn't.

"Why not? You don't like blonds?" Lane wondered.

Nate told himself he was not going to be a dick. He was *not* going to ask Lane if *he* liked blonds. Specifically sandy blonds like Trevor.

It would be an excellent change of subject because nobody ever got Lane worked up like Trevor did.

"Just not in the mood," Nate said. "It was a long week of practice."

Lane nodded in agreement. "Well, if you're not going to, would you mind if I . . ." He gestured in the direction of Ramsey, who appeared to be giving drink recommendations to Cam, Dawson, and Trevor.

Nate felt hot and cold all over. "Uh." How could he say no? And how could he stand by and say nothing while Lane went over there and hit on him?

"I'll let you think about it," Lane said, picking up his drink and patting Nate on the shoulder. "'Cause I can just imagine you're gonna stare at him a few more minutes and change your mind."

Nate wanted to tell Lane that he *wasn't* fucking staring, but before he could get the words out, Lane was gone.

Before he could decide what he was now going to say to Lane later—because he sure as fuck wasn't going to change his mind, and he couldn't imagine Ramsey wanting a repeat—Ramsey suggested they head to their private room. Nate couldn't come up with a good reason to stay out here, so he followed, reluctantly.

"This is a pretty sweet setup," Levi said, and Nate had to agree. He took a spot near the back of the room, a chair closest to the door, and tried to look anywhere but at Ramsey. For Lane, so he wouldn't be encouraged, but if he was being really honest, for himself, too.

"Told you," Wes said, smiling. "Ramsey's the best at finding places like this."

"And you're not even from Toronto," Aidan pointed out.

Ramsey just shrugged, even as Nate tried not to remember how *their* first conversation had begun. "No, but Buffalo's close. And Wes is here, so we've met up a bunch. Especially during the last year."

For a single ugly moment, Nate wondered if that was because Ramsey was sleeping with Wes. That would explain the way he'd reacted so negatively to the revelation of Nate's identity. He could be caught cheating.

But then Wes made a face, pain flashing in his eyes. "Don't," he said, and then Nate remembered that Wes had had a bad breakup.

"Chill, I wasn't going to mention Marcus," Ramsey said easily.

"Wes said you were on injured reserve," Levi said.

For the second time since he'd walked into this bar, Nate froze. This time with his beer halfway up to his lips.

*Injured reserve?* Nate's insides curdled as his brain combed through every single second of their hookup in June. Ramsey had *seemed* fine. He couldn't remember seeing him ever limp or pull back. He'd given himself physically one hundred percent. Nate was sure of it, because Nate would've noticed, even if he hadn't thought at that point that Ramsey was a professional athlete. He'd still been looking at him through a professional athlete's eyes.

"Yeah. Concussion syndrome," Ramsey said.

*Oh, God.* The rum in Nate's system soured even further.

"Had a bad one last year, right after I signed my extension. But I'd had a few before, in college, and this one lingered."

Nate recognized the tone of voice Ramsey used. He'd used it, too, his last year with the Condors, when he'd struggled with a hamstring injury that he could never seem to shake.

Awareness made him want to be nice—well, *nicer*—but then Nate thought about it. Thought about how he'd clearly been going through it in June, but he'd not said a word. Pretended. *Lied.*

He had a glass in his hand tonight. Same as he'd had a glass in his hand on *that* night.

"Didn't know you could drink with concussion syndrome," Nate said, speaking up for the first time since they'd headed to the private room.

Ramsey's gaze swiveled in his direction. Eyes that pale a blue shouldn't burn that bright, but Ramsey's did. They scorched Nate, deep down, and he knew Ramsey was thinking, too, of the night they'd met.

"This? This isn't vodka. It's just sparkling water, dude."

Sometimes Nate wondered if he'd ever seen Ramsey at all, or he'd just fallen for the myriad and shifting performances Ramsey employed.

"Ah," Nate said coldly.

"Hey, who's up for a game?" Dawson said, changing the subject as he grabbed a pool cue from the rack, rolling it between his palms.

"I'll play," Cam said immediately. Not surprising. The rook had a huge crush, visible from space, on their veteran kicker.

"Count me in too," Lane said, and, even more unsurprisingly, Trevor followed suit.

Next time, Nate wasn't going to hold back. When Lane needled him about his dry spell, he was going to needle Lane right back, and about Trevor, specifically.

"Flynn? Banks?" Dawson asked them, but they shook their heads, seemingly pretty comfortable on the couch together. Nate had been pretty sure their QB1 was falling for the Thunders' new offensive lineman, and this didn't do anything to dispel his suspicions.

"My balance isn't what it used to be. I can usually make do with darts, but not pool," Ramsey said wryly.

Nate kept telling himself he'd be fine, he could be chill, even, but every fucking time Ramsey opened his mouth, it was like getting hit with the news all over again. No time to adjust. No time to think any of this through.

"Dude, that sucks," Levi said sympathetically. "So what's it like, long-term injured reserve? Know what it's like in football but not hockey."

Nate was tempted to lean over and smack his hand right over Levi's mouth so he wouldn't ask any more sympathetic questions. He didn't need to hear any more. He didn't *want* to hear any more.

"Get paid. Do nothing. Try to recover so I can play again. That's what it's like." Ramsey sighed. "Hardest part is staying busy. Which is why I'm up here. Wes was tired of me whining about being alone in Buffalo."

Nate remembered, despite not wanting to, exactly what Ramsey had said back in June. *Kind of at a loose end at the moment,* he'd said.

That hadn't been a lie either.

Hard to say what Nate was more pissed about: that Ramsey had lied or that he'd been honest in his own way.

"He was so depressing," Wes said earnestly. It was becoming very clear to Nate just how close he and Ramsey were. Maybe he'd been wrong about the sex. But *no*. Nate knew what Ramsey looked like when he was flirting. He'd witnessed it. Fuck, he'd had all that charisma turned on him. And it was never like that when Ramsey looked over at Wes. Like he did right now.

"And we're there for each other," Wes added.

It was stupid to be jealous. Stupid to hate Lane and Levi and Aidan and even stupider to hate Wes, for getting bits of Ramsey—the real bits of Ramsey that Nate never had—but stupidity had never stopped anyone with a dick before.

"Adorable," he said dryly.

"We've known each other a long time," Ramsey said firmly.

Nate wondered if Ramsey knew all about the seething brew of emotions in his stomach. But this was Ramsey so of course he did.

"Yeah?" Aidan asked, clearly trying to defuse the situation in the most Aidan-like way.

"We went to Portland U together," Wes said.

"Hockey player and football player becoming friends? That's unusual," Dawson inserted.

"Not *that* unusual," Ramsey said. Nate swore he looked over at him, then. But then he kept talking like he'd never done it. "We've got friends who ended up together. Dean plays football for the Riptide and Brody *could've* gone pro as a hockey player. Was drafted and everything, but he decided to go to med school, like the fucking overachiever he is."

"You're still torn up about that. Brody picking science over hockey," Wes teased fondly.

"Well, *yeah*," Ramsey retorted.

Nate hadn't been able to look away from him since he'd sat down. Since the revelation of his injury. But now it *hurt* to look at him. Because clearly Ramsey missed hockey.

Hated not being able to play.

"Come on, let's play darts," Wes said. He looked over at Nate, pointedly. "You too, Bishop."

Nate wanted to tell him he was perfectly fine here, sitting back and just watching. But then Ramsey shot him a sideways look that said the exact same. That he'd be a lot happier if Nate *didn't* join them, and well, Nate wasn't going to make things easy on him.

Not when Ramsey had never made things easy on *him*.

It became very clear very quickly that Ramsey was exceptional at darts. He had a quick release and a great eye. Wes was not very good, and Nate was even, frustratingly, even worse, always throwing too hard. Feeling like he was bungling the slender darts in his big hands.

"Better luck next time," Ramsey teased as he lost another game.

Nate scowled. The guy seemed practically designed to make his life difficult.

"Be nice," Wes said, elbowing Ramsey.

"I'm being so nice," Ramsey claimed. "Taking it easy on you guys and everything."

"Doesn't seem like it," Nate complained. "Are you sure you're not cheating?"

"Hey, I did say I was better at darts," Ramsey said. He had the nerve to sound so innocent, when there was nothing innocent about him at all.

"Yeah, if you don't like losing, don't play him at cards," Wes said seriously. And yeah, Nate could see that. Ramsey would be exceptional at cards. His entire self was a poker face, an extended con that never seemed to end.

"Noted," Nate said.

"Hey, it's almost like I'm in trouble for being awesome." Ramsey seemed delighted by this fact. He slung an arm around Wes' shoulders, and Nate tried not to tense. Tried not to catalog how easily Ramsey touched his friend and even some of the other guys. How he'd gone out of his way to not touch Nate. Not once. "But we better get you home, get you to bed. Big day tomorrow."

Wes looked confused. "It is? I thought we had the day off."

"Yeah, exactly," Ramsey said, patting Wes supportively. "You have the day off before the run-through for your first big start."

Did nobody else see how Ramsey was? Sure it was Wes' start at QB, but Ramsey was acting like it was *theirs*.

Nate wanted to call him on how fucked-up that was, but Trevor spoke up first. "Dude, it's a *preseason* game."

Ramsey smacked Trevor upside the head, smiling easily the whole time. "*Dude*, I'm being a supportive friend, even though football sucks."

It was impossible to be even the tiniest bit surprised at this confession. Maybe that was why Ramsey had high-tailed it out of Nate's apartment. He'd realized Nate was that dreaded entity: a *football player*.

"What?" Ramsey said, shrugging, no self-consciousness whatsoever. "It does. It's not hockey, that's for damn sure.

Hockey, which Ramsey clearly was missing like an absent limb. Nate should feel some kind of sympathy for him, but he couldn't find it.

"Can I get pissed at him *now*?" Nate wondered.

"No," Aidan said firmly. Because of course he did.

"I like you," Ramsey declared, moving his body from Wes to Aidan.

Nate tensed, envy surging through him even as he denied, denied, *denied* that he wished it was him, not Aidan.

"You're not what everyone says you are," Ramsey said. There was a knowing look in his eyes. Like he knew if he just kicked off this conversational topic, where it would head, and where it would end up.

"What does everyone say I am?" Aidan wondered.

Of fucking course he took the bait. Aidan had been *designed* to take the bait.

"Don't listen to him, bro," Trevor inserted earnestly. "You're the best."

"No, no I really want to hear this," Aidan said with an unsurprising frown.

"Hey," Ramsey said, "are you alright? I don't have to—"

"No, tell me," Aidan insisted.

Ramsey just shrugged. "Nothing bad. Just serious. Intense. Works hard. Never takes a break. No fun." Then his face suddenly broke out into a grin, and it was blinding. That smile should be registered as a weapon. Or maybe it was just Nate who it affected that strongly. "But you're kinda fun, actually."

"Don't tell him that, it's just gonna go to his head, and his ego's already big enough," Levi teased.

"My ego's the perfect size," Aidan claimed.

Levi glanced at him, clearly delighted, and Nate knew then that they'd end up together. It was so obvious, the way they circled each other. The inevitability in the way they fit. Aidan quieter, more intense, Levi lighter and sweeter.

"Oh, it is, baby," Levi said.

Ramsey glanced over at them and then back at Nate, his blue eyes suddenly burning.

Nate glanced away first. Couldn't help it.

It was stupid he'd ever thought he and Ramsey might be something more. Like their first night together was the beginning of their journey, not the end.

They weren't Aidan and Levi, everything laid out before them, all dazzling possibility.

The group split up after that. Aidan and Levi headed back to the former's apartment. Probably to flirt more and pretend that they both didn't want so much more. Lane wanted to try some other bar, and tried to get Nate to join him, but Nate was tired and grumpy. Plus he knew from the way Lane kept eyeing Trevor that Nate wasn't who he wanted to join him anyway.

He settled at the bar for a last drink, hoping to drink it in a melancholy silence.

But of course, that wasn't going to happen. He'd just taken his first sip when Ramsey slid onto the barstool next to him.

Wes hadn't wanted to head back to his apartment without him, but the thing about Wes was that he also *knew* Ramsey, so he also knew that Ramsey was going to do what he was going to do, and there was typically nothing Wes could do to stop it.

"Don't do anything stupid," Wes said, and though he still didn't know what had happened with Nate two months ago, it was like he had a sixth sense that something was going on.

That Ramsey wasn't going to leave well enough alone and he wasn't going to leave Nate alone.

Wes probably just thought Ramsey didn't appreciate that Nate had apparently disliked him on sight, and he wasn't going to correct Wes' assumption.

"When have I ever done anything stupid?" Ramsey asked smoothly.

But Wes just rolled his eyes and tapped him on the shoulder. "*Don't* sleep with him, okay?"

Ha. *Ha.*

And this was exactly why Ramsey hadn't told Wes about what had happened in June. He'd get this disappointed look on his face. He wouldn't *say* it, but he'd be thinking it. Turned out that it was even worse in Ramsey's imagination than it ever was in reality, but that didn't mean Ramsey didn't go out of his way to avoid it.

"I'll do my best," Ramsey said dryly.

"Good," Wes said, nodding.

Then he was leaving, disappearing out the door, and there was nothing left to do but to walk up to where Nate was hunched over the bar. His shoulders seemed even broader from his perspective, the muscles in them even more prominent, his dark green henley clinging to them.

"Hey," Ramsey said, sliding into the barstool next to him.

Nate shot him a look full of disbelief and annoyance. "What do you want?"

A more sane man might have led with, "Hey, I'm sorry I wasn't upfront about my *actual* job two months ago and then freaked out when it turned out you were painfully close by association to my best friend."

But Ramsey had never pretended to be particularly sane. There was always a point to the chaos, and an end goal in mind.

This time he wasn't sure *what* the end goal was, so that was unusual, but Ramsey didn't see any reason not to go with his normal shit stirring.

"Remember me?" Ramsey said with an easy grin.

Nate grimaced. "You *lied* to me."

"Actually," Ramsey said, "I told you the truth. You just didn't want to believe it."

"This how it usually goes with your hookups?" Nate demanded.

And okay, he was clearly pissed. Ramsey had known that before he'd come up to him. Honestly, he'd known he was going to be pissed the moment Wes had told him that Nate was coming tonight, just another name on a list of them. But Ramsey had underestimated just how annoyed Nate was going to be about it.

"Sure," Ramsey said. That *was* a lie. This was not how they went, at all. First, he never let them get as close to the real him, not like he had that night in June. And on top of that, unless there was something to be gained from the connection, he rarely slept where he ate.

It was just easier to keep things neat and tidy.

The last time he'd made the mistake of hooking up with a guy too close to his actual life, it had been the Evergreens' equipment manager, and the guy had sent him two years' worth of sappy, pathetic texts before Ramsey had finally let him down as easily as he could and blocked him. At the time, it had seemed simple enough—the guy had a lot of insider knowledge of the new coach. Info that Ramsey had needed.

But in the end, it hadn't been worth it. Far too messy.

"I don't believe you. I don't believe a word you say," Nate said bluntly.

"If I remember right, I was the only one who was *completely, totally honest*." Ramsey shot Nate his most dazzling smile. The smile that had always gotten Ramsey, with a little work and effort, whatever he'd wanted.

But Nate seemed infuriatingly immune to it. "Bullshit."

"I told you I was a hockey player."

"You also told me you had a wife you were looking to cheat on. And that you were going to buy a bar."

And okay, yes, the imaginary wife *was* bullshit. But it had been a test, one that Ramsey found worked really well at sorting the assholes from everyone else.

And not only had Nate not gone for it, he'd not believed it.

He hadn't waited for Ramsey to tell him it was a lie, he'd told *him* it was a lie.

"And you decided I was Willy Nylander's dog walker," Ramsey said, using the smile again, more out of habit than the belief that it might actually work on this guy.

Nate actually had the nerve to look disgruntled he'd brought that back up. "It was more believable than what you were telling me." He glanced down, into his glass. "Never met a hockey player who looked like you."

"Probably never met another guy who looked like me," Ramsey offered.

"Is everything for you a joke?"

Not even remotely. Nothing about Ramsey's life was a fucking joke, especially now. But if he told the truth . . .no. He never told the truth.

He'd told Nate already enough of the truth the first time they'd met, and now he was paying for that honesty.

"You seem to have me all figured out," Ramsey said.

"And you seem way less pissed and inclined to run away than you did in June," Nate said, frowning.

It was like he thought by claiming Ramsey was less of a man for taking off, he'd see red and word vomit up everything.

*Ha.*

Ramsey was made of much sterner stuff than that. He'd been called a cocksucker, a girl, a *pretty princess,* and far, far worse, by dudes a lot bigger and meaner than Nate Bishop for a lot longer.

He'd been formed in a blast furnace, and Nate tossing little grenades at him didn't even dent his shell.

"Maybe I thought after all my graciousness, I deserved a slightly better lie than *I work at Tim Horton's.*"

"Yeah, a real fucking gentleman," Nate complained. He downed the rest of his drink. "I don't even know why you're here. You made your feelings clear before."

There was that *F* word again.

It wasn't like Ramsey didn't have feelings. Everyone had feelings. They were an unavoidable symptom of being human. But Ramsey's feelings weren't for anyone else but *him.* He didn't share them, ever, and he couldn't see that changing.

"Maybe I wanted to make sure you wouldn't have a few more of those and blurt out the whole pathetic story to anyone." Ramsey gestured at the glass in Nate's hand.

He didn't know why he was being so combative when he'd theoretically come over here to smooth things over. To make nice in a way that only he could.

"Why do you even care if I do?" Nate asked.

The disdain in Nate's eyes burned. Make him wish for things that weren't ever going to happen, and that annoyed Ramsey.

"I don't," Ramsey said shortly. "I was only embarrassed for you. Getting a guy like me and then bungling it."

He was *fine* with his life the way it was. He didn't need anyone else interfering in it. Wes was plenty. He had Brody still, even if Brody felt further away from him than ever, preoccupied by medical school and his big, dumb NFL player boyfriend.

He'd *had* hockey. He'd have hockey again. He had other interests and diversions. The last thing he needed—or wanted—was this even bigger, even dumber football player who thought he knew Ramsey better than he knew himself.

He was *not* Brody.

A sick pair of biceps and wet dream abs weren't going to be enough to sway Ramsey.

"Please," Nate retorted. "I was *there*. I didn't bungle shit. You were . . .you were on board. Not exactly demanding to leave after I fucked you."

Ramsey clamped his lips together. That was the worst of it. Ramsey could talk a big game. Could talk around Nate the way he talked around everyone else he'd ever met, but he couldn't magically insert himself into Nate's brain and make him forget certain things about that night.

Like how into it Ramsey had been. How he'd let Nate romance him a little, and hadn't tried to stop him even once. How he'd not been in a hurry to leave either. How he might have stayed the night, even, if Nate had never turned the kitchen light on.

Nate knew all those things, and no amount of pretending, no amount of posturing, no amount of maneuvering, was going to change his opinion.

"You're sticking around Toronto, right?" Nate asked then, before Ramsey could land on a strategy that might work. Magic was unfortunately out. The last two Etsy witches he'd tried out hadn't panned out. He hadn't been particularly hopeful they would, but it was never a bad idea to have a ringer in your pocket.

"Why does it matter?" Ramsey asked. He wasn't bitter. Bitter people had exposed weaknesses, and Ramsey's weren't, because he wouldn't let them.

"'Cause Wes is gonna keep bringing you around."

Ramsey wanted to declare that he wouldn't be, not if Ramsey had anything to say about it. Not if Nate was going to be anywhere in the vicinity.

But to avoid Nate, he was going to have to tell Wes he didn't like him. And Wes wasn't going to believe that was true, unless Ramsey decided to confess the whole truth.

And he *really* didn't want to do that. Imagining Wes' aggrieved expression was bad enough, but then he'd want to interfere. He'd want Ramsey to get some mythical happily-ever-after ending, even if his had gone to shit. *Especially* because his had gone to shit.

"Yes," Ramsey conceded. "Wes probably will want to."

"And you're not going to tell him no."

"Probably not," Ramsey said between gritted teeth. He didn't like how this guy kept seeing right through him. How had he taken a look at him and Wes and then spent an hour in their presence and figured out Ramsey's soft spot? It wasn't okay, and it definitely wasn't fair.

"So what are we gonna do about this?"

For a half a second, Ramsey wondered if he was suggesting they sleep together again. And for that half a second his body sat up and begged, saying *yes please*, but then he reminded it why that was a terrible fucking idea.

Before he realized that of fucking course that wasn't what Nate was saying at all.

"You mean, how do we co-exist in the same universe?" Ramsey asked.

Nate frowned. "Why on earth would *you* have any trouble? Were you that pissed that I was a football player?"

To Ramsey's own surprise, he found himself more than a little desperate to admit that had nothing to do with it at all. He had a strict no football player policy—but if he'd been a guy on the Bills or the Jets or the Giants, he'd have made a gracious exception.

But no, Nate wasn't on the Bills or the Jets or the Giants. He was *right here*, on Wes' team, and therefore unavoidable. And Ramsey knew himself well enough to know he'd definitely want to avoid him at some point.

He always did.

"Ask my friend Brody. I have a strict no football players policy. I love brawn, but even *I* need some brains," Ramsey said flippantly, instead of any of the confessions he wasn't going to admit.

"God, you kinda are a selfish, superficial asshole, aren't you?" Nate said. Still frowning. Like he'd actually believed otherwise, and it was a kick to the gut to realize differently.

Well, the sooner Nate Bishop believed the Ramsey he presented to the world, the easier it would be to slough him off, same as Ramsey did everyone else.

"Sure, yeah," Ramsey said, deploying the smile, again.

Nate just shook his head. "God, I was so wrong about you."

*Yes. Yes, you were.*

Maybe if Nate believed it, he'd steer clear. Make sure when they did run into each other, unavoidably, that he didn't bother even looking in Ramsey's direction.

Ramsey nodded. "Yep, you sure were."

Nate's face freezing into dismissal shouldn't have hurt. Him walking away shouldn't have hurt. But Ramsey watched him go and thought, *it doesn't hurt.*

But it did, deep down in a place where Ramsey shoved all that unpleasant and difficult emotion that he didn't know how to parse. The way it felt growing up without a single person who'd given a shit about him, lost in the foster system. When he'd realized that Daniel Hood, his foster dad at nine, only gave a shit about him because he was good at hockey. He'd never been a son to Dan, only a means to an end. The incurable loneliness until he'd figured out that a hockey team could also be a family, but only if he always made sure he was in control of it.

The devastation when he'd lost the one thing he'd ever really wanted to that last concussion.

He was still determined to get it all back, but unlike people, Ramsey didn't have control over his brain. He couldn't force it to heal.

And even if it did, he'd never get these years—the best years of his career—back. He was comfortable financially now, but money had always come fairly easily to him. Even in juniors, he'd played cards to win. That hadn't changed in college.

The new contract he'd signed a month before the last concussion had ensured he'd never worry about his bank account again, but Ramsey still thought he might trade that financial stability to be back on the ice.

But nobody knew that but him. Not Brody. Not even Wes.

Nobody, just him. And if he kept burying it down, kept reinforcing his walls so nobody could see deep enough within them, then even he didn't have to know that either.

# CHAPTER 3



*September*

It had been a great team win—everyone contributing to the thirty-four to ten victory over the Houston Texans—so Nate wasn't surprised when Aidan announced they'd be going as a team to Vault.

Nate didn't want to go to Vault. He'd done a fairly decent job over the first few weeks of the season avoiding Ramsey. Wes tended to bring him, but usually only in bigger groups and usually only when they all ended up at Vault.

There was no question if Wes would show. He was as much part of this team as anyone else, even if Aidan seemed determined to make sure he stayed on the sideline, holding his clipboard.

Nate stared at his reflection in the mirror in his bathroom and tried to justify to himself not showing up. But it was the fourth game of the year and the Thunders' fourth win. It wasn't a huge win streak but it was significant enough to be worth celebrating, and if he was absent, it would be noted.

Sterling would say something, and while they were both captains, both voted to the position by their teammates, Sterling was almost ten years older, in the twilight of his career. Everyone knew this was his last season, and next season, the defense would be all Nate's.

Maybe Ramsey wouldn't be there tonight; surely he had to have better things to do than trail after Wes.

Maybe he'd left Toronto and gone back to Buffalo. Maybe he was even back to playing hockey.

Nate pulled his phone out of his pocket and did something he never let himself do.

Googling Ramsey Andresen—when they'd run into each other in August, it hadn't taken Nate very long after to search "Ramsey hockey" and find out his last name—was a dangerous proposition. But if he didn't, he wouldn't know if he'd be around. Wouldn't be able to prepare himself for the possibility.

There was his face right there in the beginning of the results, that heartbreaking profile that Nate had begun to hate. His pulse always betrayed him when he saw it, racing even though the last thing he wanted was to still be affected by the asshole.

But as Nate scrolled down through the news about him, it didn't look like Ramsey had come off the long-term injured reserve.

He stayed strong, clicking out of the search results before he could do anything more monumentally stupid like watch his highlights again.

Turned out that the guy was actually a damn good hockey player. Not that Nate would ever admit that out loud. Or admit to spending too many late nights on YouTube with his name in the search bar.

He'd go tonight and pretend, like every other time he saw him, that he didn't like him. Because he didn't. He *didn't*.

Ramsey was a smug, egotistical dickhead, clearly enamored by his own charm.

Reminding himself of that fact, Nate headed out to Vault, catching a cab and taking it downtown.

Sure enough, there he was, in one of the corner booths with Wes again, looking cozy. Diamonds barely glinting out from underneath his collar.

It would be easier if Nate could believe Ramsey was involved with Wes. If he could even believe Ramsey was in love with Wes, even if it was unrequited. But he'd been around them enough that it was obvious there was nothing but platonic feelings there.

Well, at least on Wes' side. Clearly, Ramsey didn't *have* feelings. He was too shallow for them, like a puddle on the street.

Nate headed to the bar, and the bartender, catching his eye, poured him a few fingers of the sipping rum he favored.

He swirled his glass and glanced around, hoping that someone else would materialize so he didn't have to go over there.

He got his wish, because a second later, Sterling arrived, sliding up to the bar next to Nate.

"Hey," he said, nudging Nate. "Great game out there."

"You said that already," Nate said. Sterling had told him as the last few minutes of the fourth quarter had ticked by.

"Yeah," Sterling said, nodding. He looked grimmer than he should, considering the Thunder were riding a four-game win streak to kick off the season.

"What is it?" Nate asked.

Sterling sighed. "I don't know what to do about Jordan."

Nate had been afraid it was about Jordan Atkinson, the Thunders' rookie linebacker. He was aware of how Jordan had missed a meeting, had gotten benched for it for the first series today, and had been vocal about how that was a bullshit punishment.

It wasn't bullshit. It was necessary, especially for rookies, because they needed to understand the commitment that was required to give to the team if you were going to play professional football. This wasn't college, where coaches would let shit slide as long as a player performed on the field.

Both Coach Robertson, the Thunders' head coach, and Coach Dell, the defensive coordinator, weren't going to stand for Jordan fucking around, no matter how talented he was.

"You talked to him?" Nate asked.

Sterling shot him a look full of frustration. "Yeah," he said, rubbing his bare head with one of his hands. "I fucking tried. He didn't want to listen."

"Of course not," Nate grumbled. He sipped his rum. This was his fourth season in the NFL, and he'd been around long enough to know that talent only got you so far. He'd seen guys wash out, not because they couldn't play, but because they couldn't follow the rules.

Jordan was good, sure, but it was going to take more than some flashy play to stay on this team if he kept fucking around.

"I think you should talk to him. Friend him up. Look out for him," Sterling said as he picked up the beer the bartender had just set in front of him.

"What?" This was not what Nate was expecting. "Me? Why?"

"He could do worse than using you as a role model," Sterling said.

"What about you?"

Sterling rolled his eyes. "He thinks I'm a grumpy old man."

"You *are* a grumpy old man," Nate retorted fondly.

"Still your fucking elder," Sterling teased back.

"So what, you think he'll listen to *me*, because I'm younger? I doubt it."

"I think he'll listen to you because you're going to become his friend," Sterling said persuasively.

There were a lot of problems with that statement. "I don't—"

"Think of what would've happened in that game today if he'd actually been in position to make a play on that ball, the one they scored the long touchdown on," Sterling pointed out.

"We'd have still won," Nate said. He did not want to spend a bunch of time and energy keeping up with Jordan's twenty-one-year-old antics. Some guys got into the NFL and it was their first experience with money and fame and they went overboard.

Listening to Jordan boast about spending money in the champagne room of his favorite strip club pinged all of those for Nate.

"Yeah, but that's not always going to be the case. You wanna win a Super Bowl?"

Nate rolled his eyes. "You mean, win another one? Yeah, of course I do."

It had sucked to be traded away the summer after the Condors had done it. He'd understood why. But he hadn't *liked* it, despite Toronto becoming home in the last few years.

"Then you gotta figure Jordan out. We're gonna need him."

Nate sighed. So not only did he need to go out of his way to avoid a certain hockey player who kept hanging around, his mentor was giving him a pretty much impossible task. Control someone who didn't want to be controlled. No, actually, it was worse than that. Sterling wanted him to convince Jordan that he *wanted* to be different than how he was.

"You're good with the guys. You can do this," Sterling said, clearly trying to pep talk him.

Nate was not nearly so optimistic. "He even here tonight?"

But Sterling just shrugged, like he'd passed the problem onto Nate and he was ready to be done with it.

As Sterling took off to shake hands and greet some of the other defensive guys—notably, Jordan was not among them—Nate tapped his fingers against the bar. Trying to figure out how he could approach this situation the best.

He was so deep in thought about the Jordan problem that he didn't even notice when someone slid onto the barstool next to his.

And of course it was the last person he wanted to see.

"Hey," Ramsey said, all easy and charming, like they didn't both wish they could avoid the other.

"What do you want?" Nate asked flatly.

He hadn't been in the mood before, now he really wasn't in the mood.

"Ouch." Ramsey grinned obnoxiously. "I thought you'd be happy to see me."

"In what universe would that be true?"

"The secret one, where deep down you're obsessed with me and can't leave me alone," Ramsey said.

"You mean your imagination," Nate retorted.

"I don't need one," Ramsey claimed. "Reality's always better than anything I can think up."

Nate knew that wasn't true. He was blustering. It was obvious that Ramsey, as annoying and obnoxious as he was, *did* miss playing hockey. He didn't want to be hanging around Toronto, crashing on Wes' couch, and harassing Nate.

But of course, he was still pretending otherwise, because he couldn't go five seconds without dissembling or even outright lying about something. Even if it was something as obvious as his frustration with his injury status.

"Don't be stupid," Nate said.

The guy thought he had everyone convinced all the time that he was happy and charming and their new best friend. Nate saw through it, and so knew it was all a fucking act. Why would he even bother? Ramsey didn't *know* any of these people so it was a waste of energy to pretend.

Nate's only conclusion was that he liked fucking around with people. That Ramsey *liked* pulling the wool over their eyes. Liked controlling them and their reactions to him.

And that, more than anything else, was what led Nate right back to the original conclusion he'd made the second time they'd met: Ramsey was a manipulative asshole.

Nate wasn't going to give him the satisfaction of lumping him in with all these other poor schmucks who salivated over him wherever he went. It didn't matter how hot he was.

"Someone isn't very happy about their big win," Ramsey said lightly. "Someone is even *grumpy*. I wonder why."

"Not a mystery. It's because you're always around." Nate finished his rum and tapped the edge of the glass so the bartender would pour him another round. "You piss me off."

Ramsey had the nerve to bat his eyes. "You just wish I'd sleep with you again and you're frustrated that I won't."

"I never even *suggested* we sleep together again," Nate said flatly.

Elbowing him in the side, not too gently, Ramsey just shot Nate the smile that had no doubt won him legions of admirers wherever he went.

"Stop it," he said. "You're gonna dent my ego."

Ramsey was already leading half of Nate's football team around by the dick, even the dudes who'd never imagined they'd be into another guy. What did he need more for? What did he even need *Nate* for? The whole fucking harem was right there, available for easy plucking.

Ramsey didn't even want him. He was clearly just annoyed that Nate wouldn't fall in line and salivate at his mere existence, right next to everyone else.

"I don't know if that's even possible. Your ego seems pretty bullet-proof to me."

"You've got no idea." Ramsey paused. "But I bet you wish you did." He grinned wilder now. That look on Ramsey's gorgeous face was purely lethal. Nate's pulse throbbed, and he wanted, more than anything else, to be as unaffected as he claimed to be. After all, Ramsey looked like he didn't give a shit even if Nate hated him. It made Nate want to hate him more.

It made Nate want to actually hate him *at all*.

"Is there a reason you're over here still, trying to convince me that I still want you?" Nate asked flatly.

Something shifted behind Ramsey's eyes. A flash of truth. Maybe not honesty, but at least the act rearranging itself.

In June, Nate had wanted to see behind the act. Thought he had, for a hot moment. Then in August, he hadn't been sure if Ramsey was anything *but* the act.

He didn't want to have to reorient his understanding of the guy again.

Instead he picked up his glass. "Exactly," Nate said. "I thought so."

It was easy enough to go find Lane. To convince him and Trevor to head to one of the rooms, the one with a pool table—a game that Ramsey had admitted he couldn't play and so he'd be in no danger of joining them.

But the whole game he was distracted. Scratching when he didn't usually do that shit. Missing an obvious-ish shot that normally he'd have jumped all over.

"You alright?" Lane asked casually as he picked up his beer, finishing it after their second game. He'd already sent Trevor on an errand to the bar to get them another round, and if Nate had been paying any attention, he'd have realized that wasn't just convenience but something else.

"Fine," Nate said shortly. He hadn't been thinking about Ramsey's easy but bone-deep admission about how his balance wasn't good enough. He *hadn't*.

He didn't want to consider what was going on behind those pale blue eyes. He didn't want to feel sorry for the guy. He didn't want to think about him *at all*.

It was annoying that was easier said than done.

"You seem distracted, that's all," Lane said. He leaned against the edge of the table, and because he was such a shit stirrer—an aspect of his personality Nate typically enjoyed because Lane tended to use it against other people and not Nate—he added, "I saw Ramsey out there, by the bar."

"If you're gonna fuck him, make sure you wrap your dick," Nate said flatly.

Lane's eyes lit up and Nate realized he'd made a tactical error.

"You *do* want him," Lane insisted.

"I don't." But Nate didn't think that sounded convincing even to himself. Deciding that Lane had started it, he had no qualms about turning the tables. "And neither do you."

"Come on, the guy's insanely hot," Lane argued, but it was weak, too.

They both knew who Lane really wanted and who Lane was trying very hard not to touch.

Maybe it was mean to actually bring it up, but Lane had gone there first.

"I'm not blind, dude," Nate said, more gently this time.

"It's not . . .we're not . . ." Lane trailed off. Looked away, like he was afraid his expression would give him away.

"But you haven't hooked up in two months," Nate said.

"Neither have you," Lane argued.

"Yeah, because I'm done with hookups." He was especially done after his last one—the night he'd spent with Ramsey—had gone so sideways. "I told you that last month."

"Yeah you said it, but then he's out there being all hot and enticing," Lane said, gesturing towards the main bar.

Nate raised an eyebrow, unsure if he was talking about Ramsey or if his friend was actually admitting to having the hots for his stepbrother.

"I'm done fucking around," Nate said with finality.

"Even if it's with the super hot hockey player?" Lane questioned.

"Especially then," Nate grumbled. "He's trouble. You know it. Which is probably why you keep trying to push him at me. So you can live vicariously through whatever happens."

Lane rubbed his hands together, smiling now. "Well, *yeah*. I'd want all the details."

And this was why Nate hadn't told him—or anybody—that he'd already slept with the guy. Lane *would* want all the details. He'd want the good gossip. Everyone would. And Nate didn't feel like sharing, even though it would make sense if he wanted to parse his hookup with Ramsey down to some easily digestible, meaningless soundbites.

"He's so hot, he'd probably be shit in bed. Thinks all he has to do is lie back and look pretty."

Nate would be having a much easier time if that had turned out to be true, but he didn't want Lane getting any big ideas and deciding that he was going to go for it, his hangup on Trevor be damned.

But Lane only looked unconvinced. "I don't know, man. He could be really good. Like life-ruining good."

Nate made a face. "Stop trying to get me to change my mind."

"I'm not. Really, I'm not." Lane attempted an innocent look, which was not very successful.

"Hey, look who I found." Trevor walked back into the room, several other players trailing behind him. One of them was Jordan Atkinson. At least that would save Nate from having to text him and figure out where he was tonight.

Atkinson was the kind of thing he needed to handle if he was going to be the sole defensive captain next year, but it was hard to not resent Sterling over him dumping the whole problem into his lap.

"Hey, guys," Nate said, greeting Jack, Duke, and Jordan. Jack and Duke were depth guys on the defense—good guys who Nate liked, who he hoped that Jordan wouldn't start dragging into his own crap.

"Jordo, what's happening?" Lane asked, giving him a bro-hug.

The last thing Jordan needed was to hang around *Lane.*

Lane was smart enough—or experienced enough?—to know where the line was between raising hell and getting kicked off the team. But Jordan wasn't, and he'd take it too far. Lane would probably laugh the whole way, right up until the worst scenario.

"Heard this place was pretty sick," Jordan said.

"You wanna play?" Nate said, trying to be casual, gesturing towards the table.

Jordan shot him an unimpressed look. "Pool?"

"They've got darts too," Duke said, though Nate already thought combining Jordan's recklessness with sharp, pointy objects was a disaster waiting to happen.

"Who's winning?" Jordan asked, gesturing to the table.

"Not Bishop," Lane said, before Nate could speak up. "He's distracted."

"Yeah?" Jordan glanced over at him. "What do you have to be worried about?"

"Not worried," Nate said. *Annoyed. Preoccupied. Frustrated—sexually and otherwise.*

"Something," Lane said knowingly. He shot Nate a sideways glance. "He wants to fuck the hot hockey player, but he thinks it's a bad idea."

Nate snorted. Lane was so right and so wrong, impossibly at the same time. "No, I don't."

"So why don't you?" Jordan asked.

When they'd first met, Nate had been worried that Jordan would be one of those guys who hadn't gotten the memo and still carried around a hard kernel of homophobia, buried deep down. But it turned out, he didn't give a shit, he just cared about having a good time, wallowing in his newfound money and celebrity. Expecting that he'd be the second coming of linebacker Jesus the moment he stepped onto the field.

And he *was* good, that was part of the issue. He was almost as good as he thought he was, even.

"It's complicated," Nate said.

Jordan smirked. "Seems pretty straightforward to me. Don't be such a square, Bishop."

It was not what Nate had expected—or wanted—but if Jordan making fun of how boring he was kept him out of the worst of the hell he could raise, then Nate would take it.

"Play me, and if you win, I'll go over and talk to him," Nate said. He had no intention of losing or of talking to Ramsey, again.

"He *is* hot," Jordan said.

Trevor scoffed. "You're fucking straight, Atkinson."

Jordan just raised his hands in mock surrender. "But not blind."

It was annoying, but not particularly surprising when even the straight bro-dudes on Nate's football team could see themselves making an exception for Ramsey.

"Come on," Lane said persuasively, nudging Jordan. "Bishop's been off all night. It's your fucking time, Jordo."

Trevor held out his cue and Jordan accepted it, and Nate took that to mean it was on.

After racking the balls, he looked over at Jordan. "So, what do I get if *I* win?"

Jordan shrugged but Nate had an idea.

"You've been off all night. You're not gonna win," Lane boasted.

Yeah, he had. But if the price of losing was having to go talk to Ramsey again, he was going to fucking win.

"If *I* win," Nate said, "you're gonna hang out with me this week."

"Oooooh shit, rookie, you're in trouble," Lane called out.

Jordan made a face. "Well, I'm just gonna have to wipe the floor with you then, old man."

Nate sighed internally. He was only five years older than Jordan, but some days it felt like an eternity.

"You got it," Nate said, gesturing for Jordan to break.

He *had* been distracted all night; Lane was right about that. But Lane also probably thought he was just looking for an excuse to go talk to Ramsey, and the opposite was actually true.

It wasn't easy, locking in to the game in front of him, but Nate had learned, all the hard ways, how to do it when it really mattered.

Sure enough, twenty minutes later, Nate sank the eight ball, winning the game.

"Shit," Jordan said, glancing over at Nate as he settled a hip against the edge of the table. "Double or nothing?"

"No can do," Nate said. "I can't go talk to the hockey player twice, so I guess you're stuck with me this week."

Jordan groaned with exaggerated annoyance.

Nate felt that, too, but he *couldn't* look annoyed because this was part of his job. Would be solely his responsibility after this season.

It was going to take a lot more than a week to iron out the rookie, but Nate hoped that it would at least be a good start.

# CHAPTER 4



*October*

Nate shouldn't have come to this game. There was no excuse for not realizing that Ramsey would be at a hockey game that Wes was at, too. And he absolutely should have known Ramsey would show up and probably waltz around the suite, charming everyone in his path, hot as shit and knowing it too.

"Nathaniel," Ramsey said, dipping his head in greeting.

Not caring that Nate's name *wasn't* Nathaniel, even when Levi called him out for it.

"He knows," Nate said flatly.

But Ramsey only shrugged, an expression on his face that could only be called whimsical. "It suits you."

It didn't, because it wasn't his name. Ramsey didn't just get to change his name, because he decided to. Ramsey wasn't in charge here, despite all his feelings to the contrary.

"It does not," Nate ground out. Tried to hate him more. Tried to hate him *at all*.

But every time he thought he was making some real progress on that plan, he saw something he knew he wasn't supposed to see. Ramsey being affectionate with Wes. Ramsey supporting Dawson. Ramsey being kind to the rookie punter. Ramsey refusing to sleep with Lane when he'd finally made a half-hearted offer a few weeks back.

He was so busy trying to justify the feelings that wouldn't come, no matter how much he kept willing them to, no matter how much he kept pretending they already existed, when Ramsey turned to him and asked, "What did you think, Nathaniel?"

Nate hadn't been paying any attention to whatever bullshit Ramsey was spouting. Or what they'd been discussing. "No clue."

"Oh, that's right," Ramsey said. "Hockey's too good for you. Or you're too good for hockey? I can't remember which it is."

Nate hadn't said anything really. But it was easier to pretend he didn't like hockey players generally than to detail exactly why he didn't like Ramsey *specifically*.

"You did say you'd get him here, to Scotia Bank," Lane pointed out.

"I did. You wanna get out there after the game?" Ramsey asked, innocent expression pasted on his face.

"No," Nate said flatly.

"I don't know, I think you'd be okay out there." And there it was again. Another instance where Ramsey could've been an ass, and had pulled back, *just enough*. Just enough that it was really fucking difficult to dredge up feelings of utter hatred. Profound dislike, maybe.

"Don't fucking do that," Nate said, uncomfortably aware they had an audience. Uncomfortably aware that they were edging towards this thing between them that nobody else knew about.

"Do what?" Ramsey asked.

"That look doesn't work on me," Nate said.

But it wasn't the look. Okay, it wasn't *only* the look.

Ramsey had the nerve to look momentarily surprised. Like he *hadn't* expected Nate to pull them back from whatever precipice they were dangling on.

But Nate wasn't going to indulge any more of Ramsey's bullshit.

Before he could respond, Nate turned and walked away, leaving the group to go in search of a beer. Or maybe even something stronger. At least that was what he told himself as he rifled through the mini fridge set underneath the far-side counter.

He spent the next twenty minutes watching the game on TV and trying to avoid getting pulled into the group of Lane, Mo, and Trevor, who were all picking Ramsey's brain about the game as the second period unfolded.

At the end of the second, he finally got a text from Jordan, who'd said he was coming to the game when Nate had cornered him at lunch, insisting he come along. "Your week ended ages ago," Jordan had said, rolling his eyes. "Why do I want to go to a hockey game?"

Nate hadn't wanted to tell him the truth—that the last place he wanted to go was a hockey game, albeit for very different reasons probably—but he'd just shot Jordan his best *I'm your captain* look and told him to come anyway.

Fifteen minutes before they'd met up outside the arena, Jordan had only sent a, *not coming* text to Nate, and then hadn't answered the next three texts Nate sent, or picked up the phone call he'd made as they walked to the suite.

But now *finally*, he was responding. Of course, it wasn't like his response made Nate feel any better.

**Chill out. I'm cool.**

That was not even remotely the kind of answer that made Nate chill out.

He sighed, tapping the table next to where his phone sat as he tried to figure out what to say to Jordan that he might actually listen to.

"You don't usually frown like that at anyone except me. And I'm right here, so I know it's not me."

He hadn't even seen Ramsey approach, but there he was, a wry smile on his face. Settling in across from Nate like he wasn't going anywhere.

"It's not," Nate said flatly.

More than once, Nate had wondered why Ramsey kept seeking him out, despite him being so clear that he wasn't interested in playing

Ramsey's games. He'd eventually come to the conclusion Ramsey did it because he wasn't used to anyone not liking him. Wasn't used to being rejected when he tried to wiggle his way onto anyone's good side.

Ramsey wasn't necessarily interested in *him*. He just didn't like to lose.

"Come on, you were looking at that phone like you'd like to explode it with your mind. I've been told I'm a good listener." Ramsey deployed the smile that probably made just about everyone else putty in his hands.

It wasn't that Ramsey's incredible smile *didn't* affect Nate. It did. Just in a different way than Ramsey probably expected. There was still a hint of the *real* smile, the one he hadn't realized in June was the most authentic part of Ramsey, buried in the showy, flashy version. Nate didn't like to think of it as *fake*, but that was probably a fair-ish assessment when it came down to it.

But every time Ramsey smiled like that, Nate was still reminded of that night. When he'd known everything and nothing, all at once.

"You, a good listener?"

Ramsey shrugged, easygoing and uncomplicated. When hilariously, there was not a single easy *or* uncomplicated thing about him.

"So I've been told," Ramsey claimed.

"They probably just tell you that so you stand there and they can look at you, uninterrupted," Nate muttered.

There was another, slightly stronger, hint of the *real* smile in this one.

"Maybe," Ramsey admitted. "But I *am*, no question, probably the best problem solver you've ever met."

Now that Nate could believe. Ramsey would manipulate at least a dozen people while he solved their problems, but the problems *would* be solved.

"I'd ask if anyone ever put you in charge of something that you'd be shitty at, and then didn't help you when you started to fail but then . . ."

"I don't fail?" Ramsey grinned.

It would be mean, but for a moment, Nate considered reminding him that he was currently on long-term injured reserve. But then that hadn't been Ramsey failing; that had been Ramsey's *body* failing.

But before he could decide what to say instead, Ramsey continued, "I doubt anyone put you in charge of something you'd fail at. I don't see you as the failure type."

"I fail every day at liking you," Nate retorted, though these days it felt more the opposite.

"Fair," Ramsey said, not looking like he believed him for even a second. "But honestly, I'm good at lots of kinds of stuff, and because I am, I can tell you that *you* are too."

"That why you can't leave me alone?"

"You caught me. It's a competency kink."

"Be serious."

"Oh, baby, I am. But to add to my bona fides, I wore the C in college, too."

"The C?"

"I was the captain," Ramsey explained. His lips turned into a smirk. "It's what we call it in that other, *real*, sport."

Nate supposed he should be annoyed, but the laugh bubbled out of him anyway.

"Ah. Okay." So maybe this wasn't out of Ramsey's wheelhouse. But telling him would mean *telling him,* and Nate was already not doing a great job keeping him at arm's length.

Good enough that Aidan kept shooting him worried looks whenever they were in the same room together, but not good enough that Nate was convinced he could actually keep it up for as long as he should.

"You gonna tell me about it?" Ramsey prodded.

Nate didn't want to say, *Sterling dumped this problem on me and whenever I try to talk to him about it, he just brushes me off.* Sterling had more important things to deal with, though it was probably more like, it was his last year and he was tired of dealing with annoying rookies.

Nate sympathized. He'd only had custody of Jordan for a few weeks now, and he was already over it.

"I told you, it's this problem, and it got put on me, and I'm not . . .it's not working."

While Nate might be pissed at Sterling for this, he wasn't about to expose him to Ramsey.

"You think about asking someone else?" Ramsey asked.

Nate shot him an unamused look. "I'm not going to tell you about it."

"Dude, calm down. I wasn't saying *me*. You clearly don't want to give me any more details, and it's hard to help without them. I meant, is there someone else on the team, or maybe another friend you could run this by."

It was stupid how Nate had *never* thought of that. He'd tried so hard to make the Thunder his team when he'd been traded, but of course, he had friends still in Charleston, where he'd begun his NFL career.

"Yeah, actually." He and Deacon Harris, his mentor after he'd been drafted by the Charleston Condors, still talked pretty often. Sometimes it was just a text exchange after a game. Sometimes Deacon would call him, give him a heads-up about an opponent he'd just seen on film. Every time he did that, Deacon's husband and the owner of the Condors, Grant Green, complained fondly about how he was trying to give Nate—and the Thunder—an unfair advantage. But Deacon would just look at him, and though Grant was a certified ballbuster, both in the internet security world *and* the football world, the only one who could get him to stop whining about anything was Deac.

"There you go," Ramsey said as Nate nodded slowly. "You can say *thank you, Ramsey, you're a gorgeous and brilliant man*, now."

"Pass?"

Ramsey made a face. "Come on. I helped you, and I didn't have to."

"You chose to walk over here," Nate reminded him. Reminding him, also, of the fact that he couldn't seem to leave Nate alone.

Occasionally, Ramsey would make a pointed comment about how Nate couldn't forget their night together. And despite the fact that it was unfortunately true, he was beginning to think the opposite might *also* be true.

Maybe it was *Ramsey* who couldn't forget their night together.

Nate's neck went hot, and his fingers trembled as he picked up the phone, shoving it in his pocket. He'd call Deacon on his way home, get his perspective on the whole Jordan situation.

"Okay, you could at least say *thank you*," Ramsey bitched.

"You came over here," Nate teased instead, and Ramsey just rolled his eyes.

But Nate could feel the weight of his gaze on him as he went over to Aidan and Dawson and Cam, where they were sitting at the front of the suite, to let them know he was taking off.

Aidan shot him a concerned look. "You're leaving already?"

Nate nodded, and Aidan frowned. His expression, coupled with the fact that Aidan kept glancing back at where Ramsey was leaning, all easy charm against the tall table in the middle of the suite, made it clear he thought Nate was leaving because of Ramsey.

Well, he wasn't *not* leaving because of Ramsey.

But Nate wasn't touching that subject with Aidan with a ten-foot pole. He'd tried a few times, but he was still attempting—and failing—to be casual about it, enough that it was still easy enough for Nate to brush him off.

That might not be true forever, but at least it still held true tonight.

"See you at practice tomorrow," Nate called out to the other guys, waving as he disappeared out the door.

Still painfully aware of how Ramsey's eyes were still following him.

When he was in a cab on the way home, he texted Deacon. **You still up, old man?**

Deacon called him a second later. "Who are you calling old?" he grumped.

"You gonna call me an upstart next?" Nate joked, leaning back on the bench seat as the cab navigated the late night downtown Toronto traffic. The game wasn't over yet, but the streets around the area were still packed.

When he'd first been drafted by Charleston, and he'd met Deacon Harris, he'd been star-struck and dick-struck, harboring the world's most ridiculous crush on the guy. It had hurt, a little, when he'd realized that Deacon wasn't looking back at him but had been pining instead for the new owner of their team. But in the end, Nate could acknowledge that everything had turned out the way it should have.

"Maybe," Deacon teased. "You'd probably like that too much, though."

Deacon and Grant were meant for each other, and well, Nate hadn't met *his* ideal match yet, but he still had faith he could be around the next corner.

Especially now that he'd given up hookups and was trying to view the guys he met through a more relationship-friendly lens.

"Not anymore. Not in forever, old man," Nate insisted.

"Aw, disappointing," Deacon joked even though they both knew he wasn't, at all. "You gonna tell me what's up?"

"You gonna stop claiming I've got a secret crush on you?"

Deacon just laughed. "It's good for my ego, though."

"Like that needs any more help," Nate complained. "Yeah. I'm having . . .well, *I'm* not having the problem."

Deacon was quiet for a moment, letting Nate have his space. Something Nate had always appreciated about him.

"It's this rookie," Nate finally admitted.

"Let me guess. Atkinson."

Of course it was obvious. If Deacon had been paying any amount of attention to the Thunder, he'd probably seen it immediately. And that wasn't even counting how Jordan *had* been benched for the first series, a month ago, for missing a meeting.

Deacon, who was unofficially on the Condors coaching squad and had been a player in the NFL for almost twenty years, had likely seen that and knew there was more to the story.

"Yeah," Nate said.

"Okay, so you're a captain sure, but what about Sterling? He's the vet here. He should be handling the guy."

"He *was*," Nate said. "But he thought it might come across better—less a vet telling a rookie to shape up and more a friend watching out for another friend—if I did it."

Deacon sighed but didn't say anything. Which made it painfully obvious what he really thought of that.

"You can say it," Nate said testily. He probably wouldn't like it, but he was already a little annoyed at Sterling for dumping this problem he didn't have the skill set to deal with into his lap and then washing his hands of the whole thing.

"He shouldn't be giving it over to you. Not like that."

Nate had told himself he was not going to defend Sterling but the tone of Deacon's voice put his back up anyway.

"But—"

"No," Deacon said, even more firmly. "Sure, yeah, that's a good tactic. Pull him into the community of the team and a friend group of slightly older guys who aren't spending all their spare time fucking around."

"Why do I feel like there's another shoe you're waiting to drop?" Nate asked.

"Because there is. He should be asking you to do that, but he should still be being fucking leader."

"Deac," Nate warned.

"I've tried to be nice about it, but Sterling's phoning it in. If he wasn't prepared to play and lead the team the way he has every other year, he shouldn't be playing *or* leading," Deacon said righteously. "I knew when I was done. He shouldn't have taken that single season contract. It was a fucking money grab, especially if he wasn't committed."

"He's committed," Nate argued, though personally, deep down, he understood a little too well what Deacon was claiming.

"Is he though? Or is he just shoving all the hard shit onto you so you can deal with it?"

Sometimes it *did* feel that way, but at the same time, if he was going to lead the Thunders' defense next year, he should be able to handle anything Sterling tossed his way.

Deacon sighed again, full resignation in the sound. "Don't answer that. I'm just frustrated for you. We'll talk about Atkinson, instead."

"Yeah," Nate said.

It made sense to focus on the Jordan problem, because that was certainly, in some universe, under some unique set of circumstances, fixable. The Sterling thing? Nate couldn't imagine confronting the guy—who was a full ten years older than him, with eleven more NFL seasons under his belt, and a Super Bowl ring—and calling him out for phoning it in.

That was a great way to get his ass kicked into next week.

"So, what have you tried?" Deacon asked.

The cab pulled up to his building, and Nate got out, handing the driver a wad of twenties. Way more than the fare, but he could afford it.

The wind was fierce as he walked to the front door, and he shielded his face from it, cradling the phone against his face. "I tried being his friend, yeah? I tried reaching out to him. Making plans. Texting. Tried diverting him away from spots where he'd end up in trouble."

"Let me guess, that did jack shit."

"You got it." Nate hated admitting it, but it was the truth. And while he couldn't bring himself to admit most of this to Ramsey, Deacon was a different story.

"You go to the strip club with him?"

Nate choked out a laugh. "*No.*" He pressed the elevator button for his floor.

"I know, not your typical scene."

"You know I'm gay, I'm not gonna go to the strip club with Jordan." Though he had thought about it, more than once, for the sheer ease of at least being around to prevent the guy from getting into any more trouble.

"You're not gonna like this," Deacon warned.

"I didn't think I'd *like* it," Nate complained as he got off on his floor. "I wasn't calling you for a nice, sweet bedtime story."

"Brat," Deacon said, chuckling. "You asked for it. But really, you've tried to make him come to you, and clearly that's not gonna work. You gotta go to him."

"I was afraid you were gonna say that."

"Hey, positively, you're not gonna be tempted to hit on any of the nice ladies."

"I'm going to be there to prevent Jordan from doing it. Or at least steering him towards doing it respectfully," Nate said heavily as he swiped his key against his front door.

"You've got the gist," Deacon said. "Wherever he goes, you're going. Even if you hate it."

Nate went to his fridge, grabbed a water, and then flopped down on his big, comfortable couch. Out of the corner of his eye, he saw the framed jersey hanging on his wall.

The jersey that had made Ramsey freak out. But then, maybe he always would've left. Maybe he was never going to stay, even for the night, and anything else was a delusional fantasy.

"I do hate it," Nate grumbled. He hated a lot of things today. Starting and ending with how nice-ish Ramsey had been, and in a way that had actually felt mostly genuine.

"You okay, bud?" Deacon asked gently. "I shouldn't have to ask. How many games have you won so far?"

"All of them." Nate wanted to sound smug about it, but it didn't come out that way.

"Come on, you can't be depressed about that. So you have to go to a few strip clubs."

"A *few*? You're underestimating Jordan Atkinson's appetite for a strip club."

Deacon laughed. "That's all that's bothering you?"

Nate had not told his friend—or anyone at all—about the Ramsey situation, but maybe he should. He didn't know if getting it off his chest would actually help, but surely it couldn't make the whole thing *worse*.

"No. There's this guy—"

"Of course there is," Deacon interrupted.

"Are you going to listen or not?" Nate asked archly.

"Yeah, yeah, I'll listen," Deacon agreed, still chuckling.

Nate recited what had happened as succinctly and undramatically as possible. Seeing the hottest guy in the world across the bar. Ramsey approaching him. Them flirting. Ramsey making his desires clear. Nate deciding he didn't care—or that he could change his mind? He still wasn't clear on that, and he skipped over it. The kiss. The sex in his place. The kitchen and its aftermath.

Then running into Ramsey at the Vault team party, and realizing that he was actually a hockey player, and a friend of Wes'.

"Wait a sec," Deacon interrupted him again. "What did you say his name was again?"

"You're going to fucking google him?"

"Well, *yeah*. You said he was the hottest guy you'd ever seen. I need to verify that this is actually factual and not just your dickmatized goggles on."

Nate sighed. "Trust me, he's that hot."

"Not gonna believe you, not til I see him myself," Deacon said.

"Fine. Ramsey Andresen."

There was a second of quiet. Then, "Holy shit."

It was hard not to say, *I told you so*, but Nate was thinking it.

"Okay, yeah. You're right. Holy shit."

"Good thing Grant isn't listening in," Nate teased.

"Are you kidding me? When he gets home from the office, I'm gonna show him. You said this guy's a *hockey player*?"

"I know, right?"

"Shit," Deacon said appreciatively. "And he was good in bed?"

Nate swallowed hard. He'd tried very hard not to think about Ramsey and a bed—or a couch or a dirty bathroom or any possibly conveniently horizontal or even *vertical* surface—but that was like asking water to not be wet.

"Yeah," he said.

"No wonder you're fucked up about him," Deacon said.

"That doesn't help," Nate complained. "I don't want him, but he won't leave me alone."

"Seriously? That's what you're going with?" Deacon chuckled under his breath. "How's that working out for you?"

Fucking terrible, that was how it was working out for him.

"That's what I thought," Deacon said when Nate didn't answer. Didn't trust himself to answer.

"I know the team guys want us to get along. But every time I think about it—about playing nice—I . . ." Nate trailed off. *I think about playing way too nice.* But it was obvious that Ramsey didn't want that. He'd been so charming, but also keeping Nate at a distance. Like he didn't want Nate to get any ideas. Well, *Nate* wanted to stop getting ideas.

"You don't like it. I've been there, trust me," he said wryly.

And yeah, he probably had. Deacon's final season had coincided with Nate's rookie season—and also the season when Deacon and Grant had finally stopped circling each other and had gotten together for real.

"I'd ask you what you did to get over it, but we all know you never did." Even thinking about that fact was entirely unhelpful.

Nate couldn't say he was pining after Ramsey, but he was doing enough of *something* that the very presence of the guy, even around the periphery of his life, made him tense.

The Jordan situation wasn't helping that either.

"No, I didn't," Deacon agreed. "Are you—"

"No. *No.* I'm not anything. I just . . .he's just there, all the time. An irritant."

"Sure," Deacon said easily. But Nate wasn't sure Deac actually agreed with him.

"Nothing I can do about it. Just try to avoid him, I guess." Though he'd already been doing that. Not *that* well, and if he wasn't mistaken, he had a feeling the longer Ramsey spent hanging around Toronto, the more likely it was that he was going to end up getting a lecture from Aidan. He could *feel* Aidan worrying about it, wanting to fold Ramsey into more of their team functions, making sure he didn't feel alone or abandoned, even though he wasn't playing.

Maybe Ramsey wasn't on Aidan's team, didn't play Aidan's sport, even, but none of that mattered. Aidan was the most aggressive team captain in the history of team captain-ing, plus he had all those big brother genes.

"You could try *not* avoiding him," Deacon said, far too reasonably.

Nate laughed, but he wasn't that amused. "Why would I do that?"

"Because fighting the inevitable is still fighting." Deacon was still saying all this in this fucking calm ass tone, like what he was saying was not only sensible, it was valid.

"And then I stop fighting and what?"

Deacon hesitated.

"Exactly," Nate said. "He's not magically going to want me. He's just going to keep hanging around, being tempting and infuriating." Nate could imagine it. Nate woke up from nightmares in cold sweats, thinking about how shitty it would be if he gave in to his feelings and Ramsey only kept taunting him. Not wanting him the way Nate could want him, if he let himself.

"Okay then. Keep fighting the good fight then?"

Nate snorted. "Yeah. Okay."

"And don't be a stranger."

"It was good you dropped by the suite tonight," Wes said.

Ramsey looked up from his spot, where he was reclining on his guest room bed. Well, it was basically *Ramsey's* bed now, he'd spent so much time here.

"Yeah," Ramsey said. It had been weird, the Wolves coming to town, but he'd known it was coming, too, and that he wasn't really any closer to getting on the ice than he'd been before. With enough time, he could mentally prepare for anything, could build his walls high enough, smooth enough, impenetrable enough, that nothing could ever really touch him.

Wes kept a closer eye on the Wolves schedule than he did these days—though Ramsey had most definitely known that *this* game was coming up—and there was no way it was a coincidence that Wes had made sure the Thunder contingent came to the arena for this particular game.

"Did it help at all, or did you want to just lick your wounds in peace?" Wes asked. He pushed off the doorframe and came into the room, settling down on the corner of the bed.

It had been obvious before that Wes had wanted them here for Ramsey, even if they weren't Ramsey's team—and it was even more obvious now. It was a kind gesture, even if Ramsey wasn't entirely sure it meant anything, in the end.

He was still up in the suite, not down on the ice.

His team was still playing without him.

"It was good." Nothing would've *really* helped, but just having Wes so transparently give a shit about his emotional state helped.

"Don't lie to me," Wes said. "I saw you talking to Nate."

Wes did not know any of *that* story yet, though it was clear enough something else had happened, even to Wes, and Ramsey kept expecting to be asked about it.

But Wes kept pretending.

Hard to say if that was better or worse.

"Yeah, well, maybe I haven't given up on getting on that guy's good side," Ramsey said. Not a lie. Not exactly. If he did somehow end up on Nate's good side, he wasn't sure he'd survive it.

"Maybe you should," Wes said, sighing. "I was surprised he came."

Wes was not subtle. He should have just admitted, out loud, that he would've strongly suggested that Nate not show up to the game with the other guys.

"I'm not," Ramsey said. He could always feel Nate's eyes on him. He felt a lot of guys' eyes on him, but they weren't ever like Nate's. It was obvious Nate didn't want to be looking. That he'd rather be looking anywhere else.

But he still looked anyway and then resented Ramsey the whole time for the fact he couldn't help himself.

Wes shot him a transparently concerned look. "He's a good guy. I don't know why he hated you basically on sight."

Ramsey sighed. He knew he should tell Wes the truth, but at this point if he did it, Wes would know why he waited so long. And after that exception piled on yet another exception, so many exceptions he'd made for Nate, that he *kept* making for Nate, Wes might finally figure out why he drove Ramsey crazy.

Having to see him, his presence a forcible reminder of how it had felt that one night, and then put that aside every time, was not easy. Compounding the problem was that it had always been easy before.

"Are you ever gonna tell me why?" Wes pressed.

Ramsey hesitated.

"There's nothing," Ramsey said. Hating himself. Hating lying to Wes. The further into this that they got, the more he knew he should have told him the truth in June. *Sorry, bud, I accidentally picked your teammate up and it was really good. Until I realized who he was, I thought there was a chance he might be the exception to a lot of my rules.*

Wes sighed. "I know there's something. You're gonna tell me someday."

"Yeah," Ramsey agreed, despite not knowing if that was true, especially not with how things were going.

Wes stood, shooting Ramsey a wry look. "Don't spend too much time on screens tonight, okay?"

Ramsey had nearly reached his screen time limit for the day looking over the books for the bar this afternoon, so he just nodded.

Wes flipped off the overhead light on the way out, just the dim lamp on the table next to the bed on.

Once, a few weeks ago, after a few drinks, Levi had insisted on air-dropping him the contact info of basically everyone on the team. "Just in case you need someone," he said, "and Wes isn't around."

It was slightly ridiculous because Wes was always around, like an overeager and overprotective puppy, but it had also netted him the phone number he thought he'd never get. The phone number he'd told himself he'd never want.

Now Nate sat in his contacts, taunting him with his unused existence. The messages between them empty except for the different drafts he kept typing out and deleting.

It was so stupid. He should just delete the contact, and with it, the temptation to say something to Nate that he shouldn't.

He typed out one of his many drafts. **Hope you got the advice you needed.**

Then Ramsey deleted it a letter at a time, forcibly, pads of his fingers pressing into the screen like he could erase it from his mind.

It was the kind of painfully obvious text he'd have told everyone he knew not to send, ten out of ten times.

A flimsy excuse to make contact.

*If you have something to say, just say it,* the old Ramsey would've said.

Well, if he was taking that advice . . .

The next draft read: **I can't stop thinking about that night in June. I don't think you can either.**

That text he erased with a regretful melancholy, fingers lingering instead over each word.

He'd ask why he was like this, but he already knew. The therapist his billet mom had insisted he see, when he'd played in juniors, when she'd discovered that despite his foster kid status, he'd never been, had told him that he had a lifetime of reinforced walls that nobody could hope to get around.

At the time, he'd thought, *yes,* and *good.*

Now, at twenty-five, that thought didn't fill him with reassurance any longer.

He just felt alone. Even with Wes down the hall and Brody in his phone, all his secrets—even secrets from his best friends—threatened to bury him.

What he should really do was *leave.* Go back to Buffalo. If he did, he wouldn't keep running into the guy. Would be able to get some *much needed* perspective.

Back in June, he never thought he'd be hanging around Toronto in October. He'd assumed, maybe naively, maybe with an overdeveloped sense of *shit works out for me* that he'd be back in Buffalo, back with the team.

Even if he wasn't able to have contact or practice with the team, there was nothing stopping him from going back.

Back to his empty apartment. The empty life he'd built for himself pre-concussion that had seemed, at least on the surface, like what he'd always wanted. It had only taken a month on injured reserve to realize it was all meaningless bullshit.

If he was lonely now, even with Wes pulling his overprotective routine, Buffalo would be worse. Buffalo wasn't a solution. Normally, he'd face that problem with a clear-eyed pragmatism that every adult he'd ever met had admired.

He typed out another text he wasn't ever going to send.

**Shit sucks.**

That wasn't a very Ramsey-like text. Hardly designed to make Nate actually want him.

He deleted it again and tossed his phone next to him on the bed, feeling the beginnings of a headache that might've had its origins in his fucked up brain, or his fucked up heart—it could be one or it could be both. Probably *was* both.

He stood up and walked down the hall.

Wes was lying in bed. "Hey," he said, "everything okay?"

Ramsey ducked his head. "Do you mind—"

He didn't have to say anything more. Wes just scooted over and patted the covers. "Of course," he said, before Ramsey could figure out how to choke out the question.

Ramsey slid in next to him, settling down on the other pillow.

They did this sometimes—had done it more frequently when Ramsey had first come to Toronto—but it had always been totally platonic. It would never be anything else, Ramsey knew that now, one hundred percent for sure. He'd been ninety-nine-percent sure when he'd come to Toronto, because Wes was still painfully in love with Marcus, but after his night with Nate, he'd *known*.

It would never be like that with him and Wes, but there was still love between them. Two people who, if they weren't together, would be alone and knew it.

"You okay?" Wes asked, rolling over, grayish-green eyes full of concern.

With anyone else, Ramsey would smile and nod. He'd practically made a fucking career out of being okay. But that was the beauty of Wes. He was allowed to shake his head instead. Allowed to say, "No. But I will be."

And Wes was allowed to reach over and squeeze his arm and say back, "Yeah, you will."

# CHAPTER 5

Nate knew something like this was coming, but he was still surprised when Aidan cornered him in the hallway just outside the locker room after practice.

"Hey," Aidan said, pushing off the wall, where he'd clearly been lying in wait for Nate to head out towards the cafeteria for lunch.

Nate glanced over at him suspiciously. "What do you want?"

"Maybe I just want to say hey," Aidan said, making a face. "Why wouldn't I want to say hey?"

Nate shot him a disgruntled look. "Because I know you?"

"Fair. That's fair. I just wanted to grab you real quick and check in."

They both knew what Aidan wanted to check in about, but Nate was annoyed enough they had to have this conversation at all he was going to pretend until there was zero plausible deniability. "Oh, you want to chat about Atkinson, too?"

Aidan frowned. "What's going on with Atkinson?"

"Sterling didn't tell you?"

"Oh, he did." Aidan steered him, not towards the elevator that led to the floor with the cafeteria, but one of the empty meeting rooms. Again, it wasn't surprising as much as it was annoying. "Told me you were taking care of it. Are you not?"

"I am," Nate said. He'd been to three strip clubs in ten days, and he hadn't *hated* it, though the whole point of it had been pretty lost on him.

"Good, good."

Aidan leaned against the first row of chairs in the auditorium-style room. "I'm glad, but Atkinson isn't why I wanted to check in."

"I know," Nate said.

"If you—" Aidan broke off, shaking his head. "You don't want to talk about it."

"I think you'd be the first person to get that," Nate muttered.

"I am, but sometimes we gotta take one for the team." Aidan gave him a hard look.

"He's not on our team."

"No, he isn't," Aidan said frankly. "He's not really on *any* team right now, and that sucks."

Nate wanted to say how that wasn't his problem. He was desperate for it to not be his problem. But it had, inevitably, been his problem since June.

His problem because his brain and some other organs he refused to identify kept making it his problem.

"Yeah, it does," Nate said instead.

"I talked to Wes a few days ago and he told me Ramsey's not going back to Buffalo anytime soon."

Nate had known it, but it still sucked to hear it, laid out in black and white like that. He needed Ramsey to be okay, not just because that would mean Ramsey would go back across the border, but because it meant he would be *okay*.

"Okay."

Aidan made a frustrated noise deep in his throat. "Tell me what your deal is with him, because he's not going anywhere. I want him around, even if you don't."

The last thing he wanted to do was tell Aidan Flynn about his sex life, but maybe he could . . .well, he could say *something*. "I met him before," he said, hoping he could keep it nebulous.

"Oh yeah?" Aidan crossed his arms over his chest and just looked unamused.

"Yeah." Nate still wanted to leave it there.

"So what? You hit on him and he turned you down and you're bitter about it now?"

"Not even close," Nate scoffed. Then realized a second too late that he should've worked a little harder to keep a poker face. But that was the problem with Ramsey—he blasted through any attempt Nate ever made at disinterest.

"Ah, so you slept with him and he ditched you."

It had been so much more than that, but Nate supposed that if you had to boil it down to the basic series of events, that was it. He nodded.

"I worry about Levi if he ever has to keep a secret from you," Nate added.

Aidan just laughed. "That's the thing though—he doesn't have any. That's the beauty of a relationship."

Nate's heart ached. He'd pretended for so long that he didn't want that, but he did. He *still* did. But Ramsey had taken up residence in his blood, and no amount of exorcisms seemed to be able to evict him.

Maybe if he wasn't around, Nate could start to get over it, could go back to his intention of finding a boyfriend. Of falling in love. But how could he even think about that, when the only person he could think about was Ramsey?

But he wasn't going anywhere. Aidan had just confirmed that, and now he felt stuck between a rock and a hard place.

"Yeah, I know," he said shortly. "You good now?"

"Wait," Aidan commanded, catching his arm as he began to turn away. "We're not done."

Nate could shake his grip off. It was strong, but Nate was stronger. Nate was a captain, same as Aidan. He could tell him to fuck off.

But this was *Aidan Flynn*. When Nate had been in high school, Aidan had been tearing it up in the NFL, winning Super Bowls. If Deacon ever found out that he'd brushed Aidan off, he'd never hear the end of it.

Even if Deacon didn't necessarily *like* Aidan—too many years of healthy competition had made that a stretch—he would insist Aidan had earned respect. Especially in this scenario.

"What?" Nate asked testily.

"So you slept together and it was what, really good? And now you're torn up about it?"

"No," Nate retorted.

"He was shitty to you when he left?"

"You have a real future in interrogation after the football thing," Nate grumbled.

"Thanks." Aidan's tone was dry. "So my brother keeps telling me."

"Riley's rarely wrong."

Aidan's blue eyes, burning brightly, bored into him. "Don't change the subject."

"I—"

"You were. Riley's not a *get out of jail free* card."

Nate sighed. "Sure yeah. He told me the score. I thought I could accept that, even though it wasn't really what I wanted. But then after, I thought it might go differently. It *was* going differently. Then he figured out who I was."

Aidan grimaced. "Ouch."

"Yeah, it didn't end well after that."

"He seems to be trying to be friendly," Aidan said cautiously.

"That's just his way. He doesn't like that I don't like him." Nate wasn't going to go into Ramsey's whole ridiculously charming fa-cade or how it was as flimsy as those old film sets they'd built on Hollywood back lots. Nothing behind them. Or even worse, a bunch of bullshit that Ramsey didn't want to be seen.

"You haven't considered trying to bury the hatchet and becoming friends?"

*Friends.* That was fucking rich.

Nate didn't dignify that with a response and Aidan winced. "Okay, yeah, I know it sounds stupid."

"It's fucking ridiculous," Nate corrected in a hard voice. "I can't be his friend. I couldn't ever be his friend."

He wanted him too much for that, the desire tearing through him with claws.

"But I want you to come around, and I want him to keep coming around," Aidan said, like he was just going to pretend Nate hadn't said that at all.

"Nothing stopping either of us," Nate argued.

Aidan shot him a look. "You know it makes things difficult when you're not even trying to pretend to be nice."

"Is that what you're asking me to do? Pretend?"

"Fake it til you make it? Maybe he'll surprise you?" Aidan pretended false positivity it was obvious he didn't feel.

And Nate shouldn't feel guilty. He was allowed to not like a guy. He was allowed to show it, if he wanted to.

"Doubtful but I'll think about it," Nate agreed, finally.

"Was it serious?" Aidan asked. The one question Nate didn't want to answer.

"Nah," he lied. Or did he? Nate wasn't even sure if he even knew the truth anymore.

Aidan sighed. "You know why I'm asking this."

"Because he's alone. And his team's basically left him behind. Maybe we're not his team, but we could be."

"I thought you might," Aidan said. "You do get it."

"I'd be fucking blind not to," Nate muttered.

"But, despite all that, if you . . .if it was a real problem, a significant issue, I would be willing to discuss it. Like, if you had feelings for him. If you loved him."

Aidan had preached to him as the consummate leader before Nate had ever been traded to the Thunder. He'd seen it up close and personal lots of times since then. But he didn't think he'd ever seen it done as deftly as Aidan was doing it now. Being there for Ramsey, while also reminding Nate that he was most important. That he was still, *always*, one of theirs.

He could lie; he could tell the truth.

Nate hesitated.

If he said he had feelings for Ramsey, Aidan would let it go.

If he said he loved Ramsey, if he actually said the shit out loud that haunted him deep into the night, then how would he ever get over it?

Besides, he didn't love Ramsey. He didn't *know* Ramsey.

But he might've, if Ramsey had ever let him.

"No," Nate said. "No feelings, other than a bruised ego." He didn't say the *L* word out loud, because he wasn't sure he could.

Wasn't sure he *should*.

Aidan wasn't the sharpest when it came to emotions, but if Nate stuttered, if his face looked as awful as he thought it might, then he wouldn't be able to hide all the *what-ifs* that haunted him.

Aidan just nodded. "Okay, then."

Nate should've expected that wouldn't be the end of it.

But a week went by, and then another, and Nate didn't get complacent, exactly, but he was distracted by the Jordan problem and losing himself in the rhythm of the season. By late October, he thought Jordan might be warming to him, but maybe that was just because he was willing to go on a tour of Toronto's strip clubs with him.

Tonight, they weren't at the Wild Leopard or the Neon Light. They were at Vault, Jordan over by the bar, Nate keeping half an eye on him and half an eye on where Ramsey had just appeared.

Whenever the team came to Vault, he was always here, an undeniable presence Nate couldn't avoid. Tonight, he'd expected that nothing would be different, and sure enough, there he was, sliding through the crowd, doling out his charming smiles like candy.

He met Nate's eyes and Nate tried not to tense.

It was stupid, but he kept waiting for the inevitable moment when he saw Ramsey and his pulse didn't race.

Today was not that day.

And even worse, Ramsey seemed heading in his direction. Taking an indirect route, but that didn't matter, because every time Ramsey glanced over at him, it was obvious Nate was his ultimate destination.

Usually, Ramsey was not this obvious, and Nate buried the flash of concern that he wasn't okay.

But then Ramsey was at his side, glancing up at him with those unearthly blue-ish silver eyes, sweater matching them almost perfectly, a glittering diamond-encrusted chain just peeking around his collar.

"Bishop," he said, nodding at him.

Nate swallowed down the complicated soup of emotion that Ramsey always churned up in him. "Playing nice, huh?"

"I thought that's what I *always* do," Ramsey retorted mildly. Not bothered, like he never was, by the edge of Nate's voice.

"Yeah, wonder if you can actually fucking stand any of us," Nate muttered. He hated how he didn't know if it was all an act or not. If Ramsey's semitransparent interest tonight was even genuine.

And if it wasn't, why was he even bothering?

"Oh, but you're my favorite, Nathaniel," Ramsey teased, like Nate hadn't said anything at all.

That was new, and Nate hated it.

"Hey, Nate, I was going to ask you something," someone said, and Nate glanced over, surprised that not only Dawson was standing there, but Cam, too. He'd been so hyper-focused on Ramsey, he hadn't even noticed them walk up. "You got a minute?"

Maybe Dawson had been deployed by Aidan—he knew they were longtime friends, and it wouldn't surprise Nate at all if Dawson had been tasked to make sure everyone stayed politely neutral—but Daws was a good guy, and Nate wasn't going to tell him to fuck off.

Especially if Dawson actually had a legitimate question to ask.

Still, he'd barely gotten his carefully doled-out portion of Ramsey and he didn't want to leave him just yet—even as he felt a desperate need to get away, to get clear, forever even, rising in him.

Dawson led him towards one of the empty high-top tables, and Nate resisted the urge to glance back at Ramsey once, twice, and then finally gave in as the desire hit him the third time.

It didn't help that Ramsey was looking right back.

Nate tried to shake his mind clear of Ramsey's spell but it was hard. It was always hard. "So, what's up?" Nate asked.

"Uh, you might've heard I had to fire my lawyer."

Nate buried his incredulity that Dawson had dragged him over here to talk about *lawyers*. Focused instead on the fact that Dawson had needed one at all.

He'd gotten royally fucked over by his ex-wife, then his ex-father-in-law, and now it seemed by his lawyer.

Poor dude. Nate would feel much sorrier for him, but he seemed very cozy with the rookie punter, so it was hard to feel *too* sorry for him.

"Yeah, I did hear. That sucks, man. Sucks that people keep taking advantage of you."

"Thanks," Dawson said, tapping his fingers on the tabletop. "I was wondering if you had any recommendations. Knew anyone who was really good at handling contract stuff. And wouldn't be against seeing me through the rest of this trial with Ackerman."

Ackerman was, Nate was pretty sure, the guy who'd stolen all his money. His ex-father-in-law.

Luckily, Nate did actually have a dynamite lawyer. A guy he actually trusted. "Yeah, my guy's great. I'll text you his number."

Dawson smiled gratefully. "That's awesome."

"No prob."

Nate told himself not to do it, but he couldn't help it. He glanced back, to where Ramsey was chatting now with Wes and Mo.

"You seem like a real helpful guy," Dawson continued.

That wasn't what Nate was expecting to hear, though it felt good to hear that instead of the opposite that he usually got from Sterling. "I do?"

"Well, yeah. I've been through it, sure, but it sounds like that guy's been through it too." And of course, *of fucking course*, he waved in Ramsey's direction.

He'd give Dawson a minimum of credit. At least he'd come up with a relatively legit question before he segued into what he'd clearly dragged Nate over here to discuss: Ramsey.

"Not you too," Nate retorted.

"Listen, I don't know what your issue is—"

But Nate was done hearing about it; he was definitely done talking about it. "Yeah you don't," he interrupted Dawson. "And you're not gonna. Did Aidan suggest that you talk to me? I can handle my own shit."

*Yeah, sure, you can, but you haven't been. That's obvious, from how everyone's jumping on you about this.*

"Of course you can. And no, of course Aidan didn't put me up to anything. *Would* Aidan do that?" This was all delivered in an especially soothing tone, like Nate was a spooked horse that needed calmed.

Well, fuck that.

"No. He'd never want someone to pull something off where he failed." He didn't mention that Aidan had *already* tried.

"Exactly. We're just both saying similar things, because it's so obvious."

God, of course it was. Nate had *known* it, even as he hadn't been able to hold himself back, to make his own feelings more opaque.

"What's so obvious?" Nate challenged.

Dawson shot him a look brimming with sympathy. "That you want to go talk to him."

It was like a hit to the solar plexus. Nate had experienced so many of those, over the years. Was able to slough them off, now, almost always. Like they'd never happened. But this blow had force and weight, thanks to Dawson's blunt honesty, and it stung, too. Humiliation blooming inside his stomach.

Everyone knew. Everyone knew, and everyone wanted to *help*.

"I absolutely fucking don't," Nate retorted. Praying that if he said it with enough vehemence, that might make up for the obviousness of the lie. "That guy is a menace. Always showing up and throwing his weight around, like anybody gives a shit about some washed-up hockey player who can't get on the ice."

It was an objectively awful thing to say. Ramsey's situation could've happened to any of them. They both played intensely physical professional sports. It was the root of why Aidan was trying to fold him into the team. It was why Wes had made sure he wasn't alone.

It could've been Nate or Aidan or Mo. Any of them could've taken one hit too many, their careers balancing precariously after.

It had been too harsh and mean, and cruel in a way that Nate *wasn't*.

He didn't know who he hated more in that moment: Dawson for making him say it, or himself for saying it.

In the end, it was no question that it was the latter. Still, he wasn't going to stick around to see the soft reprimand on Dawson's face.

He picked up his drink and left, not watching where he was going. Ending up in one of the smaller private rooms, with a conveniently unlocked door, off a hallway that made up one of the spokes off the main bar.

Draining the rest of his drink, Nate set it on the empty side table and paced back and forth in front of it.

He'd known as soon as those words were out of his mouth that he shouldn't have said them. But he couldn't go back to Dawson now and say that he hadn't meant them at all. That he hadn't meant any of the heartless, spiteful crap he'd been spouting ever since he'd run into Ramsey again and realized who he was.

It wasn't right. Part of him wanted to go apologize to Ramsey for how much of an asshole he'd been. But if he did, he didn't know which Ramsey he'd get. The Ramsey from June, who'd let him see, even briefly, behind all those smooth, charming walls, or the Ramsey after, who'd seemingly been on a quest to prove to everyone that he was perfectly okay.

But Nate was cursed to see right through the act, torn between being pissed that Ramsey insisted on the lie at all and worried that Ramsey clearly believed the lie was necessary.

"What did Dawson say to piss you off?"

Ramsey had either entered the room silently or Nate had been so distracted by his unruly thoughts that he hadn't even noticed.

He shut the door behind him, and Nate tried not to tense.

"What does it matter?" He'd just been feeling guilty for being shitty to the guy, and now here he was, doing it again. Why? It was so much easier to be shitty, to reduce this emotional stew boiling inside him down to annoyance and anger than it was to try to identify each individual ingredient.

Ramsey just shrugged, seemingly unbothered. "You seemed pretty upset. Dawson looked worried."

Nate wanted to ask why *he* was here, and not Dawson, but the answer was obvious enough. Dawson knew he'd pushed too hard and would back up. Ramsey didn't know where the line was—or he knew, and he didn't give a shit.

"I'm tired of everyone telling me how I should act," Nate finally said. He didn't add, *to you*, but he thought it was pretty obvious that was what everyone kept interfering over.

"Ah," Ramsey said. "They want you to be nice to me."

"Don't you want that?"

Ramsey looked at him, and there was a little more of the real Ramsey in his face, now. Not entirely, but Nate had spent the last two months memorizing each and every version, cataloging how much of the truth he was seeing.

Hating how miniscule the percentage was, each and every time.

"I don't care either way," Ramsey lied.

It made Nate want to stomp over to him, wrap his hands around his gorgeous neck and *wring* it.

"Lie to everyone else, but not to me," he spit out.

Ramsey had the nerve to look surprised. "How do you know—"

"I *know*," Nate interrupted.

"Oh. Okay." Ramsey looked unnerved now, licking his lips and glancing away. "I . . .I guess so, yeah. It would be nice. I keep trying to be friendly."

"Friends," Nate barked out, an amused laugh punctuating the word.

"Yeah, it's stupid, isn't it?" Ramsey said, baring his teeth in a smile similar to Nate's unamused chuckle.

"They're just so persistent," Nate said, giving in and sighing, relaxing a hip against the side table. "I had to endure Aidan's lecture two weeks ago, and now Dawson."

"They mean well."

"Doesn't mean it's not annoying as fuck."

Ramsey's smile was more relaxed now. More real. "If you think Aidan and Dawson are annoying, come hang out with Wes sometime when he thinks he can convince you to do something you don't want to do."

"Worse?"

"Oh my God, you have no idea," Ramsey confessed. "And honestly, it's nice sometimes, but mostly like you say, it's annoying as fuck. Especially when he doesn't . . .when he has no idea what he's talking about."

Nate considered telling Ramsey that he'd told Aidan at least the bare facts of their first meeting, but he had a feeling Ramsey wouldn't like that, and he also didn't particularly want to bring up, into this surprisingly chill moment between them, the reminder that they'd had sex once.

"Right."

"So we've got a few options," Ramsey said.

"Options for what?"

Ramsey rolled his eyes, but his glance over at Nate was full of fond affection. Nate wanted to believe it was real, that he meant it, that it wasn't just another act designed to placate Nate, to wrap him around Ramsey's fingers so he could control him better.

"Come on, you don't want to continue this way," Ramsey said.

He didn't, but he was also justifiably concerned about letting Ramsey make plans to shift the narrative.

"Of course not," Nate said. He was tired of well-meaning teammates interfering. But what he was most tired of were his own fucking reactions.

Maybe Ramsey would suggest they come up with a way to avoid each other, and that would take care of the latter, too.

"We should just pretend that we're friends now. I've been trying, but you keep pushing back," Ramsey said, with a frank glance over at Nate. Like this was all *his* fault.

"*I* keep pushing back?" Nate retorted.

"See? That right there. All you had to do was say, *sure, Ramsey, sounds good.*"

"Maybe I'm not as good at faking it as you are," Nate said. It was kind of shitty. Not as shitty as what he'd said about Ramsey to Dawson earlier, but then, he was working on a sliding scale right now.

But Ramsey didn't even look slightly offended. He actually looked *pleased* instead. "Nathaniel, *nobody* is as good at faking it as I am."

"I can't believe you're gonna brag about that like it's something worthwhile."

But Nate could. He *could*.

It was why Ramsey alternatively made him want to tear his own hair out and wrap his hands around his neck. Pull him in and . . .*well*.

"Don't mistake the ability to see through some of my bullshit to mean you actually know me." Ramsey said it in a faux-stern tone, but Nate had a feeling he'd actually pricked something deeper there. Ramsey wasn't happy about what he'd said.

Guilt pulled at Nate, again, and he was so tired of it.

He didn't apologize, but he did say, "Okay, so, you want to just, what . . . pretend we're okay with each other. Pretend we're friends?" There was a big problem with that one—well, more than one. Several, in fact.

Starting with the issue that he'd *just* told Aidan that he could never be friends with Ramsey.

Finishing with that Nate wasn't entirely sure he could pull off a casual friends vibe. Not when it came to Ramsey.

"Eh," Ramsey said, shrugging. "I'm not sure that's gonna work. You're never going to be able to not look at me like you don't want to tear my clothes off."

Nate squawked in outrage. "I don't—I really—I *don't*."

But he probably did. He was thinking about it, anyway.

Embarrassing that it showed on his face. Embarrassing that Ramsey had recognized and then identified that look so easily.

"I was going to say, before you freaked out, that despite all my acting skills, I couldn't pull that off either."

Nate reared back. Not sure he'd actually fucking understood. "What do you mean?"

"You know what I said," Ramsey said steadily, like he hadn't just admitted to wanting to rip Nate's clothes off, too. *Again*, actually.

"But—"

"Keep up," Ramsey said impatiently. "Don't play dumb football player with me. I'm predisposed to think that, but I've never been able to believe it with you."

Now that *was* flattering. Maybe even more flattering than Ramsey wanting to get him naked.

"Okay, so you want to . . ." Nate swallowed hard. This was a terrible fucking idea. Of all the insane plans that he'd imagined Ramsey might trot out, them sleeping together—even *continuing* to sleep with each other—was not even on the list. It was so far deep into crazy pants territory that Nate hadn't even considered it.

"Pretend that we're fucking? Yeah."

"You're insane."

Ramsey shrugged. "You want them to leave us alone. You can't pull off being casual friendly. This is the easiest solution."

Nate's jaw dropped. "To pretend to be fucking?"

He'd been right before. Talking about sex with Ramsey was horrible. Catastrophically stupid, really. To say the word *fucking* made him think of all the things he'd shoved down hard into the box. Even if the lid had always refused to stay closed, at least they'd been contained.

They weren't contained now. Him saying it, them *talking* about it, had incinerated the box and now they were all floating around his head.

Too many memories. Too many fantasies.

"Yep," Ramsey said, like this was nothing. Like it was a perfectly logical solution to their problem.

"I . . .that's honestly the worst plan I've ever heard. Nobody is going to believe it."

"And what, they're going to believe that we're suddenly friends, all bloodless and desireless?" Ramsey snapped back.

He'd been keeping a tight leash on himself, Nate realized.

Then he realized, too, that maybe this was getting to Ramsey the same way it was getting to Nate. That made the whole idea even worse, and it had been fucking cataclysmic to begin with.

Nate forced himself to take one deep breath and then another. "They're not going to believe it, because they're not going to believe that I'd be okay just casually fucking you."

"If I wasn't the king of problem solving, we might actually have an issue." Ramsey had tightened his leash again, and now he just sounded pleasant, like they were discussing the weather outside. "Also, positively, we're not back in Portland or in Buffalo, where the easiest solution might be too difficult to prove particularly convincing. But we're not, so . . .there it is."

"There *what* is?" Nate was afraid to ask. The more casual and easygoing Ramsey seemed to get about this, the more totally insane his ideas became.

"We don't pretend we're just fucking. We're . . .I don't know, what's the step between just fucking and like, soulmate-boyfriend shit, like Aidan and Levi?"

Nate's jaw dropped even further. "You want to pretend to be *dating* now?"

"Okay, so casual dating, yeah," Ramsey said, nodding to himself like Nate had not said anything at all. Like this was all plausible, and not absolutely batshit insane. "That makes sense. I can see that. I've not done any of it so I wasn't sure, but that was probably what I would have suggested."

"Wait, you've *never*?"

Ramsey shot him a look. "This should not surprise you."

It really shouldn't. Ramsey had told him everything he needed to know back in June. But then, it was hard to conceive that *that* Ramsey—the one who didn't exchange phone numbers or do second nights or get involved romantically at all—was willing to fake date him. Not only was willing, but had been the one to suggest it.

"Maybe I'm still surprised from everything else," Nate said.

Ramsey laughed. Not the fake, *I'm charming everyone in my aural vicinity* kind of laugh, but a real laugh. Nate was cursed, and blessed, to be able to tell the difference.

"That's me," Ramsey said wryly. "Full of surprises."

But Nate wouldn't have said that, at least not before tonight. In fact, other than the startling reveal that Ramsey was a pro hockey player, nothing he'd done had ever brought even mild astonishment. He'd been exactly the overly-charismatic-and-knew-it guy that Nate had imagined him to be.

It hadn't been even remotely shocking that he'd wiggled into Nate's social circle, without seeming to break a sweat. If Ramsey wanted something, he got it. And always, it felt like there was an ulterior motive with him.

Of course that made Nate wonder what Ramsey's ulterior motive was with this whole fake dating thing. Sure, getting Nate's teammates and Wes off their backs was appealing, but this was a lot to do just to make that happen.

"Why are you even suggesting this?" Nate asked bluntly.

The corner of Ramsey's mouth quirked up. Nate wished the memory of kissing it was hazier, but it was crystal clear still.

"You worried about me?" Ramsey asked.

"Maybe I'm worried about *me*."

Nate was aware Ramsey had deliberately not answered the question, but he'd be stupid to assume he could make Ramsey, of all people, tell him something he didn't want to.

Maybe Ramsey refused to admit it, even to himself.

"Don't try to convince me you're an asshole, Nathaniel. I won't believe you."

"Even though I've been a dick to you a bunch of times?" Nate asked archly.

But Ramsey just shrugged. "Maybe I deserved it. Some of it, anyway."

That wasn't right either, though. Ramsey had told him the score before Nate had ever kissed him. And when he'd done it, he'd embraced Ramsey with eyes wide open. He'd *hoped* something else would happen, sure, and he'd begun to believe that maybe it might, before they'd walked into the kitchen together. But who was to say that hadn't been Nate's wishful thinking overflowing?

"You told me the truth that night."

Ramsey gazed at him. Nate was mesmerized, in spite of himself. In spite of definitely knowing better. But then, that was the whole idea now, wasn't it? He was *supposed* to be mesmerized. Admittedly, not when they were alone, necessarily, but they'd need to practice, right, in order to pull this off?

"Yeah," Ramsey admitted.

"And I laughed at you."

"I especially liked the bit where you called me Willy Nylander's dog walker."

He couldn't mean that. "You don't mean that."

"Hey, maybe *you* aren't aware, but I know how much Willy spoils those dogs."

It was still humiliating, when Nate thought about it. "You just let me go on and on, digging myself into a deeper hole."

Between one blink and the next, Ramsey was suddenly in his space, hands up on his shoulders, gazing up in Nate's eyes. His own glinted with amusement. Before, Nate would've shucked him off in a hot second, because they weren't doing this any longer, but now he guessed . . .well, they were practicing right? That had to be what Ramsey was doing, because he didn't do anything without a purpose.

"Hey, listen, if I was actually offended, I wouldn't have suggested we hook up that night," Ramsey said.

He was tall, but Nate was taller, and Nate couldn't help the perverse enjoyment of seeing Ramsey gaze up at him like this.

He *was* beautiful, especially like this. But it was funny, because his beauty, while an undeniable, constant, insistent reminder, wasn't what kept Nate fascinated by him.

It was all those tall, slippery, impossible to climb, impossible to de-molish walls, and how every once in awhile they'd shift just enough for Nate to get a glimpse of what might be behind them.

"What, you have a kink for people who laugh at you?"

Ramsey's pink tongue flicked out, wetting the bottom of his even pinker lip. Ten out of ten times, Nate was sure that was one of the most effective tools in his not-inconsiderable arsenal. And yeah it worked on Nate too, even as he fought against succumbing to the weaponized gesture.

"You think you were laughing at me, Nathaniel?"

"Well, yeah. What do *you* think I was doing?"

"Come on. We were laughing together." Ramsey shot him a look like he couldn't believe he had to explain this.

"You really believe that."

"You thought you were so funny and clever, and you *were*. You just weren't playing with all the information."

Nate shouldn't resent that reminder. He *hadn't* been. Ramsey had made damn sure of that.

But like Ramsey knew he was edging towards annoying Nate, he pulled back, just enough. "But," he continued, "now you are. It's me and you, on the same side, now."

Nate knew he should tell Ramsey to forget the whole insane idea. It didn't even make that much sense. But the idea of being on the same side as Ramsey, of finally being in on the joke with him, was so appealing it was hard to imagine him deciding he didn't want to. Because he want-ed to, desperately. And then there was the extra temptation of getting Ramsey where he wanted him. Right in his space. Closer than anyone else had ever had him before.

"You're crazy," Nate muttered, which was emphatically not *we can't do this* or *we shouldn't do this* or *this is a huge mistake.*

And Ramsey knew it, because he grinned, wild and free for a split second and Nate's heart hiccupped.

"Yeah, okay. But you're down, though?"

It *was* a huge mistake, clearly, if his internal organs were to be believed, but that wasn't what he was saying out loud.

"Sure," Nate said.

# CHAPTER 6

Ramsey should've sensed that he was riding too close to the edge. Should've predicted that in this kind of mood he'd do something inherently stupid that he couldn't take back.

But suggesting to Nate that they fake date to get their friends off their back felt so inevitable, Ramsey wasn't sure that even if he'd seen it coming from a mile away that he could've dodged it.

He and Nate had been on a collision path for so long it was probably a miracle that Ramsey hadn't lost his mind and suggested something like this ages ago.

The next morning after, he sat at the kitchen counter, drinking his coffee and eating his eggs, watching Wes as he blended up his daily protein shake.

It still felt weird that he wasn't bulking—had been specifically told *not* to do it, in fact, so he wouldn't gain too much weight before he got back on the ice.

"You disappeared for awhile last night," Wes said, not looking up as he worked the blender.

Ramsey knew that Wes would give him some kind of opening.

Last night Nate had wondered when they were going to start their charade. If they were going to walk out of the room and begin right then, convincing everyone they'd ducked into that private room specifically for some alone time.

But Ramsey told him no.

It made sense, sure, but it had been too fun to watch the flush rise on Nate's cheeks when he'd retorted fondly, "Like I would ever let you pull me into a bathroom for our first hookup."

Nate had cleared his throat and nodded along.

"I'll go first and you can leave later. We'll be in touch about our upcoming plans."

Nate had mouthed along with *upcoming plans*, and had tried to say something about how Ramsey didn't have his phone number.

Ramsey had only pulled his phone out of his pocket and texted him, the first actually sent text in the thread he'd been haunting for two months, **Yes I do.**

Nate's expression had been priceless.

Ramsey wasn't proud necessarily, but he was still thinking about it eight hours later.

"Yeah, I was chatting with Nate," Ramsey said casually.

Wes' head snapped up.

"What? You were just *chatting* with the guy who's been giving you shit since the moment you started coming around the team?"

"Yeah. He's a cool guy, actually." It was hard to fool Wes, because he saw through him in a way almost nobody else did, but he could easily paste a smug expression on his face and mean every bit of it. "Not sure he'll keep giving me shit anymore, though."

Wes' jaw dropped. "Are you fucking serious? No. You're not. You can't be."

"When am I ever *not* serious?"

"Um, all the time?" Wes stared at him over the blender. "Why didn't you say this last night? Why didn't you tell me *first thing*?"

But Ramsey just shrugged, easy and casual. If he'd rushed to tell Wes, excited like an overgrown puppy with his first crush, Wes would never have believed it.

Telling Wes and Wes believing it was the trickiest part of this whole charade.

"What happened?" Wes looked fascinated. Worried, yes, but also extremely interested. "You know he's a good guy, right?"

Ramsey rolled his eyes. "And what, I'm not?"

"No but you're the fuck them and leave them type," Wes said sternly.

"Maybe, maybe not."

Wes looked even more boggled. "*What.*"

"Maybe everyone's been right."

"I'm sorry, *what*," Wes repeated. He came around the island, giving Ramsey a hard look the whole journey.

"Maybe I—*we*—just needed to do something else," Ramsey said nebulously.

Wes put his hands on Ramsey's shoulders, his hazel eyes full of dubious concern. "And what would that be, exactly?"

There was a part of Ramsey that wanted to squirm away. To not say any of it. It wasn't like he *enjoyed* lying to Wes. He wouldn't enjoy lying to Brody either, and there was no question the first person Wes was going to text about this was Brody, despite his west coast time zone.

"How am I supposed to know yet?" Ramsey said, wide-eyed.

But Wes just shot him a look. "Don't play that innocent bullshit routine with me. I know you too well."

He did, and Ramsey had figured that it wouldn't work, but it had been worth a try.

"It's not like I've done this before," Ramsey confessed. It was the truth, and he'd long since discovered that some carefully chosen truths were always more effective than the most well-constructed lie.

Wes' expression softened. "No, you haven't. You like him?"

Every muscle in Ramsey's body tightened. Wes must have sensed it, and thankfully, he misinterpreted it—or at least misapplied the conclusion—because he said, "Okay, yeah it's too soon for that, for you. Baby steps, right?"

Ramsey swallowed hard. "Yeah, sure."

"If you like him, though, it's okay," Wes said casually.

There was no question that in addition to all the exclamation points Wes was going to send Brody, he was going to add, *and Ramsey LIKES him.*

It made Ramsey squirm, but he wasn't sure he hated it. Or that it would be a lie.

Undoubtedly, Nate fascinated him. He wanted to know how his brain and his heart worked. He wanted to pick them apart and then put them back together until he understood everything about them. That was similar enough to liking him, right?

"Okay," Ramsey said.

"But, we don't have to talk about it. When are you seeing him next?"

"Not sure," Ramsey said honestly. He'd told Nate they were playing it by ear, after he shot Ramsey that adorably affronted look about the phone number.

"Well, you should text him," Wes said, returning around the counter to the blender with his protein shake.

"Yeah?"

After emptying the blender, Wes took it over to the sink to rinse. "Well, yeah, you should. Especially if you do uh . . .feel that way we're not saying you're feeling."

While Wes' back was turned, Ramsey rolled his eyes. He loved his friend, but Wes could be ridiculous.

"If we're thinking along those lines," Ramsey said, "I've got something to say too."

Wes turned back, smile bright. "Yeah?"

He had no idea what was coming, that much was obvious.

"You should text Marcus."

Wes froze, plastic cup full of smoothie halfway to his lips. "What?" he barked.

"If you love him still, you should text him. That's just your own advice, right?"

Wes looked pissed off and betrayed. "And say what? Sorry, guy, guess I miss you a lot? Guess I was full of shit when I said it would be okay if we went our separate ways?" He huffed out a frustrated breath. "Seems like the wrong thing to send over text."

"Then call him up and say it," Ramsey said.

"You remember what I said. What we agreed to, when you basically moved in here," Wes reminded him in a hard voice.

Yeah, Ramsey remembered. He'd brought up Marcus, Wes' ex, once, and Wes had lost his shit. It was the only time he and Wes had ever fought.

"Yeah," Ramsey agreed, feeling guilty though he wasn't sure that he was right to. It was just Wes' wrecked face. The way he always looked like he was missing a part of himself, but knew he wasn't ever going to be able to find it and put it back where it belonged.

The fight had been bad enough that Ramsey had actually felt the need to apologize, something he almost never did. But Wes had been so upset, despite that he *clearly* was dying to do what Ramsey suggested and contact Marcus, that he hadn't felt like he had any other choice.

He also hadn't had much of a choice when after the apology, Wes had made him promise that he wouldn't talk about Marcus or make any other suggestions or interfere in any way. Ramsey had already promised *himself* he wouldn't interfere in a way he normally would, but Wes had extracted the additional promise that he wouldn't even bring it up. Because, Wes said, Ramsey had never been in love. He'd never even dated anyone. How could Ramsey know it was "so easy" to just send Marcus a text if he'd never been there before?

Ramsey couldn't say that was entirely why he'd suggested this whole fake dating slash fake liking charade to Nate, but it was definitely an added bonus.

If Wes thought Ramsey had similar feelings, for the first time ever, maybe the promise no longer applied.

Maybe he *could* get away with suggesting to Wes that he put everyone out of their misery by telling Marcus that he freaking *missed* him.

"You *promised*," Wes repeated, more emphatically this time.

"I know, but—"

"No buts," Wes said, and the look on his face was enough that Ramsey decided it was best to let it go. Tackle this another day, and in another way, maybe.

Wes sighed, picking up his shake again. "I know," he continued, "you just want everyone to be happy the way you're happy, but it's just not happening, okay?"

Ramsey wanted to tell him that he wasn't really particularly happy right now, but if he did that would undermine this whole thing, and what was the point of doing it if he 1) couldn't get Wes off his back about Nate and 2) figure out a way to make it work to Wes' advantage, or at the *very least,* convince him that this cold war between him and Marcus was very stupid?

So instead Ramsey agreed. "Yeah," he said. "Really happy."

Wes shot him a look.

"Okay, that was overstating it a bit," Ramsey agreed. "How about *fairly* happy?"

"Better," Wes grumbled. Then he brightened. "Text him."

Ramsey finished his coffee. "That wasn't even a question."

"No, it wasn't," Wes agreed.

"I wouldn't have told you about it if I thought you were going to be so bossy."

"Yeah," Wes said, leaning against the counter, "let's talk about 'it'."

"You told me we didn't have to," Ramsey complained.

"That was before you started to refer to your feelings—or your whole deal with Nate—as an *it*."

Ramsey rolled his eyes. "I don't *know* what it is yet. We talked. We came to a . . ." *An agreement to fake like each other.* "We agreed that maybe what we'd been doing up to now wasn't working."

"It's not a business negotiation," Wes said incredulously.

"Of course not."

"Then why does it sound like it is?"

Probably because Ramsey didn't know how to even describe something that was more than flirting with the express intention of sleeping together shortly after, or him trying to get something he wanted.

"I don't know," Ramsey said, drumming his fingertips on the counter, trying not to sound testy.

Ramsey was good at lots of things. Lots and lots of things. Hockey, obviously, and arranging things to everyone's benefit. Being a friend to Wes and Brody. Maintaining a killer poker face. Putting people at ease. Looking fucking amazing. Just glancing at a situation and knowing how to improve it without anyone being the wiser. Making money.

He was good at so many things it had never occurred to him that he might not be good at this, too. The only reason he hadn't been sure was because he just hadn't done it before.

"Yeah, you do. You never do this. You're not going to be good at it."

Ramsey sighed with exaggeration. "There's lots of times I haven't tried something and I turn out to be fucking amazing at it."

Wes rounded the counter and smacked him on the side of the head. Hard enough it stung a little. "Come on," he said. "I know you're like ridiculously smart, but don't be an egotistical jackass about it."

"Okay." This was why Wes was valuable. Well, *this*, and many other things.

Not for the first time, Ramsey missed Brody, who was across the country and not as readily available to puncture his ego.

He was always gentler about it than Wes was.

"So what else happened?" Wes asked. "Did you kiss him?"

Ramsey hesitated. He *had*, but not last night.

"No," Ramsey said.

Wes looked surprised. "You didn't?"

"Well, I wasn't sleeping with him last night." That made perfect, logical sense.

But Wes smacked him again. "Are you joking? Actually, don't answer that."

"What? Why?" Ramsey didn't like thinking he'd screwed up. Even in the imaginary roleplay that he and Nate hadn't actually engaged in. The fake memory where they'd talked and flirted and admitted, maybe not with words, that they actually liked each other. That they liked each other, *for real*.

"Kissing isn't *only* something you do before you have sex with someone," Wes said with an exaggerated patience.

"Okay, that's . . .uh . . .good to know." Ramsey hated feeling like he wasn't doing things right. That he'd broken some kind of unspoken rule.

"Text him," Wes ordered again. "Text him and tell him you want to see him tonight."

For a split second, Ramsey wanted to argue. Wanted to tell his friend that he wasn't going to take orders about this, but then why wouldn't he? Whether it was fake or it was real, he didn't know what he was doing. Maybe Wes' happily-ever-after had splintered apart, but he'd still had it for years. He still knew way more than Ramsey did.

So instead of arguing, Ramsey pulled his phone out. There was already a text from Brody there. How on earth had Wes managed to text Brody without Ramsey noticing? But he clearly had, because Brody had sent him a whole string of question marks, followed up by a **what the fuck, dude? you go and fall in love and don't even TELL ME.**

"I can't believe you told Brody I was in love with Nate," Ramsey told Wes, aggrieved. "Now he's never going to leave me alone about it."

Wes shot him an unapologetic look. "Shouldn't have brought up Marcus then."

"You play dirty," Ramsey muttered.

"And I learned from the best," Wes agreed dryly.

"Fuck, okay. I'll text him." Ramsey didn't say who *him* was, but he thought it was pretty obvious it was *not* Brody.

He didn't expect Wes to check his texts, but Ramsey still made sure he kept up the charade as he typed a message out.

**I'm glad we talked yesterday and that we're on the same page now. We should hang out tonight.**

"Oh my God," Wes said, absolutely looking over his shoulder, with zero shame.

"What?"

"You can't send him *that*. You sound like you're still arranging a business meeting. I would ask if you know how to flirt but you flirt every fucking day, with everyone around you." Wes hesitated. "Do you not know how to flirt with someone when you like them?"

"Of course I do," Ramsey insisted. But he was secretly, terrifyingly worried that maybe he didn't. He could flirt with lots of people, sure, and like Wes said, he did it all the time. But Nate was not *everybody*. He and Nate already had enough water under the bridge that it felt weird to employ his usual tactics, to fall back on his normal patter.

Nate wouldn't like it; Ramsey wasn't sure *he* would like it.

"You totally don't," Wes argued.

"Maybe I don't have to be good at this," Ramsey said. "Maybe I just have to show up looking hot and kiss him and it won't matter."

Wes' expression was unimpressed. "Alright. You try that. See how well that works out for you."

"I will," Ramsey said, glad that this wasn't actually real, and he wasn't depending on his face and his skills in the bedroom to close the deal.

Normally, he wouldn't have worried for even a second, but maybe Wes was right, and he kinda sucked at this.

He pressed Send.

"There," he said, turning to Wes. "Are you happy now?"

"Yes." Wes looked smug. "I can't wait to tell Brody how bad you are at this."

Ramsey groaned.

Nate was not surprised to get the text.

What he was surprised about was the contents. Stilted and awkward, nothing like the in-person Ramsey who was so amazing at charming anybody and everything within a mile radius of his person.

**I'm glad we talked yesterday and that we're on the same page now. We should hang out tonight.**

Nate looked at the text. It said it was from Ramsey. It was right under his stupid, smug, **Yes, I do** text.

But it sounded nothing like him.

**I'm sorry but did a pod person send this?** he sent back.

A second later, another text showed up. Nate could practically *hear* the exasperation in it. **Wes was trying to help me. Insisted I text. All part of our little scheme.**

Nate just laughed, leaning against one of the weight machines. It was technically a day off, after a game, but he rarely took one off. Especially now, in the heart of the season. Coming into the gym and working out some of the soreness of the game actually helped him recover better. Keep his body moving, the way it was meant to be moved.

**Doesn't explain how shitty you were at texting,** Nate sent back.

**Do you want to hang out or not?** was Ramsey's answer.

Nate actually did, but he was enjoying pushing Ramsey's buttons—especially when it felt like the last two months had been *Ramsey* pushing *Nate's*.

**Yeah, I think I could make some time. You don't want to just pretend you're coming over to my place?**

**Who says we're not going to mine?** Ramsey wanted to know.

**You live with Wes. Is he going to supervise our date?** As Nate typed out his reply, he couldn't help but grin. This was the flirtatious

Ramsey that he knew. That he liked, deep down, in spite of every reason not to.

**I liked you better when you were nicer**.

**Lies.**

Nate tucked his tongue into his cheek and typed out a second text. **That mean you're coming over tonight then? Six? I'll get takeout. We can watch something on TV and pretend to make out.**

He was ready for Ramsey to claim they wouldn't be pretending to do that at all, and he was going to have to shut that down, because the one conclusion he'd come to since agreeing to this ridiculous farce was that he could pretend to like Ramsey and he could pretend to date him but he couldn't do those things while sleeping with him for real.

But to Nate's surprise, Ramsey didn't. Instead, he replied with, **Ok.**

Nate asked next, risking bringing up that night two months ago. **You remember where I live?**

It was annoying, but Ramsey deliberately didn't engage with that. He just sent a bloodless thumbs-up text, and that was the end of it.

After, though, Nate's pulse was still high and his blood was still buzzing. Ramsey churned him up, even when he wasn't trying to. Even the stupid swagger-less text he'd started out with had done that, and it had only gotten worse from there.

Nate considered sending Ramsey another text, telling him to forget it. That it was a bad idea. It still felt like mostly one.

But it also felt irresistible, a chance to be in on the joke with Ramsey for once, and God, even though Nate should know better, he apparently didn't.

He finished up his workout and went to grab lunch from the cafeteria. Dawson and Cam were there, sitting at one of the tables with Cam's dad, Marty, the special teams coordinator, and Coach Dell, who was Nate's coach and ran the defense.

For a second, he considered stopping at their table and sitting and eating. Nate knew he'd be welcome, but he had film to watch.

Next week they were playing the Eagles, and he needed to be prepared. Anticipate the schemes the coaching staff was already probably putting the final touches on. Deacon had taught him that to be overprepared was to be just prepared enough, and he'd been trying to impart that wisdom on some of the younger guys.

Obviously some of them were doing better with it than others.

Jordan was one of the guys he practically had to drag kicking and screaming into the film room.

Speaking of Jordan . . .when Nate was halfway through the film he'd scheduled himself to watch today, he pulled out his phone and texted the bane of his existence.

**You coming in today?** he asked, despite already knowing the answer.

Jordan didn't text back right away. Despite that it was noon, there was a strong possibility he was still in bed. Recovery was important sure, but Nate had tried to stress to him more than once that wallowing in bed half the day was not the same as a solid recovery routine. Had also added, more than once, that what had worked for him in college was not necessarily going to work for him going forward. That being twenty was different from being twenty-five.

But Jordan always rolled his eyes and told Nate that he was too stuffy. Too serious. Too disciplined.

Nate didn't like to think he was *just* those things, but he also knew that those things were going to make it possible for him to play deep into his thirties, barring injury, whereas if Jordan didn't figure it out, he'd be lucky to *see* thirty in the NFL.

Finally, when he was just about finished up, Jordan texted back. **Nah bro. How can you even think about football today? Such a solid fucking win.**

Nate rolled his eyes. **Football is my job and your job, that's why. God, you are such a fucking loser.**

Nate was not really expecting anything else, but it still stung. Maybe he *was* a loser. Maybe he had asked for all of this by being overly conscientious and responsible. But then both Deacon and their teammate Jem Knight, now both retired, had been when Nate had come into the league as a rookie, and their dedication had been both inspirational and aspirational.

If Nate wanted a career like Deacon or Jem's, then it was right there for the taking, with the right amount of hard work.

**Yeah, a loser who's gonna run circles around you tomorrow.**

**Probably, bro. Love ya anyway.**

Jordan didn't love him. He knew Jordan barely tolerated him. But it still felt better that they'd managed to move on from, *you're such a fucking loser.*

Nate gave that last text a thumbs-up, his heart beating a little faster at how reminiscent that felt of how Ramsey had responded to him, and stood.

He had two hours to get home, clean up a little, order takeout, and get his shit together so that Ramsey wouldn't catch him unawares.

# CHAPTER 7

IT HAD FELT LIKE two hours was plenty of time, but Nate felt like it sped by. He'd just managed to pull on a T-shirt after his shower when the doorbell rang.

"Aw," Ramsey cooed the moment Nate opened the door, "you left a message with the concierge that I was your new boyfriend."

Nate spluttered. He had most definitely *not* used the word boyfriend to describe Ramsey's position in his life. Dating, sure, but not *boyfriend*.

They weren't doing that, fake or otherwise. Ramsey had specifically said *casual dating* last night and Nate had agreed.

"That isn't what I told him," Nate said, ushering Ramsey inside.

But Ramsey only shrugged, like he was unconcerned that before this moment, he'd probably never slept with the same person twice and now he was rolling with being someone's boyfriend.

Specifically *his* boyfriend.

Nate searched for something to say but his mind was blank. Extra, super-duper blank.

Those two words, put together, and the fact Ramsey was back in his apartment after the last two months was short-circuiting his brain. A thrill kept spinning through him at the thought, and he kept having to push it aside.

Ramsey walked right in, skirting past the doorway to the bedroom and into the living room with its jerseys on the walls.

The jerseys that had tipped Ramsey off to who he was back in June.

Nate tried not to tense as Ramsey gazed at the Thunder jersey under its glass. He was sure he was going to say something about it. Some casual, defusing-the-tension sort of remark that didn't make light of that night but somehow managed to reduce its importance.

But Ramsey didn't. He didn't say anything at all. He just turned away from it, finally. "So, what's this about you feeding me?" he asked instead.

Nate didn't know what to do with that. He'd been so sure he knew what direction Ramsey was going to take, and now that he hadn't, he felt extra flustered.

Why *hadn't* Ramsey said anything about it? He'd looked right at it. They both knew he had.

"Uh yeah, sure. I was going to wait to order until I knew what you were interested in."

"Asian's always a safe bet," Ramsey said lightly. "Sushi? Chinese? Thai?"

That was how they ended up leaning together over the kitchen island, staring at Nate's phone as Ramsey experienced zero qualms in clicking any kind of sushi he thought sounded good.

"Are you really gonna eat all that?" Nate questioned as he added another roll to the cart.

Ramsey shot him a faux-wounded look. "Are you doubting me?"

"Yes. Always," Nate retorted dryly.

"I'm gonna remember you being a shitty date," Ramsey said, grinning. "Being cheap. Questioning my food choices."

"You don't even know what a shitty date is. You've never even been on one."

"But I still know what a good date is. I've watched the Hallmark channel and both my best friends remind me every fucking day what romance is."

"Both of your best friends?" Nate questioned. He only knew about Wes. Maybe he shouldn't have asked; maybe he didn't really need to know any more about Ramsey than he already did, but he *wanted* to know more about Ramsey.

It was a similar kind of alarm ringing in the back of his head that had sounded when Ramsey had casually suggested they fake whatever this relationship was between them. But just like then, it didn't stop Nate at all.

"You know Wes," Ramsey said, and Nate nodded, fully aware that Ramsey was hesitating.

"If we're accusing anyone of being a shitty date, a *good* date would at least be willing to tell me something about himself," Nate said.

Ramsey made a face. "You're going to meet him in a few weeks."

"I will?"

"Well yeah. He'll be coming here with his boyfriend, who plays for the Riptide. Dean Scott."

"You know the guy who's dating Dean Scott?" Nate told himself the awe in his voice was only a casual sort of appreciation for the guy's insane football skill, and Ramsey wouldn't make more of it than that.

But of course, Ramsey only rolled his eyes. "Not you too," he said.

"What?" Nate replied self-consciously.

"Don't tell me you've got a crush on that guy. *That guy*, ugh," Ramsey muttered. "You think you're gonna do your friend a solid, get him a good roommate and maybe dislodge, just a little, the stick that's crawled up his ass. Instead, he ends up *falling in love* with the guy and quitting hockey so he can moon over him all over Southern California."

Nate raised an eyebrow. "Yeah?"

"*Yeah*," Ramsey repeated with emphasis. "I'm still annoyed about it."

"He really quit hockey so he could follow Dean Scott?" It really said something that this was the most interesting and most remarkable part of everything Ramsey had just said.

"Well, *no*, not technically. Technically Brody quit hockey so he could go be a brilliant doctor."

"That's a little different," Nate pointed out.

Ramsey smacked him lightly on the shoulder. "Not you too," he complained.

"Just saying."

"Anyway, they'll be here, and I'm sure they'll want to meet you. I can only imagine the texts Wes has already sent him."

Nate raised both eyebrows. "Texts?"

"Oh, Wes is just . . .torn between insane excitement and complete disbelief and feels like he has to share that with someone or he'll explode."

"Over you pretending to casually date?" Nate supposed he shouldn't be surprised.

Ramsey rolled his eyes. "Not *pretending* according to him."

"Right." Could anyone blame him for tacking on *pretending* every single time his brain stuttered over *dating*? His heart and his brain and his cock kept wishful thinking the opposite.

"Back to our date." Ramsey fluttered the eyelashes over those lethal blue eyes in his direction. Even in a T-shirt and jeans, he was so beautiful Nate could barely believe he was even real and standing next to him in his apartment.

Surely he was a mirage that would vanish as soon as Nate touched him.

But Nate reached down, hand curling around his hip, half because he wanted to, and half because he wanted Ramsey to push him off, and Ramsey just leaned into it.

"You want anything else?" Ramsey asked instead, gesturing towards the phone.

"You ordered half the menu," Nate bitched.

But Ramsey just shrugged and kept clicking through, holding the phone up so Nate's Apple Pay would recognize his face.

"Oh," Ramsey said, glancing at the screen. "You got a text—I didn't mean to—but who's Jordan?"

"Shit," Nate groaned, plucking the phone from his hands. "A teammate. A rookie teammate."

"Ah." Ramsey's noise was full of understanding, even though Nate had barely said anything. But maybe that was all that was necessary.

"So him sending you a text about how hopping the Wild Leopard is, that's normal?"

"Yeah, unfortunately." Nate let go of Ramsey's hip, skirting around the island so he could pull two bottles of water out of the fridge.

He opened one and slid the other in front of Ramsey. "You want something else. I've got a few other things. Juice. Milk. Sparkling water."

"This is fine," Ramsey said. "Let's talk about your Jordan."

"He's not *mine*," Nate said emphatically. Sterling would probably disagree with that assessment. He'd gone out of his way to make Jordan Nate's problem.

"Don't worry, Nathaniel. I'm not jealous." Ramsey grinned. "Especially of a guy who thinks the best way to hit on you is to suggest you hang out with him at the Wild Leopard."

"He's not *hitting* on me," Nate clarified. He shouldn't probably tell Ramsey any of this, but if they were actually, for real, dating, then he probably would.

And maybe, if he was struggling on what he should and shouldn't say, what he should and shouldn't do, he could just fall back on that solid foundation.

Pretending, but well, *not* pretending, at the same time.

Ramsey raised an eyebrow. "He went out of his way to tell you where he was."

"He thinks . . ." Nate wasn't sure why this made him sound so flustered. "I guess he thinks I had a good time, last time we went."

Ramsey started to laugh. "But you're *gay*."

"I know." Nate grimaced.

"Is he . . .slow?" Ramsey asked it nicely, at least.

"No, he's just . . ." Nate sighed. "I think he's lonely and away from home, like really, *really* away from home for the first time, and he's homesick and doesn't know what to do with it."

"Maybe," Ramsey said. "You ask him about it?"

"Are you joking? I can barely get him to talk about football. Nevermind anything personal except what dancer he wants to take to the champagne room next."

Ramsey was still laughing, but instead of that making the whole Jordan situation worse, and making Nate feel guilty for not handling it better, it felt good, like a pressure valve release.

"God, I know," Nate added, slumping across the counter, smiling now. "I'm the worst fucking person to help him, and here I am trying despite that."

"Are you the worst person?" Ramsey asked, sounding like he already knew the answer.

"Well, *yeah*," Nate said. "I'm gay, like you said. It's not like I'm actually enjoying our little strip club trips. And it's not like I'm actually any good at convincing him to try anything else."

"And you're doing this because?" But before Nate could tell him, Ramsey snapped his fingers and straightened. "Shit, this is the problem that got put on you."

Nate winced. He hated thinking of Jordan as "the problem" but well . . . if the shoe fit . . .

"Yeah," he admitted. "Can't believe you remembered that."

Ramsey shot him a look. "You can't?"

Okay, that was a good point. Nate had spent so much time and energy cataloging every interaction they'd ever had he could probably repeat them all, word for word. But that was *him*. He'd never imagined that maybe Ramsey felt the same.

"I didn't know you were paying such close attention," Nate said, forcing himself not to squirm as he said it.

But Ramsey only shrugged. "You said it yourself, I'm good at pretending."

Nate was dying to ask what else he was pretending about, but that felt too personal even for a *real* first date.

"I should text him back." Nate changed the subject instead, because that was a hell of a lot safer.

Nate stared at his phone screen, unsure what he should say. He never knew what to say to Jordan, and they didn't understand each other at all. Nate had come into the NFL determined to do anything and everything he needed to be successful. He'd never have dreamed of fucking around the way Jordan was doing. And if he had, Deacon would've smacked him upside the head, told him to stop being so fucking stupid, and in thrall of the guy and all his accomplishments, Nate would've done it immediately.

But that wasn't what Jordan was doing.

A second later, he felt the warm press of a body next to his, and he looked over in surprise to see that Ramsey had slid right next to him.

"What are you gonna say?" Ramsey asked, casually, like it wasn't a big deal that they were pressed together, hip to shoulder.

It was a big deal to Nate. He was lightheaded with the feel of having Ramsey this close, again.

"I don't know," Nate confessed. If he'd known before Ramsey entered into his bubble, he definitely fucking didn't know now.

"Hm." Ramsey hesitated. "You could tell him to have a good time—"

"But what if he *does*?" Nate asked with a grimace. "He probably fucking will, and then I'll have to go bail his ass out, and I don't want to do that."

"And fuck up our date? Hell no. We have sushi coming, and you're going to pretend to try to hold my hand on the couch later," Ramsey said.

Nate swallowed hard. "I am?"

"Well, why wouldn't you?" Ramsey's glance over was arch. "Do you not want to hold my hand?"

Nate wasn't going to answer that question. Not for real. "You ever done that before? Maybe you're going to be shitty at it."

Ramsey rolled his eyes. "It's hand holding. I think I can rock it."

"Might have to practice," Nate suggested.

"No advantages for you there," Ramsey retorted fondly, his smile deepening into something real.

"None whatsoever," Nate lied, returning the smile.

"We'll have to do it until we get it right. Have to be convincing to everyone else, right?" Ramsey said.

"That's the idea." Nate had to look away. It would be too easy—*so* easy—to get lost in Ramsey's eyes, in the way his body felt pressed against his own.

"So, you can't tell him to have too much fun," Ramsey said, like he knew he'd pushed Nate as far as he could. "You could warn him."

"Ugh, and be accused of being boring and stuffy again? No thanks."

Ramsey nudged him with his hip. "You aren't boring and you aren't stuffy."

"Tell *him* that," Nate complained. Not secretly glad at all that Ramsey had said it.

"Next time," Ramsey promised, then hesitated. "Though the examples I'd probably supply wouldn't be teammate approved."

Nate's skin flushed hot. "Probably not."

"At least the first—and best—one," Ramsey added, shooting Nate a look that was vaguely apologetic.

"Right," Nate said. Like yes, they'd already had sex. He didn't need the reminder. He thought about it all the time. He'd thought about it all the time even when he'd been trying to resent Ramsey's presence. Now? It was virtually impossible not to fixate on it constantly.

"You could threaten him," Ramsey suggested slyly. "Tell him you're gonna destroy his ass in practice this week if he fucks this up for you."

"I don't know if he'd even believe that."

Ramsey looked surprised for the first time since Jordan had come up. "Oh, come on. Yeah, he would."

"You saying I'm scary?"

"Terrifying," Ramsey declared dryly. He didn't hesitate in plucking the phone out of his hands though, fingers flying over the screen as he typed out a message. When he returned it to Nate, he hadn't sent the message. It was still sitting there in drafts, cursor blinking.

**Have fun but not too much. I have a hot date tonight and trust me, you don't want to interrupt it.**

"Hot date, huh?" Nate asked.

Ramsey's expression didn't even waver. "How would you describe it?"

For a moment, Nate considered telling him that sushi delivery and holding hands on the couch probably didn't crack his top ten, but then he'd never done those things with Ramsey either.

Hadn't even let himself dream about it.

"Fair," Nate finally agreed. He pressed Send and then set the phone screen-down on the counter. "Come on," he said. "The food won't be here for another half an hour or so. I think that's plenty of time for hand holding practice."

He held his hand out, not sure if he was calling Ramsey's bluff or his own.

Ramsey looked at his hand, looking as unsure as Nate had ever seen him, but then that look wiped clean, like it had never existed. "You're sure I'm capable of it on an empty stomach?" he teased lightly.

"Let's just give it a try, anyway."

Ramsey's gaze flicked to Nate's eyes, and then back to his hand. He exhaled softly. "Alright," he said and fit his hand into Nate's.

Nate had big hands, and Ramsey's weren't small either, but they still fit flawlessly together. Their callouses sliding together, Nate's from the weight room and Ramsey's from so many years of stickhandling. Different, maybe, but still complementary.

"See?" Nate said, squeezing Ramsey's hand as he led them to the couch in the living room. "Not terrible."

Ramsey's chuckle was a little unsteady, and when they sat, Nate didn't miss the few inches that he left between them, or the way he didn't let go of his hand.

"You want to watch something?" Nate asked. "A movie? TV show?"

Nate should've known that Ramsey wouldn't take the hand hold-ing crack lying down. "Oh," Ramsey said, "I know there's an early game on. Minnesota versus Vancouver."

"Vancouver doesn't have a football team," Nate said, pretending ignorance just to experience the cat-stole-the-cream smile that Ram-sey gave him.

"No, they don't," Ramsey agreed. He turned towards Nate. "Do you know how much fuck ass football Wes has made me watch in the last three months?"

"No?" But Nate could imagine.

"You owe me this, Nathaniel."

"I kinda think *Wes* owes you this," Nate argued, even though he knew exactly what he was going to end up turning on the TV: Minnesota versus Vancouver.

Hockey, and not football. And he was probably going to pretend not to like it, all the while secretly enjoying every moment. Not because he liked hockey particularly but because he'd like watching Ramsey watching it. He'd hoard every moment Ramsey let down his guard, to lean in and explain some particularly confusing penalty to Nate.

"But Wes isn't even here," Ramsey said, with a wide-eyed inno-cence that was so goddamn good Nate might've believed it was true and real, even if he hadn't personally experienced just how innocent Ramsey wasn't.

Nate groaned, at least ninety percent of it fake as hell, and picked up the remote. "What channel? The fuck ass Canadian channel?"

Ramsey elbowed him. "We're in Canada, you idiot," he said.

That was fair. He navigated through the ESPN app until he found the game.

The first period was just starting, and Nate was rewarded by Ramsey settling in more comfortably next to him. Relaxing, not all the way, but more. *Enough.* At least for now.

Ramsey's hand was warm and a little damp in his as they watched the Canucks play the Wild.

"What's particularly special about this matchup?" Nate finally asked, during a break in the action. He didn't want to confess that after meeting Ramsey for the second time, he'd started watching more hockey. First out of a perverse need to prove it was stupid, much stupider than football, and then second because it was the only way he could figure out how to be close to Ramsey when he'd never felt further away.

"The Canucks versus the Wild? Nothing particular. It's just on. And the Wolves are playing the Canucks next week." Ramsey paused. "Part of their Canadian trip."

"Ah." Nate wanted to ask why he was bothering watching this game if he wasn't going to be playing in the game next week, or even going on the road trip. But that was something that he'd realized over the last few months—Ramsey would share, fairly easily, that he was a hockey player and that he was on long-term injured reserve, but anytime anyone asked anything specific, or wanted him to talk about it, he'd perform evasive maneuvers.

Nate couldn't blame him. If he was stuck, injured, away from football, with no end in sight and not any clear idea when that would change, he'd be going crazy.

He definitely would not want to discuss it.

"You can ask, you know," Ramsey said, making a face, his voice much edgier than usual. "I can tell you want to."

"I didn't think *you* wanted to talk about it."

Ramsey didn't take his eyes off the screen. "I don't," he said flatly.

"Then why would you tell me I can ask about it?" Just when Nate thought he understood everything about Ramsey's prickliness, something new cropped up and surprised him.

"You want to, I can feel it, and it just sucks waiting for it. Wondering when you're gonna ask. Trying to figure out what I'm going to say."

"You figure it out yet?"

Ramsey looked over at him, and now he looked surprised. A hint of an unexpected smile on his face. "Not really."

"Then I'm good. How about this? When you figure it out, you come tell me, okay?"

"You're weird." Ramsey was chuckling now, though, and that black cloud that had threatened to descend was already clearing up. Nate patted himself on the back.

"And you're normal?"

Ramsey squawked. "I put up a very good front, fuck you very much."

"Yeah, sure, for everyone else."

Sighing, Ramsey relaxed back onto the couch, his shoulder actually brushing Nate's now.

Another few minutes ticked off the clock, and they sat in silence, watching the game. Still holding hands. The longer it went on, the more comfortable it felt. The more familiar.

The more Nate wasn't sure he could learn to live without it when this whole charade finally ended.

Then Ramsey said, "You were surprised I suggested this."

"Watching hockey? Holding hands? Having sushi at my place?"

"Doing this at all," Ramsey clarified. "But that's why. It's . . .it sucks sometimes."

"What? Being a victim of your own act?"

Ramsey shot him a hot glare.

"What?" Nate retorted. "You are, kinda."

"What's annoying is how perceptive you are."

"But if I wasn't perceptive, I wouldn't be here. *You* wouldn't be here." Of course, Nate knew that he bought every second of Ramsey's time and attention with that inherent understanding. Didn't mean he *liked* it, though.

Was it so wrong to want Ramsey to want to spend time with him not because he felt seen by Nate, but because he just plain fucking *liked* him?

"True," Ramsey said, sounding more cautious than normal. Like he was going to pick every word out of his mouth. But then he didn't say anything else.

And it sucked, sure, but shutting Ramsey up sucked even more.

"Explain this to me," Nate said, blindly waving at the screen.

"You want me to explain a power play to you?"

Maybe Nate should be embarrassed, because he actually knew what that was.

"Sure," he said.

"It happens," Ramsey said, faux seriousness oozing from every word he said, "when someone from the other team is very, very naughty and gets punished for it."

Nate barked out a laugh. "Seriously?"

"You seriously wanted me to tell you what a power play is," Ramsey retorted fondly. "I told you, that stupid football player routine doesn't work on me."

"Okay. Fair."

The Wild's power play ended, still no score, and to Nate's surprise, Ramsey spoke up again. "I *will* tell you about offensive zone entries, if you're interested."

He said it so casually, like he wouldn't care one way or the other. But Nate saw it for the olive branch that it was, and there was never going to be any circumstances he didn't accept it.

"Sure," Nate said.

He followed about seventy percent of Ramsey's detailed lecture, which Nate thought was pretty impressive, considering that he'd only been watching hockey for less than two months.

"Why aren't they trying to do that now?" he asked, gesturing to the screen, after Ramsey finished.

"Oh, that's the fourth line," Ramsey said.

"So? Do they not count? Do they not try to score?"

Ramsey shrugged. "Sure, they do. But they eat up minutes. They keep the other team from scoring, but generally those guys aren't exactly scoring powerhouses." He turned towards Nate, and he felt fully relaxed now. "You know you have starters, and how sometimes for a play or two a backup comes in to give the starters a breather?"

Nate nodded.

"Well, that's what the fourth line—and sometimes the third line—is for. The top six, they're the major players. The starters."

"What are you?" Nate caught himself just in time from asking *what were you?*

Ramsey barked out a laugh. "*Not* a forward. I play defense."

"Legit," Nate said, squeezing his hand. With someone else he might've fist-bumped them, maybe as an excuse to touch them if he liked them, but he was already holding Ramsey's hand.

"It's a little different in hockey."

"You don't say," Nate said dryly.

Ramsey grinned. "We're allowed to score points."

"So are we," Nate retorted, though he had yet to do that in his career. But maybe someday he'd hit the end zone with a fumble or an interception.

Someday *soon*, hopefully.

"Not like us," Ramsey argued. "And we get to run the offense, when our team's on the power play."

"Did you do that?"

"Yeah, I ran the power play at Portland U. And right before I got hurt, I was transitioning from the second to the first power play for the Wolves." Ramsey sighed.

"That sucks," Nate said, "but you're going to get back to that." What else was there to say? Maybe he couldn't promise anything, but he wanted to. Anything to erase that hateful wrinkle between Ramsey's eyebrows.

"Soon, maybe," Ramsey said, the edge of his voice suddenly rough. He didn't move away, but Nate could feel the line of his body tense up.

With anyone else he was dating—or "dating"?—Nate would know how to divert the subject, or even cheer them up. But if he kissed Ramsey again . . .well, he couldn't do it and not mean it.

Which meant he needed to do something else. Anything else.

"Uh, I bet the food is nearly here," he said.

*That's so shitty; couldn't you do better?*

But he couldn't, because the game was currently on a commercial break, and what was he supposed to do? Ask Ramsey to talk about it, when he clearly didn't want to?

Ramsey looked over at him, wry smile blooming across his face. "God, you are kind of shitty at this. What are you gonna ask me about, the weather next? It's Toronto. It's balls cold, and it's gonna get colder and then colder still."

"I thought I was so good you couldn't stay away," Nate said with faux outrage.

Ramsey rolled his eyes, but he'd relaxed, enough.

"Seriously, though, the food should be here shortly." And when he checked his phone, sure enough, he'd gotten a notification that the delivery guy should be here any minute. He was just about to open his mouth and tell Ramsey this, when the doorbell chimed—the concierge with the food, no doubt.

"I got it," Ramsey said, jumping up before Nate could.

Nate half-expected Ramsey to bring the bags of food to the living room and they'd spread it out on the coffee table, but he didn't. He took it to the kitchen island instead, making himself at home in Nate's condo, going through every cupboard until he found plates.

"Do you mind if I have a beer?" Nate asked, making a mental note that if—*when*—they did this again, he'd have better non-alcoholic beverage options.

Ramsey shot him a look over the plastic containers he was unpacking from the bags. "Why would I?"

"No reason," Nate said lightly, detouring to the fridge and grabbing one, popping the top.

"If you start treating me like someone who's broken, I'm gonna break you," Ramsey retorted.

Nate considered saying that he'd be shocked if Ramsey was able to, and then he realized that Ramsey wouldn't need to best someone physically to break them. He'd probably have a half dozen ways in the back of his mind that would destroy Nate's life, creatively and completely, and Nate would never be the wiser.

He must have seen that knowledge dawn on Nate's face, because Ramsey just nodded in satisfaction and said, "Exactly."

"Okay, I won't," Nate said, settling down on the barstool next to Ramsey's. If he was different—more like, if this thing between them was different—he might tuck his ankle around Ramsey's. Enjoy the feeling of them touching all through dinner.

But this thing between them wasn't different. He'd agreed to it, even though Nate knew it might be like an exercise in frustration and denial.

So far, that was seeming pretty accurate.

They were halfway through the significant haul of sushi, Nate trying to focus on eating and not on the deft way Ramsey maneuvered his chopsticks, when Ramsey spoke up. "Wes does that."

"Wes does what?" Nate asked, not sure he was following.

"Treats me with kid gloves, like I'm broken and I won't ever get fixed. Like a stray dog that got lost and won't ever be found."

Nate spluttered. "You're not lost, and even if you were—you said it yourself, it's not forever."

"He means well. And sometimes it does feel good. But most of the time it just drives me nuts."

"Then why are you here?"

The corner of Ramsey's mouth quirked up. "Believe it or not, it was worse being back in Buffalo."

Ramsey didn't say it, but it was clear that despite Wes' hovering, which Ramsey himself said got old, that it was somehow better than being alone.

"Well, I'm glad you're not—" Nate cut himself off. Ramsey knew he was perceptive—that he saw through a lot of his bullshit. But he didn't need to point it out, blatant and cruel. Not like that. "I'm glad you're not there," he repeated, finishing the sentence in a way that softened it, at least a little. "Glad you're here," he added.

Ramsey smiled, small but real. "Yeah, me too."

# CHAPTER 8

THEY HAD JUST FINISHED up eating when Ramsey suggested that they watch the third period of the Wild-Canucks game. Nate offered his thoughts on that, more to see Ramsey smile and argue than because he genuinely didn't want to watch it, then his phone buzzed.

Ramsey had already ensconced himself on the couch. Nate pulled his phone from his pocket and winced as he glanced at the screen.

**Shit ur gonna be pissed.**

Yeah, he probably was gonna be pissed. He wanted to sit here on the couch with Ramsey and hold his hand as Ramsey explained some obscure hockey concept to him as they watched a game between two teams he didn't give a single shit about.

Nate thought that pretty much said it all.

"What is it?" Ramsey asked as Nate walked into the living room, because apparently he had a sixth sense for trouble.

Trouble like Jordan Atkinson.

Nate was already typing out a response: **what happened?**

He was also seriously considered just calling Jordan, and he might have, if he thought there was a chance in hell he might actually pick up the fucking phone.

"That rookie at the strip club sent me a text," he told Ramsey. "Something about me being pissed."

Ramsey looked unimpressed. "He should be more worried about *me* being pissed."

"Yeah, but he hasn't met you yet. He doesn't know that you'd probably barely blink while you destroyed his life."

"Aw, you say the sweetest things, Nathaniel," Ramsey cooed.

Before that kind of comment would've ratcheted Nate's temper—and probably the undercover arousal he kept pretending he didn't feel—up. But now he just let Ramsey's somewhat perverse sense of humor wash over him.

His phone dinged again, and this time Nate didn't waste a moment before looking at it.

**can you come?**

Nate groaned out loud.

"What?" Ramsey asked, but before Nate could tell him, he'd neatly taken the phone from Nate's hand and was looking at the screen himself.

"Can I?" Ramsey asked, glancing up.

Nate wasn't sure that Jordan had ever listened to anything he'd ever said, so Ramsey could hardly do any worse. He shrugged.

Ramsey nodded sharply and returned to the screen, tapping out a message quickly and decisively. Less than thirty seconds later, he passed the phone back to Nate. There was an unsent message sitting on the screen.

**not until you tell me what's happening**

Nate pressed Send. Lifted his head to look at Ramsey, who just shrugged. "You'll go regardless," he said matter-of-factly, "but it'll be good to be prepared when we go in."

"When *we* go in?"

Ramsey looked at him. "Come on, do you really think I'm going to let some stripper-obsessed rookie upstart ruin my date? I don't fucking think so."

For a split second, Nate nearly argued with him, because Jordan wasn't Ramsey's problem. Wasn't what he'd signed up for, even remotely, even if he'd signed up for Nate. *Volunteered* for Nate, really, which was a thought that even when it vaguely crossed his mind, still made Nate hot.

But if Nate was considering it, Ramsey *might* come in handy. He had an unreal ability to charm and indisputably knew how to defuse a situation.

"Okay," Nate said. "Let's go."

"Wait," Ramsey said, reaching for his arm. Nate always forgot that Ramsey was strong too, a professional athlete, until obvious moments, like this, when with a single grip, he could keep Nate in place.

"What is it?" Nate asked.

"Let's see what he says first."

Nate relaxed, and then to his surprise, Ramsey released his grip but instead of letting go, his fingers trailed down his arm and tucked into Nate's, tangling them together. Squeezing once, then twice.

Nate swallowed hard as their eyes met. He wanted to lean in and kiss Ramsey. Stop fighting this thing between them. It had been soul-shaking enough the first time, but Nate didn't think he'd be able to keep to his feet now.

But it was still Ramsey who looked away first.

Then Nate's phone buzzed and Ramsey shifted closer to him, so he could read the screen too.

**just some shit.** And then after, instead of explaining what *any* of the shit was, Jordan just sent him a location.

*Fuck*.

Ramsey sighed, which was exactly how Nate felt. They grabbed their coats, and a minute later, they were out the door.

"You ever been there?" Ramsey asked as they headed downstairs. He was on his phone now, and as they rode the elevator down to the ground floor, he tilted it towards Nate so he could see he was getting them a ride to the Wild Leopard.

"A few times," Nate admitted as they exited the elevator.

He wasn't surprised when Ramsey did a double take. "You've been to the Wild Leopard," he stated baldly. "A *few* times."

"Not out of personal choice," Nate said.

Ramsey grinned. "You *are* a good mentor, going to look at all those hot naked ladies, when you don't give a shit about hot naked ladies."

"Right?" Nate snorted under his breath. "Totally fucking wasted on me."

"He gets that right?" Ramsey asked.

"Oh, he knows." Nate pushed the door open, holding it for Ramsey.

"Car should be here in two," Ramsey said. "Blue Tesla sedan."

"I wish he would've given me some kind of clue," Nate said, pacing in front of the building.

"He did warn you, at least."

"I should've known better," Nate grumbled.

"If you're gonna tell me you'd have taken me on a date to the Wild Leopard, I don't believe you."

"No, I wouldn't have." Nate shoved his hands into his pockets. He'd been here for two seasons now, and the bitterness of the November cold still took him by surprise. Ramsey had let go of his hand in the elevator, and now he almost wanted to reach back for it, for warmth. Or at least that was the lie his uncooperative brain wanted to believe.

"So what, you'd have ditched me for your problem rookie?"

He wouldn't have done that either. Ramsey had to know it. He shouldn't be making Nate admit it, but he seemed to want to.

Nate just didn't know why.

He didn't need to. He'd already positioned Nate exactly where he wanted him, and Nate wasn't moving. Not until he had a compelling reason.

"No," Nate said.

Ramsey smiled, the edge of his lips curling smugly in a way that should've been unappealing but instead was just wildly hot.

"You're insane," Nate added.

"Heard that before."

"You ever believe it?"

Ramsey shot him a look. "Nathaniel, I knew it was true before anyone ever told me."

Of course he did.

The blue Tesla sedan pulled up, and ten minutes later, they were climbing out in front of the Wild Leopard. It was upscale, at least, no neon outside and a classy vertical sign on the edge of the brick building, lit dimly, the gold edges shining in the darkness.

At least it didn't seem like Jordan's trouble had followed him outside, and there were no visible cops.

The bouncer at the door must have recognized him, because he didn't say anything, just gestured them inside.

It took a second for Nate's eyes to adjust to the dim light inside, but the moment they did, he began scanning the different booths and the stages for Jordan.

"What does he look like?" Ramsey asked, and he'd shifted closer. So close they were pressed together.

"Tall. Gangly. Dark hair. Brown skin. Cocky as hell."

Ramsey nodded absently.

Then Nate spotted him over by the farthest stage, lounging on one of the big leather chairs, a cluster of half-naked strippers around him, all laughing at something he was saying. His hands waved animatedly in the air, and he was smiling.

"Strange," Ramsey said coolly after Nate pointed him out and they started to head over. "He doesn't *seem* to be in danger."

There were no cops. No bouncers. No clear or obvious red flags of any kind. Just Jordan Atkinson hanging out at the strip club, with the easy confidence of a guy who dropped enough money here he knew he'd be welcomed with open arms, no matter what the fuck he did.

Nate saw red. Tried to breathe in and breathe out as they finished walking over, hoping to give himself some perspective and also give Jordan the benefit of the doubt. But it was hard.

It was especially hard when they finally walked up to Jordan, and he looked over at them, surprised.

"Oh, shit, you came," Jordan said.

"I came," Nate said flatly.

The circle of strippers around Jordan shifted and that must have been the first moment he caught a glimpse of Ramsey next to Nate, because his jaw dropped open a little.

Nate always wondered if Ramsey was used to that kind of attention, or if you *could* get used to causing a stir wherever you went.

"Holy shit, you *were* on a date," Jordan said.

"I was. I *am*," Nate said flatly. He'd been annoyed, sure, but more worried. Now he was just pissed. What was Jordan's *problem*?

"And with *him.*" Jordan looked wowed, and that should've been a sop for Nate's ego—even if it wasn't a legit date—but all Nate felt was something like rage, because he'd obviously dragged him here and nothing was really wrong.

"What's the deal?" Nate demanded. "You wanted me to come here, so here I am. What's wrong?"

There was a flash of panic on Jordan's face, but it was gone so fast, replaced by that smug overconfidence, Nate wondered if he'd seen it at all.

"Who said anything was wrong?"

"You did, you idiot," Nate ground out.

"Actually—"

Ramsey shot him a quelling look. "You just wanted him to show up here."

"No," Jordan protested but there was an insincere quality that Nate clocked right away. "Listen, if you wanna know, there was a super hot guy here earlier, and I thought you might want to meet him."

Ramsey snorted under his breath.

"Clearly," Jordan continued, glancing over at Ramsey, "you don't need that kind of help."

"Clearly," Nate said, frowning. He wasn't sure he believed Jordan's story, but what was he supposed to do, call him a liar?

"Well, you're here now," Jordan said. "Sit down. Have a drink. Enjoy the nice ladies."

Nate laughed, unamused. "Are you serious—"

But Ramsey unexpectedly tucked himself into Nate's side, glancing up at him. "We should," he said, interrupting Nate. "At least for one drink."

Nate didn't know what to say. He couldn't tell Ramsey in front of Jordan that he had no intention of spending any longer here than he had to, and he also didn't want to tell Jordan that Ramsey wasn't drinking. That was always Ramsey's secret to share.

"Alright," Nate said, giving in. "I'll go grab us something to drink." He didn't really want to leave Ramsey alone with Jordan—though he wasn't entirely sure which one he was most worried about—but he'd go himself to get the drinks, so Ramsey wasn't forced to talk about his injured reserve status.

"Put it on my tab," Jordan suggested, grinning. He patted the chair next to him. "What did you say your name was again?"

"I didn't," Ramsey said smoothly, "but I'm Ramsey Andresen."

"Jordan Atkinson," Jordan said. He was still staring at Ramsey like he was an object he didn't quite know how to quantify. And dude, the guy had *no idea*.

Ramsey looked up at Nate after he sat, and gave Nate a slight nod, telling him that he was okay.

And of course he was okay. Ramsey was endlessly adaptable, always at home everywhere, charming and at-ease, even at a strip club when he had no interest in the women parading in front of them.

Nate turned to go to the bar and realized after he'd given the order to the bartender—a beer and a sparkling water with lime—that the ultra-confident Ramsey was the act. Was he really okay underneath it? Nate didn't know. He'd begun to get tiny glimpses of the real insecurities and fears that lay beneath the front, and instead of scaring him away or turning him off, Nate only wanted to know more.

But God only knew what Jordan might say while he was gone, so he grabbed the drinks as quickly as they were set on the bar and headed back.

"Your boy's a hockey player?" Jordan said as he handed Ramsey his glass. "Seriously, man?"

"Seriously," Nate said.

Ramsey chuckled under his breath. "You sure this kid's straight, Nathaniel?"

"Fuck you, I love pussy," Jordan said, full of righteous energy.

"Nobody's doubting that," Nate said dryly.

"You're just . . .like really fucking pretty," Jordan said, eyeing Ramsey up and down.

Ramsey barely glanced back, almost bored with the amazement in Jordan's voice. And maybe he was. Maybe this shit happened to him every single day, and having people pant after him was beyond even routine, just totally boring.

"Doesn't mean I couldn't kick your ass," Ramsey said easily.

And Nate, that night back in June, had seen his naked body. Had seen the strength of it. Jordan was strong, too. Nate knew it, because he shared a weight room with the guy, but Ramsey's body was a weapon designed for one purpose. He hadn't seen it back in June, because he hadn't ever watched more than a few minutes of hockey before. But now that he had, Nate understood the specifics.

"Oooooh, I like him," Jordan said. He nudged Ramsey. "Maybe you should be worried, Big Dog."

Ramsey raised an eyebrow. "Big Dog?"

Nate flushed. "An old nickname."

"Dude, *no*, he's been Big Dog since he was in college."

"Thought I could leave it there," Nate grumbled. He *had*, but then Jordan had showed up. He hadn't gone to Wisconsin, but Indiana, which was in the same conference, and Nate had been a legend in some of those locker rooms.

Jordan had cut his collegiate football teeth on stories about Big Dog, and so when he'd showed up here in Toronto, that was how he thought of Nate. And of course, that meant the nickname came back in force.

"Oh, it's adorable," Ramsey said, shooting him a sly smile. "Gonna call you that from now on instead of Nathaniel."

"Sick, dude," Jordan said.

"I take it back. Actually, I don't hate Nathaniel at all," Nate said.

"He's kind of a whiner, isn't he? Is he actually . . .you know . . .*fun*?" Jordan asked Ramsey.

This was outrageous but not really all that wrong. Nate *was* boring. Boring made for a damn good football player, which mattered more than being the entertainment for some rookie. But he *wasn't* sure what Ramsey would say.

"Oh, he's plenty fun," Ramsey said coyly, shooting Nate a hot look from under his lashes. The kind of look that meant, *we've fucked and we're gonna fuck again later.*

God, Nate wished the second part of that was actually true.

But if he took Ramsey to bed, every line would blur, even fuzzier than they already were.

"Oooooh," Jordan said, punctuated by a loud cackle. "So it's like that, huh?"

Nate couldn't exactly give Ramsey a nudge and let him know that Jordan was the second biggest gossip in the locker room—second only to Aidan—and tomorrow, at practice, Jordan was going to be opening his big mouth, telling everyone about Big Dog's date with the hot hockey player.

"It's like that," Ramsey agreed, with a sharp nod. He drained the rest of his glass. "We'd better let you get back to your ladies," he said, standing.

Nate was only halfway done with his beer, but he followed suit, unsure what was going on, but willing to follow Ramsey's lead.

Ramsey reached down and took Nate's hand. "See you around, Little Dog," he said to Jordan with a wink, and then he was leading slash towing Nate out of the club.

"What was that about?" Nate managed to hold his question in until they were outside, Ramsey calling them another Uber.

Ramsey glanced up from his phone. "What was what about?"

"We didn't need to stay."

Ramsey didn't say anything, so Nate plowed ahead. "And we didn't need to lay it on that thick for him either. He's the second biggest gossip in the locker room and—"

Ramsey looked up again. His bluish-silver eyes were gleaming, shadows falling on the unreal curves and planes of his face. "And tomorrow, he's going to crow about how he met the guy you're dating and I'm hot and charming and a hockey player? Yeah, I know."

Nate should stop being astounded by the way Ramsey just *knew* things.

"Oh, don't look so surprised," Ramsey teased, nudging him. "I live with Wes, remember? And while he can be absolute shit at communication, he talks a lot to avoid talking about the thing he doesn't want to talk about, so I know a lot about the team. Hadn't put a name with a face before now, though. So that's Jordan Atkinson."

"My pet problem," Nate grumbled.

"He's not a problem," Ramsey said, and yeah, he still wasn't used to hearing these truth bombs drop from Ramsey's lips.

"What do you mean, he's not a problem? He *is*. He totally led me to believe there was a problem at the club. He's missed meetings. Curfew. He practically lives at the strip clubs. He wants to go rogue on the field and isn't particularly interested in being coached, because he already thinks he's God's fucking gift to a defensive scheme. Sterling *and* Coach Dell are both *on my ass* about it. He's a total fucking problem."

But Ramsey just shrugged again. "Not really." He gestured towards the street as a car pulled up to the curb. "Look, there's your car."

"My car?"

"Yeah, I got something to take care of too," Ramsey said. "An actual problem. So I'm gonna go a different direction."

Nate was still trying to parse that the date was over, so abruptly, when Ramsey reached over, pulling the rear car door open. "Text me when you get home," he said, a casual order.

He might've argued with that, but it was easier to just nod, and say, "You too, okay?"

He went to slide in, but at the last moment Ramsey caught his hand and Nate turned back.

"You—" Ramsey murmured and then shook his head fiercely, like he was trying to clear it. But whatever the point of it, it must not have worked, because he was leaning in and brushing a brief kiss against Nate's cheek.

Nate froze, but Ramsey was already letting go, and the driver was meeting his eyes in the rearview, asking to confirm the address.

Then the door was closing behind him, and Ramsey was gone.

He nearly craned his head, to see if he could catch just the figure of him, but he held himself back at the last moment. It wasn't going to provide him any additional clarity on what the fuck had just happened.

When he got home, he pulled his phone out of his pocket, opening it to his text convo with Ramsey. But he didn't know what to say. He wanted to ask, *why did you do that? Nobody was watching.*

But if he asked the question, he might get an answer, and not knowing felt like it might be more preferable to hearing something he didn't *want* to hear.

Maybe it hadn't even been anything. Maybe Ramsey kissed his friends on the cheek all the time. Maybe that was the typical way he said goodbye to Wes, and when he kissed Nate, it didn't mean anything.

He should just ignore it. Pretend it didn't happen. But the feeling of it was still spooling through him, the imprint of Ramsey's lips against his skin.

For one more moment, Nate let himself feel it, and then he pushed it aside. They'd had a good night, despite all his frustrations with Jordan, and he wanted to focus on that. Not on what he *hadn't* gotten.

This was good, and this was enough, and maybe sometime, in the distant future, Ramsey would be a friend. Probably not a close friend, because it was clear his future was playing hockey, even if he wasn't doing that right now.

His brain reassembled into the correct order, he sent a text. **Back home. Don't forget to do the same.**

Ramsey sent a little saluting emoji and then added, **you're not a bad casual date, Nathaniel.**

And if that jumbled Nate's orderly brain into a different, much more uncooperative arrangement all over again, well . . .only he knew it.

# CHAPTER 9

WHEN RAMSEY'S PHONE RANG halfway through him scrambling himself some eggs, he glanced at the screen with a resigned sigh and tucked the phone between his ear and his bare shoulder.

"Took you long enough," he told Brody.

"Eff you too." Brody sounded exhausted, and Ramsey didn't need to do the time zone math to know it was crazy early in California, where Brody lived with his boyfriend.

"Expected to hear from you at least half an hour ago," Ramsey said.

"You don't wanna know what I was doing half an hour ago," Brody retorted, sounding marginally more awake now.

"Gross." The dish back was automatic. Ramsey could hardly bitch at his best friend for his big, hot football-playing boyfriend when . . .*well*.

Not that Nate was his boyfriend. He wasn't even his fake boyfriend. He was his . . .well, his . . .big, hot football-playing casual dating guy. Big, hot football-playing *fake* casual dating guy.

And that was a real mouthful that he wouldn't have told Brody, even if he was telling him the whole truth.

"Got a lot of room to talk these days," Brody said smugly.

"That didn't take you very long." Ramsey was resigned. He had given his best friend so much crap about Dean it was only fair that he had to take it back.

"Shoe's on the other foot now, huh." Brody paused. "You wanna hear the texts Wes sent me about it. Cause oh boy, there's some good ones in there."

"I imagine," Ramsey said dryly. He flicked off the stove and grabbed his plate, loading it up. "Let's get this over with, okay? I have a PT appointment this morning."

Maybe it hadn't been kosher to use his intricate knowledge of his best friend and his big science brain and his even bigger heart against him, but Ramsey wouldn't be Ramsey if he didn't try.

"How's that going? I know you said the GyroStim was working—" He broke off abruptly. "Oh, you fucking asshole."

"What?" Ramsey asked innocently.

He could practically hear Brody roll his eyes through the phone. "You know exactly what you did. Don't fucking change the subject."

"I didn't—"

But Brody knew him way too well to believe it. Nobody else, except Wes, knew him better. "Bullshit," Brody said, laughing under his breath. "You forget that you can't run me like the way you run everyone else on the fucking planet."

"Doesn't mean I'm not gonna try," Ramsey muttered.

He settled down at the island, setting the phone on the counter next to his plate of eggs and putting it on speaker.

"I'm just trying to figure out what your angle is in all this," Brody said and Ramsey's mental antenna pinged.

"What do you mean?" he asked carefully while trying not to sound careful.

"Oh come on, you don't actually *like* this guy," Brody said. "You don't do that."

Maybe Ramsey had taken Wes' relatively easy belief in his and Nate's charade for granted.

"And what, I can't change?" Ramsey argued.

Brody hummed under his breath.

"Didn't you change too, when you met Dean?"

"That's not fair," Brody complained.

"You told me so many times you didn't want to get involved with anyone. You were perfectly happy being solo, and then you met Dean."

"You mean, *you* shoved Dean into my lap."

"Well, to be honest, I sort of think of you two as the other way around—"

Brody interrupted him with an outraged noise. "I really don't want *you* thinking about it."

"Come on, I'm not *that* cold-blooded." He wasn't going to tell Brody that he'd only thought about him and Dean objectively, wondering, like he always tended to do, how they might fit together. He'd bet that they'd be exactly what each other needed.

It was always satisfying to be proven right, but then there was being a little *too* right. Not that he'd wanted Brody for himself—Brody was too sweet and naive, and a *friend*, and Ramsey never played around where he ate—but he'd never, ever expected what happened. One of the few times he'd truly been taken by surprise.

"Still don't like it," Brody said. "But apparently you've got your own football player these days, so now you don't have to fantasize about mine anymore."

Ramsey spluttered.

"You didn't tell me about him," Brody continued, not sounding hurt, his tone still so casual, "and I can't figure out if that means he doesn't mean anything or that you were worried I was going to clock just how much he does mean to you."

"Stick to what you're good at, science boy," Ramsey said, but he was suddenly a little worried.

"Psychology is a science, dumbass."

"A *soft* science," Ramsey retorted.

"Are you fucking joking right now? No, don't answer that. I can see exactly how it is." Brody paused and Ramsey's fingers clutched, damp with sweat and sudden nerves, around his fork. "We don't have to talk about it. So tell me about your physical therapy. How's it going?"

"Symptom free for three weeks and counting. Feeling good. I feel like . . ." Ramsey wet his lips, not wanting to say it, even though he knew Brody wanted to hear it. But what if he jinxed it?

"Feel like what?" Brody prompted. And maybe he'd let Ramsey go about Nate, but he wasn't going to ever let him down easy when it came to his health.

"I feel like maybe it's finally clearing. Maybe . . ."

Brody had been in California for the entirety of Ramsey's injured reserve stint, but unsurprisingly, he'd been as involved as possible. He was the one who'd come to Ramsey and suggested the GyroStim that had saved Sidney Crosby's career.

Even found the closest one to Buffalo, that just happened to be in a hospital in Toronto. "And," Brody had said, "you're already there most of the time, so it works out."

At that point, he hadn't told Brody that he'd been crashing in Wes' guest room, not wanting to worry him, but then he shouldn't have been surprised either that his two best friends had been talking about him behind his back.

"Maybe?" Brody prompted.

"You know what I'm saying." Ramsey didn't want to say it so bluntly.

"Yeah," Brody said. He'd been a hockey player. He knew how superstition was baked into hockey DNA. "But God, that's so great. I'm so happy for you."

"Well, I'm not sure yet. But things are promising."

"When are you getting back on the ice?" Brody asked.

"Not sure yet, but hopefully soon. Maybe in the next week or so? Balance is so much better," Ramsey admitted. "But the Wolves want me to stay up here, and keep using the GyroStim, so they've been talking to the Leafs about letting me use their practice facility during off-hours."

"And," Brody added slyly, "I bet you're wanting to stay up in Toronto anyway."

"Brods," Ramsey warned.

"You can't tell me that's not part of it."

"I want to play hockey again."

"Well, no shit, of course you do."

"That's all I'm saying," Ramsey said.

"And all *I'm* saying is that you're probably extra motivated."

Ramsey sighed. "I thought you didn't think I was legit interested in Nate."

"Oh, is that his name?" Brody asked innocently. "Are you telling me about him now?"

"Dick," Ramsey hissed.

But Brody just laughed. "How'd you meet him?"

For a split second, Ramsey wanted to tell Brody the whole truth. He'd not even been tempted to tell Wes—probably because Wes was too close to the whole situation—but he felt a nearly impossibly huge yearning to be honest with *someone* about it. Someone who'd understand. Who'd make all the right sympathetic noises and then kick his ass from here to Buffalo about it.

The only person who could do that would be Brody. But he knew Brody and Wes talked, specifically and mostly about *him,* which was a situation he was only tolerating, and if he told Brody, Wes would eventually find out and then kick ass in a way he didn't need.

"At the bar," Ramsey said vaguely. That *was* true.

"Wes said he didn't like you on sight. That ever happened to you before?"

Ramsey laughed because what else was he supposed to do? He couldn't say, *actually, he liked me too much. But more than that, he saw right through me.*

"Oh, sure," Ramsey said lightly, though he wasn't sure that *had* happened before.

"Bullshit," Brody said. "You wrap everyone around your little spider fingers. It's what you're best at. Weaving the right web, at the right time, for the right person."

Most of the time Ramsey was grateful for his skills, but when he contemplated how hard he'd worked to try to get Nate to ease up, he only felt a deep-seated frustration.

"Well, it didn't work on him. Hasn't worked on him," Ramsey said.

The only thought that eased it was flashes of memory from last night. Nate smiling as he added too much sushi to the online order. Nate and him on the couch, holding hands. Nate teasing him, more gently than normal. Nate actually listening when Ramsey talked about hockey.

Ramsey would have said, unequivocably, before this that none of that would have particularly interested him. Maybe it would have even bored him.

But he hadn't been bored at all.

"Seems like something must have. Wes told me you guys went on a date last night. You, a date. I can't even imagine it."

"You want me to tell you about it, so you *can*," Ramsey guessed.

Brody laughed. "Well, *yeah*. No shit. This is big."

Ramsey was tempted to say again, *but you don't believe it*, but if he kept bringing it up, kept picking at that thread, Brody would eventually get even more suspicious than he already was.

He couldn't figure out what to say. *Was* it big? It didn't feel big, maybe because it wasn't really real. But if it *was* real, it would be big, wouldn't it? That Ramsey would be panicking. Terrified that someone who wasn't Wes or Brody might see behind his carefully reinforced walls.

But before he could decide which angle to take, Brody continued. "I'm trying to figure out why you're not freaking out more."

"How do you even know if I am?"

"Fair. Except I don't think I've ever really seen you freak out, before. Maybe a little, when I told you I was going to med school. But that was about *you*, not about someone else."

Ramsey wanted to argue this was also about him, but that argument wasn't going to do him any favors either. He didn't need to give Brody any more reasons to be suspicious.

What he couldn't do was tell Brody he was taking all of this in stride, because if it was real, he wouldn't be.

"I don't know how much Wes told you," Ramsey hedged, instead.

"That you and him kept slicing into each other, before suddenly, you show up one morning and are like, we're all good and we're dating now." Brody paused. "You realize how fucked up that is, right? The one guy who doesn't like you, and that's the one you want?"

"That's not why," Ramsey protested. Because if that was actually how it was, that *would* be a little fucked up. Ramsey could imagine his old therapist from his teen years having a field day with that one.

"Then what is it about him? Sure, he's hot."

"I'm gonna text Dean and tell him you said that."

"*He* told me that he thought he was hot. Your guy's one of the guys Dean's been following."

"See, *that's* hot. You know I have a competency kink."

"I know you do," Brody said steadily, but still he didn't sound particularly convinced.

"So maybe that's why."

Brody huffed out a laugh, edged with frustration. "Why does it sound like you don't even know why you like him?"

Ramsey didn't want to answer that question, because he wasn't sure Brody was actually wrong. He was usually so good at parsing through all his emotions and identifying each and every one. Cataloging them, then slotting them where they could be of the most use. But Nate had never fit into any of his known boxes.

He'd tried, of course, but Nate was always wiggling away, evading not just analysis but dissection, too.

"Maybe I don't," Ramsey finally confessed.

Maybe the truth hiding in the lies would be enough to convince Brody.

Brody was silent for a long moment. "Huh," he finally said. "Wild. Okay. Maybe you *do* like him."

Ramsey was not going to look too closely at the fact that the one thing he'd told his friend that was absolutely true was the one thing that had convinced him this thing with Nate was real.

"Why would I date him if I didn't? I've liked plenty of guys, and I never dated *them*," Ramsey insisted.

"But here's the thing, I'm not sure you really did. You liked that they liked *you*."

Ramsey swallowed hard.

Being seen was always a double-bladed pain. It sliced with an unexpected delight, but it could sting, too.

"That's what I mean," Brody said reproachfully. "You've never done this before. You're in new ground here. It's okay to panic about that, a little."

"But not too much right?" Ramsey asked flatly.

"Or a lot," Brody corrected gently.

"Well, then if you're going to allow it."

"Wes says he's a good guy. Solid. So I'm not going to worry too much that he's going to fuck you up," Brody said.

"Thanks," Ramsey said wryly.

"And I'm not gonna suggest that Wes warn Nate that *you* might fuck *him* up," Brody added.

"Hey, fuck you," Ramsey said. He left everyone better off than they were when he'd stumbled onto them. Nate had been the one exception, and he supposed it wasn't all that surprising that Nate was *still* the one exception.

"You don't know what you're doing," Brody reminded him. "And you flailing around, you might hurt him without meaning to."

"I don't *flail*," Ramsey argued, though in a certain light, what he'd been doing all fall, and then by insanely suggesting they pretend to be getting along—*better* than just getting along, really—was the textbook definition of flailing around.

"Alright," Brody soothed. "And you did say your balance was a lot better."

"As good as it ever was, these days," Ramsey insisted. And that was true physically. But he did feel off, a little out of step, with Nate. No matter how much he tried to get them on solid ground, it kept wobbling out of his control.

"Good," Brody said, approval seeping into his voice. At least there was that. Brody was settled. Wes was curious but not in a pointed way that was difficult to handle.

"See, I'm all good," Ramsey reassured. Brody agreed, to his relief.

But even after Ramsey hung up, he still wasn't sure that he *was* balanced. Not really.

There was last night, when he'd kept everything casual and easy and *fun*, all the way up until he'd needed to say goodbye, and his hands and his mouth had tingled. Desperate, even though it was stupid and pointless, to touch Nate with intention.

He shouldn't have kissed him, even on the cheek.

But that had felt like the less nuclear option.

Nate hadn't mentioned it when he'd texted him later, so Ramsey told himself he'd brushed it off, called it the same kind of thing as the hand holding. It wasn't a big deal.

Except it was, because it felt like Ramsey was learning a new language that he'd never spoken before, and he couldn't believe how easy it flowed from his mouth.

He'd expected it to be painful and difficult, vowels impossible to form, but it was the exact opposite.

He got ready for his PT appointment and headed out, walking because despite the cold, Ramsey thought he could use the bracing air to clear his head.

Marsha Evans was his physical therapist here in Toronto—recommended by the Wolves organization and seconded by the Leafs—and he'd been working with her for months now. She'd arranged for him to visit the clinic that owned the equipment that Brody had suggested he try out.

She'd been a little skeptical at first, but then she'd read up on Sidney Crosby's history, and after, she'd become one of GyroStim's biggest proponents.

"Hey, bud," she said briskly as he walked into the clinic's gym and hung his coat up on the hook on the wall. "How're you feeling?"

They always did this check-in at the beginning of every appointment. Only once had Ramsey not told her the complete truth about how he'd been feeling, and after he'd nearly fallen twenty minutes later, doing an exercise he probably shouldn't have been doing, she'd sat him down and given him a blunt lecture.

"Don't fucking lie to me, ever again," she'd said.

And he hadn't.

"Good. Balance good. Not feeling tired or drained. No headache."

Marsha nodded. "You've been making real progress."

"Chance I could get back on the ice next week," Ramsey said casually, the opposite of how he actually felt about it.

Marsha looked over at him, her normally no-nonsense face breaking into a bright smile. She knew just how hard he'd worked for this. How much he'd wanted it. "Oh yeah?"

"Yeah." Then he was grinning too, just as big, if not bigger. "The Wolves have been talking to the Leafs about possibly letting me skate at their practice facility. They're still working out the arrangements but Dr. Thompson feels like I've been doing well enough it won't possibly trigger a relapse." He looked over at Marsha. "I'm assuming you're going to agree with Dr. Thompson on this. I know you send him reports."

She shot him a knowing look. "You think I'm kicking your butt but not being honest about it to Dr. Thompson? I'm telling him everything, buddy. Probably even stuff you don't want him to know."

It was impossible not to laugh about that. Ramsey didn't know that he could have, a few months back, when it seemed like he was never going to get better, and he'd be stuck on the sidelines forever, but now that the whole nightmare was nearly in his rearview, he actually could.

"Even that time I almost fell over during—"

Marsha shot him another quelling look. "Oh, I sure did."

Ramsey made a face. "Why am I not surprised?"

"Why do you think I told you to start having sex horizontally?" Marsha raised an eyebrow. "And I'm gonna expect that you followed instructions."

"Yeah." What he didn't tell Marsha was that he hadn't hooked up much—or really, at all—since then. That had been the hookup before he'd met Nate, and he'd felt so good that night, he'd been careful.

And then after? Well, he didn't want to blame his dry spell on Nate, but it was absolutely Nate's fault. Nate's fault for being the final nail in the coffin of the guy he'd used to be.

"Come on," Marsha said, gesturing towards one of the big mats laid out across the floor. "Let's do your stretches and work on your balance exercises. Maybe you're nearly cleared for ice time, but that doesn't mean you're gonna be phoning it in."

"I'd never assume that," Ramsey said, giving her his best serious face.

But she just laughed. "Remember when you thought you could run my shit?"

"I never thought that," Ramsey claimed as he walked over to the mat, and carefully—he could never be too careful, or take for granted his basic balance, again—went down on one knee and into one of his stretches.

"Who are you kidding?" Marsha crossed her arms over his chest, pinning him with her best no-nonsense look. "You run everyone's business, all the time."

Ramsey just shrugged, a little sheepish in a way he wasn't about his skills, most of the time.

He owned how good he was at working people, at getting what he wanted and needed, and making sure it didn't just go one way, but that he always returned the favor.

Not many people he'd met saw through him. Wes. Brody, sometimes. Marsha, for sure. And Nate.

Most of all, Nate.

"Come on, pretty boy," Marsha chided, nudging him with her knee. "Let's get those stretches in."

Ramsey re-focused, on what was the most important thing. Not Nate, but hockey.

Specifically, *getting hockey back.*

# CHAPTER 10

Nate was getting ready for Tuesday's practice, tugging on his jersey over his pads, when a loud voice cut through the low-level chatter of the locker room. "Yo, you guys should've seen the guy the Big Dog brought to the Wild Leopard last night."

Nate froze.

He'd known this would happen sooner rather than later, especially with Jordan involved—the guy didn't know how to keep his mouth shut, nevermind when he had a juicy piece of gossip to share—but wasn't prepared for it to come out *this* quickly.

"What?" Levi piped up. Because of course it was Levi. "Nate brought a hot guy to the strip club?"

"And how do *you* know the Wild Leopard's a strip club?" Aidan drawled softly but pointedly.

Levi just laughed though. "Babe, it's called the *Wild Leopard* and it's somewhere Jordan went. Not very difficult to put two and two together and get four."

*Yes,* Nate thought, *let's talk about Jordan and his affinity for trashy strip clubs instead.*

But then Wes piped up. "You took Ramsey to a strip club? A strip club with *women*?"

The cat was out of the bag now.

Levi catcalled. Mo shot him a knowing look. Lane exclaimed, "Are you fucking serious?"

And okay, that was fair.

"You took the hot hockey player out?" Dawson asked.

Nate flushed. "I didn't take him out."

"Kinda seems like you did," Dawson pointed out.

"We stayed in, until . . ." Nate glanced over towards Jordan's locker. "Until *some people* decided it was a good idea to cry wolf and fuck up the mood."

"Oooooh," Levi chimed in. "There was a mood to ruin?"

*Just tell them the truth. Whether it was intended to be real or not, it felt damn real.*

"Fuck yeah there was." It wasn't a lie. He'd been looking forward to watching the third period of the hockey game with Ramsey, even if it was a hockey game. Frankly, he'd probably have been willing to watch a spelling bee if it meant Ramsey was next to him, his warm calloused hand fitting so perfectly in his, offering all his unexpectedly humorous, pointed analysis.

"Wow," Lane said. "You finally melted the ice king?"

"He's not cold," Nate complained. He'd never been cold to Nate, even if Nate had been shitty to him. Turning Lane down, which Nate had most certainly noted with interest, did not make Ramsey icy or cold.

"Yeah, you're a little bitter, bro," Trevor chimed in.

"Fuck you," Lane retorted fondly, glancing over at him.

"Ew," Trevor said, but he didn't sound as convincing as he should be.

Nate internally sighed, wondering when *that* was going to hit the fan—but then, even when it did, it would *thankfully* be Aidan's problem, not his.

He had his own hands full, with Jordan.

"I thought you didn't like the hot hockey player." Dawson was clearly not going to let this go.

"Maybe he was just bitter the act wasn't getting him anywhere," Levi said, chuckling under his breath.

"Obviously that's not it," Nate said. He told himself Ramsey wouldn't be mad if he sold this. That was the whole point, right? "Because he was on *my* couch last night."

A chorus of *oooohs* echoed through the locker room. "Get it," Mo called out.

"And maybe," Nate added, mentally apologizing to Dawson, who'd only had eyes for the rookie punter, anyway, "he wasn't interested in you because you kept referring to him as the hot hockey player."

But Dawson seemed completely unbothered. "Fair," he said. He exchanged a knowing glance with Cam. Clearly neither of them were too upset about Dawson striking out with Ramsey—if he'd ever tried, at all. Nate wasn't sure he even had.

"So this is what, serious?" Lane asked.

Nate felt the question on the back of his tongue, bittersweet.

Forced himself to shrug, making the movement easy and casual. "We're just having a good time."

"And why shouldn't you?" Lane said knowingly. He came up and slapped Nate on the back. "Congrats, man. You deserve it."

Like Ramsey was a fucking trophy, to be passed around to the most deserving.

Nate tucked his desire to bare his teeth away. It would be so obvious how he felt, that his feelings ran deeper, if he said what he was thinking.

He shouldn't have worried though, because there was another person in this locker room who gave a shit about Ramsey.

"Maybe it's Nate who deserves him," Wes said quietly.

Nate glanced up and met Wes' interested gaze. Tilted his head, acknowledging Wes' comment but not saying anything.

Wes must have seen what he was looking for in his expression because he just nodded back, approval blooming across his face.

He wasn't surprised when halfway through practice, Aidan cornered him.

He'd known that wouldn't be all of it. Not after Aidan had taken an especial interest in tucking Ramsey into the Thunder family. And especially after that conversation they'd had a few weeks ago.

"Hey," Aidan said, approaching him on the sideline.

Nate was over here because the linebackers were working against the offensive line and he was keeping an eye on Jordan, because it wouldn't be the first or last time he pulled a shitty move, even against a teammate.

Wes was in, taking the snap, because nobody wanted Aidan to get accidentally demolished in practice.

"Hey," Nate said, trying to match Aidan's easy tone, but not sure he did it. He knew what this was about, and it was difficult not to brace himself for it.

"So you're dating Ramsey, now, huh?"

"Is that what we're calling it?" Nate asked, despite knowing perfectly well what they were calling it. He and Ramsey had even gone out of their way to define what it was, just so they knew what to tell everybody.

"Why don't you tell me?" Aidan still sounded perfectly friendly, but there was an edge to his tone now. Like he really thought he needed to defend Ramsey against Nate. Like Nate might fuck up Ramsey.

Well, news fucking flash, if anyone was getting fucked up here, it was Nate.

"We're dating," Nate said and if it came out a bit more bluntly than he'd intended, well, sue him.

Even after the charade was over, he'd know what it felt like to touch Ramsey. To hold his hand. To feel his lips against his cheek. Every single time he sat on his couch, he'd be able to look over and remember what it was like to have him right there, exactly where he wanted him.

"Ah." Aidan looked like he had something he wanted to say, but he wasn't saying it.

Nate sighed. "You can say it, you know."

"Well, I had trouble getting you to even admit you *liked* the guy," Aidan said. "And I know you two have a . . .well, a *history*."

"Yeah." Nate was not surprised that Aidan was going to tiptoe around the truth, even though it was just the two of them standing there.

"I don't know which I'm more surprised about, that you got out of your own way, or that you managed to convince Ramsey to change his mind."

"I'm not an idiot. Or incapable of charming anyone." Nate knew how gruff he sounded.

*Except I'm totally an idiot, because I stupidly agreed to his plan. The plan he had to come up with, because I couldn't charm him.*

"Of course not," Aidan said and gave him an awkward pat on the arm. "Clearly you pulled it off."

Nate decided he was done with this. He'd played really nice, before this. And he *liked* Aidan, but he couldn't tolerate another moment of this. He'd only admitted the truth to Aidan to begin with because he thought it might get him off his back about Ramsey. But that had backfired, spectacularly.

"Kind of the way you pulled off Levi?" he questioned innocently.

Aidan made a disgruntled face. "I think the whole team knows I nearly fucked that up."

"Exactly," Nate said.

"You're an asshole," Aidan said, but he was grinning now. "Maybe I *can* see how you managed to charm Ramsey, even if he wasn't interested in being charmed."

That hadn't been Nate's point, but he wasn't going to be mad that it had worked out unexpectedly well.

"Thanks," Nate said smugly.

And okay, he might be fake dating Ramsey, but he was still *dating* Ramsey.

Seemed like an accomplishment worthy of taking a victory lap over.

Aidan opened his mouth, probably to give him some other variation of a hard time, but before he could say anything, a commotion on the field grabbed both of their attention.

Nate identified the source of the problem immediately. It wasn't even particularly a surprise. There was a reason he'd been over here to begin with.

He was going to kick Atkinson's ass from here until next week.

"Shit," Aidan muttered, turning and taking in the situation instantly.

Jordan was facing off against Ross Acker, who was the starting left tackle who'd become the starting right tackle after Levi had taken his spot during training camp. He hadn't handled that transition particularly well, but now the line was much more solid. Still, on top of Acker's normally prickly attitude, Jordan had clearly bested him and was now getting into his face about it.

Shit was right.

Aidan turned to him, just as Jordan shoved Ross back. "You wanna handle this or—"

"I got it," Nate muttered. He wasn't going to send Aidan out there. Jordan wasn't smart enough to avoid pulling something catastrophically stupid, like getting in the face of the Thunders' Super Bowl winning QB1.

He stalked over, gaze pinned to where things were escalating between Jordan and Ross, despite several teammates, including Levi and Duke, attempting to separate them.

"Atkinson," Nate barked out, voice as hard as he could make it. "What the fuck are you doing?"

But Jordan didn't pull up. He was still running his mouth. Variations of *old* and *fuck* and *total shit* were being thrown around and Nate buried his wince and steeled himself, heading right into the fray.

He grabbed Jordan by the neck and used a good chunk of his strength to drag him away.

"What the fuck are you doing?" Nate demanded again. "Have you lost your goddamn mind?"

"He called me slow," Jordan announced sulkily. "When *he's* the slow one. Slow and old—"

Levi, who had ahold of Ross now, suddenly struggled as Ross tried to break free and come after Jordan, who had apparently never heard of staying quiet while you were fucking ahead.

"Fucking *shut up*," Nate said and risked Jordan overcoming him by removing one of his hands from around Jordan's bicep and slapping it across his mouth. "Are you stupid? I don't care what he said to you, or what he is, you don't fucking do that. Ever."

Jordan mumbled angrily around Nate's hand.

Nate wasn't willing to risk removing it though.

"What's going on here?" Shit. It was Coach Dell, the defensive coordinator, who'd come over to see what the fuss was about.

Now he was going to have to hear from Sterling that he hadn't quieted Jordan quickly enough or got to him fast enough to get him to shut his fucking mouth.

"We got it handled," Nate said.

"Yeah," Levi agreed. Thankfully, Ross had seemingly gone quiet, all the fight seeped out of him, and he wasn't even being held back anymore.

Coach Dell looked from Nate to Jordan. "Tell me," he said anyway.

Jordan opened his mouth but Nate just smacked him. "What *you* have to say doesn't matter," he said flatly.

"Fucking unfair," Jordan muttered under his breath.

"No, he's right," Coach said. He wasn't a bellowing presence in the room, almost never yelled. Was most effective when he was deploying this mystical fucking look that made it look like you'd disappointed him so epically that you could only redeem yourself by fixing it for next time.

He was one of the best coaches Nate had ever had.

"Still bullshit," Jordan said, raising his voice more.

In the two years since they'd been together, Nate had gotten to know Coach Dell and felt like he was even pretty good at predicting what he'd do in any given situation.

Coach turned to Nate. "You wanna tell him why?"

Oh, he sure fucking did.

"Sure, Acker was running his mouth. He's been at this a long time. Not surprisingly he knows how to get a rise out of you. Couldn't beat you on the ground, maybe, so he goes to the next best thing. He makes you lose your fucking temper. Which you did, spectacularly."

Coach Dell nodded, mild expression on his face still, and Nate let him take over from there. "And you know what's gonna happen when that goes down in a game?"

Jordan glowered. He didn't need to answer, because this had been one of the cons on his draft sheet. Coach and Sterling and him had dug in on all their new rookies, and Jordan's temper—on and off the field, on top of his stupid antics—had been an undeniable red flag. But their GM and Coach Dell, too, had thought they could work on it. Could fix it, even. "Lots of guys think they're hot shit in college," Dell had pointed out quietly. "And they adjust to the NFL fine. He just needs a strong mentor."

Nate had stupidly assumed that would be Sterling but of course it hadn't been.

"I'll tell you what happens," Coach said when Jordan didn't answer. His tone had grown firmer. Not quite steely, but intent. The tone he used when you were *going* to pay attention to what he said, or else suffer the consequences. "The guy's gonna bullshit you the whole game. He's gonna push you. And then at the worst moment, when we get a third down stop we really fucking need, he's going to pull it out, the comment you can't handle, and you're going to get flagged. Automatic first down. And if you really lose it, like you did today, you're looking at an ejection. Fines. Game suspension, even."

At least Jordan looked partially cowed by that concise recitation of possible events.

So far, he hadn't gotten more than a handful of penalties and none of them had been ones they couldn't ultimately afford.

But that would change.

"And," Coach Dell added, tone going pure steel now, even though he never once raised his voice, "that is your teammate over there. He's your brother-in-arms. And if you ever lay one hand on one of your brothers again, I will make you wish you didn't get up this morning. Is that clear?"

Jordan ducked his head.

"What was that?" Coach Dell asked pleasantly.

"Yes, Coach." When he raised his head, Nate decided Jordan looked at least *mostly* contrite. There was still a temper burning in his eyes. Embarrassment, maybe. Humiliation that he'd been called out like that by his coach.

Nate wasn't sure how he'd respond to that. If it would be now, or if he'd wait, slow-burning coals banked in his stomach.

He'd need to keep an eye.

Fuck. An even *closer* eye.

Coach Dell nodded, and he walked off.

"Don't say it," Jordan ground out.

"I wasn't going to say shit," Nate said. "You ready to get back to the drill or do you need another minute?"

Jordan looked over at where Ross was standing, looking fairly relaxed from his posture.

"I'm good," he said.

"Okay." But Nate wasn't going to be stupid and just observe. He wasn't a linebacker, but he tapped himself into the drill anyway.

Jordan kept it together, at least, and then practice ended.

Nate hoped that he'd heard the last of it from Aidan but on his walk up to the locker room entrance, Aidan swooped in at the last second.

"You handled that well," Aidan said.

Nate wasn't sure if he was buttering him up for whatever new interrogation he'd thought up during the last quarter of practice or if he really meant it.

"Mean it," Aidan added, nudging him with his shoulder. "It's not easy to defuse a situation like that and have everyone be able to go back to practice like it didn't happen, but you managed it."

"That was mostly Coach Dell," Nate said, but he felt the warmth of the compliment still. Aidan was kind of a pain in the ass, but he was also one of the best leaders he'd ever had the luck to play with.

"Not just him," Aidan said firmly.

"Well, thanks." Nate was still bracing for the other shoe to drop.

"About what we were talking about earlier . . ." Aidan looked over at him. "I *am* happy for you, if you're happy about this. And I have to think you are, because I think everyone noticed that you weren't exactly thrilled about how things had worked out between you two, before."

"Yeah," Nate said. There was so much he could say about it, but he didn't know what he *should* say. But in the end, when he boiled it down to just, *are you happy about this?* The answer, no hesitation at all, was *yes.*

"And," Aidan added, "that makes things a lot easier."

Nate froze. "What do you mean?"

Aidan just shrugged. "Well, it *did* make things like tonight's get together awkward, but it won't be anymore, now that you'll be coming together."

Nate was still frozen. He wasn't sure he'd moved—or breathed—in the last thirty seconds. "What?"

He'd known, of course, that this would be necessary. This thing with Ramsey was going to have to be more than telling people about them and practicing hand holding on his couch while they watched a hockey game. But he hadn't really thought about what it would mean to have to pretend to be crazy about Ramsey in front of everyone.

*Pretend. Yeah. About that.*

It was difficult enough to remind himself that this was all a charade. Nevermind after he had to do everything he craved, deep down in a place he refused to acknowledge.

"Shit, did Levi not talk to you? He was supposed to." Aidan had the nerve to look mildly annoyed before his expression bled right back into that now typical lovestruck awe that Nate knew the whole team was still trying to adjust to.

"He might have," Nate said. He'd been preoccupied. "I haven't checked the group chat."

"Well, we're having a thing at my place tonight. Video game tournament of sorts. Pizza. Snacks. That kinda thing."

"You really are a real boy now," Nate said.

Aidan smacked him on the arm. "Be nice."

"That was me being nice." And also distracting from his current internal meltdown. "And Ramsey's going to be there?"

"He said he would be. I guess I just assumed you two would be coming together. Did he not mention it to you?"

Nate bit off the comment that he and Ramsey were *dating,* not attached at the hip, not like *some people on this team.*

They were supposed to be leaning into this, not fighting against it.

"We've . . .uh . . .been a little busy," Nate said.

Aidan flushed and shot Nate a knowing look. "I know how that is."

Nate *hadn't* meant it like that, like they couldn't get out of bed and wandered around their lives like lovestruck, sex-drunk idiots. But he supposed if Aidan wanted to assume that, then he wasn't going to correct him.

"Right."

"So, tonight. Seven. Don't get distracted and be late," Aidan teasingly tossed over his shoulder as he headed into the locker room.

Well, *shit.*

Now Aidan thought they were fucking all the time. What was going to happen when Wes pointed out that Ramsey hadn't spent a single night in Nate's bed yet?

Nate pushed that thought aside. If he spent any more time theorizing—*daydreaming*—about Ramsey in his bed, he'd be totally fucking useless.

The more pressing issue was why Ramsey hadn't told him about tonight.

But sure enough when he reached the locker room and his phone, there was a text from Ramsey on it.

**Hope you're ready for our couple debut,** it read.

Sure, yes, he'd known this was coming. It was the natural conclusion of the plan he and Ramsey had hatched together. Or, really, the plan *Ramsey* had hatched and he'd been stupid enough to go along with.

But he'd thought he'd have time to prepare. To shove everything he was *not* faking deep down and lock it away.

A few hours from now was not enough time to do that. Not even close. Of course, now that Nate was really thinking about the whole thing objectively, a few days or a few *weeks* might not have been enough time.

**You could've told me,** Nate texted back.

**And then you'd panic and declare that you weren't going.**

As Nate stripped off his practice jersey and his pads, he made a face, annoyed at how well Ramsey had read him.

**It's gonna be fine,** was on his phone when he came back from the showers. **Just follow my lead.**

That did not make Nate feel *that* much better.

What he should do is demand that they make an actual plan. Set boundaries. Agree on a few very specific instances of PDA—like the hand holding they'd been practicing, for example—and stick to those.

But Nate was stupid and didn't say anything, just sent Ramsey back a thumbs-up along with a, **pick you up at 6:45.**

**Don't be too eager,** Ramsey teased, the text coming in on his drive back to his condo.

Nate groaned out loud in his car. But there was no way to avoid this, no way to temper it until it became less insane.

That ship had sailed the moment he'd given in to Ramsey's insanity.

He parked in the garage, took the elevator up to his floor, checking the time as he let himself into his condo.

He had an hour before he had to grab a cab to Wes' place to pick Ramsey up. Normally, he'd wear sweatpants and a T-shirt to go to Aidan's to play video games, but this was supposed to be a date. He was supposed to be putting in effort for Ramsey—and Ramsey was a guy who looked like *that*. Even the guys on the team who had zero ability to dress themselves would be able to look at him and go, *yeah, whatcha doing about that, Big Dog?*

What *was* he doing about that? Well, he could throw some jeans on.

He'd just picked out a long-sleeved henley in a dark maroon color that he thought made his arms look pretty good, when there was a knock on his front door.

Nate wasn't expecting anyone, but after he opened the door to Ramsey, he supposed he should have.

"Hey," Ramsey said, his smile a small secretive tilt of his lips. "I thought it just made sense for me to come over to your place first."

Nate wanted to be annoyed, but it was hard to be when Ramsey looked like that. Light blue knit cap pulled down over his blond curls, making his eyes more a stormy gray than blue, and his silver puffer jacket emphasized the broadness of his shoulders and the narrowness of his waist.

"At some point I'm going to regret giving your name to the doorman," Nate grumbled, but Ramsey barely blinked as he ushered him inside.

"It makes sense," Ramsey continued like he hadn't said anything, "because if you picked me up, we'd have to bring Wes."

"You don't want to third wheel Wes?"

"It feels mean," Ramsey said softly.

"Oh, because of Wes' ex?" Nate didn't know that whole story, but whatever had happened, it seemed Wes was still dealing with the fallout.

"Something like that," Ramsey said. He held out a six-pack of beer. "And I stopped by the corner store and got us something to bring."

"Such a good guest," Nate half-joked. "Maybe I should always take you with me."

"Maybe you should," Ramsey said, his chin tilting up towards Nate, the look in his eyes serious.

But that couldn't be right. Ramsey couldn't really mean that.

Nate cleared his throat. Not letting himself dwell on a faraway future where he didn't even have to ask but just took it for granted that when he was invited somewhere, Ramsey would be at his side.

"Thanks," Nate said. "We don't have to leave yet—we could watch something on TV—" He'd been considering turning on the Stars Caps game from last night because the recap had seemed pretty good when he'd read about it, but before he could suggest that, despite the high potential for Ramsey giving him shit about watching hockey, Ramsey interrupted him.

"I thought we could also discuss what the plan is," Ramsey said.

"The plan?"

Ramsey unzipped his jacket and hung it up next to Nate's much more basic navy blue jacket. "Come on." He gestured towards the kitchen. "Let's talk about it."

Nate wasn't sure he wanted to talk about it. He wasn't sure he wanted to just *do* it either.

He hadn't decided yet which was going to be worse—the talking or the doing—but apparently Ramsey had already decided.

Nate took a seat on one of the barstools, watching as Ramsey opened Nate's fridge, humming under his breath as he took in the sparkling water that he'd started stocking since that first time Ramsey had come over.

He pulled out one of those for himself and a beer from Nate's stock, opening it with a quick flick of his wrist, setting it in front of him.

Was it weird Ramsey was becoming so comfortable in Nate's space? Nate didn't know whether he hated it or loved it.

"So," Ramsey said, taking a sip of his water, "do you have any hard limits?"

Nate wanted to confess that this whole thing was a hard limit; not because he'd dislike it or it would make him painfully uncomfortable, but because he'd like it all too much.

But it was too late to do that. Everyone already thought they were dating, and whether they did this tonight or in a few days or next week, it was happening.

"I don't know," Nate said.

"Can I touch you?"

Nate rolled his eyes. "Have I stopped you yet?" They'd held hands. There'd been casual touching when they sat on the couch watching the hockey game. Sure, it had made Nate feel like setting his skin on fire, but he'd done it.

He could handle it again.

Even if it was not casual and more purposeful.

"No." Ramsey tapped his fingers on the counter. He looked like he wanted to say something but was holding back. Nate almost told him to spit it out, but if even Ramsey was worried about voicing something out loud, maybe it was better if he didn't.

"I don't know what you're worried about," Nate mumbled.

But he actually did.

Ramsey shot him a look. "You don't?" he asked, tone full of disbelief.

And okay, yes. He did. He absolutely fucking did. What had been his first thought when Ramsey had suggested this insane plan?

*I can't do it, not if it's not real.*

"Okay, fair," Nate conceded gruffly.

"So I can touch you? And you're going to touch me?"

Nate had been right. Talking about it was actually excruciating.

"Sure," Nate said.

"What about—"

"No," Nate said. He couldn't sit here and listen to Ramsey choreograph all their PDA.

"You don't know what I was going to say," Ramsey asked a little testily.

"You were going to say, *what about kissing*, and I was going to say hell no to that suggestion."

Ramsey made a face.

Nate wondered if he knew why he'd said that, but Nate wasn't going to go into any kind of detailed explanation. It would be so fucking embarrassing to confess, *I can't fake that, not with you. Not when I want to do it for real.*

"You didn't mind it in June," Ramsey said, and yeah, sure he hadn't. He'd fucking loved it.

"This is different," Nate said stiffly.

"Fair," Ramsey agreed.

Nate took a long gulp of his beer and was in the middle of swallowing when Ramsey continued with, "What about sex?"

Attempting to clear his throat, Nate wasn't sure he could breathe. "What *about* sex?" he finally managed to choke out.

"Are we having it?" Ramsey asked the question in the most casual, blasé voice.

"*No.*"

A flash of frustration passed over Ramsey's face. "I meant in our fake relationship, Nathaniel. *Obviously.*"

"Obviously, yes," Nate ground out. He added, before he could stop himself, "Do you really think a guy would be dating you and not get you into bed?"

Ramsey tilted his head. "You said it, not me."

"Exactly." Nate finished his beer. They had practice tomorrow and he should pace himself. Be an example for the rest of the guys on the team, but it was hard to imagine getting through the next few hours—Ramsey burying himself even more deeply under his skin, *on purpose*—and doing it without the hazy veneer of alcohol.

"Then I think that's everything," Ramsey said. He took another sip of his sparkling water. "Was there anything specifically you wanted to cover?"

God, Nate hadn't wanted to cover any of this *in the first place*, even as he was forced to acknowledge that at least they'd discussed the limits ahead of time. Ramsey knew his feelings on kissing for their teammates now, at least, and he wouldn't be blindsided by that. But he had a feeling Ramsey had already known his stance on that. Why he'd asked anyway, why he'd specifically gone out of his way to have this conversation . . .well, Nate didn't know but he wasn't stupid enough to ask.

He'd long since learned the lesson that you didn't ask questions you weren't ready to hear the answers to.

"No, that's it," Nate said.

"Alright." Ramsey plucked Nate's empty bottle and, draining his own can, rinsed them both out in the sink and threw them away in the recycling bin.

Nate watched this whole thing, wondering how it was, *when* it was that Ramsey had gotten so comfortable in *his* condo. He'd only been here a handful of times. But he'd done it, so easy, like he'd absolutely known. Like he'd paid close attention to every detail he could, before.

But again, Nate wasn't going to ask, because he couldn't imagine *that* answer would be any better for his peace of mind.

"You ready to go?" Nate asked instead.

Ramsey nodded, and ten minutes later they were in a cab, heading towards Aidan's building, which was maybe only a mile away, but it was cold and getting colder. Welcome to Toronto in freaking November.

The car pulled over to the sidewalk, let them out, and as they took the elevator up to Aidan's floor, Nate found his hand hovering just behind Ramsey. Instinctually shifting into the kind of mode where he might put a reassuring hand on his back, even if the guys they were going to see weren't just Nate's teammates but had become Ramsey's friends as well.

Found himself asking, "You good?" as they stood in front of Aidan's door, after knocking.

Ramsey glanced back at him. "Why wouldn't I be?"

It was a fair question, because nothing about Ramsey ever screamed, *I'm unsure and uncomfortable.* The guy seemed to own every situation he was in, sliding easily into each and every one. But Nate could never stop wondering deep down if that was because it was true, or if it was because Ramsey wanted everyone to believe it was.

What good was seeing through some of Ramsey's walls if he couldn't figure that one out?

"No reason," Nate said, and then Levi opened the door.

"Hey guys," Levi said warmly, tugging first Ramsey and then Nate in for quick hugs. "So good to see you. Especially here. *Together.*"

"Can we like . . .uh . . .*not* make that a big deal?" Nate murmured under his breath as Ramsey headed towards the living room, carrying their beer contribution.

Levi tilted his head. "Why would you not want to make a big deal out of it? Man, you got *that* guy. I'd be crowing about it from the rooftops." He paused. "Well, frankly, I *have* crowed about it from the rooftops."

Levi sure fucking had. He'd bagged Aidan Flynn and even a few months in, basically never wanted anyone to forget it. An adorable combination of smug ego and uncomplicated awe.

"Yeah, you really have," Nate said, hoping that would be the end of it and Levi would let him off the hook.

But before Nate could head after Ramsey into the living room, Levi caught his arm. "Seriously, though, bro, why wouldn't you?"

"It's just . . .uh . . .complicated."

Levi frowned. "I was under the impression it was *not* complicated. That you were dating. Like nothing super serious, but like, *enjoying* each other."

Of course Aidan had told Levi his suspicions from earlier today. About how they were apparently constantly fucking all their feelings out. Well, maybe it was good that he and Ramsey had established that in this fake relationship of theirs, they were definitely having sex.

"Uh, yeah, right. Of course. Definitely." Nate inwardly grimaced.

Levi nudged him, chuckling. "Say less, bro."

They'd been moving towards the living room, where Aidan and Levi had fit about twenty large football players—well, nineteen large football players and one semi-large hockey player—and Ramsey, talking to Dawson and Cam, glanced up as Nate walked over.

"There you are," Ramsey said, the way he looked over at Nate proprietary and the hand that he set against his waist even more.

Nate might not have noticed, but he was too used to cataloging every minute shift that crossed over Ramsey's beautiful face.

"Here I am," Nate said, letting himself sink further than he normally would into Ramsey's touch. Right now, it was not only allowed, it was welcomed.

"Was wondering when we'd see you," Dawson said, smirking.

"You saw me for hours earlier today," Nate pointed out.

Dawson's pointed glance snagged on where Nate and Ramsey were touching. "Not like this."

Cam nudged his boyfriend. "What he *means* is we're happy for you two. It was inevitable."

"It was?" Ramsey gazed up at Nate with wide, innocent eyes. Clearly playing. Nate knew enough to know *that* much.

It was cute, damnit. It was so fucking cute.

"You both know it was," Dawson said, laughing. "From the moment Nate decided he didn't like you, we all knew it meant something else."

Nate swallowed hard. He'd worried about how much he'd like this, but they'd been here less than ten minutes, and he was already swamped with a desire for this to be how it was, all the time.

For Ramsey to gaze up at him with his blue eyes and mean every bit of surprise and awe in them. Like he hadn't expected it either, but he should have known that they'd end up here either way.

"What did it mean, huh?" Ramsey asked him. Still looking at him *that* way.

"I don't know what you mean," Nate said, unconvincingly.

Could someone be terrible and fucking awesome at this at the exact same time?

Ramsey just nudged him, shooting him a brilliant, private smile. "Yeah, you do."

Yeah, he did.

"I thought—" What he'd *actually* thought was that Ramsey had lied to him. Had been in on the joke and the only one standing on the outside was Nate. Like he'd wanted and wanted and *wanted,* but Ramsey had been perfectly okay just walking right out the door. But Nate couldn't say any of that. "I thought I wanted to know him and he wasn't going to let me," he finally said.

Ramsey's expression softened. "Back then I definitely wasn't going to."

Was he talking about June? Or was he talking about when they'd met again? Was it the truth? Was it a lie? With Ramsey, it was impossible to know.

But Ramsey wasn't done. "But now?" He shot Nate a smile that Nate would believe, one hundred out of one hundred times, was *real.* "Now I want to let you."

Nate's throat tightened. He couldn't come up with a lie fast enough. So he just tugged Ramsey in even closer, his arm settling around Ramsey's waist, like it belonged there.

Ramsey tipped his head up, and Nate didn't know if he was the worst actor in the world, or the best.

"Aw, you two are disgusting and adorable. I *told* you," Dawson said, nudging Cam. "I feel like you owe me at least three dinners for arguing with me."

"Me?" Cam just laughed. "*I* told *you*, but you said they just wanted to get each other into bed."

Ramsey's hand slid up his back. "Maybe we did," he teased. Tucked his head half into Nate's chest. They'd agreed on casual touching, but this felt a lot more than just casual.

Purposeful, and not just because Dawson and Cam and a dozen of his teammates were watching.

"Hey, you two," Aidan said, calling over. "Stop flirting and come over here. You're both up in the next round."

"Oh, is this actually a serious tournament?" Nate asked. Somehow his hand had ended up tangled up in Ramsey's. They'd done that before, just the two of them, but it felt like *more* now, meaningful to be doing it in front of everyone, in a way that it hadn't before.

Aidan just shrugged. "What's serious?"

But Levi nudged him, laughing with delight. "This is Aidan. Does he know how to do things that aren't serious? He made a whole chart and there's a ranking and everything. Seeding, even."

"Where'd you put me?" Nate asked, not surprised in the least.

"On the bottom," Aidan said primly, and Nate spluttered.

"Feels unfair," Ramsey murmured, pressing the side of his body against Nate's. Supportive, that was all it was. But Nate was having trouble believing it.

"You good for playing?" Aidan asked Ramsey.

"Okay if I just watch? Haven't played in awhile—" He broke off, and Nate knew what he wasn't saying. He hadn't played video games since his concussion.

"You can be my lucky charm, baby," Nate said, glancing down at Ramsey. He told himself it was just a distraction from Ramsey's admission, but as Ramsey gazed back, Nate wasn't convinced that was true.

What was even true anymore. Were they doing this to make his teammates and Ramsey's friends more comfortable? Or were they doing this because they *wanted* to do this?

"Yeah, he sure can," Dawson called out. "Gonna give him a good luck kiss too?"

Nate stiffened. That was the one line he couldn't cross. He already knew he couldn't. He'd told Ramsey they couldn't.

But Ramsey was Ramsey, unbelievably quick. Always landing on his feet, like a cat. "Come on," he said, voice dropping into a seductive purr that made Nate's tongue thick in his mouth. "I'm gonna give you a really good kiss."

Nate froze.

Before Nate could protest though, or Ramsey could lean down and actually do it, he was tugging him aside down the hall. Out of sight.

Like whatever good luck kiss Ramsey was gonna give him was gonna be so good he didn't want anyone else to see.

"Sorry," Ramsey murmured into Nate's neck as Nate pressed him into the wall.

If anyone peaked around the corner, they'd see them five seconds out from a heated embrace. Theoretically.

"Don't be," Nate reassured. "It's . . .I'm okay."

"Are you?"

Nate squeezed his eyes shut. He wasn't okay. He wanted him. Cock embarrassingly hardening in his jeans from a little flirting, and even the suggestion that he could kiss Ramsey.

"I will be," Nate said roughly.

He knew he should take a step back. Get some air. Get some fucking perspective.

But Ramsey was so perfect like this, caged in by Nate's bigger body. Those blue eyes on his face, like they couldn't look away even if they wanted to.

Ramsey reached up and tapped his cheek with his fingertips. "I wouldn't have."

And that was the thing; Nate *knew* he wouldn't have crossed the line. He didn't know when it had happened, but he trusted that. Trusted *Ramsey.*

Considering how long he'd carried his frustration and resentment for what had happened on the night they'd met, that was astounding.

But not really all that surprising. He'd been heading here, every time they'd seen each other since.

"I know," Nate said. "I trust you."

Ramsey's face softened, astonishment in his eyes. "You do?"

He shouldn't say it. Should swallow it back. But he couldn't help it. "I think . . .I think I *am* getting to know you."

Nate watched as Ramsey swallowed hard. But he didn't look away. "Maybe you are," he admitted.

Nate knew he should say something else. Puncture this mood, anyway. Yank them both back to the land of sanity. Remind them they were just faking this whole thing.

But before he could, Levi poked his head around the corner, sly grin on his face. "Y'all are too much," he said. "You should be relieved Aidan sent me instead of himself. *He'd* dump cold water all over you."

Nate wanted to laugh and say, *maybe we need it,* but he didn't. Instead he stepped away. Couldn't look at Ramsey, the long, gorgeous line of him up against the wall.

"Good thing you did," Ramsey said lightly. He gave Nate a playful shove the rest of the way. "I think you're definitely going to win now, baby."

Nate wasn't so sure about that. His brain still felt submerged in what had just happened between them. What he'd almost done. Because sure enough, when he let himself think about it, he'd been not even twenty seconds away from saying, *fuck everything* and kissing Ramsey, despite everything he'd said he didn't want to do.

"I think so too," Nate lied.

But still, when he finally got into the living room, among the catcalls and pointed comments, he surprised himself by winning the whole goddamn tournament.

The whole time, Ramsey gazed at him, knowing, and Nate wasn't sure that he'd been wrong, after all.

# CHAPTER 11



FIVE DAYS LATER, IN Philadelphia for a Sunday afternoon game, Sterling pulled Nate over at the end of warmups.

"He good?" Sterling asked.

Nate wished he didn't know who *he* was. Wished he could pretend ignorance.

But there was an intensity in Sterling's dark brown eyes that told Nate that he wouldn't find the joke particularly funny.

Still, Jordan always seemed fine, at least up until things went sideways.

"Sure," Nate said.

Sterling frowned. "Bishop, you know we can't let him get out of control."

Oh, he knew. It was annoying that Sterling was now chastising him like this was his first fucking professional game.

"I got it," Nate said testily.

"I checked in with him last night, after the walk-through. Wanted to make sure that after that incident at practice this week there isn't going to be any more bullshit."

Nate wished Sterling hadn't done that.

He'd kept an eye out for Jordan this morning, the way he always did. Thought he'd been perhaps a bit quieter than normal. Withdrawn. Not laughing with the other guys the way he usually did before a game to stay loose.

He hadn't seen enough to be worried, necessarily, but now that observation coupled with Sterling's admission made something unsettled spike in his stomach.

"What did he say?" Nate asked.

He'd been annoyed since the first time Sterling had asked him to keep an eye out for the guy. But the more he got to know Jordan, the more he'd realized that Sterling would've been the worst choice. Nate didn't know if he was a *good* choice, necessarily, but he had to be better. There was something about Sterling—his stern, overly serious demeanor or the authority that he wore like a cape?—that seemed to set Jordan on edge even more.

"He said he was fine." Sterling didn't look all that happy about it though. Clearly, it had not been a particularly productive conversation.

Nate internally sighed, eyes already scanning the sideline, because he was going to have to make time in the next five minutes to check in with Jordan and somehow defuse the bomb that Sterling had inadvertently set.

"Yeah, he can be full of it when that's the answer," Nate agreed.

"Well, watch out for him," Sterling warned, like he hadn't just created an additional problem that Nate was now going to have to fix.

"Will do," Nate said, between gritted teeth.

He spotted Jordan over by the bench and headed over the moment Sterling gave him a dismissive nod.

"Feeling good?" Nate asked, as he approached where Jordan had both hands braced on the back of the bench. He looked like he was stretching his calves.

He'd learned, through plenty of mistakes, not to ask Jordan if he was okay.

Asking Jordan if he was okay only made Jordan assume that Nate thought he was *not* okay and always made him additionally prickly. A lesson that Sterling had unfortunately not learned yet.

"Yeah," Jordan said.

Nate wasn't sure what else to say, because he couldn't talk to the guy if he didn't let him in, but then Jordan added, "I wish you'd tell Sterling to mind his own fucking business."

"You could always do that," Nate suggested.

But Jordan just laughed. "Yeah, right," he said, but at least he sounded a little lighter than he had a moment ago. He was smiling now. Not quite to the normal level of bullshit joking he'd do with the guys before a game, but close.

A total fucking win and Nate would take it.

"You *could*," Nate joked. "You could also walk barefoot over some glass. I wouldn't exactly recommend it."

"That's why you should tell him," Jordan said.

Nate just rolled his eyes, though. "I think you're overestimating the difference between how Sterling feels about you and how he feels about me."

"Dude, no," Jordan said, and his voice was more serious than Nate had anticipated. "He respects you so much. You're like, in his good books forever."

Nate wasn't sure that was true, but he was more than a little pleased Jordan actually seemed to think so.

"Well, thanks," Nate said, shrugging. "But I'm still not bailing your ass out if he wants it in a sling. So keep that in mind, okay?"

Jordan just went back to his stretches. "Dude, I got this. Don't need to worry about me. Not at all."

Nate hoped so. He really fucking hoped so.

The game began, and Nate took his spot on the defensive front four, hyperaware in a way he normally wasn't of Jordan's position behind him.

Obviously, he'd been keeping an eye on the rookie since the beginning of the season, but during a game, Sterling in his free safety spot had a much better vantage point to make sure Jordan was in position and taking care of his responsibilities.

But on the first snap, the right tackle locked Nate up, catching him off guard when he tried a move Nate hadn't anticipated from the film he'd watched, and Saquon broke free from defensive containment, cutting quick and hitting open space.

Nate finally shucked the tackle and pivoted, to try to reach the play.

Goddamn it, Barkley was fucking fast. He was already ten yards down field and Nate wasn't fast enough to catch him—though that didn't mean he wasn't going to try.

Still, Nate's stomach sank because while Jordan was currently closing the gap between him and Barkley with the burst of speed that had set him apart from the rest of last year's linebacker draft class, he'd clearly *not* been in a position to stop him right away.

*Shit.*

He did track him down, Nate reaching the pile about a second too late. Jordan popped up from tackling Barkley to the ground. He didn't meet Nate's eyes, and worry pinged deep down in Nate's gut.

That had been easily a twenty-five-yard gash for Barkley. Not the way they'd wanted to start the game, that was for sure. Nate had lost count of the number of defensive meetings he'd been part of this week where they'd planned everything around the central plan of *don't let Barkley beat you on the ground*.

Well, so far that was not working.

Sterling caught Nate's arm before they got reset for the next play. "Atkinson was out of position," he said under his breath.

"Yeah," Nate agreed.

"I gotta talk to him."

"He'll adjust," Nate said. Jordan could be stupid about a lot of things. But Nate had seen the high football IQ that he possessed. He'd eventually be able to run the defense, if he could get out of his own goddamn way.

But that was always the trouble, wasn't it?

Sterling didn't look convinced though. "If he doesn't, I'll talk to him," he said.

Nate didn't think that was a good idea, but he also wasn't willing to correct Sterling mid-game. Besides, he didn't think he'd have to. Jordan would adjust. He'd been playing well this year, if a little erratically. But that was to be expected for a rookie. He was still learning the ropes of the NFL. Nobody was ever perfect and definitely not during their first season.

Sure enough, on the next play, the Eagles handed the ball off to Barkley again—it was what Nate would have done, if he was in charge of the offense, considering the Thunder had just given up a big run play—and it was better, but still nearly a ten-yard gain.

This time, Nate shucked the right tackle off better, adjusting for the new move the guy tried, and he was actually the one who caught Barkley, tackling him to the turf.

Sterling's hand was the one Nate grabbed to help lift himself up.

"I'm gonna," Sterling said, but Nate shook his head.

Yeah, Jordan should've been there. He definitely should have been in a better position than Nate to make the tackle.

"Let me," Nate said.

Sterling shot him a look.

"Just . . .I think it'll go over better coming from me," Nate said.

Sterling's expression was still full of doubt, but he nodded.

There wasn't time for Nate to say anything, because the Eagles were already getting set, and it didn't matter anyway, because Hurts dropped back.

But before he could throw the ball, Duke was on his other side, eluding the tight end that was trying to block him, and a second later, Hurts was on the ground.

The Eagles bounced back the next play and got the first down. But then, between a dropped pass and Nate *finally* getting the better of the right tackle, tackling Barkley for a loss in the backfield, it was third down. The Eagles were just inside their field goal range, and Nate was determined that they wouldn't get the first down. They'd stop them here.

He realized a second too late, as he set his position, that the only coverage that AJ Brown had was Jordan. A really fucking fast receiver to only have a linebacker on him, even a linebacker as quick as Jordan was.

Nate huffed out a breath and tensed his muscles, waiting for the snap count.

He didn't bother saying a prayer. God wasn't going to do shit about this. This game came down to man versus man, and if Jordan couldn't handle it, well, as sucky as it would be to find out, the Thunder *should* know if he needed more help than he was getting.

Maybe he wasn't ready to start yet.

The center snapped the ball and Nate pushed off, driving with the strength in his legs and his stomach, pushing back on the right tackle.

He got a glimpse out of the corner of his eye as Brown took off, running a route designed to get the first down.

Nate finally got around the tackle, but Hurts threw the ball a second before he got there, right in the direction of Brown.

*Fuck.*

But to Nate's shock, Jordan kept up with Brown, at least enough to leap up and at the very last second, bat the football away.

It was a dynamite play, made even better by the fact that Jordan wasn't a corner, designed to defend passes one-on-one with the league's best receivers, but a linebacker.

After the team gathered around Jordan, celebrating his defensive stop, Sterling broke away and caught Nate's eye as they jogged back towards the sideline.

The Eagles set up for the field goal attempt and after grabbing some Gatorade, Nate headed in the direction of where Jordan was slumped on the bench, one of the backups excitedly re-narrating the play, adding comments in about how fucking amazing it had been.

It had been really good, but Jordan didn't need this backup inflating his ego even more, especially not when Nate had to lay down some hard truths.

"Yeah," Nate said as he approached, "it was a really fucking great play, wasn't it?"

The backup nodded emphatically, eyes a little wider now that he realized who'd spoken. "Sure was," he agreed.

"Shouldn't have come to that, though." He gave Jordan a hard look. "Barkley shouldn't have been able to rip that run off at the beginning."

Jordan shrugged mechanically, the light in his eyes dimming a little.

God, Nate really fucking hated this part of his job. But in this case, it was better him than Sterling, who would come down like a ton of bricks, with none of the subtlety needed to soften the blow. Some guys handled that okay, but it was becoming clear to Nate that Jordan was not one of those guys.

The backup melted away, heading further down the bench like he already had an inkling of how this conversation was going to go.

"You were out of position," Nate said. Maybe more bluntly than he'd intended, but what else was there to say?

"Receiver ran a pick on me," Jordan said. "Got me tied up a little. Was a second too late to intercept Barkley."

"And you were still out of position," Nate said. If he'd been in the right spot, even a receiver—especially a receiver—shouldn't have been able to disrupt their defensive play.

"You think so," Jordan complained.

Nate huffed out a frustrated breath. There were times he wanted to just leave Jordan to Sterling's not-very-tender care. Let him deal with *him*. Instead of Nate, who kept trying to be a friend. Who kept trying to give him the room and the grace Nate knew he needed to grow.

He wasn't doing it for Jordan's thanks, but he wished that Jordan might at least recognize that it could be a lot, *lot* worse.

"I know so," Nate said.

"I dealt with it in the end, didn't I?" Jordan retorted.

Okay, that was something, at least. At least Jordan seemed to realize Nate was right. Didn't want to admit it straight out, but he at least *saw* it.

Nate wasn't surprised though, because again, Jordan had the football brain he needed. He just didn't fucking use it enough. Let his ego get in the way.

"An unbelievable play doesn't cancel out every mistake," Nate reminded him.

Jordan made a face. "Whatever, man," he said.

Nate walked away not sure if he'd made a dent. He was hopeful, at least, but not convinced.

Still, when they took the field after Aidan took the Thunder's offense down the field, Dawson hitting a matching field goal, it seemed that Nate's optimism wasn't misplaced, because Jordan's position was better.

This time they didn't let Barkley rip off a big run, and after only one first down, the Eagles were forced to punt.

It was one of those games, Nate thought as the final minutes ticked down, that left you weary and exhausted to the very marrow of your bones. Each and every yard for both teams had been hard fought.

They hadn't given up another big run to Saquon Barkley, and they hadn't even given up a big play to Hurts, but the special teams guys had given up a big punt return in the third quarter and that had set them up for a fairly easy touchdown, no matter what Nate and his guys had tried to do to stop it.

And for the first time in what felt all season, Aidan and the offense had been stymied, barely able to put drives together.

Cam was getting more work as a punter than he had all season.

Games like this happened. It was just football. Sometimes the breaks didn't fall your way, and a team was better suited or even better prepared to handle what you were good at. That seemed to be the case today.

Nate had just hoped that in the end, it might go their way. But it didn't.

They lost by three, the Eagles hitting one last field goal.

Nate's body ached as he tipped his head back in the showers.

He dressed, dealing briefly with the media questions, and half an hour later, they were filing onto the plane, a quiet, subdued bunch.

It was only their second loss of the year, but that didn't mean it didn't suck either.

Especially because it felt like this one should have been the Thunder's kind of game.

Even Jordan, joining the card players at the back of the plane, was quiet-ish.

As he slumped into his seat, Nate was grateful because he didn't have the energy to fucking deal with his bullshit tonight.

He pulled out his phone and turned it on, letting all the messages filter in.

One from his dad, telling him that he'd played great, and sometimes the breaks didn't go their way.

Another from his agent, congratulating him on his two tackles for loss and his sack in the fourth quarter. Wisely, Ian didn't bring up the actual game result, because they'd been together a long time, and he had to know that if Nate had to choose between individual stats and team success, he'd pick the latter every single fucking time.

A text from Deacon. **Good game, tough loss,** was all it said. Deacon would understand. Deacon *always* understood.

Nate scrolled through the rest of the texts—various friends and family members peppered with some old college teammates and even a few from guys he'd played with on the Condors—but his thumb froze when he got to one particular text.

He hadn't expected to get one from Ramsey, and when he opened their conversation, his stomach fluttered, because there was way more than just one.

Ramsey had clearly been texting him throughout the whole game.

There were easily a dozen texts here, and Nate could easily identify what had driven Ramsey to send each and every one.

He'd started with something about Jordan being out of position—Nate would have to give him some shit for watching enough football this year to know that much—and then he praised him for that crazy batted pass of Brown's. He made a comment or two about Nate's prowess, including his third quarter sack, that made Nate's heart beat a little bit faster, and then he wrapped up the whole analysis of the game by only saying one thing.

**Hard fought loss. Keep your head up.**

The plane took off, and the plane quieted more.

While Nate was scrolling back and through the messages, reading them three, four, five times—that last time through was between him and his phone—another text popped in.

**Don't kill the rookie, okay? He's going through it.**

Nate hummed under his breath. This wasn't the first time Ramsey had made an allusion to understanding what Jordan was going through.

He wanted to know why Ramsey believed it. Wanted to understand what Ramsey had seen that Nate had somehow missed.

**Thanks,** Nate replied, **and I'll take that under advisement.**

**Knew I picked a smart guy to fake date, Mr. Big Vocabulary.**

But before Nate could reply that he might be a football player, but he wasn't stupid.—he'd gone to college, and unlike some of his teammates, he'd actually gone to some of his classes—another text arrived.

**Seriously, though. Camera caught you giving him a lecture after that first drive, and I hope you took it easy on him.**

**Why should I?** Nate asked, really curious what Ramsey would say.

**Because you're not an asshole like the other captain. Also—that's so fucking weird. Who makes the decisions if you're both captains?**

**You know who gets the final say and it's not me, Hockey Guy. The vet always.**

But Ramsey hadn't answered his question, and now Nate had even more so he texted again. **Why do you think Sterling's an asshole?**

**Vibes**, Ramsey said, **and the way Jordan tenses whenever he looks at him.**

Shit, so it wasn't just his antenna perking up about how uneasy Jordan was about Sterling.

**Not just me, then.**

**If it makes you feel better, I don't think it's anything the guy's done or said that's put the rookie's back up.**

**You wanna explain?** Nate asked.

Of course, though, Ramsey was slippery.

He should have one of those signs near him at all times. *Slippery when wet.*

But he should really, *really* not thinking about a wet Ramsey, especially not on a plane full of his teammates and coaches. *Especially* not after a bad loss.

That way lay absolute insanity.

He was already going out of his mind, trying to keep his hands and his thoughts to himself.

Every casual touch Ramsey gave him lit him up from the inside, and at one point, Nate wasn't sure how much more he could take without breaking and doing something he absolutely shouldn't.

The worst part of it was that he was fairly certain that Ramsey wouldn't even be disappointed. It even seemed like Ramsey might actually *welcome* it, which was not doing Nate's peace of mind any favors.

Ramsey finally replied. **Sorry,** he said, **I had to talk Wes off the cliff. And no, not really.**

The thoughts flashing through his brain like uncooperative flashcards—Ramsey wet, Ramsey laughing up at him, Ramsey naked in bed underneath him, Ramsey's lips against his cheek—made Nate reckless.

He wanted to claim that he'd tried to avoid it, but if he was being really honest, it hadn't been so hard to break him down.

**If I was there, I bet I could get you to tell me.**

**Probably,** Ramsey texted back. **Too bad you're not. Sounds like a fun time.**

Nate groaned under his breath, his head hitting the seat cushion behind him. If he didn't know better, he'd think Ramsey was trying to seduce him. But if he was, wouldn't Nate know it? *And* if he was, wouldn't he have suggested something else besides fake dating?

Not for the first time, Nate wished he understood the guy a little better—even though Nate had a feeling that he understood him better than most.

**Don't tease me,** Nate texted back.

**No. Besides, you started it.**

Nate typed out one letter at a time, deliberate and slow. *And I'll finish it,* but he before he hit Send, he sat there for a minute and just stared at the message. At what it would mean. Was he just slotting into the place Ramsey wanted him to be? Going along the path Ramsey had laid out for him already? And if he was, why was that so terrible?

They already knew how good the sex would be. Nate had a feeling that it might be even better, now that they were getting to know each other.

But what was going to happen when Ramsey went back to hockey and Nate had to shake himself out of the daydream he was currently floating through?

Nate didn't know, and that was the thought that made him delete the text, one letter at a time.

**You okay there?** Ramsey sent.

*No,* Nate wanted to send. *You're changing everything. You're changing me. And I can't even hate it.*

But he didn't send that either.

# CHAPTER 12

Ramsey had been thinking—and wishing and dreaming and fantasizing—about this day for a very long time.

He leaned over and pulled his skate laces tight despite doing it twice already.

Still, it was hard to believe that after all these months, these interminable, never-ending months, he was finally here again, gearing up and ready to get back on the ice.

"Take it easy, okay?" Marsha said to him. "You don't have to rush it. You've got time. Just enjoy this, okay?"

Ramsey nodded.

She'd been his first phone call after the email had come through, Dr. Thompson confirming that he was getting back on the ice and that he had a standing practice slot at the Leafs' practice facility every morning for the next month.

His second had been to Brody.

He'd texted Wes only a long string of exclamation points. He didn't have to detail what he was so excited for, because Wes, front and center for almost all of Ramsey's misery, would know exactly what he was talking about.

Next he'd opened his conversation with Nate. The last message Nate had sent was in response to, *You okay there?* He'd only said, **Yeah, on our way home.** Frustratingly cutting off their little flirtatious banter.

Nate was smarter than Ramsey sometimes. Because Ramsey hadn't wanted to stop, even though he'd known better. He'd wanted Nate to show up at Wes' door with his friend and say, *we've got somewhere better we need to be. Like my bed.*

But of course he hadn't. He was becoming *that* guy. That embarrassing, obvious guy who he'd cautioned so many other guys from being.

All it had taken was pretending that Nate was his *boyfriend* for it to not only feel like it was true, but for the desire for it to be true to sit real and undeniable, under his breastbone.

Ramsey finished tucking his lace in and stood, letting out a deep breath.

He was ready. He was really fucking ready.

Marsha was standing by the entrance to the rink. "Hey, bud, you good?"

Ramsey looked over at her, and that was the only warning he had before no-nonsense Marsha hooked her arm around his shoulder pads and tugged him into a quick hug.

He couldn't remember the last time he'd been hugged by someone who wasn't Wes. Brody, sure, when he'd seen him briefly this summer, but that was it.

The football guys all gave him bro hugs, brief and thoughtful maybe, but not the same.

Easy casual affection was the one thing he'd found in the hockey world when his foster dad had dragged him into it at nine but since he'd come to Toronto, he'd been missing it and hadn't even realized it until Marsha was tugging him close. She held him for a longer moment than he expected, not letting him go, fingers digging into his sweater. It was an old Wolves practice jersey, goldenrod and red and black.

Finally she pulled back, something soft lurking in that frank brown stare of hers.

Ramsey was suddenly very sure that she knew more about him than he realized. Maybe she'd even known this whole time, and she'd managed to bury that knowledge down deep. Didn't let it impact any of their interactions.

From the beginning he liked her, but now, there was a bone-deep appreciation and affection. Both that she knew and also that she never said anything.

"Proud of you," she said, and he opened his mouth to say something typically self-deprecating, but before he could, Marsha continued, her tone firming. "But that doesn't mean you're back on the ice and everything's all hunky-dory now. You still gotta work hard. *Keep* working hard."

Ramsey swallowed hard. "I can do that."

She nodded sharply. "You'd better."

Patting him one last time on the arm, she gestured towards the ice. "You'd better get out there, bud."

Ramsey didn't need another invitation. He took his first step, hesitant but sure, and then he was skating, again, cold breeze whistling in his ears. The ice was fast and smooth, his blades cutting through it like nothing. Like it wasn't a big deal, like he hadn't been dreaming about this for months and months. Sure at some point that he wouldn't get it again.

For the first rotation around the rink, he just let himself feel. The wind. The ice. The chill. The blades beneath his feet, slicing sharply.

Joy filtered through his whole body.

He knew what people liked to say, sometimes, when they got catty and mean. That he only wanted hockey because of what it could do for him. That he'd only played to get into his foster dad's good graces. That he'd only excelled so Daniel wouldn't send him back into the system.

But from the first time he'd stepped onto the ice, Ramsey had found a home that he'd gotten lucky enough to experience in the first nine years of his life.

It wasn't just the ice. Or the game. It was the team, which became his family.

It was one of the reasons he'd resisted leaving college, though the Wolves had told him they wanted him after his junior year.

He'd just begun to amalgamate into his *new* Wolves family when the second concussion had hit him, *hard*.

The doctors had never been able to explain why he'd been able to shake off his first one, his senior year of college, so easily, but the second one had sidelined him and sidelined him and *sidelined him*.

Until he'd genuinely begun to wonder, in the dark corners of his mind, the shadowy parts he couldn't hide from, if he was never going to make it back again.

But here he was. Back again, and fighting to stay back.

He and the Wolves training staff had discussed certain drills that they wanted him to do. Easy things, really. But as Ramsey rediscovered skating again, everything felt new and beautiful and exciting again.

By the time he got off the ice, he felt lit up with joy. Practically glowing with it.

Marsha gave him one look and said, "Had fun out there, huh?"

"Yeah. *Yeah.*" Ramsey felt wild with it, almost like he was nine again and he was high on the thrill of finding something he loved that much.

Or, in this situation, finding something he loved that much *again*.

The joy spiraling through him made him reckless. Made him crazy.

Made him pull his phone out when he got back to the locker room. Before he even started shedding his gear, he unlocked it. Pulled up his convo with Nate.

It was precisely the kind of text he'd unequivocally tell everyone he knew not to send. An excuse to open dialogue. No purpose in it whatsoever except to get attention, and Ramsey had never begged for anyone's attention in his whole life.

But he felt dangerously close to begging for Nate's.

**Had a really fucking good day.**

He forced himself to put the phone down. To take off his gear carefully, piece by piece. Head to the showers.

Wouldn't let himself pick it up again until he was dressed in a pair of loose sweats and big thick sweatshirt, bundled up against the November chill.

When he did, Nate had replied.

**Yeah? You wanna tell me about it?**

And that was the biggest problem. The one that Ramsey was wrestling with, the one that he turned over and over in his mind and couldn't seem to find an appropriate solution to. Maybe the *only* problem he had never found an appropriate solution to.

What to do about Nate and how he seemed to be the first person Ramsey always wanted to talk to.

It didn't make any fucking sense. Nate wasn't his oldest friend or his best friend, or really any kind of friend at all. But he felt drawn to him in a way he couldn't explain. Couldn't quantify.

The situation at Aidan and Levi's the other day had just solidified all those feelings into something hard and inescapable inside him. Something he couldn't avoid, even if he wanted to.

Did he even want to, anymore?

Ramsey tapped his fingers on the screen. Useless. Not sure what to say. Knew what he wanted, *desperately*, if he was being honest with himself. In the end it was the fear that made him text back.

**I'll bring over takeout?**

That was better, right? More casual. More like the "dates" they'd already done, and less officially date-like. Not that Ramsey had any real idea of what a real date might be like, besides the obvious stuff. Dinner and a movie. Holding hands. Making out in the back of the theater. Well, he hadn't done any of that stuff. Well, *mostly* any of that stuff.

A second later a text came in. **Sure.**

Then, another one. **We can practice our hand holding again. Stars v Leafs on tonight. Thought you might wanna watch it.**

Before he could think, before he could *overthink*, Ramsey typed out, *more interested in practicing something else.* But before he could—before he could even *think* the phrase, *maybe we're done with practicing and ready for the real thing now*—he deleted the message.

In the end, he took a page from Nate's book and kept it simple. **Sure.**

But his whole walk to the car, and on the drive to the sushi restaurant to pick up food, Ramsey was thinking about it. Didn't want to be, but *was.*

*Still* thinking about it, if he was continuing the trend of being a little too honest with himself.

In June, Ramsey slept with him because he'd wanted to, sure, but also because he'd hoped by shoving Nate into a conventional box, he could deal with him. But that had never worked, had it?

Even shoving him into an unconventional box by suggesting they pretend to date hadn't worked.

Nothing had worked, and now here he was, knowing better than to send stupid texts but doing it still. Knowing better than to go over to Nate's condo, a complicated pool of desire and affection in the base of his stomach, but definitely doing it anyway.

He was feeling too fucking good to be cautious.

He'd *skated* today.

That thought buoyed him all the way from the restaurant to Nate's building and up to his door. To the point that he wasn't even sure anymore that the fizzing happiness bubbling away inside of him wasn't just about the progress he'd made on his recovery but maybe who he was going to get to tell about it.

Nate opened the door right after his first knock, like he'd been waiting. Like he'd been standing near it, just as eager as Ramsey felt.

"Hey," Nate said, holding the door in as Ramsey walked in, toeing off his shoes and handing the bag of takeout to Nate as he pulled off his heavier coat.

"Hey," Ramsey said, shoving his hands into his pockets so he wouldn't do something monumentally stupid and totally out of character—*additionally* out of character—and grab for him.

Lose himself in the uncomplicated joy of the way he already knew their bodies fit together.

It would be so easy. It would be *so* good. But Nate had said he didn't want to cross the line, so Ramsey wasn't going to be the one to do it, no matter how much he wanted to.

"Come on in," Nate said, gesturing towards the living room. "I put the game on—but first, tell me what was so good about today."

The words burst out of Ramsey, like he'd been holding them in too long. "I got back on the ice today. Got to skate, *finally*."

It had felt real when he was doing it, but there was nothing more real than opening his mouth and telling Nate. Watching the knowledge filter through Nate's brain in real time, and his *smile*—Nate had given him real fucking smiles a handful of times before, sure, but Ramsey was pretty sure it had never been like this before, not since June—it was lighting up parts inside of him that had been cold and dead for so long Ramsey might've even forgotten they existed.

Maybe they'd *never* existed before.

"Oh yeah? *Yeah?* God, I'm so fucking happy for you," Nate said, and he was pulling Ramsey into his arms before Ramsey could take a step back. Before Ramsey could be smart about this after all.

But maybe like their first meeting, this was all predestined, and there'd been no way to avoid it, not really.

Not when Ramsey fit into Nate's embrace like he'd been designed for that purpose, only. Nate's big strong arms around him like that first breathless step on the ice. Like a snipe from the blue line that went right over the goalie's shoulder pad. Like a perfectly blocked shot. Like the bone-deep satisfaction of waking up every morning and knowing that his life was arranged exactly as he wanted it to be and nobody else but him knew how he'd done it.

Nate tipped his head down but didn't let go, and their eyes caught.

Ramsey's pulse thumped unevenly. He should say something; make a joke. But the last thing he felt like doing was laughing. Not when Nate's dark eyes were so intent on him and then his grip tightened around Ramsey's waist. Not only *not* letting go, but holding on tighter.

"Nathaniel," Ramsey murmured breathily. Not sure, for the first time in what felt like forever, how on earth he even intended to finish that sentence. What it even *meant*.

"I told myself I wouldn't do this—" Nate broke off with an abrupt head shake and that was all the warning Ramsey got before Nate dipped his head and kissed him.

It was the kiss version of that smile. A kiss that tasted like joy, flavored with inevitability. Softer and sweeter than he'd anticipated but somehow even better than it had been before.

They'd kissed in June and that had been good. So good, Ramsey had thought about it long after he should've forgotten about it.

But this was even better.

Nate made a muffled noise in his throat, fingers digging into the sweatshirt fabric pooling at his waist, and something wild and new flared inside Ramsey's stomach.

It had been awhile for him—after June, he hadn't felt like going out and picking up, though he'd steadfastly ignored what that meant and why he was blowing off guys who approached *him*—and that had to be the reason it felt this way.

Both urgent, like if he didn't drag Nate to his bedroom, he might combust, and easy, like they had all the time in the world this time.

Like it wasn't just going to be once, but enough that maybe in a million years, all of this wouldn't feel like he was being remade from the inside out.

Nate kissed him deeper, and Ramsey let himself get lost in the kiss. In the perfect interplay of his mouth and Nate's mouth, and the way his tongue curled around Ramsey's, like it not only belonged in Ramsey's mouth, but that it *owned* Ramsey's mouth.

Normally that might not be a turn-on but everything about Nate did it for him.

Always had.

Which was why he hadn't been able to leave him alone, even when he thought Nate was dangerous to not just his peace of mind, but the way he'd carefully and deliberately constructed his life. Even when he thought Nate would resent him forever for leaving how he had in June.

None of that had ever mattered.

Nate broke off, as the back of Ramsey's head tipped back against the wall. He was breathing hard. They were *both* breathing hard.

Ramsey wanted to gather him in closer. Pull him back. Lock him in so he'd never stop kissing him.

"I told myself—"

"You're gonna give me a complex about how you don't want me," Ramsey teased, because it was easier than saying it for real. Than questioning, *why are you still fighting this?*

He didn't want Nate to put the brakes on now. Didn't think they *could*, but Nate was deliciously stubborn. He might still try and Ramsey wasn't going to survive that. Didn't he know that Ramsey and his normally exceptional self-control was hanging on by a thread here?

Nate laughed, eyes crinkling, like he couldn't imagine a world in which that was actually true. "*I* kissed *you*."

"Both times," Ramsey reminded him. Reminded *himself*.

"Shouldn't *I* be the one bragging about that?" Nate wondered. His hand had found Ramsey's hair and was currently ruffling through it affectionately. But there was a hint of something more in the touch. Like it would only take a moment for the vibe to change completely. For Nate to bury his fingers in Ramsey's curls and *yank*.

"I don't know, shouldn't you be?" It was hard not to smirk. Not to feel a real kind of way about that. Lots of guys—more than Ramsey really could count, or remember, even—had wanted him over the years, but he'd never felt like that was anything special. Not until Nate had chased him out of the bar.

"I don't take it for granted. Having you, like this," Nate murmured and kissed him again, soft and lush.

He wouldn't. He *didn't*.

Ramsey's mouth went dry, his whole body tight with want.

But before he could really sink into it, Nate pulled back.

His fingers drifted lower, down the side of his face, tracing the bow of Ramsey's lips. Unbidden, Ramsey's mouth opened. If he was panting, the only two who would ever know about it were Nate and himself.

And while that might have been unacceptable at some point, Ramsey was finding it difficult to care right now. Not when what he'd wanted for so long—wanted and told himself over and over that he shouldn't get, that he *wouldn't* get—was right here, within reach, Nate's muscles flexing under his touch.

"Do we need to talk about it?" Nate asked.

Ramsey didn't want to talk about it. He just wanted to *do* it. He knew Nate did too. He could feel Nate's hard cock pressing into his hip. Could feel how tightly leashed Nate's whole body was, coiling around his arousal. Keeping it controlled.

He was tired of Nate controlling it. So tired of controlling *himself*.

"What is there to talk about?" Ramsey played stupid. It wasn't his best moment, but also, most of his blood was no longer in his brain and he was *this* close to finally getting what he'd been craving, again.

Nate shot him a knowing look and did the worst thing in the world: he stepped away.

Ramsey did not make grabby hands and try to pull him back, but he *wanted* to.

"We said this wasn't real. That we weren't dating, for real," Nate said, his voice rough. Frustrated.

Well, that made *two* of them.

"I think *I* said it wasn't real," Ramsey said impudently.

Nate rolled his eyes.

"That was only because I couldn't get you to even talk to me," Ramsey said, and it felt like a truth had just shaken free. A truth he wasn't sure he'd wanted out there, but now that it was, he couldn't take it back. If he even *wanted* to take it back.

He'd been fighting this for so long. Months of Nate being pissed at him. Months of snide comments and a simmering resentment. Probably an *earned* simmering resentment, because Ramsey had ditched him the moment he'd panicked at who he was hooking up with.

Funny how Nate being Nate Bishop, defensive captain of the Toronto Thunder, was now somehow *less* pressing than the fact that he was Nate Bishop, guy playing frustratingly difficult to get.

Nate shot him a baffled look. "That isn't true. That can't be true."

None of those were questions, but Ramsey's head bobbed still, nodding.

He'd lost control of himself, which Ramsey supposed was all inevitable. Eventually, he should've known he'd run into the one person who made him a babbling idiot.

"Wait a minute, *is* that true?" Nate took a step closer. "That's not bullshit?"

Ramsey's mouth was so dry. He didn't know how to do this. "Why does it matter?"

Nate shot him a chiding look. "It fucking matters to me." He pressed him, full body against Ramsey's, to the wall. Then kissed him again. Deliberately, and Ramsey would've thought it was like a taunt, but he'd seen the look on Nate's face—that open, naked want broadcast for anyone who wanted to see it—and knew it wasn't. "If it isn't bullshit, then I'd do that again."

"Just once?" Ramsey asked, mustering up the most innocent voice in his roster. But it didn't work. It came out all wonky. Which . . .not surprising, considering he wasn't sure he could feel his fingers or his toes. He wasn't cold, though; the opposite, in fact.

Burning alive just from the look in Nate's dark eyes.

The hopeful possibility that Ramsey might want this too.

And he thought he might, but he didn't know *how* to want that.

Still, maybe it just came down to the one truth he *could* say out loud. "When I skated today," he said, hating how his voice trembled, but he couldn't help it, not anymore, "I was so fucking happy. And you were the first person I wanted to tell. That's not bullshit."

Nate didn't say anything. He just leaned in and kissed Ramsey again, hands rising to frame his face. Ramsey's eyes fluttered shut. Feeling everything and nothing at the same time.

The kiss spun on and on and then broke and then re-formed and formed again. Like Nate had *also* been storing up each and every time he'd wanted to kiss and he'd buried the impulse down instead of indulging, and now there were so many to share.

Nate's hands buried in his hair again and this time he did tug, tilting Ramsey into the position he wanted. One and then another and finally, a third.

It was amazing how he'd kissed before, but it had never felt like this before, like Ramsey was being turned inside out every time Nate's mouth slanted over his, sure and true.

Ramsey didn't know who moved first, but it felt like the most natural progression in the world to shift his weight to lead—or follow?—Nate down the hall to his bedroom.

He'd been in here once before, last June. So much of it felt the same. Ramsey's knees giving out and landing him on the edge of the mattress and Nate looming over him.

But everything felt new and different, too.

"Take this off," Nate murmured against Ramsey's mouth, tugging up the hem of his sweatshirt. "Need to see you, sweetheart."

Ramsey let Nate tug the thick fabric up and over his head, and then they were kissing again, hot and heavy. He reached for Nate, pulling his T-shirt off, finally getting to map out all that hot skin, rippling with muscle, with his palms.

When Nate crowded him on the bed, fitting himself between Ramsey's thighs like he was born to be there, the skin-to-skin contact made Ramsey lightheaded.

He'd wanted before. Sex was something he could always fit into easy-to-process boxes, but that was sex with strangers. Just two bodies—or sometimes more—colliding together.

But everything with Nate felt heightened, like it was too big to hold, nevermind to fit neatly into a label that Ramsey understood.

He'd be okay just making out like this, rubbing up against Nate's gloriously muscled thigh, even coming in his pants, when six months ago, he'd have laughed at something so childish.

But the actual act mattered less. The way he looked mattered even less than that.

He wasn't worried about making a stupid face or being too desperate or letting all his naked desire show.

He just wanted to feel it. Wanted to *keep* feeling it.

"What do you want?" Nate asked in a hushed, rough whisper. His hand was still buried in Ramsey's curls but it had gentled. The way he was looking down at Ramsey was reverent. Almost awed. Like he couldn't quite believe that they'd made it back here.

That made two of them.

"I just . . ." Ramsey panted in the air between them. Why had they stopped kissing? He didn't want to stop. He never wanted to stop.

And maybe it was okay for Nate to know that. A kernel of real truth, something Ramsey had buried and buried and couldn't any longer, because it was sprouting, growing past his control.

"Tell me," Nate said gently. Ramsey reached over and tugged Nate's T-shirt off.

Nate's gaze softened, even as it heated more. "Tell me," he insisted again.

The kernel cracked open. "Kiss me," Ramsey begged.

"Always," Nate said and leaned in, pressed skin to skin, and kissed him.

They collapsed onto the bed, Nate pressing him down into the mattress, and Ramsey groaned into his mouth as Nate's thigh wedged between his legs again.

They were both in sweatpants, but just the pressure was glorious. Lighting him up from the inside out.

Another Ramsey, an *old* Ramsey, would be already thinking of how to flip the power in the situation. How to shift focus, because Nate was all over him, every single bit of his attention like a laser on Ramsey.

Impossible to hide.

He dug his fingertips into Nate's broad shoulders and let himself relax into the feeling of Nate's mouth sliding over to his neck, then lower to his collarbone. To his chest, then his abs.

By the time Nate hit the waistband of his sweatpants, Ramsey was sweating and squirming.

Nate's eyes flicked up to his. They were so dark in the dim light of the room. "You want me to touch you?"

Ramsey swallowed hard. He knew what Nate wanted. He wasn't going to go past the point of no return without Ramsey's permission.

But speaking it out loud would make it real. Would mean he couldn't hide any longer.

No more pretending that it was just sex. That Ramsey just wanted to get off. If that was all it was, he'd have been hooking up the whole summer and through the fall. He wouldn't have pressed the big red button blinking in the back of his mind, and *made* Nate pay attention to him the only way he could.

Because what he'd intended was to tell everyone they knew that they weren't just fucking, or even friends with benefits, but *romantic.*

Maybe Ramsey didn't know how to do this. Maybe he'd be absolute shit at this—he'd certainly never done it before, never even *wanted* to do it before—but Nate made him want to *try.*

"I want you to touch me." Ramsey expected his voice to come out wavering and unsure. He *felt* unsure, like the concrete foundation he'd set his whole life upon was suddenly trembling. But instead, he sounded unbelievably certain. Desperate yes, unsure *no*.

Nate's whole face melted, fond affection blooming across it. This was what Nate had been hiding the whole time, behind a front of annoyance and frustration. He'd wanted this too, and he hadn't thought he could have it.

"God, baby, wanna touch you so bad," Nate murmured, and didn't waste any more time. He tugged Ramsey's sweatpants and his briefs down, and a second later, Ramsey gasped out loud as Nate's mouth licked up his length, sinking him into that tight white heat.

His whole adult life, and frankly probably before that, Ramsey prided himself on his self-control. His ability to keep his shit locked down, when the moment came, and to only lose it when he *chose* to. But he already knew that wasn't going to happen right now.

Right now he was going to lose himself, not just at how skillfully Nate was sucking him down, because he *was*, but because it was *Nate*.

Ramsey groaned, pleasure spiking, hips rolling restlessly, because he couldn't figure out how to keep his shit together.

Reaching out, Nate pinned Ramsey's hip with a hand, hot and heavy. *Strong*. Ramsey made a questioning noise.

Nate lifted his head and his gaze met Ramsey's. "Stay," he said gruffly. "Just . . .take it, baby. Okay?"

Ramsey's mouth dropped open a little. That was the last thing he'd expected Nate to say.

It was Nate's turn to groan, deep in his throat. "Shit, I need you to be less . . ." He trailed off.

"Less?"

"Less hot. Less fascinating. Less infuriating."

"I'm not—I'm letting you—" Ramsey didn't understand. Wasn't this what Nate *wanted*? He'd assumed, sure, but Nate had seemed to very much be enjoying the situation until this point.

"Exactly," Nate said.

It hit Ramsey like a blow to the chest.

Nate understood that this was not how Ramsey usually conducted his hookups.

He understood that this was an exception. That *Nate*—as a concept, as a persona, as an experience—was an exception.

And Nate *craved* it.

"God," Ramsey whined and fell back against the mattress. Undone, and that was before Nate even got his cock back in his mouth.

"So fucking gorgeous like this," Nate murmured, between long sucks, pulses of heat vibrating through Ramsey's limbs.

He still couldn't feel his fingers or his toes, and he'd worried for a split second that meant something was wrong, but now, he was beginning to see that maybe that meant something was very right.

This, *Nate*, was very right.

He was on a hair trigger, barely able to hang on to the self-control he'd spent a lifetime curating, and then Nate tucked him deeper into his mouth, tongue curling around the head, and Ramsey lost it.

If he was being honest, as he groaned out his orgasm, he hadn't even *wanted* to hang on to it. Not anymore.

Maybe he'd had more skillful orgasms, but he'd never had one that felt like that before, like he'd been emptied out. When Ramsey glanced down at Nate, that cavern at the center of him filled back up, all lightness and joy.

Nate was hot, sure, definitely one of the more attractive people that Ramsey had ever slept with but that wasn't why he wanted to sleep with him.

It didn't even feel like it made the top ten.

Ramsey made a greedy hand motion and kicked him gently on his back with his heel as he crawled up Ramsey's body.

They kissed, Ramsey tasting himself on Nate's tongue. Then Nate pulled back. Ramsey didn't need any more instruction. He reached down and was about to wrap a hand around Nate's cock. Wanting, more than anyone else, to make him feel good—to make him feel like *this*—too. But before he could, Nate batted his hand away and did it himself.

Ramsey couldn't help the way he pouted about it.

"Sweetheart," Nate said roughly, "I just want you to lie there. Look perfect."

Yeah, that was not a surprise. Nate was not the first guy to want that.

But then Nate kept going. "So fucking beautiful when you smiled at me tonight. Like I was seeing the real you. Like you *wanted* me to see the real you, and I—"

"You did," Ramsey said and watched, mouth hanging open, as Nate began to come, then, spurting all over his chest in hot wet pulses.

"Fuck," Nate said with feeling and collapsed against him. Not crushing him, not exactly, because Ramsey wasn't small either, but hemming him in.

Any other time, Ramsey would've kicked him in the leg. Told him to get up. Insisted on them cleaning up.

But this felt . . .well, it felt *nice*. Especially when Nate tucked his face into Ramsey's neck. As the seconds ticked by, Ramsey could feel Nate's heartbeat slowing, and then somehow, aligning with Ramsey's own.

Ramsey knew he should say something. Ask the inevitable question. *Does this change anything?* But he didn't need to ask it, because the answer already felt like it was reverberating inside him, like someone had just hit a gong: *it changes everything*.

Finally, Nate lifted his head. "Are you freaking out?" he asked.

Ramsey did smack him then. "*No*."

"You get that this . . ." Nate hesitated. "We can't—"

"We can't go back, I know. I get this changes everything, yes." Ramsey barely held back an eye roll. Of course Nate was going to ruin this perfectly nice post-orgasm cuddle session by stating a bunch of obvious truths.

"And you're *not* freaking out," Nate stated rather than asked. His gentle tone was both touching and frustrating.

And yes, Ramsey did understand why he might be worried. God knew they'd both fought against this—in particular it felt like he'd done everything in his power to both bring it to fruition and also push it away as an impossibility—but it had happened, now.

No changing it, even if he wanted to change it. And he didn't.

"No, I am not freaking out," Ramsey said carefully, with as much dignity as he could muster with come smeared across his stomach and a two hundred and fifty pound football player plastered across him.

Nate pushed up onto an elbow and stared down at Ramsey. He was grinning. "Good. 'Cause I'm gonna want to do that again."

"You said so," Ramsey said.

Nate frowned in confusion. "When?"

"After you kissed me in the hallway," Ramsey reminded him.

"You did mean it, didn't you?"

Ramsey nudged him again. Sure, this was all new to him, but he didn't like or appreciate how many times Nate was questioning him. "You *know* I meant it."

"God." Nate sighed happily. "I was the first person you wanted to tell." He flopped over onto the mattress next to Ramsey.

Ignoring the mess he was making, Ramsey rolled over, unable to help his own answering grin. "You gonna take out a billboard about it?"

"I should. I bet there'd be a lot of disappointed guys out there."

"A lot," Ramsey agreed, smirking.

Nate just laughed though, which settled another part of Ramsey that he hadn't realized he'd needed settled. Ramsey couldn't change his past—it was part of him, and he wouldn't even necessarily want to change it—but he couldn't date someone for real if they were going to stew about it. If they were going to be jealous.

Instead, Nate just seemed smug about it.

"That shouldn't be cute, but it is," Ramsey admitted.

"What, feeling damn good about the fact that it's *me*?"

Ramsey nudged him again. "Yes."

"Get used to it, baby." Nate leaned in and kissed him again.

"That should also not be cute," Ramsey said.

"Me calling you baby?"

Ramsey nodded, and Nate's expression softened into seriousness.

"Do you not like it? I can call you something different—"

"No, no," Ramsey said. "I . . .I wouldn't think I would, but I do. I do like it. It feels good. Real. Like you're really dating me."

Nate's brown eyes softened into fondness. Ramsey didn't think he could look away even if he wanted to. "Baby, I *am* dating you for real."

Ramsey had known it. He'd known it from the moment he'd told Nate the truth about how he'd been dying to tell him about today.

He'd known he'd wanted it for even longer.

Nate had to know that, but Ramsey still felt he should say it. "I want you to know how much it kills me to say this, but I'm not going to be good at it."

"Dating me?" But Nate just started laughing without even waiting for Ramsey to answer. "I don't want you to be anything but you, okay?"

"Easier said than done, when you get annoyed with me," Ramsey grumbled.

"And I'm still going to want to date you, even if I get annoyed. That already happened, didn't it? You freaked out and ran away, and I was annoyed about that for awhile. Few months, easy. And guess what, the moment you showed up again? *Boom*. Still wanted to fucking date you."

It was impossible to keep the smile on his face from growing bigger and wider, completely breaking through containment.

"Yeah, baby?"

Nate just chuckled. "Yeah, baby."

# CHAPTER 13

RAMSEY DECIDED IT WAS weird because of how *not weird* it was.

He kept waiting for his freakout. When they ate the takeout on the couch, the Stars and Leafs playing hockey in the background, Nate's arm slung across his shoulders casually. As if he hadn't even noticed it, he just wasn't ready to let go of Ramsey.

And, it turned out, Ramsey wasn't ready for that either.

When the game finished, Nate looked at him. Easy, still. In the back of his mind, Ramsey knew it was because Nate was still concerned he was going to panic and bolt. It was difficult to blame Nate for that, though it was still a little embarrassing, because Ramsey kept waiting for it himself. And it kept not happening.

"So," Nate said.

But even though Ramsey understood *why* Nate might be concerned, he wasn't going to let him off the hook entirely. "You can stop looking at me like I'm a horse that's gonna spook," he teased, elbowing him gently in the side.

Nate flushed. "Sorry."

"Don't be," Ramsey admitted. "I keep waiting for it, too."

"If you want to—"

"I don't want to," Ramsey said. And to his own surprise, *meant* it.

"Alright. So, you want to stay? I have to get up early."

"I should too." He had things to do. A workout to get in. Wes' inevitable gloating to endure. Several resumes to review for the bar.

"But you want to stay?" Nate looked shocked.

Okay, that was fair, but Ramsey still made a face. "Why is that so hard to believe? I *told* you . . ." He trailed off. What had he said? It felt like he'd said too much, but also not enough, before they kissed.

Nate raised an eyebrow. "You told me?"

"I told you I wanted to be around." Ramsey was having trouble meeting Nate's dark eyes, because it felt like they saw all the way through him, like bolt of electricity right through him. Exposing all the tender, sweet parts of him that Ramsey hadn't even been sure he possessed until this year.

But no matter how much he'd pretended they didn't exist, no matter how hard he'd shoved them down, they were surfacing now.

Nate had brought them out, without even trying.

"Okay," Nate agreed, and it was easier even than Ramsey had thought to trail after him back into the bedroom.

Not for sex, but for *sleep*.

Nate unearthed a spare toothbrush from his cabinet and they brushed their teeth side by side.

Such a domestic scene would have been enough to send him running and screaming, but then Nate nudged his foot, smirk on his face, and it was all the reminder Ramsey needed that he'd wanted and wanted and *wanted* and now he was here.

Why would he want to leave?

He'd done that once, and it certainly hadn't worked. It had never made Ramsey want Nate any less.

They went to bed, to *sleep*.

Ramsey was sure at this point that the enormity of this action would hit him, and a hundred things would bother him enough to keep sleep at bay, but to his surprise, the steadiness of Nate's breathing and the smell of him on the sheets combined with the exhaustion of a good day, the *best* day, to send him into drowsiness immediately.

Nate didn't touch him, but the way he looked over at Ramsey, the foot or two of mattress between their bodies, was good as a touch.

The sweet, intimate kind.

"Night," Nate said softly, and Ramsey didn't think he was imagining the wealth of meaning in just that one word.

All the things he wanted to say, and wasn't, because he was still afraid the heartfulness would send Ramsey running to the door.

Maybe in time, Ramsey could convince Nate—and himself—that none of it would.

He was still thinking about it as he drifted off into sleep.

Woke up to Nate's alarm, gentle but insistent, and then the sound of Nate rolling over, shutting it off.

Without any more warning than that, a warm body was encasing his, and Ramsey sighed as Nate's breath ruffled the curls at the base of his neck.

"You're still here," Nate said, tone gravelly with sleep and full of wonder.

"Don't sound so shocked," Ramsey said. But he was shocked, too. He was *still here.* He'd stayed the night, and the world hadn't imploded. Nothing terrible had happened. He'd let someone that wasn't part of a very select inner circle, friends who'd never let him treat them like any of the others, see him at his most vulnerable.

And even more shockingly, he didn't feel freaked out about it.

Nate nuzzled his scruff onto Ramsey's neck, and he shivered. "When you said you had to get up early—"

Nate just laughed, though. Laughed and his hand found Ramsey's cock, hardening against his thigh. "Baby, I gave us enough time for *this.*"

By the time Ramsey let himself into Wes' apartment a little over an hour later, he was feeling damn good.

Wes was in the kitchen and heard the door open.

"Hey," he called out. Insistently.

Ramsey rolled his eyes. He knew what kind of conversation this was going to be, and he didn't know if he felt better or worse about it happening, considering the last time they'd talked about this, none of it had been true.

But it was true now.

Ramsey gave in to the inevitability. Maybe if he didn't avoid it, it would suck less.

"Hey," Ramsey replied, sauntering into the kitchen. He grabbed a mug and poured coffee.

Wes leaned back against the counter, smirking. "Late night? Early morning?"

"We don't have to do this, you know." But there was no way Wes wasn't going to do it. He'd probably been looking forward to it for weeks now, ever since Ramsey had told him he and Nate were casually dating.

"Oh, I think we do."

"I don't need a lecture on how to be safe."

The look Wes shot him was a little galling. "Don't we?"

"Please. I get tested. You know Nate gets tested. And there's always condoms."

Wes pushed off and Ramsey should've expected it, but he smacked him upside the head. "You idiot, I'm not talking about *sex*. No, you're the last person I need to lecture about safe sex. I'm talking about your *heart*. Because apparently you have one after all."

"That's unfair," Ramsey said automatically.

Wes' expression softened. "You're right. It *was* unfair. You've always had a heart. You're one of my best friends. One of the most loyal. You'd give me the shirt off your back, if it came down to it."

"I'd even brave the dragon in his cave and suggest you call Marcus," Ramsey muttered under his breath.

"I heard that," Wes said, drumming his fingers on the counter.

"I meant you to," Ramsey retorted.

"Don't change the subject, okay? Sure, you have a heart. But you show it so rarely, it's like you wanted to pretend it didn't exist."

"It exists," Ramsey ground out.

"And I'm *glad* it does. Glad that you're showing it to someone who isn't me. Who isn't Brody. Someone who isn't your teammates."

"You mean *romantically*." One hundred times out of a hundred, that word would've gotten stuck in Ramsey's throat, but he actually managed to say it now without it feeling like it was choking him.

Nate was different; Nate made *everything* different.

"I do," Wes said, nodding. "So that's why I'm saying, are you being safe with your heart?"

"This sounds like the beginning of a terrible self-help book," Ramsey said, sipping his coffee.

But Wes was not going to be deterred. "The harder you try to *not* talk about this, the more determined I'm going to be to do it."

Ramsey did not say anything about Marcus—okay, he did not say anything *else* about Marcus—and thought that he should win an award for his hard-won discretion.

"That's obvious," he said instead.

Wes had the nerve to roll his eyes. "Really, I'm happy for you."

"Good, 'cause it seemed more like you just wanted to lecture me."

"I know how easy it is to just let things go along, when you're happy. To let everything else fall away. But the everything else is the really important shit."

Wes rarely sounded bitter. He would admit, usually under duress but never excessive force, how much he loved Marcus still. That he'd been the one to screw it up. He never even sounded angry at Marcus, for what Ramsey considered his half of the implosion.

But his voice was hard now. Implacable.

"What are you talking about?" Ramsey asked carefully. He wasn't sure what Wes was about to say, but he had a feeling he wasn't going to like it.

"Like how does this thing *work* when you go back to Buffalo?" Wes asked.

Ramsey froze. "I don't know. I didn't think—"

"Yeah, you didn't think." Wes shoved a hand through his hair. "That's why I'm doing your thinking for you. Which, I have to say, is *not* a situation I saw coming, but here we are."

Ramsey opened his mouth and snapped it shut again. "I'm skating, sure, but who knows when I'll join the team again and we're . . .it's not serious."

"You stayed the night at his place. You've never done that before. You've never *wanted* to do that before," Wes said slowly. Carefully. And that was the thing that finally made Ramsey do a double take.

*Wes* saying it so carefully.

"It's not a big deal," Ramsey claimed but the words didn't feel genuine, even to him.

Wes shot him a look. "You don't even look like *you* believe that."

That was fair. He didn't. It *was* a big deal.

"It's a fucking big ass deal. And I don't say that to freak you out—"

"No?" Ramsey rolled his eyes, but Wes continued.

"I *don't* say that to freak you out. I just don't want you to carry on, blissfully happy, and then get the shit kicked out of you by life and circumstances out of your control."

"Wes—"

"No, don't," Wes said stoutly. But Ramsey ignored him—the same way Wes had ignored him so many fucking times, when missing hockey had threatened to overwhelm him—and set his coffee down, wrapping his arms around his friend and hugging him tightly.

"I'm always gonna," Ramsey said into his shoulder.

Wes shuddered out a breath, and it was only when he seemed calm again that Ramsey let go.

"Listen, I get this freaks you out. It *freaked* you out."

"Real life destroyed my life," Wes said quietly.

"I know." Ramsey wasn't going to go into how it had been so much more than *only* circumstances out of Wes and Marcus' control. Wes didn't want to hear that right now.

"That's why I'm so worried about you."

"It's sweet, but I'm good, thanks," Ramsey said bluntly.

Wes gave an exaggerated sigh. "You *think* you're good."

Ramsey wasn't going to go into detail about how the last few weeks hadn't been legit so they'd only *just* started dating. He couldn't say he wouldn't ever be serious about Nate but right now? He was still trying to wrap his mind around that they were actually doing this for real.

He wasn't sure when he'd actually be able to rejoin the team in Buffalo, and he didn't know if Nate would even want to keep dating. Maybe he'd get sick of Ramsey's bullshit. That wouldn't be very surprising, especially because, like Ramsey had confessed last night, he didn't think he'd be very good at this.

"I don't know anything yet," Ramsey said with exaggerated patience. "We just started doing this."

"Weeks ago," Wes retorted.

"Yes, yes, weeks ago, definitely." Ramsey was never going to be able to come clean. But maybe he could distract Wes. "Which is why I think I need some help."

"Some help?" Wes sounded unamused as he turned back to the coffee machine.

It was the only indication Wes hadn't slept well last night. Ramsey wanted to ask him if it was because he'd had bad, restless thoughts or if it had been his absence that had thrown Wes. But he didn't ask, because again, sometimes it was better not to know the answers to questions you weren't ready to ask.

"I mean, yeah. You know how to date someone. You dated Marcus forever, and you two were happy."

Wes shot him a look.

"What? You *were*. I'm not even suggesting anything here, only stating facts."

"Sure you are," Wes said steadily.

"I'm just saying, you're really good at this dating thing." Ramsey was not going to bring up that if he'd actually been that good at it, maybe he and Marcus could've made it work despite life and circumstances both being a bitch. "And I could use some help in that department."

Wes leaned against the back counter. Watching as his coffee brewed. "You're asking for advice. *Dating* advice."

"Who else am I gonna ask?"

"It's not that I think there's a better person to ask. It's shocking that you acknowledge there's something in the world that you're not good at."

Ramsey huffed out a sharp breath. "If I was really that egotistical, I would never get better at anything."

"Oh, please. You came out of the womb brilliant at a whole list of things. It's one of the most annoying things about you."

"I know," Ramsey agreed. "I don't know why anyone likes me. I'm insufferable."

Wes laughed, finally. First laugh he'd gotten out of him since he'd gotten home, and clearly Wes had been braced for the discussion, same as Ramsey had been.

Ramsey just hadn't anticipated that he'd needed to be prepared for the angle Wes had ultimately taken. And he *should* have. He'd just been . . .well, to use Wes' annoying terminology, *happy*.

"You are," Wes agreed, but now he was smiling too. "What do you want to know?"

"I want to be good at dating. Nate deserves my best, and since I've never done it before, that doesn't seem likely."

"Has he complained?" Wes asked archly.

"Please," Ramsey said.

"I know, that was a stupid question."

"But he *might*," Ramsey added.

"Maybe someday," Wes said, still sounding amused. "And if he does, just give him a blowjob to shut him up. Those, you *are* good at."

"This is not helpful." He had at least expected that Wes would have some good advice for him, and it would distract Wes from what was going on. But the problem was Ramsey's questions had only served to narrow Wes in even more tightly.

"Well, give me a specific thing you aren't sure about, and maybe I can be more helpful," Wes said.

"I . . .I want to plan a date." He didn't, actually. He and Nate's non-dates—grabbing takeout and eating on the couch, holding hands or with Nate's arm slung over his shoulders, listening to Nate reveal bit by bit just how much hockey he'd been watching surreptitiously—were going well. They both had a good time. Add in the great sex, and it wasn't a combination anyone would complain about.

But there was a part of Ramsey that kept thinking, *but we could do better, right? There's more to dating than this. There has to be.*

"You want to plan a date," Wes repeated deadpan.

"Don't say it that way," Ramsey complained. "I can plan things."

"Exactly," Wes said. "You're fucking amazing at planning things. You're scary good at it. I don't know why you'd ever think you'd need *my* help."

"But it's a *date*. I don't do dates."

"Yeah, if you were trying to teach someone about having a hot hookup and leaving them wanting after, you'd be golden." Wes shot Ramsey a smirk over his shoulder as he poured his coffee.

"Fuck you," Ramsey retorted, but he was smiling too. "I'm multi-dimensional."

Wes raised an eyebrow. "Oh yeah? Then why are you asking for my advice?"

Ramsey sighed. "I just . . .I want to do right by him. By me, too."

"Of course," Wes inserted slyly.

"Just if you had any suggestions or ideas," Ramsey said, hoping this would be the end of it. He'd initially thought, why not ask, because it would give Wes something to think about—anything but how freaked out he was about any possible parallels between Ramsey's situation with Nate and his own.

Wes sipped his coffee. "Be thoughtful," he finally said. "Do things he likes. Do things *you* like. Dating is about meshing your two lives together."

There was a part of Ramsey that wanted to make a face. He didn't want to mesh his life with anyone else's, even Nate. He liked his life. It was exactly as he'd arranged it to be—at least if he got hockey back—and he enjoyed it that way. He would have done things differently if he didn't.

Nate was, always, a wild card he never saw coming, no matter how much he prepared for his eventual appearance.

"Don't tell me you like your life the way it is. You wouldn't be here in Toronto if that was true."

And *God*, Wes wasn't wrong.

"I've changed things since I got here," Ramsey argued.

Wes shot him a look. "Sure. But the fact you can't leave him alone, maybe take that as a sign that you *don't* know everything."

"Honestly, I love you, but also fuck you," Ramsey said. He wasn't sure he'd actually learned anything helpful, but it was certainly a new way to look at it. A new angle to consider.

Wes just laughed. "Love you too, babe."

"You seem to be in a pretty good mood even though we lost last week."

Dawson slid into the seat next to him and nudged him with his shoulder.

Nate had been sitting in the biggest auditorium in the practice facility, ostensibly getting ready for the week's walk-through, but in reality staring at his phone.

Wanting to text Ramsey. Knowing he didn't have a good reason, but wanting it anyway. Though, if he was being really honest with himself, that had been a thing for the last few days. Longer than that, even. But for the last few days, after they'd agreed to date for real, it had been a near constant need simmering under his skin.

When would he see Ramsey again? When would he talk to him again? Would Ramsey send him a text while he was at practice, just because he could, because he knew Nate wouldn't be around, and it was okay if it was transparent?

"It wasn't a bad loss, and we're gonna bounce back this week," Nate said, but he knew what Daws was getting at.

Daws also knew what he was getting at, and he only nudged him again. "Please, that's not why you're looking all starry-eyed."

"I don't—"

But Dawson didn't let him finish. "Bud, you can't argue with me about this, because I've been there, been right in your shoes, pretending that what's happening isn't what's happening, but newsflash, it's fucking happening."

"What's happening exactly?" Nate wondered. But he was afraid he knew. He had eyes, didn't he? And it was nearly impossible to miss how Dawson looked at Cam, at how they rotated each other, alone in their own little cozy loving world.

It was similar to Aidan and Levi, but different, too. A reflection, maybe, of how different they were as couples.

What kind of couple were he and Ramsey going to make?

"Please," Dawson said. "You're in love with him."

Nate choked on his breath.

"Don't even bother denying it. You were staring at your phone like you couldn't wait to talk to him. Like if you yearned hard enough, what you wanted would just materialize."

"I don't yearn," Nate insisted, frowning. What else was he going to call what he'd been doing for weeks? For fucking *months*?

"Sure," Dawson said, chuckling under his breath. "Deny it all you want to, but you know who you're really denying in the end?"

"Your inner gossip?"

"Shut up, that's not me. That's Aidan. And Levi. Or Aidan-and-Levi cause they're like some package deal kind of shit these days."

"Sure it's not." Nate was relieved he'd managed to distract Dawson, but there was still that bright fucking red exclamation point in the back of his head, an alarm that wouldn't stop blaring, whenever he thought of what Dawson had said.

"Don't think I didn't notice that you changed the subject," Dawson grumbled.

"I don't want to talk about it," Nate said, as nicely as he was able, with half of his brain melting down at the possibility that Dawson might be right.

"Of course not," Dawson soothed. "Forget I said it." But the smile he shot Nate as the coaching staff headed towards the front of the room told Nate that he knew exactly how impossible that was going to be.

Coach Dell started the walk-through with a reiteration of the three tenets that he wanted the whole defense to remember for this game against the 49ers.

*Containment* – specifically of Christan McCaffrey and the 49ers' insanely dynamic run game.

*Patience* – the Thunder weren't going to win every battle, but the idea was they'd win the war in the end.

*Work together* – Coach Dell was always preaching that their defense had all the pieces they needed to be successful, they just needed to execute but even more importantly, they needed to rely on each other. Let their weaknesses and strengths complement each other.

By the time Zane moved onto the offensive game plan for the week, Nate felt even more externally confident and certain that they'd prepared well for the week. Jordan was playing well, if a little scattered, but he usually pulled it together on game days, and Nate was hoping that this week would be no different.

Plus, now he'd figured out that something about Sterling bothered Jordan especially—put him on edge—and Nate would know to watch out for that. Keep an eye on Jordan and steer him away from Sterling unless there was no way to avoid it.

With his own game plan in place, he touched base with Sterling, checked in with Jordan, met Aidan's eyes across the room, giving him a brief nod of acknowledgment and then headed back to his apartment.

Toronto was one of the few teams in the league that didn't require players to stay in a hotel the night before home games, and Nate intended to take full advantage of that. A nice hot shower to relax his muscles. Watch some TV. Spend a long, restful night in his own bed.

Maybe a few texts with Ramsey. Maybe he could even gently encourage Ramsey to send him a good picture, under the guise of wishing him luck. Give Nate something to look at when he lay in bed thinking about the guy he was almost probably, certainly not in love with.

They'd just decided they were dating. The last thing Nate needed to do was freak Ramsey out by throwing out words that would certainly send him running the other direction.

He made it home in decent time, and, after parking in the basement lot, headed up in the elevator to his floor.

To his surprise, when he input his door code into the pad, it beeped insistently at him, indicating that the door was already unlocked.

Nate tensed. The door definitely should have been locked. In fact, he'd set the pad to the highest security setting—to lock the moment it shut.

Carefully, he turned the handle and slid through the small opening he'd made. But the moment he fully entered the entry, he knew it wasn't going to be a problem and all the sudden tension leaked out of his body.

Admittedly, he didn't know *why* Ramsey was in his kitchen, humming under his breath in that distinctive way of his, or why the house smelled of tomatoes and garlic, but it wasn't some crazed fan, at least.

"Hey," Ramsey said the moment Nate walked into the kitchen. He was stirring a pot of something that smelled delicious on the stove. "I'll be out of your hair in a minute. I just wanted to stop in and um, fix my favorite pre-game meal for you. For tomorrow. You know, before *your* game."

Nate raised an eyebrow. This was not what he'd expected at all.

"You broke into my apartment to fix me dinner?"

Ramsey ran a hand through his unruly blond curls. It pulled his T-shirt up, showing off his flat, muscled stomach. Nate sucked in a breath, still feeling unsteady and awed that this guy—this clever, unpredictable, brilliant, *gorgeous* guy—was his. *Yeah,* the voice inside his brain, the one that sounded painfully like Dawson, said, *you're not in love with him at all. Not even a little.*

"Yeah?" Ramsey looked briefly ashamed, before that expression melted away, replaced by his usual self-confidence. "Yeah. I didn't *break* in. Not my fault you're kind of lazy about how you plug in your door code."

"Good thing I wasn't doing it in front of someone I cared about keeping it a secret from, then," Nate teased. He reached out and to his pleased delight, Ramsey let himself be pulled into his embrace.

"Good thing," Ramsey said, voice muffled by Nate's shoulder. He pulled back a little. "I meant it though. I'm sure you've got your regular routine, and I don't want to mess it up, but I just thought it would be nice, or, um, thoughtful, even to have dinner waiting for you. And if you don't want to eat it tonight—"

Affection swamped Nate. He loved the calm, self-possessed Ramsey. The one who charmed everyone, who made it look easy as breathing, even as Nate knew it wasn't. But he liked this Ramsey too. The one who wanted to be kind and thoughtful, but didn't know how to do it without being clearly nervous about it.

"Hey," he interrupted gently, placing a finger on Ramsey's mouth to keep him from rambling, "it's fine. It's good, even. Maybe . . .maybe time to start a new routine, even."

Ramsey's eyes softened. It was unreal how Nate had ever believed he was coldly calculated. He *could* chess-master the hell out of any situation but it wasn't ever cold. It was burning hot, every bit of his machinations suffused not by how little he cared, but how much.

"How would this new routine go?"

"Hmmm." Nate tilted his head. Then leaned in and brushed a kiss across Ramsey's mouth. He tasted like basil and garlic. Like he'd been sampling the sauce, wanting it to be perfect. "We can start with that. You got any ideas?"

Ramsey's grip on his shoulders tightened and his body swayed closer, pressing up against Nate's.

"I can think of a few things."

Ramsey kissed him this time, soft and lush, drawing it out until Nate's head was swimming with an intoxicating combination of lust and something so much sweeter. An emotion that he didn't want to name, even though he was becoming more and more sure he knew what it was.

Maybe what it had *always* been.

"That's good, too." Nate broke off with a gasp. And sucked in another breath when Ramsey dropped to the floor. Tugging Nate's sweatpants down with him.

"Yeah?" Ramsey looked up, the blue in his eyes slowly getting swallowed by the pupils as he stroked Nate's rapidly hardening dick. "How about this?"

Naturally, Ramsey was good with his hands. A deft, skilled touch.

This would've been plenty. Frankly, even a non-sexual text from Ramsey might've been enough to get him going when he'd gone to bed later tonight. He'd imagined a picture being the most he could hope for.

But now he had Ramsey tilting his head up, looking at him from under his lashes, like he knew exactly what he looked like, and stroking his cock like he was born to do it.

"I think this is a nice touch, how about you?" Ramsey's tone had gotten breathier, and his face looked like a freaking wet dream come to life, but none of it felt manufactured. From the way he kept squirming, like he couldn't help how much it turned him on to have Nate like this, to the obvious erection tenting the front of his gray sweatpants, it was clear he was one hundred percent into this.

Into *Nate*.

That was the fucking ego boost of a century, but that wasn't even why Nate loved it so much. It was everything else about Ramsey.

The carefully hidden thoughtfulness and generosity and loyalty that ran through him, deep, that he'd begun to allow Nate to see.

Then Ramsey slid an inch closer and Nate's fingers dug into Ramsey's curls, tightening as Ramsey took his cock into his mouth.

And as good as Ramsey had been with his hands, it was nothing, *nothing*, compared to how good he was at this.

"So fucking amazing," Nate breathed out unsteadily.

Ramsey hummed around his length, doing something sinful and incredible with his tongue. Pleasure fizzed through Nate's body, and Ramsey groaned hard when Nate's fingers sank even tighter into his hair.

It was hard to even know what was more arousing. The incredible visual of having Ramsey on his knees for him like this or how fucking insane he was at sucking cock or the fact that it was happening *at all* after so many months of never believing that it would.

Ramsey's fingertips dug into Nate's thigh, and Nate, who'd been trying to keep his eyes away from how spectacular Ramsey looked like this with the hopes of prolonging the dirty joy of it even a few seconds longer, had to look down. Then he saw Ramsey grinding against his own palm, a damp patch obvious on the gray fabric of his sweatpants, and that was it. Game fucking over.

He tensed, nudging Ramsey's head with his touch, making it clear he wasn't lasting much longer, but Ramsey didn't budge, and a moment later, he tumbled headfirst into an orgasm he wouldn't forget anytime soon.

Ramsey was panting and a moment later, Nate's softening cock just slipping from the heat of his mouth, he made a shocked sound and came too.

For a second, neither of them moved. Nate because he didn't trust his body or his brain. Maybe he'd scoop up and carry Ramsey to his bed, tie him down, and never let him leave. Whisper sweet nothings in his ear until he stopped being afraid, stopped worrying that this wasn't real and wasn't lasting.

But then Ramsey stretched and Nate easily caught him up, lifting him to his feet. "I . . ." Ramsey's eyes were still wide, shocked. Like he couldn't believe he'd come like that either. Somehow Nate knew it wasn't *that* surprising that he'd given Nate a blowjob in the kitchen. But the rest? Nate knew he'd be stuck on that.

"Damn, I think that's gonna have to be my new routine," Nate teased, tugging Ramsey close so he couldn't wiggle away.

Ramsey's head tilted closer to his. He still was looking over Nate's shoulder, not meeting his eyes, but he also wasn't running.

"I think . . .I think you should go strip down. Find some clean clothes—"

"Your clothes aren't going to fit me," Ramsey said matter-of-factly.

"No, but I'm going to enjoy seeing you in them anyway," Nate said, deciding that if Ramsey was being blunt, he could meet him there.

The corner of Ramsey's mouth tilted up in a smile. "Yeah?" He still seemed a bit sheepish. Embarrassed, clearly.

"It's going to be hot," Nate said steadily, "but you know what was even hotter?"

"Hmm?" Ramsey asked.

"Watching you get so worked up you came in your pants, just from blowing me."

Nate had never seen Ramsey blush before, but he was rewarded now, with the reddish tinge creeping across his cheeks. "Come on," he said.

"I mean it," Nate said, leaning in and giving him a quick, hard kiss.

"You don't have to say that for me," Ramsey scoffed.

Of course Ramsey was going to be a tougher nut to crack than that. "How about I'm saying it because it's true?"

Ramsey stared at him for a long moment. Nate felt like he was trying to see straight into his soul, into his heart—and maybe he could. Maybe what Ramsey saw there was going to freak him out, but there was no way to change how he felt.

But instead of tensing or finding another reason to run, Ramsey relaxed.

"Alright," he said. He raised an eyebrow and asked archly, "*Anything* I want to wear?"

"Sure," Nate said, already turning to the pot on the stove. "I'll get dinner plated up."

When Ramsey came back ten minutes later, Nate shouldn't have been surprised, but he still burst out laughing and then had to pin Ramsey to the counter and kiss him about it, fingers digging into the sweatshirt with Nate's name and number emblazoned on the back.

"You're incorrigible," Nate said when he was finally able to drag his mouth away from Ramsey's.

Ramsey grinned. "Just the way you like me."

And Nate was beginning to realize how true that really was.

# CHAPTER 14

NATE SHOULDN'T HAVE BEEN even the tiniest bit surprised that waiting for him after the game against the 49ers was a whole string of texts from Ramsey.

He'd been offering more and more opinions of late—similar to how Nate was feeling more comfortable speaking up when they watched hockey together—but this was a new high.

**Have a good game,** was the text that kicked off the thread.

Then, **looking hot, baby.** Followed by, **is it wrong to get turned on watching you tackle some other guy to the ground?**

**Especially when that guy is McCaffrey.**

Nate laughed out loud, and several teammates glanced over his way, including Wes.

"He doing it to you now, too?" Wes asked, gesturing towards the phone in Nate's hand.

"Texting me during the game? Yeah."

Wes grinned. "It's a sign of love."

Nate knew what he meant—that it was a sign that Ramsey gave a shit, not that he *loved* him—but it was hard to stop his brain, but more his heart, from grabbing onto that turn of phrase and believing it meant what he wanted it to mean.

"Yeah," Nate agreed. Not asking more. He wouldn't want to do it here regardless. He could already sense that the half of the locker room not currently celebrating the win against San Francisco were all paying attention to what he and Wes were discussing. And Nate didn't need to give them any more gossip ammunition.

He turned his attention back to the string of texts.

**Fucking killer tackle for loss. Shit baby, you're good at this. You sure you don't wanna become a hockey player?**

Nate laughed again.

Then, **you're gonna have to talk to Jordan again—he was out of position. Gave them that first down, plus more.**

Inwardly sighing, Nate scrolled and there it was. He'd had a feeling the cameras had caught him talking to Jordan on the bench after that drive—after the 49ers had scored their only touchdown of the game—and sure enough, there it was.

**Shit, of course you already know that. You're a good C.**

The first time Ramsey had referred to him as the "C" Nate had asked what that meant. "Captain," Ramsey had clarified. "It's what we call it in that other, real sport."

Nate had only been able to laugh. Especially now that he knew that Ramsey respected what he did, just liked to give him shit about it.

A pattern that had definitely begun to go both directions.

**He seems better after you talked to him.** That text came in about fifteen minutes after the last one, about the time it had taken the Thunder to go on their next offensive drive, score a field goal, extending their lead to thirteen.

And yes, when the defense had taken the field again, Jordan *had* been better, but it was worrisome that he had to keep making these corrections.

He knew he was going to end up having to talk to Sterling about it. Probably Coach Dell too. They would see it all on tape and Nate hoped that Jordan was ready to have a *long* week of practice.

He could shelter him only so much. Didn't even *want* to shelter too much, because no matter how much natural skill Jordan possessed, he was going to have to take coaching better.

**It's still crazy to me how long your shifts are. Wait, they're not called shifts, right?**

Ramsey was getting better at parsing out plays—that was probably entirely due to Wes playing so much tape in their apartment—but his terminology still sucked.

**Nope,** Ramsey texted next, before Nate could decide they needed to have some kind of sexy flashcard session in bed, **I was right. They're not called shifts. Drives. Huh. That's weird. You football guys are so weird. Hot, but weird. Also a fan of the pants. Especially you in those pants.**

Twenty minutes later, **damn baby, you shut them right down. Guess that good luck blowjob did its work.**

**I know I said it last night, but make sure everyone comes out to Vault tonight. You earned a decent celebration.**

**Decent? That's all I (we) get for holding the 49ers to thirteen points?**

**Could've held them to zero,** Ramsey texted back.

Nate just laughed, not feeling bad at all about the result or how he'd played. By the time the 49ers had scored their touchdown, the Thunder defense had been hanging back, mainly trying to prevent big chunk plays, which of course, Jordan had essentially given up, by being out of position.

They'd recovered well after that, shutting the 49ers offense back down and only allowing one more field goal in the fourth quarter, but it had been a wake-up call that the game could've gone a different direction.

**I'll keep that in mind for next time. Gotta put that work in to earn a legit celebration.**

**Oh,** Ramsey texted back right away, **never said it wouldn't be legit. I'll meet you down there?**

**Sounds good.**

Before he headed to the showers, he turned to the room and raised his voice, "Big party tonight at Vault. Ramsey wanted me to let everyone know they're welcome and they'll be on the door list."

"Oooh, look at you," Lane teased, whipping a towel in Nate's direction, "being Ramsey's good little errand boy."

Nate knew it, knew someone might say that, but the truth was, he didn't mind.

In fact, he *liked* it. Felt Ramsey's touch, his presence, resting over him like a cloak.

So it was easier than Lane probably expected for Nate to turn to him with the best shit-eating grin in his arsenal and say, "Better me than you, bud."

Lane made an outraged noise, but Trevor was laughing next to him, and Nate wondered, not for the first time, when Lane would clue in that maybe what he was looking for was closer to home than he realized. But *Nate* wasn't going to be the one to start meddling in the demon twins' drama.

Not when he was still trying to figure out his *own* relationship.

Nate took a shower, washing the sweat and dirt of a game away, and after doing some media, headed out in a cab with Lane, Trevor, and Dawson.

"Cam's going to go grab his dad and meet up with us at Vault," Dawson explained when Trevor asked where Cameron had gotten to.

"Yeah, you're usually inseparable," Trevor pointed out, clearly missing the ironic observation that he and Lane were *also* usually inseparable. Even as they bickered and gave each other a mountain of shit, Nate realized he couldn't even picture a time when they hadn't been right next to each other.

"Speak for yourself," Dawson retorted, and *yeah*. Of course he was the guy who was going to say the thing they'd all been fairly careful not to say.

Trevor made a face and Lane chimed in, "What's that supposed to mean?"

"Nothing," Nate soothed.

Lane shot him a look across the bench seat. Nate had taken one side, and Lane the other, shoving Dawson into the middle because he was smaller. Dawson had squawked about that, claiming he was big where it counted, and *yeah*, if you saw the way Cameron was walking around like his head was in the sex clouds all day, that was not something anyone was currently doubting.

"You're not the one who said it," Lane argued as the cab pulled to a stop outside the alley that contained the Vault entrance.

They all piled out, and Nate sort of hoped that might be the end of it, but of course it wasn't. When they got inside, the doorman waving them inside casually, not even bothering to ask their names or if they were on the list. But then Nate *had* been at the head of the line and he had a feeling Ramsey had made sure that if anyone was going to be recognized from the Thunder, it was going to be Nate.

Still, Ramsey wasn't anywhere to be seen yet, as they headed towards the bar, and Nate pulled out his phone, shooting him a quick, **where you at?** text before the bartender could approve him for his order.

But before he could answer, Lane pounced first. "What was that about, in the cab?" he asked Nate in a low voice, sliding in at least two inches closer so they wouldn't be overheard.

"Seriously?" Nate asked, glancing up and clocking where Trevor was. Yeah, unsurprisingly, not *that* far away. Which meant that Lane at least suspected what Dawson had been talking about, and he didn't want Trevor to overhear when he asked about it.

Nate mentally sighed. He was going to need to send Deacon a very nice bottle of whiskey or something to make up in arrears for all the difficulty he probably had caused him when he'd been young and very stupid.

Was it not enough that he had to deal with Jordan's idiocy but now Lane was going to add to it too?

"What?" Lane whined. "You know I don't like it when people say mysterious shit."

"It was not that mysterious," Nate said, after giving the bartender his order. "You know exactly what Dawson was saying."

"If I knew, I wouldn't be asking," Lane said sulkily.

"Okay, you're ninety-five-percent sure you knew and wanted that five percent certainty."

"I just don't know why it's a big deal. We're friends."

"You're brothers," Nate reminded him.

"*Step*brothers," Lane retorted instantly, which really, didn't that say it all? Nate really was about five seconds away from straight-up demanding Lane think about why that clarification was so key, but then he felt a hand slide up his arm, intimate and sure.

He glanced over at Ramsey, his cobalt blue sweater making his blue eyes impossibly even bluer.

"Hey," Ramsey said, "congrats." And Nate didn't waste a moment, leaning in and kissing him. He kept it brief, unsure how Ramsey felt about obvious PDA—though he could probably guess. Next to him, Lane made a frustrated noise, and a second later he was gone.

"Is he okay?" Ramsey asked, settling easily into the place Lane had occupied next to him at the bar. It felt so right, so natural, to wrap an arm about Ramsey's waist and tuck him in next to him.

Ramsey went easily so he must not have minded either.

"Oh, he's demon twin-ing again."

"Demon twin-ing?"

"Don't tell me *you've* missed that he and Trevor, his stepbro, have got some real tension between them. Tension of the sexual variety."

"Oh yes, that," Ramsey said somewhat dismissively. "Don't tell me you're going to get in the middle of that."

"Trust me, I don't want to," Nate said. Then paused. "Wait a minute. Are you—*you*—seriously suggesting that I shouldn't be meddling?"

Ramsey just shrugged though, apparently aware of the irony of the situation, but unwilling to shoulder it. "That's something even I wouldn't get into the middle of," he said. "Families and sex. Scary combo."

Nate couldn't disagree with that. "You just get here?"

"Oh, no. I've been here for hours," Ramsey said. "There was a supplier issue with the napkins I had to get sorted out."

Nate paused, repeated in his head what Ramsey had just said. "Wait a minute."

Then it was Ramsey's turn to freeze. "Oh. *Oh.*"

"You didn't mean to tell me that. You didn't mean to tell me that you help run this place."

"Uh, actually," Ramsey hesitated. "I'm a part owner? Majority owner, in fact?"

The thing was, Nate *knew* he didn't know everything about Ramsey yet. That he was still waiting for Ramsey to unpack some—or *most*—of his closely hidden secrets. But this was one that he'd never seen coming.

"Wait. *Wait.*" Nate was still reeling, but of course Ramsey hadn't stopped talking.

"I was just going to advise on the gaming room," Ramsey said, "but then I did the walk-through while they were still putting the interior together and I made a few suggestions." He shrugged, like investing in a bar wasn't a big deal. "And then towards the end of the process, someone had to buy out, and I'd just signed that big contract with the Wolves, and I had the money, so I figured why not?"

"Why not," Nate stated blankly.

Ramsey flushed a little. "I wasn't going to tell you. The only one who knows is Wes, and that's only because there was no way to avoid it. But I didn't really want anyone else to know."

"Why not?" Nate repeated, but this time he made it a question.

Nate could count on one hand the number of times he had ever seen Ramsey's mask truly slip. It was slipping now, even as he watched Ramsey try to gather himself. "I really wasn't going to tell you."

Nate nudged him. "Is that supposed to make me feel better? Because I gotta tell you, it doesn't really."

"Shit, you're right. Told you I'd be terrible at this." Ramsey made a face. And for a second, Nate really saw him. Saw all the insecurities and anxieties. All the churning that went on beneath Ramsey's smooth exterior. And maybe that should have made him like the guy less. Should have made it impossible to love him, but instead, Nate just felt a swelling tenderness. A recognition that Ramsey was human too, even as he tried to convince everyone he was actually superhuman.

"You're not terrible," Nate murmured. "But I wanna talk about this." Ramsey tensed.

"Not in a *bad* way," Nate said. "Just . . .you own this place, apparently. Can't you wave a magic wand and get us into one of the private rooms?"

"I got just the thing," Ramsey said and took him by the hand, leading him towards one of the narrow hallways and into a room lined with floor-to-ceiling bookshelves.

Nate took in all the books and the big wide window seat at the back of the room with its long, gathered velvet drapes.

"The door doesn't lock, but it's the library. Nobody comes in here," he added. "Especially during the nights when the place is overrun with football players."

"Hey," Nate retorted instinctively, but Ramsey only grinned.

"Not better when the Leafs come in either," he admitted.

"Better," Nate said. He propped a hip against the back edge of one of the couches. "Okay. Tell me why you didn't want anyone to know."

"I . . ." Ramsey hesitated for so long Nate actually wondered if he wasn't going to tell him, after all. "I did think about it, before everyone came here for the first time. Even considered how I'd do it. Like casually, like it wasn't a big deal."

"It's a big deal," Nate interrupted.

"That I own it? Or that I didn't tell anyone?" Ramsey said it so matter-of-factly, but the cracks in his composure were obvious now, once he'd begun to recognize them.

"Both?" Nate ran a hand through his hair. "We all *like* you, Ramsey. You know?"

"Come on," Ramsey teased, "you didn't like me at all, at first."

This was so blatantly untrue, Nate didn't even know where to begin, but he knew he should say something to reassure Ramsey.

"At first? I actually liked you way too fucking much."

Ramsey's mouth dropped open in surprise—and Nate didn't think very much surprised him.

"I did," Nate repeated firmly. "The night we met, I liked you so fucking much. I liked you so much I nearly didn't have sex with you because I wasn't sure I could deal with you leaving after and never getting your phone number. Never getting to see you again."

"But you *did* have sex with me." Ramsey had adopted that teasing, flirtatious tone again. The one he seemed to think would distract Nate enough that he'd throw everything else out the window. Historically, it was probably crazy effective. Nate felt himself wavering, despite absolutely knowing better.

"I did," Nate said, and then added bluntly, "and then you freaked out."

Ramsey sighed. "I miss when just me saying the word *sex* was enough to distract you."

"How do you know it isn't?" Nate was thinking of last night, already, images of Ramsey on his knees in front of him, the way his blue eyes had gone fuzzy and soft when he'd come.

"If it was, I could tell," Ramsey complained.

It was time for Nate to confess some of his own truths. "It distracts me, okay? But don't—"

"I wouldn't." Ramsey grinned.

Nate couldn't help the commiserating smile he gave him. "You absolutely would."

"Okay, I absolutely would." Ramsey's dimple emerged. Adorable and sexy, at the same distracting time. And Ramsey had thought he wasn't distracting. He was the *most* distracting.

"But you won't," Nate continued, shooting Ramsey a stern-ish look, "because you won't get to hear how much I liked you."

"You said you did. But then you didn't like me at all, when we met again."

"Not true," Nate confessed gently. "I liked you even more. I liked you so much that I couldn't deal with the fact that you'd let me make such a fool of myself."

"But you didn't."

"I didn't know that though. I didn't *believe* that I hadn't." He hesitated. "And now I'm remembering what else you said. First you told me you were in town to research a bar. Buying into a bar. That was *this* bar, wasn't it?" At this point Nate wasn't going to let himself feel stupid. He just *wasn't*. But it was hard to push those feelings away. The voice that screamed at him that this whole fucking time, Ramsey had been lying to him when he should be telling the truth and telling the truth when he was supposed to be making shit up.

"Yeah," Ramsey said, and of course he didn't even look sheepish at having *that* discovered.

If Nate was sane, he shouldn't have ever trusted Ramsey. Nothing Ramsey had ever done would make him feel like he'd made the right choice in taking him at face value.

But then Nate remembered a half-whispered confession. *I was so fucking happy. And you were the first person I wanted to tell. That's not bullshit.* Ramsey insisting that he didn't have to deal with his Jordan-sized responsibilities alone. Ramsey suggesting he call Deacon and get advice, if he wouldn't accept it from Ramsey himself. Ramsey letting himself into his condo, into the heart of his life, so he could make his favorite pre-game meal for Nate. Staying the night, even though he'd never done it before.

But Nate wasn't sane. Dawson was right, and Nate was actually insane. Insanely in love with Ramsey.

"Don't be mad, okay?" Ramsey tacked on, and Nate looked closer. While he'd been having his enormous realization—though it wasn't really that enormous, was it, because it had been building for a long time now—little cracks in Ramsey's composure had begun to show.

Ramsey *really* cared if Nate was upset.

"I shouldn't have done that, I know, but it was fun, and a joke and it didn't feel real, even as you felt like the most real thing I'd run into, in so long . . ." Ramsey trailed off, blue eyes intent and serious on Nate's.

Nate wanted to reassure him that no, he wasn't mad. That he didn't *like* it, that he would've much rather Ramsey had come clean that night. That he'd not run out of his condo the moment he'd realized that Nate was Nate Bishop, defensive end of the Toronto Thunder. But that he *understood* too.

Ramsey didn't share all the parts of himself with anyone. Nate didn't know why yet, though he knew there must be an overriding reason, tucked away somewhere in Ramsey's history. Maybe Wes was the only one who knew. Maybe Wes was the only person Ramsey truly let in.

And Nate had been painfully adjacent to Wes.

The play life that had seen Ramsey pretend that the thing he was wasn't the truth at all, but a joke, had been about to collide with his *real* life.

"You were the most real thing I'd run into in awhile too," Nate admitted. "Come here, okay? I'm really not mad. I wish you'd told me—"

"I did tell you," Ramsey said, a trace of his usual impudence back in his tone, even as he slid closer, tucking himself into Nate's arms like he belonged there. And that was for Ramsey's benefit, Nate realized, not just *his*.

"You didn't mean to," Nate corrected, but so gently. He knew it had been a slip up. That much was obvious. But yes, he *did* believe that Ramsey would've told him about it at some point.

"I . . .I'm not so sure about that," Ramsey confessed, so quietly into Nate's shoulder.

Nate pulled back, just so he could see Ramsey's face. "What do you mean?" He thought he understood, but he wanted to be sure.

"Sometimes I . . .sometimes I can't get out of my own way. I've been doing it so long, on my own. Protections between me and the world, it just feels natural. I don't even realize I'm doing it, a lot of the time. Most people can't see through it."

"But I did."

Ramsey nodded. "You did. Even from the first night. I'd never met anyone who could see through me, the way you did. Well, no. That's not true." He huffed out a breath. "Wes did."

"You said—" Nate's mind raced back to that June night. "You said it wasn't a single guy. You said it was a couple." As soon as he said it, realization dawned, hard and bright and inescapable.

"Yeah," Ramsey said, "it *was* a couple. But they broke up, and I got Wes in the divorce."

"Jesus," Nate said, more than a little shell-shocked. "And the other guy—"

"Gone." Ramsey said it succinctly. "Those are Wes' secrets to tell."

"I get it."

Ramsey relaxed another fraction into Nate's embrace. "Yeah?"

"Yeah." Nate paused. "What did you mean when you said you hadn't meant to tell me the truth about your position here tonight?"

"I mean, sure, I didn't *mean* to. It did slip out. But don't you wonder how sometimes we subconsciously protect—or unprotect—ourselves?"

"You think that big brain of yours wanted to tell me and so it did?"

Ramsey's teeth bit into his lower lip. "Not my brain. No. That would stop me. For sure."

There was only one thing that might override that enormous chess master brain, and it was Ramsey's heart.

Nate felt his own lodge deeply in his throat. "Oh."

"Yeah." Ramsey leaned in, and it wasn't hard at all—maybe one of the easiest things he'd ever done, in fact—to kiss him about it. They didn't need to talk about it. Not yet. Maybe Ramsey never could. If it was only this, forever, then Nate would accept that.

Ramsey telling him, *I was so fucking happy. And you were the first person I wanted to tell.*

How could he ever be disappointed if that was true? And it *was* true. Nate could feel it in the tentative but sure way Ramsey met his lips. The way he lost himself to kissing him back. Tipping his head, Nate's hand reaching up to cradle it.

They kissed for a long time, until Nate felt breathless and mindless with the feel of Ramsey's mouth on his mouth.

It had been so good that first night, but the intensity of now, the way he *knew* Ramsey now and was beginning to see even more of the real guy behind the facade, made it even better.

He wasn't just kissing that really hot guy he'd met in the bar, but Ramsey, with that big brain and that ride or die loyalty to Wes, to wanting the guys to come into this bar and welcome them but not know it was him who was doing it.

Ramsey was an enigma and a contradiction, but he was becoming *Nate's* enigma. Nate's contradiction.

And he never wanted to let him go.

Ramsey pulled back, pupils huge in his blue eyes. "Let's . . ." He sank even white teeth into his swollen bottom lip. Nate wanted to do that. Nate wanted to drag him by his hair, back to his condo, and not let him leave the bed all night long.

But that wasn't going to lead to even a decent *team* celebration? Between the two of them, it would be more than legit. The *most* legit.

But Nate had responsibilities, and so did Ramsey, now that Nate realized the truth.

"I want to," Nate said. "So fucking much. But I can't leave. Not yet."

Ramsey's expression turned sly. He tugged Nate in the direction of the bench seat that ran all the way across the back of the room. "We could here," he suggested.

And *God*, Nate wanted to. Wanted to pull that sweater off. Get his hands on all of Ramsey's gloriously bare skin. Everyone who said he was hot in clothes had never seen him naked—and Nate was prepared to go to war to make sure that was a situation that didn't change.

He felt greedy and possessive that it was only him now that could know Ramsey like that. The past didn't matter. But right now? For all those days and weeks and months in the future? Ramsey was *his*. At some point he'd become hockey's too, but even then, Nate hoped—hoped so fucking hard—that he would stay Nate's too.

"I don't know." Nate hesitated. There was a door but not a lock. Not that he cared about getting caught. Everyone he knew here would probably expect it at some point or another. You didn't date a guy like Ramsey and not let him tempt you into a few questionable decisions.

But that semi-possessive streak flared again, and Nate decided that no amount of arousal, no desperate need to get off, was ever going to equal the risk of someone walking in and seeing *Ramsey* like that.

Not when that Ramsey was all for him, now.

Not just his body. Not just his mind. But Ramsey had said it himself, the *other* thing that might intervene to pave the way to Ramsey's potential happiness.

"What if I told you that we wouldn't even be the first," Ramsey teased.

"Really?" Nate supposed he shouldn't be surprised. This was a bar. People did stupid things in bars. Especially in bars with rooms with unlocked doors.

He'd been in his share of gay clubs in his life and *yeah*. That was not a surprise at all.

"Oh, I won't even tell you who it was, but *that* revelation would really surprise you." Ramsey chuckled under his breath. He leaned in and kissed Nate again, but this time it wasn't a purposeful kiss. A kiss meant to go somewhere. A kiss, instead, to tide him over through the end of the night.

"Come on," Nate complained.

But Ramsey only smiled. Gorgeous and perfect and *real*. And in that moment, all Nate's. "Nope. Not gonna say. Prerogative of the owner. Maybe you can take me home in a few hours and sexually torture it out of me."

"I'm going to hold you to that," Nate said seriously. What a fucking great idea.

God, Nate might have loved him even more in that moment. Not only that he'd read between the lines and knew what Nate wanted, even though Nate hadn't really wanted to admit to the worst of his impulses. But to make it a game between them. A game they'd both *very* much enjoy playing.

Nate let his hands drift down. Get a nice firm grip of Ramsey's gorgeous ass. "Good," he said, heavy with promise.

# CHAPTER 15

Ramsey deliberately went out of his way to set this meeting for a time when he knew Wes would be at practice. It wasn't that Wes wouldn't be supportive—he'd be the opposite, in fact—but he'd hover.

If he hovered, he'd see exactly how nervous Ramsey was about this conference call, and as much as he usually didn't mind Wes seeing his vulnerabilities, this felt different.

Not something he could share with others. Instead, this felt like a journey he'd been undertaking by himself, fighting off all the demons in his head with only his own hands and his own wits.

Wes wanted to be there for him. Nate wanted to be too. Ramsey knew that, but he wasn't ready to share it.

Wasn't sure he'd ever be ready.

He dressed carefully. When he wasn't playing, Ramsey usually avoided team-branded merchandise, but today he dug in the back of the guest closet and pulled on one of his Wolves sweatshirts. The one with his number on it. Forty-three, stamped in white on the black background. Impossible to miss. Impossible to deny.

*I'm still a member of this team,* it declared, so much louder and so much more obviously than Ramsey would've ever felt comfortable doing himself.

His foster dad would've told him to do it anyway, but Ramsey was too used to hiding the deepest desires of his heart away.

When he pulled up the meeting invite on his computer, perched on one of the barstools in Wes' kitchen, his agent was the only other person who'd logged on yet.

"Looking good, Ramsey," Bartholemew Smith III said, nodding in approval.

He didn't specifically say that Ramsey's team-branded sweatshirt with his number stamped over his heart was a smart choice, but he didn't have to.

He and Barty were a good pair. When Ramsey had needed to sign with an agent pre-draft, he'd met with half a dozen. Barty had not been among them. Ramsey had potential, yes, and he was going to hockey powerhouse university Portland University, but a defenseman, even an offensively minded defenseman, had not been on his radar.

"Yeah," Ramsey nodded. That was the beauty of Barty; he understood at least half of Ramsey's moves. Which might not have been a lot, but it was still more than most people.

"You ready for this?" Barty asked, tapping his fingers on the polished hardwood of his desk.

"Born ready," Ramsey replied, making sure his voice was steady. Controlling himself the way he'd been doing his whole fucking life.

Barty nodded in approval. He never had to worry about Ramsey going off script. In fact, Ramsey was usually the one making up the script.

That was exactly why, tired of the small mindedness of the agents he'd met with, he had reached out, making himself impossible to avoid. The move had impressed Barty, and everyone had been surprised when Bartholemew Smith III, used to cherry-picking first overalls and the big superstars in their prime, had signed a d-man not expected to go in the first round at all.

But then, he'd stayed in college, honing his skills, and by the time he'd hit the Wolves' roster, he'd been the best version of his hockey self.

Good enough, *ready* enough, that he'd killed it his first season. Third most points on the team, an exceptional plus-minus. Finalist for the

Calder, even at his relatively old age. Barty had told him he could get the contract they wanted if Ramsey had delivered. And Ramsey had delivered, all the way up until the second to the last game of the year, when that asshole from the Sens had taken him out.

"You really were. I've got all the reports from Dr. Thompson and also your PT there in Toronto. Back on the ice, even. You're going to be ready to come back soon." Barty kept his tone mild. Maybe Brock Rossbury wasn't on the call yet, but that didn't mean either of them were ever going to let down their guard. This was all carefully pitched small talk. He and Barty had already had a phone call yesterday about this meeting and hashed all this out. Discussed every line of those reports.

"That's the idea," Ramsey said.

"I still think you should've come down here. Weather's so much better in Florida," Barty said mildly. "Hayes could've gotten you into the Sentinels' practice facility."

"I'm good here," Ramsey said. "At least until I'm ready to go back to Buffalo."

The video conferencing window chimed, and Brock Rossbury's face appeared next to Barty's.

Ramsey straightened.

"Morning, Ramsey. Barty," Brock greeted them in his mild-mannered way.

Rossbury had not been the GM when the Wolves had drafted him five years ago—that change had happened two seasons ago—but Ramsey liked the guy. Admired that he also had figured out that you could get more accomplished with honey than with vinegar. He didn't yell. Didn't scream. Even during a string of losses that had essentially taken them out of playoff contention last season.

"You're looking good. Good color. Strong." Brock couldn't tell any of that, probably, but Ramsey had noticed his eyes catching on the number emblazoned on his chest. And when he had, his chin had lifted a bit, the corner of his lips tilting into a small smile.

"Feeling good," Ramsey said.

"I can't tell you how glad we all are here to hear that," Brock said.

Didn't bother prevaricating at all, which *was* something Ramsey didn't quite understand, though he could appreciate it. Could appreciate the lines Brock Rossbury drew in his own organization.

When it had become obvious that the coach he'd inherited *did* feel like yelling in retaliation for missing the playoffs was only allowed, but acceptable—and not just yelling, but personal attacks and brutal bag skates—Brock had relieved him after the season had drawn to a close.

Ramsey had only talked to the new coach a few times, but he seemed more cut from the same cloth as Brock Rossbury himself, and Ramsey couldn't wait to play for him.

Though, truthfully, at this point he'd be willing to play for the devil himself if it meant he was back on the ice and back with the team.

"Can't be more glad than I am," Ramsey confessed. That was one of his secretly, tightly held truths, but it wasn't anything Rossbury wouldn't already expect.

Ramsey was a hockey player. Of course he wanted to play hockey.

"I'm sure," Rossbury said, smile growing a little more. "Let's talk about your medical reports. The GyroStim did what we needed it to do, it seems."

"Yeah," Ramsey agreed. Barty had been quiet so far but then that wasn't surprising because it was what he and Barty had agreed on yesterday. Truthfully, he hadn't really needed Barty here for this; he was only present because it would be weirder if Barty wasn't.

"Headaches gone. Balance back. Returning to the ice. Your PT specifically put a note that in the few ice sessions you've had so far, your drills looked great." Rossbury paused. "She's not a coach, of course."

Ramsey shrugged, as easily as he could. Even though it wasn't easy at all. "Only a lifelong Leafs fan."

Rossbury chuckled under his breath. "Poor woman."

"Trust me, she feels it," Ramsey said.

"I floated the idea to Barty of sending you to Syracuse for a conditioning stint."

Yeah, Rossbury had. Ramsey hated the idea of it. He didn't want to go to the AHL. He wanted to be back on NHL ice. Playing in NHL games. Earning the contract extension he'd signed right before the Sens game.

"I don't need that." It was unlike him to be so dead set against something—at least verbally, when working his opponent around to his own opinion was usually far more effective—but Ramsey wasn't willing to take the chance he couldn't pull it off and he'd end up in Syracuse for the rest of the season.

It was only mid-November. The NHL had only been playing for six weeks. He could come back by Christmas and play like he'd lost no time at all. Ramsey felt *sure* of this.

"I know you don't think you do."

Ramsey exchanged a quick glance with Barty, who gave him a minute shake of his head. Okay, so Barty hadn't told Rossbury that Ramsey didn't want to go to Syracuse, so Rossbury must have figured that out all on his own.

"I—"

"Ramsey, let's be honest with each other," Rossbury interrupted with a light, resigned sigh. He pulled his glasses off and polished them on his shirt. It was easy to forget he'd been a player himself, because he often looked like a guy who'd only ever crunched numbers, though that was not true. He'd played for the Wolves himself, for fifteen years.

"I'm being honest," Ramsey said. He was not going to get annoyed, even as he wanted to. Rossbury didn't have a clue how much more uncharacteristic honesty he was currently getting from Ramsey.

"You are," Rossbury agreed. "I know you don't want to go to Syracuse. But you also want to play hockey. For a long time, I'm going to assume."

For a long moment, Ramsey wanted very much to hold on to all his cards. On to all his walls. Not let Rossbury see beneath them. It was a habit born of too many childhood lessons. Tough to let go, though he knew he should, especially in this moment.

It took effort to do it. To do it and relax after doing it.

"For a long time," Ramsey agreed.

"Cliff, the assistant GM, thought Barty here negotiated so tough because he's Barty, and also because you give a shit about the money, but I told him he was wrong."

Ramsey twitched. He hadn't realized that Brock Rossbury was *this* observant.

"Cliff," Rossbury continued, "was also under the mistaken impression that Barty runs you, like he does basically all his clients—"

"Hey now," Barty interrupted, annoyance flashing across his face.

"Barty, we've been friends a long time. Don't try to pretend Ramsey's like all your other clients."

Barty shot Ramsey a sympathetic glance. "Alright, I won't."

"You took him when it didn't even make sense for you to add him to your stable. And that's panned out, but as much because Ramsey here is maybe the smartest hockey player I've ever seen—certainly the most strategic—as much as he's actually got the skill and the drive to back it up."

Ramsey didn't thank Rossbury for noticing both of those things, but he was thinking it. Flushed inside at being so *seen*. It was a good and bad feeling. One he was still getting used to. Brody and Wes had shown him the beginnings of it. Nate was furthering it. But that didn't mean Ramsey was used to it yet. Didn't mean that it sat easy on him. The opposite, in fact.

But he forced himself to accept it. It was different with Rossbury than it had been with Brody and Wes, who'd slid easily and eventually under his defenses, and very different than Nate, who'd bombarded them until Ramsey *wanted* to wave the white flag.

No, for Brock Rossbury, Ramsey was going to have to let them down out of his own accord. And he'd done a lot easier things.

"You're not wrong, as usual," Barty said, with a genuine smile. "Told you he was a good guy," he added, directing that to Ramsey.

What he'd actually told Ramsey was that he'd have difficulty doing his usual running-circles-around-everyone routine with Rossbury.

They hadn't had much interaction last season, but now that they were, Ramsey was beginning to see that for himself.

"Listen, at the end of the day, we want you to play hockey. We want you to play for *us*, and we want you to do it for a long time," Rossbury said, with the air of a man who felt totally comfortable laying all his chips on the table.

Ramsey, who'd been trying to keep Nate and his inevitable geographical presence in Toronto a non-consideration during any of this, listened and didn't think the GM was lying.

He wanted Ramsey to play hockey for Buffalo. For a *long* time.

And barring whatever he and Nate were doing—it was still so new it was hard to even put a name on it, to put feelings to it, though that seemed to be happening no matter how Ramsey grappled for the brakes—that was what Ramsey wanted too.

There was no reason to *not* say it. "That's what I want too."

It was all he'd wanted for so fucking long, it seemed ludicrous to prevaricate because of Nate. But no matter how ridiculous it was, there was a split second where Ramsey wanted to.

If Wes was here, he'd be making concerned faces at Ramsey from across the room. Overlaying his own past nightmare onto Ramsey and Nate. But then, that was *another* reason he'd made sure to take this call when Wes could not possibly overhear it.

"Good." Rossbury nodded, expression full of pleased certainty. "I'm glad we're on the same page. I know you're not interested in going to Syracuse—"

"I'm not," Ramsey said.

But Rossbury just chuckled. "I suppose I shouldn't be surprised when I inherit a genius and then he tries to outsmart me. Or out-stubborn me."

Ramsey supposed he could argue with that, but he wasn't going to. Why would he? The guy *saw* him. There was nothing to do but embrace it.

Wes had always told him that someday change would come and he'd be forced to make considerations and space for that change.

"You shouldn't be," Barty said, laughing too, now.

"Let's ramp up your drills. Your on-ice conditioning. I'm going to have our staff send over more instructions to your PT. I wouldn't normally put more on someone without the experience, but you say Marsha has the hockey knowledge. She'll do. And then in a month, we'll bring you to Buffalo. Put you in a non-contact jersey. Try you out in a few practices. See how it goes."

Ramsey saw the challenge for what it was. *Prove it to me,* Brock Rossbury was saying, *and you can have everything you want.*

Ramsey had never been given that chance and *not* gotten everything he'd wanted, and he wasn't about to start now.

"That sounds good to me."

Rossbury nodded, looking pleased.

Ramsey should be pleased too. And he *was*. This was everything he'd wanted. But there was still that stray thought. The one he kept banishing that kept coming back around, anyway.

He knew this plan would give him more time around the Leafs' staff. Giving them an opportunity to scout him without ever letting Rossbury in on the vague possibility that kept haunting his brain. The vague possibility that kept telling him, *you should stay here, in Toronto. For Nate.*

It was insane, which was why Ramsey kept dismissing it. He'd never shaped his life around a man, certainly not a relationship, and he wasn't going to start now. But if this plan of Rossbury's gave him options, then who was Ramsey to turn his nose up at them?

That was not something Ramsey had *ever* done.

"I'll have them send a new package over, in the next day or so," Rossbury said. "You having any trouble getting ice time? Do I need to talk to the Leafs' GM?"

Ramsey shook his head. "Nope, they've been great."

"Good. Good. I wasn't sure about you doing this rehab in Toronto but it's worked out great. Obviously the GyroStim was there, but I think being around a good friend helped too."

Normally, Ramsey might've dismissed this as ridiculous sentimentality, but being around Wes *had* helped. Being around Nate, also, but then Rossbury didn't even know of *his* existence.

At least not yet.

Ramsey shoved that thought away, *again*.

"I agree," Ramsey said.

Rossbury laughed, the sound startled out of him. "Should I record that?" he teased gently.

Barty had the nerve to also find this amusing, and normally that might put Ramsey's back up—being the brunt of a joke—but he found that he was smiling too.

"Maybe," he admitted.

"Next time," Rossbury said.

And a minute later, the call that Ramsey had been hoping for and dreading in equal measures was over.

He and Barty both hung up from the video conference and less than ten seconds later, his phone rang. It was Barty, of course.

"Couldn't have gone better," Barty said in lieu of a greeting.

"Agreed," Ramsey said. He hesitated though. He should tell Barty about the possibility of him staying here. From the brief conversations he'd had with Mal and Elliott, there was room on the Leafs' roster for a good defenseman. They were wanting to trade for one before the deadline.

Ramsey could be that guy.

If he didn't tell Barty, then Barty couldn't even amalgamate the possibility into their future plans.

But if he told Barty, then Barty would want to know why, and *he* would not be convinced that Wes was enough of a motivation for Ramsey to turn his back on the team that had stuck by his side all through this concussion hell.

"Then it's settled," Barty said and Ramsey let out a hard breath, not contradicting him. Not sure he could. Not yet.

Nate might still get sick of him. Maybe his feelings wouldn't deepen.

But Ramsey heard the flimsiness of both those arguments, even in his own head. Nate seemed more enamored than ever, their relationship was *solid*, and Ramsey could already imagine falling even deeper. Maybe he'd never been here before, but he could still recognize the landscape.

"Yeah," Ramsey agreed. "It's settled."

But deep down, he wasn't sure that was true at all.

Nate was pretty sure he'd taken leave of his senses.

Under *what* scenario did he think it would be a good idea to spend not only hours outside in Toronto in mid-November, but to do it on a sheet of ice, with blades strapped to his feet?

And not by himself, hoping nobody recognized him and witnessed his abject humiliation, but *next* to someone who was so good at this he'd made a fucking career out of it.

But Nate wanted to do it. He'd planned this. He was insane for doing it, maybe, but Ramsey made him want to do insane things. Probably because he was pretty sure he was insane about Ramsey.

"When I looked up this address, I thought I must've been hallucinating."

Nate looked up from his phone where he'd been scrolling absently through Instagram to see Ramsey walking towards him with a knowing smirk on his face.

And yes, he had expected this. There was a reason he'd only sent an address and told Ramsey to dress warm.

He'd assumed that Ramsey would Ramsey and look up the address himself, but he wasn't going to be the one to give the surprise away.

"No. You weren't," Nate said. He hesitated when Ramsey stopped in front of him. Nobody would be surprised if he kissed Ramsey. Nobody would be surprised if Ramsey kissed him back. But they hadn't discussed the public PDA component of their relationship. Nate wasn't the *most* recognizable professional athlete in the Toronto area, but he wasn't undercover either. Maybe Ramsey wouldn't be anywhere else, but this was hockey-mad Toronto. Especially when they were literally standing next to an ice rink and Ramsey had a hockey gear bag over one shoulder.

But Ramsey just dropped the bag, rolled his eyes, and tugged him in. The kiss wasn't short or brief or really PG-rated.

Nate found himself sinking into it. Wishing that he hadn't planned this date.

Admittedly, he'd already been doing that.

But right before he considered whimpering or begging, Ramsey pulled back, his blue eyes so bright. Joyful. "That," he murmured, "was for bringing me to the outdoor rink, even though you're going to hate every second."

"You don't know that," Nate argued.

Ramsey shot him a look. "Baby, you're gonna hate it, and it's okay." He dropped his voice even more. "It was still really fucking sweet."

"Maybe I'll be a freaking skating genius," Nate muttered.

That seemed unlikely, but he didn't like how everyone—not just Ramsey, but *everyone*—thought he was going to suck at this. He had good balance. Exceptional reflexes. He was a professional athlete for fuck's sake. Maybe he wouldn't be *good*, but he was at least going to hold his own.

"Sure," Ramsey said. "And I'm gonna take the field and play wide receiver."

"You wouldn't be bad at it," Nate argued loyally. Ramsey had good hands and great instincts for the field of play.

"No, I'd be fucking amazing," Ramsey said, grinning as they headed over to a row of empty benches. "You're an 11 right?"

"Why?"

Ramsey rolled his eyes. "I brought you skates, dummy. You don't wanna use their cheap ass rentals."

Oh. Yes. Skates.

Nate stared down at the pair of brand-new skates that Ramsey pulled out of his open bag. "Where did you even get these at such short notice?"

"I'm sponsored by Bauer. They love me. This face sells a lot of hockey gear, baby. Told them I needed a pair overnighted to me."

It was surprisingly thoughtful.

"Besides," Ramsey added with a smirk, "you're with a hockey player now. You need skates."

Nate almost declared this was the first and last time he was ever getting on the ice, but considering he'd actually planned this *and* he had no intention of letting Ramsey go, not anytime soon, clearly that was not going to be true.

Best to get used to it. Actually, best to get *good* at it.

"Alright," Nate said, accepting them. "You think I should be wearing hockey skates."

Ramsey, who'd pulled his own much more worn skates from his bag, glanced over at him. "Did you want to wear figure skates?"

"Isn't there something else? Like something in-between?"

Ramsey burst out laughing. "Babe, *no*. You'll like these. They're good stuff. Had them sharpened at the practice rink this morning. Just enough. You should be good." He paused. "Well. The *skates* should be good."

"Hey," Nate retorted without heat.

Patting him on the leg, Ramsey turned back to his own skates, lacing them up with quick, expert motions. Nate wondered how many years he'd been doing this. He'd heard talk of some guys getting on the ice before they could walk.

Maybe a question to ask once they were on the rink and Nate needed to distract Ramsey from how *not* good he was going to be at this.

It wasn't hard to figure out the skates. Except that Nate had just gotten the first on when Ramsey stopped him.

"No, no," he corrected. Then sighed. He'd already gotten his skates on, unsurprisingly. "Let me."

"What—" But before he could ask what Ramsey meant, he was standing up, as steady as if he was on his own two feet, and tucking Nate's skate boot between his legs. Leaning down, and Nate let out a surprised yelp as Ramsey tightened the laces.

"You're not gonna be on your edges, so you don't need them that loose," Ramsey said under his breath. "Tighter will be better. Trust me."

"I do," Nate said, realizing as he said it that of course he meant it.

Ramsey must have realized it too, because his eyes flicked up to Nate's, big and wide and so fucking blue.

"Yeah, I do," Nate repeated more firmly this time. "Wouldn't be doing this otherwise."

*This* could mean the ice-skating. Or it could mean this whole relationship, and Nate realized that he meant both.

Maybe Ramsey realized it too, because he was quiet as he finished tightening the laces on Nate's first skate and switched to the other.

"There," he said, letting Nate's foot drop to the ground after one last reassuring tug on the laces. "Better."

"Thanks," Nate said and tilted his head up.

Ramsey smiled, a small, private thing that, despite the frigid temperatures, made Nate feel warm inside. Outside too, like the two of them were tucked away in a cozy bubble that nothing and nobody could burst.

He leaned in and brushed his mouth across Nate's cheek. "Anytime," he said. "You ready to skate now, baby?"

Was he *ready*? Nate didn't know about that, but he was going to do it anyway.

He stood and only Ramsey grabbing his arm saved him from toppling right over. And they were on solid fucking ground still, his skate blades sinking into the rubber mats scattered around the outdoor rink.

"Shit," Nate muttered.

"Give it a sec," Ramsey said, gently, with much more reassurance than Nate expected. He'd been such an ass about how hockey had to be easy, so easy anyone could do it, and here he was, unable to even stand up while wearing skates.

"I—" Nate cut off when he wobbled again. But then he felt like he steadied a bit. Enough to keep upright. "Okay. I think I'm okay."

Ramsey raised an eyebrow but when he spoke, he was still being nicer than Nate probably deserved. "Just take your time," he repeated. "You're good."

Nate let out a breath. Got his bearings and yeah, he really was going to be okay.

Still, Ramsey didn't let go of him as they walked towards the rink. "Don't be a hero," Ramsey murmured under his breath. "Take it slow. And if you're going to fall, just let yourself fall, okay?"

"I'm not going to fall," Nate said. But then he took his first step onto the ice and promptly, immediately fell on his ass.

Ramsey leaned over him, and now he *was* laughing, under his breath. "Shit, babe, you *did* go right down, didn't you."

Nate made a face but took Ramsey's arm when he held it out. And he'd known Ramsey was strong, but it was another to experience it, as Ramsey hauled him like he weighed fucking nothing.

"Yeah," Nate grumbled.

"Told you. Go slow," Ramsey counseled gently. "Come on. Try not to step but to glide."

It took him a minute, but Nate felt like he got a handle on it. But of course when he did, that was the moment they reached the curve of the rink.

"Shit," Nate exclaimed. "We gotta—"

"You got this. Just follow my lead."

Nate wasn't going to do anything else, because he really didn't want to hit the ice again. Unsurprisingly, it was hard. And cold.

They cautiously, gingerly, skated around the first curve. Okay, he'd done it. Nate relaxed a fraction. Loosened his death grip on Ramsey's forearm, and when he did, Ramsey looked over at him, eyes dancing with delight.

"You good, baby?"

"Better," Nate said. Now that he'd gotten the hang of the balance and the rhythmic motion of the skating, it *was* easier. He'd never be fast. Or agile. Or *ever* be able to play a game while on skates, but maybe he wouldn't embarrass himself.

"Yeah, you're a natural," Ramsey teased.

Nate barked out a laugh, then regretted that, because of how it shifted his weight and made him wobble terrifyingly.

"I mean it," Ramsey said seriously. "You took to it faster than I thought you would."

Several people, all clearly experienced skaters, fast and nimble, skated past them at a much quicker clip, and Nate didn't miss how Ramsey eyed them.

"You can . . .you know, skate without me. I'm good. Really."

But Ramsey just shot him an incredulous look.

"I mean it," Nate reassured him. "I'm not gonna die without you holding me up."

"Maybe later," Ramsey said casually. "I'm good right here. We came to skate together, not for you to watch me skate circles around you."

There was a part of Nate that desperately wanted to tease back that he couldn't, even if he wanted to, but there was no way that was even remotely true.

Ramsey absolutely could, and *would*.

But he wasn't, and that was pretty sweet, actually.

"How long have you been doing this?"

Ramsey glanced over. "This?"

"Skating. Were you one of those kids who started skating before they can walk?"

Ramsey gave a short laugh. It was such a strange detour from his earlier sweetness that Nate did a double take, nearly falling over in the process.

Reaching a hand out, Ramsey caught him just in time, his hand closing firmly around Nate's arm.

"Hey, you okay?" he asked.

Nate was sure he was concerned. But he was also semi-convinced Ramsey was trying to change the subject.

"So did you?" Nate repeated.

Ramsey made a face again. "Did Wes tell you?"

"Did Wes tell me what?"

"I mean, it's not like it's a secret. I'm sure it's in my Wikipedia."

"What is?" Nate was so confused; torn between wishing he hadn't brought it up in the first place, and also terribly curious what had Ramsey acting this way.

Ramsey sighed. "My . . .well, my foster dad taught me to skate. And I wasn't young, I was actually old for it. Nine, in fact."

There'd been more than once that Ramsey had surprised him. But Nate didn't think he'd ever been as surprised as he was in this moment.

But *God*, that explained so much. Ramsey had been a foster kid.

"No, I didn't know. Wes didn't tell me. And I didn't read your Wikipedia."

"Come on," Ramsey said, clearly trying for a teasing, affectionate tone, "why not? I think my feelings are hurt."

That was easy enough to explain. And easier than dealing with Nate's suddenly complicated emotions about finding out yet another secret that Ramsey hadn't ever told him. Though him keeping this quiet at least made a lot more sense than the fact he was part owner of Vault.

"I didn't because I kind of thought—*hoped*, anyway—that anything that the world knew about you, you'd want to tell me yourself."

Nate felt rather than saw Ramsey flinch. Realized how that sounded. And added, before Ramsey could freak out even more, "But I get why you didn't share this. That's . . .that's a big thing. A private thing. And until the last few weeks, I can't say we were ever friends."

"We were never friends," Ramsey agreed easily. He seemed to have relaxed some, at least. "It's not that I didn't want to tell you. I *did*. But it's also a hard thing to bring up, especially when you're not used to talking about yourself."

Nate took that to mean what he assumed it meant—which was that Ramsey was unused to telling any of his hookups anything that was personal or private about himself.

But he'd wanted to tell Nate. That much was obvious, from the yearning in his voice.

"I get it," Nate said softly. "That must've been hard."

"Being a foster kid or having my foster dad be my hockey coach?" Ramsey asked wryly.

"Yes?"

Ramsey chuckled. "Sort of, yeah. I bounced around a lot. But then at nine, when I ended up with the Hood family, and the dad, Daniel, figured out I could skate? Could play when I stopped falling over every five seconds? I was safe."

It was painfully easy to read between the lines. Ramsey had only been safe with that foster family as long as he played hockey. As long as he *excelled* at hockey.

"It's kind of amazing you didn't end up hating it," Nate said gently.

"Loved it from the first moment I got on the ice." Ramsey's voice was a mix of wistful joy. "I guess I was lucky that way."

"Better than lucky, I'd say," Nate said.

"Never wanted to be anything other than a hockey player, the moment I hit that ice. And I was behind, so I had to work harder, and I learned, too, that if I used my brain and worked smarter, that was even better."

Nate could see that. He could imagine Ramsey being eleven or twelve and already smarter than everyone around him. A kid that didn't have any advantages except that big brain, trying desperately to level the playing field until it was fair.

But even then, it was probably never *that* fair.

"That all makes a lot of sense."

The corner of Ramsey's mouth quirked up as they made their way around another turn. "Yeah? You feel like you're close to unlocking all my secrets?"

Nate actually thought that maybe he was—he'd take at least some of the credit, but if Ramsey hadn't ever wanted to share, he never would have. As for him? Nate knew he wasn't much of a mystery, not like Ramsey was, but it was undeniable that Ramsey knew him now, inside and out.

Ramsey probably knew that Nate had already fallen in love with him. He'd probably known it the moment it happened and Nate couldn't even be angry about that. All he felt was a dizzying kind of relief that Ramsey must know how he felt and he still kept wanting to be with Nate.

Nothing had sent him running for the hills. *Yet.* Maybe *ever.*

"Maybe I am. Maybe I like it."

"Just like it?" Ramsey's smile was fully back now, light and joyful, and Nate wanted, suddenly and stupidly, to throw caution to the wind and tell him the truth.

*Actually, I love it. I love you.*

Because that was what his feeling had to be right? This bright bubble of light that seemed to be permanently lodged under his breastbone, that only glowed fiercer every time he looked over at Ramsey.

"No," Nate said and didn't elaborate.

Ramsey only smiled harder, and didn't ask him to, which to Nate's mind was definitely all the confirmation he needed that Ramsey knew the truth.

Knew the truth *and* was doing the opposite of panicking about it.

"Can I ask . . ." Nate trailed off. Knowing he probably could. But still feeling unsure how to do it.

Of course Ramsey understood what he was asking, instantly. "Why was I a foster kid?"

Nate nodded.

"That's pretty much the one thing everyone wants to know," Ramsey admitted wryly. "The nice answer is my mom died, and there wasn't a dad in the picture. The not-so-nice answer is she was a drug addict, probably couldn't figure out who my dad was from the sheer number of possibilities, and then she did die, from an overdose."

"God, I'm so sorry." Nate wondered if he shouldn't have asked.

But Ramsey only shrugged. "It's awful, for sure. But if I'd ended up with her for longer? Who knows what I'd have gotten dragged into." He looked over at Nate and squeezed his hand. "I wouldn't be a professional hockey player. I wouldn't own a bar. I wouldn't have ever met Wes. I wouldn't be here, with you. Whenever I want to get angry about the things that happened to me, I remember all of that too. I remember that I built my own goddamn life, exactly how I wanted it."

"Yeah, you did." It was so fucking impressive. So many people looked at Ramsey and saw only the pretty face. Or assumed, because he was a hockey player, that he was dumb as hell.

But the more Nate saw of him, the more secrets he uncovered, the more in awe of the guy he was. The deeper he fell in love with him.

"Hey, you good? I'm gonna stretch my legs a bit." Ramsey shot him a mischievous look. "And maybe show off for the super hot guy who brought me here."

Nate nodded. "And the super hot guy is pretty sure he's going to be very impressed."

"Pretty sure?" Ramsey confirmed.

Nate didn't have to see any of Ramsey's skills to know, without a doubt, that he was great, but it was still fun to paste a skeptical look on his face and watch as determination flooded Ramsey's features.

"You got it, baby," Ramsey teased and took off like a shot, suddenly whizzing around the rink with quick, efficient movements. Dazzling Nate as easy as breathing.

Then he did it backwards, a shit-eating grin on his face as he passed by Nate.

"Impressed yet?" he called out.

"Very," Nate said, and Ramsey's smile softened. Took on that private tilt to it that Nate hadn't seen him give to anyone but him.

And, not for the first time, he thought—but really, genuinely started to believe—that this thing between them might not just be something, but might be *everything*.

# CHAPTER 16

"I can't believe you wouldn't get me the inside scoop," Nate grumped good-naturedly as Ramsey moved around the kitchen, preparing his chicken parm for the second time on a night before a game.

"I think even if I asked Brody to pump Dean for info on the game, he wasn't going to give it to *me*. Not since we started dating," Ramsey said as he stirred the sauce.

When Ramsey had offered, Nate had slyly suggested that not only should the chicken parm be a home game tradition, but a blowjob in the kitchen too. Ramsey had only shot him an amused look and promised he could do one better.

Anticipation was simmering at the thought, right along with his tomato-basil sauce, but he wasn't going to give away the game just yet.

It was too fun teasing Nate.

"But you didn't even *try*," Nate said. He was so cute like this. Ruffled and soft, hair messed up from Ramsey's fingers when they'd kissed hello. Sitting on one of his barstools, looking at Ramsey as he cooked then dinner, like he was the greatest thing in the whole universe.

Maybe Ramsey wasn't the best at this dating thing, but he was *trying*. At least Nate didn't seem to have very many—or *any*—complaints. Ramsey wasn't naive enough to think that was a permanent situation, but for now, he'd take it.

"Are you saying you need me to get you an inside scoop to beat Dean and the Riptide?" Ramsey asked archly.

Nate shook his head emphatically.

"Good," Ramsey said. "Because I didn't start dating a football player only for him to not be the greatest football player ever."

Nate laughed, the sound tugging at that brightness that seemed permanently lodged in Ramsey's chest these days.

He was specifically not asking himself what that feeling was. Not because he was scared of the answer. Nope. That wasn't it at all, because Ramsey didn't shirk from things. He'd never shirked from things. He'd always faced even the most difficult situations head-on, and this was no different. Didn't matter if both Wes and Brody kept telling him he was delusional. Brody would see himself, tomorrow night.

"I'll beat the Riptide for you, baby," Nate promised.

Even though they both knew that the Riptide was a tough opponent and that Nate couldn't *actually* promise that. It still made that warm place inside Ramsey burn a little hotter.

"You'd better. I gotta hold my head high with Brody, after."

"Oh, speaking of that." Nate slipped off the barstool and headed into the living room. Coming back a minute later with a package. "I got something for you."

He slid it across the counter and the bashful excitement in Nate's face had Ramsey setting the wooden spoon down and coming to investigate immediately.

It was from the Thunder team store, and Ramsey had a feeling he knew what was inside, before he opened it.

"I know you're not a football fan," Nate said, "but I thought, for the game, because your friend Brody will be there—"

Nate stopped, as Ramsey shook the jersey out. As expected, it had Nate's name and his number on the back.

If anyone had asked him a month ago if he'd be willing to wear not just a football jersey, but his *boyfriend's* football jersey, Ramsey would've told them they were absolutely fucking crazy. But then back in June, when he'd first met Nate, he hadn't ever imagined willingly watching a whole football game without bitching the whole goddamn time. But now he was not only willing to do it, he was analyzing the play and texting Nate a whole string of comments during the game.

When Brody had texted him, asking if he was interested in watching with him, he'd said yes, despite how much crap his friend was going to give him.

"You don't have to wear it," Nate said hurriedly, and Ramsey realized he'd been standing here staring at the fabric for too long, a weird mix of incredulity and happiness swirling through him.

He was not only doing this, he was *happy* doing this.

"I want to wear it," Ramsey said and then pulled his T-shirt off. "I better check the sizing."

"Well, you usually wear something underneath, the fabric's scratchy. That's an authentic game jersey—I would have given you one of mine, that I've worn, but you're smaller than me—"

"Nathaniel," Ramsey interrupted as he tugged the jersey over his head. Sure enough it fit great. And at least the color would look fucking killer on him.

Nate's pupils had already dilated though. Probably imagining what Ramsey looked like from the rear, Nate's name and number on his back.

Nate's gaze jerked up. "What?"

"I think we need to workshop this outfit," he suggested, pushing the waistband of his sweatpants down until fabric pooled at his ankles.

Sure enough, Nate's jaw dropped as Ramsey stepped out of his sweatpants, now clad only in Nate's jersey and his briefs.

"Don't move," Nate said, voice dipping low and roughening. "I'm taking a mental picture for every lonely night in my future."

"Oh baby, they aren't going to be any lonely nights." Ramsey had still been turning over the geographical problem over and over in his head, and even if he was based in Toronto, the hockey and the football schedules were going to be tough to navigate.

If Ramsey was doing this—and it sure seemed like he was doing it, that *they* were doing it—he wasn't going to let physical distance fuck them over.

"No? So you're never going to go anywhere else to play hockey?" Nate teased.

He seemed unconcerned, which was fine. Ramsey could be concerned for both of them. That was generally how it worked, anyway.

"Funny you'd assume that we wouldn't still be having sex. It's called FaceTime sex, baby."

Nate shot him a hot look as he rounded the island. It was easy for Ramsey to melt into his touch. Easiest thing in the world. Slightly harder but even more rewarding for Ramsey to jump onto the counter, wind his arms and legs around Nate's powerful body. Lean in and murmur into his ear as Nate's mouth found the sensitive curve of his neck. "No need for FaceTime sex right now, though."

Nate didn't need any other instruction. He picked Ramsey up and less than thirty seconds later, Nate was depositing him on the bed and stripping his shirt off.

But when Ramsey's hands went to the hem of the jersey to tug it off, Nate stopped him with a dark, intent look.

"No," he said. "You're keeping that on."

Ramsey couldn't help but tease. "Am I though? You said it, it's kind of scratchy—"

Nate silenced him with a hard, hot kiss. Pressing Ramsey into the bed in exactly the way he'd wanted. Nate's tongue in Ramsey's mouth, stroking his insistently, hands smoothing over the fabric of the jersey, like Ramsey might still be tempted to take it off.

But anything that got Nate this hot, his cock a burning hot line against his bare thigh, was worth it in Ramsey's book.

He'd always imagined that sex so many times with the same person might get boring, but so far, it was actually even better each and every time. Different too. Sometimes it was heartfelt. Sometimes quiet and intimate. Sometimes hot and sexy. Sometimes playful, and Ramsey experienced laughing through sex for the first time.

How could he get bored when there were so many varieties, and Nate seemed determined to try it every way?

Nate pulled back, Ramsey still tasting him on his tongue. "What do you want, baby?" he murmured. "Didn't you say something about big plans?"

Oh yeah, he had. The jersey had distracted him, but Ramsey was adaptable, and the jersey actually added a fun, sexy wrinkle.

"Nathaniel, I want you to fuck me. In your jersey." Ramsey fluttered his eyelashes. "How does that sound?"

Nate's jaw dropped and he leaned in, kissing him again. Hot and wet and perfect, his mouth saying without words just what he thought of that idea.

The kissing was really fucking good—Ramsey had never been tempted to forgo the sex part for the kissing before—but the idea of wearing this jersey as Nate fucked him and then wearing it to the game stuck with him. Smugly looking over at Brody, while only he knew what had happened in it?

That got him so fucking hot he didn't want to waste a second making out when he could be being fucked into next year.

"Come on," he panted into Nate's ear, fingernails digging insistently into his broad shoulders.

"Impatient?" Nate teased.

And normally, playing at impatience could be fun and sexy, but he wasn't actually playing around this time when he nodded.

Nate leaned in and gave him one more kiss before pulling back and not just grabbing the lube but shedding his sweatpants too.

Ramsey went to turn over, because what was the point of doing it in this jersey if Nate couldn't see the name on the back.

The very idea of *belonging* to anyone, even playacting at it during sex, would've normally been the opposite of hot, but Nate was apparently magic *and* had a magic dick, because Ramsey wanted to give him that.

But Nate stopped him. "No," he said, shaking his head as he tugged Ramsey's briefs off. "Like this. I wanna see your eyes."

Was it any wonder that some of Ramsey's wires were getting crossed? The hottest, sexiest guy in the world, even by football player standards, was going to make him come hard *and* was saying earnest, sweet shit like that and *meaning* it.

"Get to it, then," Ramsey demanded.

Nate rolled his eyes, but a minute later was between Ramsey's legs, gently rolling up the hem of the jersey so he could slide his cock into his mouth as he got his fingers inside him.

Even one of Nate's fingers was better than two of his own. And two? Ramsey swore his eyes rolled to the back of his head.

He kicked a heel against Nate's back. "I'm ready. I'm really fucking ready."

But Nate would never be rushed and this was no exception. "Not yet," Nate said, but his voice sounded frayed at the edges, hopefully losing the lock he usually kept on his self-control.

Ramsey groaned as Nate gave him a third. Slow and inexorable, pushing in and fucking him softly, then harder as his body adjusted around them.

"You're good at this," Ramsey said, panting.

He normally wouldn't be so eager to pump a hookup's tires, but Nate wasn't just a hookup. Maybe he hadn't ever been a hookup.

And he really was fucking amazing at this. Lighting Ramsey up from the inside out, his own self-control beginning to splinter.

"God, fuck me please," Ramsey begged.

But Nate was on his own timetable, and it was at least half a dozen more eye-rollingly good thrusts later before he was pulling his fingers out and slicking up his cock.

"You sure you want it like this?" Ramsey asked with the last of his composure.

Nate didn't say anything else, just pushed in, answering without words, his gaze warm and intent on Ramsey's face.

Like he never wanted to look at anything else.

"Knew you'd look good like this," Nate said as he slipped the rest of the way in.

*God*. Ramsey was so full and not just physically. That light inside him kept growing and growing until he wasn't sure how to contain it any longer.

"So fucking perfect in my jersey," Nate continued, voice growing rougher and rougher as he began to thrust. Tilted Ramsey's leg back so he could get an even better angle, and Ramsey couldn't hold his moan in any longer.

Even if he'd wanted to, he wouldn't have.

It felt too good. Too *right*.

If he was being very honest, how it had felt that night back in June had been nearly enough to send him running for the hills, nevermind this very jersey.

But now he was wearing it, and he was going to keep fucking wearing it.

"You close, baby?" Nate panted.

He reached for Ramsey's cock, his fingers tangling in the fabric of the jersey, but Ramsey didn't even need that. He batted his touch away, shifted his angle, and let Nate's thrusts carry him the rest of the way there, orgasm hitting him hard and fast.

"Nathaniel," Ramsey wailed and Nate gasped out a laugh, and followed right after him.

"Fuck," Nate groaned a minute later, the sound echoing against Ramsey's neck. "We made a mess out of this jersey."

"That's what a washing machine is for," Ramsey said with a low, tired chuckle. He felt wrung out, in the best possible way.

"Why do I have a feeling you're not even going to bother washing it?" Nate hummed. "You're gonna end up wearing it and smugly staring over at Brody the whole time, thinking of me fucking you in it."

"Ew that's gross," Ramsey exclaimed, smacking him on the shoulder blade. "And I would absolutely do it, but Brody would kill me."

"What he doesn't know won't kill him?" Nate offered. Ramsey could hear the smile in his voice.

"Buddy, don't worry. You've staked your claim on me. I'm already wearing your jersey."

Nate sighed happily. "Yeah, you are, aren't you?"

Brody let out a half-gasp, half-yell the moment he spotted Ramsey entering the suite.

Ramsey knew it was coming. Had already prepared half a dozen fairly good chirps back for when Brody inevitably gave him so much shit for what he was wearing.

But somehow, faced with his other best friend and his incredulous, shocked, and *thrilled* expression, Ramsey couldn't dredge any of them up.

Instead, he just pulled Brody in a big hug, his fingers digging into the fabric of Brody's jersey.

Brody's was blue too, but ocean blue, with the swirling wave logo of the Riptide on the front and Scott on the back.

"Hey, we match," Brody said, voice muffled by Ramsey's shoulder.

Ramsey pulled back and met Brody's eyes. He looked tired. Tired but *happy*. Not for the first time, he wished he could've convinced Brody to take another path, but he was no longer convinced that path would've been as fulfilling or given Brody as much joy.

"You get one minute to say anything," Ramsey said.

"Oh wait. *Wait.* This isn't Wes' jersey is it? Oh my *God*," Brody exclaimed, hooking his head over Ramsey's taller shoulder and letting out a squeal. "You've officially lost your mind. Are you okay? Are you Ramsey? *Really* Ramsey? Or have you been replaced by a pod person? Pod people?" A crease appeared between Brody's golden brown brows.

Ramsey smacked him in the chest. Right over that stupid wave logo. "Did you really think I'd start dating Nate and finally wear Wes' jersey to a game? I know you and Dean have been together like three years now, but I really wonder what kind of boyfriend skills you're bringing to the table."

Brody's jaw dropped. "*Boyfriend*, huh?"

"You have one, you should know what it's like."

It was a little funny, watching Brody flounder like this, especially when Brody was one of the smartest, most intelligent people he knew. Zero common sense, though. Dean had gotten all the life skills in their relationship, for sure, but still with that huge ass brain, Brody seemed floored.

"I do. *I* do. But I didn't think *you* would ever."

"I think you're nearing your sixty-second limit," Ramsey warned. He wandered over to one of the mini fridges set underneath the counter. Scanned through it until he found the light beer he was looking for. He could officially drink now, but he'd found he'd gotten out of the habit over the last year.

Still, this was a big day. One beer wouldn't kill him, especially a light one.

He popped the top off.

Brody was still staring at him like he was one of Brody's experiments, needing analysis. "I don't understand what's happening. You *look* like Ramsey—though weirdly happy for a guy who hasn't gotten back on the ice yet."

"I *am* back on the ice. Remember? I texted you. Last week." Ramsey hoped that maybe the change of subject, especially a subject that was medically adjacent, might be enough to distract Brody from Nate.

"Don't change the subject," Brody complained. He leaned against the high top table in the middle of the suite. "You're such an ass."

"I'm just saying, you *knew* this was happening."

"I know you were fucking him," Brody said. Ramsey wouldn't admit it even under threat of a red-hot poker, but he missed pre-Dean Brody. The nun Brody, the even more naive Brody, who couldn't say the word *fucking* without blushing.

"I told you we were dating," Ramsey said mildly.

"You did. So did Wes. But we both sort of assumed that was only because he resisted all your other advances. Not that it was *serious*. Not that you would show up to his game in his *jersey*. Like his *WAG*."

"Hey," Ramsey retorted.

"Yes, an outdated and horrible term. But still applicable here." Brody crossed his arms over his chest. "What the fuck, Ramsey?"

"I can't believe you think I'd tell him we were dating just to get into his pants."

It had *kind* of been that way. But Brody didn't need to know that. At least Nate had been in on it.

"Admittedly, you've never had to do that before, but Wes told me that Nate was tougher. Maybe the toughest challenge you've had yet—"

"Nate's not a challenge." It wasn't like Nate had told him *no thanks* and Ramsey had seen red and done whatever he could to get the guy into bed. If he'd wanted sex, he'd have found sex. Admittedly, probably in another bed that wasn't Nate's. And that would've been a damn shame.

"Holy shit," Brody said, his eyes going wide again. "You like him. You *love* him."

Ramsey choked on his beer. "You don't know that."

"Uh, yeah, I do. It's pretty damn obvious." That settled, of course Brody changed the goddamn subject all on his own. "So you're skating again. What does Rossbury think?"

"I convinced him to not bother sending me to the AHL." That was not entirely true. It could still happen, but only if Ramsey showed up to the Wolves' facility and wasn't game-ready. And that would *never* happen.

"Wow, really?" Brody leaned over and rummaged through one of the fridges, grabbing his own beer.

"There's caveats," Ramsey allowed.

Brody rolled his eyes. "You gotta show up in a few weeks? A month? In game shape. Ready to play."

Maybe Brody had never gone to the NHL but he could've. He'd been drafted and gone to two developmental camps with the Canes. But when push had come to shove, he'd decided he'd rather be a doctor than a professional hockey player.

Ramsey still didn't really understand it, but he'd also learned, the hard way that year, that he didn't have to understand things to respect them.

"Yep, that's what we discussed," Ramsey confirmed.

"And how's that going?"

"Good." He was sore, most days, but a good kind of sore. Slowly but surely getting his speed and agility back. He'd worried, just a little, that his puck handling, always a strength of his game, wouldn't come back the same as it had been before the hit, but so far, every-thing seemed to be coming back.

He'd even taken advantage of the more basic drills to up his precision even more.

Maybe he'd even come back from injured reserve better than be-fore he'd left.

"For a little while, I thought you'd have to find something else to do," Brody said gently.

That had been the worst-case scenario. There'd been plenty of long, lonely nights where Ramsey wondered if that would be him. But that wasn't the kind of thought he ever shared, even with Wes, even with Brody. Maybe he'd tell Nate, someday.

"And what would I even do? Professionally run people's lives?" Easier to make it a joke.

But Brody just shook his head. Still thoughtful. "You have Vault. And I have a feeling that whatever you wanted to do, whatever opportunity came up, you'd be fucking great at it. Wes says the bar is doing amazing."

Ramsey didn't know about amazing, but it hadn't hurt that it was now the favored spot of all the pro athletes in town. Auston Matthews had just booked a private room for Anthony Stolarz's birthday party. The balance sheet was solid, even with the expensive remodel they'd done of the space, and the insane rent price of being in downtown Toronto. Nevermind the rising costs of everything else.

"Yeah, we're doing well. And it's been a good hobby while I've been here," Ramsey agreed.

"Just a hobby?" Brody asked, raising an eyebrow. "You don't want to become a hospitality mogul?"

Ramsey didn't miss that Brody hadn't asked if he could. Only if he wanted to be. "Not really." *I want to be a hockey player.*

Brody smiled, just as the volume of the music in the stadium reached a fever pitch. "Hey, guess it's time," he said, gesturing towards the front of the suite. "You want any tips on how to be a WAG?"

"You're not a WAG," Ramsey protested. "You're a medical student, about to graduate and head to your first residency."

"Are you *sure* you don't want any tips?" Brody teased as they took their seats in the first row of the box.

"I'm sure the first rule is don't mingle with and definitely don't sit with WAGs from other teams," Ramsey retorted.

"Yeah, you'd be a shitty WAG anyway."

"Maybe I'll make Nate *my* WAG," Ramsey said. "Plenty of hockey left even if the Thunder make it deep into the playoffs."

"You're good, but not that good," Brody said righteously.

"Hey, I know you're used to having the best football-playing boyfriend, but that doesn't mean it's *always* going to be that way."

Brody made a face. "You would make a competition."

"At least they're not ever on the field at the same time."

"You figured that out?"

Ramsey elbowed Brody in the side. "Come on. I've never been *that* clueless."

"Close, though," Brody joked.

It was easy for Ramsey to spot Nate as the sea of white and blue trimmed jerseys swarmed onto the field to the top decibel range of AC/DC.

"He *is* big," Brody said thoughtfully.

"I'm assuming you're talking about Nate, and not your monster of a man."

"He's a gentle giant—except when I don't want him to be," Brody argued, going a little pink as he said it.

Ramsey decided there was no point in keeping the comment to himself any longer. "I miss when you were practically consigned to a nunnery."

"No, you don't," Brody said, his grin and his blush both equally bright now.

"Actually, I do. Because I could give you shit before, and now I can't."

"Disappointing," Brody said, not sounding disappointed at all.

"I hope that you told Dean to not like kill our quarterback or anything. We kind of like him, and I don't want to see what happens if Wes has to actually put the clipboard down."

"I did, but Dean just grinned at me. So maybe message not received? Besides, if Wes had to play, he'd be awesome," Brody declared loyally. "Did you invite him tonight?"

Despite many reservations and an actual *pros* and *cons* list that Ramsey had written while he was in the office at Vault and then burned *additionally* just to be safe, yes, Ramsey had invited Wes to their get-together tonight.

It was only too bad that Mal and Elliott, playing with the Leafs now, were out of town. Otherwise, it would've been a real party.

As it was, now, it was going to be two couples and then Wes.

Because that wasn't going to be a mess or anything.

"Yeah, I invited him, and when it goes bad, I want you to acknowledge it was *your* idea."

"It would've been worse if we *didn't* invite him. He'd be so left out, and for what? Just because he doesn't have a boyfriend?" Brody argued.

That was the conclusion that Ramsey had come to too. He'd ended up underlining it twice on the *pro* side of his list.

"He'll put a good front up while you guys are there. But it's after I worry about."

"Maybe it'll motivate him to reach out. You told me you thought he should."

Ramsey sighed. "I wish that was true, but he seems determined to be a martyr for the rest of his whole fucking life because Marcus told him he was picking football over him."

"But he wasn't?" Brody frowned.

"That's debatable," Ramsey said. It wasn't his business—but of course he knew exactly where Wes and Marcus had gone right, and exactly where they'd gone wrong. "I don't think either of them anticipated that he would bounce around so much in the first year."

"Speaking of that," Brody said, not very casually, "what are *you* going to do about that?"

Warmups were just finishing up. Ramsey looked away from the field for a second and gave his friend the toughest look in his arsenal. "Are you fucking joking?"

"No?" But there was a hint of guilt in Brody's voice.

"Don't come here and do Wes' dirty work, okay?"

"He's just trying to prevent you from making his mistakes. And obviously I'm not against that either."

"Obviously," Ramsey retorted snarkily.

"Ramsey, it *is* a concern. In what, three weeks, a month? You're going to be back in Buffalo, and there'll still be months left in the football season."

"And?"

"*And*," Brody stressed, "you've never had a relationship before. Nevermind a long-distance relationship. Wes and Marcus—"

"I told you, don't come here and parrot Wes' self-fulfilling prophecies. I've got it handled."

He hadn't talked to Nate—he hadn't known how, especially when Nate had to know the inevitable geographical separation was coming and hadn't said anything either, like it was truly not a big deal—and he hadn't quite been able to stomach telling Barty about the possibility of a trade. Not when Rossbury and the Wolves had been so supportive. When they'd done everything that Ramsey had ever wanted. They'd stood by him through everything, even when it might've been easier, simpler, more convenient, to move on.

"Do you?" Brody questioned.

"Yes," Ramsey snapped. Painfully aware that the more vehement he grew, the more suspicious Brody was going to be. The more inevitable it was that he'd tell Wes all about this conversation.

Brody was easier to dismiss than Wes.

Wes was paranoid and haunted by his own past mistakes and saw Ramsey as a way to set history straight.

*Stupid*.

"Okay, we don't have to talk about it," Brody conceded. "But at least tell me you and Nate have talked about this. Long-distance isn't so difficult, if you guys *communicate*. You know what that is, right?"

"I know how to use words, yes," Ramsey ground out.

"Alright." Brody didn't sound convinced, but that made sense. He wasn't stupid and couldn't have missed that Ramsey hadn't actually answered the question.

There was no way he wouldn't be reporting back to Wes. And after tonight's dinner, there was every chance that Wes, upset and sad and lonely, would refuse to let Ramsey brush the subject off again.

"It's really not that far. Only what, an hour? Two, tops?" Brody continued.

"Depending on the traffic, the middle of that, depending on where we'd each be coming from," Ramsey said guardedly.

"Right. That's no big deal. I'm looking at a residency at hospitals over an hour out. We know it'll be tough, but Dean and I are going to make it work."

Ramsey said it before he could realize how stupid *he was*. "That's because you two are disgustingly, incurably in love."

Brody poked him with his elbow and shot him a brilliant smile. "And you're not?"

# CHAPTER 17

Nate had known this game would be tough. The team had all mentally circled it on the schedule from the preseason. Before the preseason, even.

The Riptide were historically a tough opponent and a great time. Even flying across the country and the inherent difficulties of that didn't mean they wouldn't bring a knock-down, brutal, semi-dirty fight.

Nate hadn't been wrong.

Both offenses had been locked down by the opposing defenses for much of the game. Dean and the Riptide defensive line had terrorized Aidan all game long. He'd barely had a second to throw before his linemen were being overwhelmed.

But Aidan was gritty and tough, and Nate had watched from the sideline, deep into the fourth quarter, the score still so close at six to three, as Aidan led the Thunder down the field and with a beautiful quick little slant to Trevor had put the Thunder up three, with four minutes left.

"Sorry I couldn't drag out the clock any more," Aidan said to him, as they'd watched Dawson and the kicking team run out to make it four.

"You did your best. Eight-minute drive and you got the TD," Nate said, slapping Aidan on the back. "You did your job. Let us do ours."

Sterling had the defense huddle up and made it clear nobody was getting behind anybody. Their *one* job was to make sure they took away any ability to get a long play, and to make that happen, the Thunder defense couldn't take a risk. Couldn't play as instinctually as they normally would. They were running this drive totally by the book. The Riptide had a great quarterback too and an even better receiver and a coach who was willing to go for it on fourth down.

When Sterling was done issuing instructions, Nate turned to Jordan. "You good, man?" he asked.

Jordan wouldn't be directly responsible for covering the biggest threat—wide receiver and insane playmaker Chase Riley. He might be a year or two past his prime, but he was as wily as ever, with a still-dangerous burst of speed. But even though Jordan wasn't a cornerback or a safety, he'd be covering the middle of the field. If someone was going to slip containment, it was going to be Jordan's responsibility to track them down. Stop them. By any means necessary.

"Yeah, I'm good," Jordan retorted, tone edgy like he thought Nate was questioning his readiness. Nate wasn't, but he needed to make sure Jordan understood.

In a lot of ways, Nate had tried to be a shield over Jordan. Protecting him from the way the team and the media and the fans could come down on new guys—guys still trying to find their way in the challenging and unsettling landscape of the NFL—but if he fucked this drive up, fucked this *game* up, Nate wouldn't be able to. Not anymore.

Wouldn't even be sure he wanted to.

"You're sure?"

"You questioning me, Big Dog?" Jordan demanded.

But Nate wouldn't be swayed. He had to make sure. Maybe they had a winning record. Maybe they'd only lost three games so far this season, but this was a good team. A team that was practically guaranteed to be in the playoffs. A team they'd need to be able to beat if they had any chance of going all the way, the way Nate so desperately wanted to.

"No, but I'm making sure you know your place," Nate said.

The moment he said it, he knew it was wrong.

Knew instinctively, even before Jordan flinched, that he'd phrased it wrong. He wanted to take it back, to explain better what he'd meant—that it wasn't that he didn't trust Jordan, but that it was part of his *job* to make sure that Jordan knew to do his.

But before he could explain and make it right, Sterling was gesturing their group onto the field. It was time.

Usually, it was easier for Nate to empty petty frustrations and distractions from his mind. Easy to lock in and focus on the next play. But he felt a little slip of unease wiggle through him, no matter how he tried to clear it. Taking his position, he leaned over and listened carefully for the snap count.

When Phillips, the Riptide center, snapped the ball, Nate pushed off and immediately saw the quarterback—Sam Crawford, 2x Super Bowl champ and 3x league MVP—drop back and wind his arm up for the throw.

Nate collided with the right tackle, bouncing off him in a calculated move, and then spun around his bigger body, evading his attempts to grab him for a second time.

The tight end came in, trying to get him, and he wasn't a match for Nate, not with a full head of steam and all his strength behind him, but it didn't matter, because he provided just enough time for Crawford to throw the pass.

Nate's head whipped around, eyes tracking the ball as it spiraled through the air, and for a single, heart-stopping second, he thought the tight end, sliding out of his position right in the middle of the field, where *Jordan was supposed to fucking be*, was going to catch it. But at the last moment, Jordan appeared, leaping up and batting it away.

The stadium erupted, and the corner of Nate's mind that had been buzzing with the anxiety that Jordan might fuck this up, relaxed.

Especially when on the next down, Nate hit the gap a little quicker than he had the first time and flushed Crawford out of the pocket before he could even have a chance to toss the ball downfield.

It wasn't a sack, but Crawford still threw the ball away, out of the hands of any receivers. Especially receivers named Chase Riley.

Third down, Crawford tossed a quick slant to the Riptide's running back, but Jordan was there again, tackling him before he could get the first down.

It was fourth and six.

"Keep it up," Sterling exhorted them in the huddle. "We've got this."

Nate felt the last bit of tension leave him. He hadn't been entirely sure if they *did* have this—how many game winning drives had Sam Crawford led this team on? Too many for Nate to remember and at least a handful had been in the playoffs. One to win the Super Bowl. It was stupid and dangerous to count the Riptide out, not until the last seconds ticked off the clock.

But they had this in the bag.

Jordan was playing great. The defense was a well-oiled machine.

On fourth down, Nate expected they'd slot that tight end to block again, hoping to give Crawford a few extra precious seconds to throw, and he was right.

Nate spun around the right tackle and got delayed just long enough in a block by the tight end, clearing him as Crawford threw the ball deep.

Not deep.

Deep-ish.

In the soft spot of the coverage. Exactly where Jordan had been covering. Or where Jordan *should* have been covering, if he'd been in the correct position.

He was not in the correct position.

Instead, he was all the way over on the other side of the field. Too far to catch or even chase down Riley when he crossed over, caught the ball mid-stride, and took it for another twenty-five yards.

Sterling was the guy who finally brought Riley down.

He shot Jordan a look but didn't say anything before they huddled up again, briefly, before the next play, the clock ticking down, which meant that they barely had a chance to catch their breath before the Riptide offense was getting into position for their next play.

Clearly they didn't want to just be in field goal range—because they were nearly already there—and they were still pushing.

They wanted to win the game.

Nate was determined that it wouldn't happen. But as one play slipped into the next, he realized that it might not matter how much he didn't want it to happen.

The Riptide were inexorably pushing towards the goal line. Closer with every play. Time didn't even look to be that much of a factor.

He pushed the last of his energy into the final two plays, trying to get to Crawford and get the sack.

But at the last second, Crawford stepped around him and tossed a short little screen to the running back, who dove over the line.

There were still forty seconds, but that was asking too much of the offense, and the game ended less than five minutes later.

Jordan was alone on the bench, towel over his head, and Nate considered going over to him. Reassuring him that he hadn't fucked up, even though that would've been a lie.

Aidan and Levi joined him on the way into the tunnel. "Tough breaks, man," Aidan said.

Nate had gotten out of the habit of apologizing for when the defense let the offense down, but it was so hard not to do it now, especially when it *was* their fault they'd now notched their third loss.

"Yeah," Nate just agreed. It sucked. Maybe they were still on top of the division and still had a nice lock on the number one seed for the playoffs, but now the Riptide—a powerhouse in the AFC too—owned a tiebreaker over them. Never a good feeling.

"Don't let him beat himself up too much, okay?" Levi said quietly, and Nate could only nod and hope that Jordan would actually *let* him do that.

Nate hadn't been entirely sure about the whole situation when Ramsey had broached the idea of having a double date dinner post-game with Brody and Dean.

"The Riptide isn't even heading back to California," Ramsey had explained when Nate had wondered how that might work, considering that teams usually expected their players, especially star defensive ends, to travel with the team right after the game. "They play Buffalo next week, in Buffalo, so they're just staying on the east coast. They can just take a different flight, meet the team in New York."

That had been the only excuse Nate could come up with for why it might not be a great idea. The general concept didn't bother him; in fact, he was surprisingly interested to meet this ex-hockey playing best friend of Ramsey's who'd quit playing to become a doctor. But the fact that the ex-hockey playing best friend was dating one of the best defensive players in the NFL? Nate hadn't been entirely sure he'd want to sit down and break bread with Dean Scott, no matter how the game went.

They'd greeted each other fine, meeting up in the shadowed restaurant atrium, exchanging *great games* and Brody insisting on hugging Nate, which had made Ramsey hiss at least one semi-serious threat under his breath.

It was only then that Ramsey had realized Wes had decided he wouldn't show up to dinner.

Brody winced as they were shown to their table. "He said he was tired and that he'd grab breakfast with us tomorrow morning, before we fly out. I think . . .I think it might have been too much for him."

"He could've told me," Ramsey argued.

Nate and Dean had ended up pulling up the rear as Brody and Ramsey tipped their heads together to discuss, as they called it, *the Wes Problem.*

Nate was used to exchanging, at the bare minimum, generic small talk with other players, but he hadn't been sure what to expect of Dean.

Then Dean turned to him and said, "I hope your rookie, Atkinson, doesn't beat himself up too much about that play."

For a second, Nate didn't know how to react or what to say. He bristled, a little instinctively, at the reminder that the Riptide had won and the Thunder had lost, but then that was swept away entirely by gratitude that Dean gave a shit about the feelings of one of the players on Nate's team.

Specifically the player that Nate had been trying to mentor, but Dean couldn't possibly know that.

"I hope so too," Nate said quietly, shooting Dean a look that hopefully spoke volumes about his gratitude.

"Hard to be a rookie," Dean said, voice gruff. "'Course, you guys are a great unit. Veteran. Solid. You're doing a great job with him."

It felt bitter on Nate's tongue as he admitted, "Not good enough."

But Dean just shrugged. "Sometimes it takes time. Sometimes it takes something like today to remind a guy of what they need to do."

Nate didn't want to say that it was instead more likely that Jordan would spiral—either on or off the field, or possibly *both*—but that was his gut feeling.

"Hopefully," Nate said as the hostess led them to the private room that Ramsey had reserved. Over the last week he'd rotated through four or five possible restaurants before finally settling on this one. Nate had asked him one night why the actual restaurant mattered so much, but hadn't known how to answer when Ramsey had admitted this was his first double date and he just wanted it to be perfect.

Nate took a seat next to Ramsey, Ramsey reaching out and squeezing his thigh. "Hey," he said in a low voice, "is Jordan okay?"

"I don't know," Nate admitted, and that was the best-case scenario.

He'd tried talking to Jordan right after the game but Sterling had gotten to him first, and that meant that by the time Nate had arrived on the scene, Jordan had been intractable and taciturn. Not interested in talking.

He'd worried, at first, that he might need to cancel this dinner and babysit the guy, to keep him from going off the rails, but then he'd disappeared and hadn't answered any of Nate's texts.

He hoped that meant he'd go to the Wild Leopard or one of his other favorite strip clubs, spend too much money on private dancers in the champagne room, maybe blow even more cash on some top shelf booze, and call it good. That wasn't ideal, but he wouldn't get into *too* much trouble that way.

"I just wanna say," Brody said, after they'd ordered drinks and an appetizer, "this is *very* exciting for us." He nudged Dean, who echoed much less enthusiastically.

"Babe," Brody said, shooting him a look.

"What? I'm confused. Are we excited that Ramsey's finally stopped hitting it and quitting it or that when he did, he picked another football player?"

"Yes," Brody said triumphantly.

Ramsey made a scoffing noise, but he did admit, "That's fair. I knew you two would enjoy a good laugh at my expense so it's good we're getting it out of the way quick."

"Well, *I* knew that it was gonna take someone special to tame our favorite wild child, so I'm personally not that surprised—"

Brody probably would've kept going, but Nate had felt Ramsey stiffen next to him, and frankly *he* didn't like that either.

Time to say so.

"I didn't tame him," Nate interrupted.

Three sets of eyes swiveled towards him, and to Nate's own surprise, the set that looked the most astonished was pale blue and belonged to his boyfriend.

"What?" Ramsey said.

"I didn't tame anyone. You're still wild. You're still amazing. Just not by yourself, anymore," Nate said, suddenly awkward. He hadn't been prepared to make a confession like that, especially in front of Dean Scott, but the truth was, he'd never ascribed to any of that bullshit masculine conformity.

If Ramsey needed Nate to stand up in front of the whole goddamn world and proclaim how fucking amazing he was, then Nate would do it gratefully, and with the awe that Ramsey *deserved*.

For a second, nobody at the table said a word. Then Ramsey's hand reached out and squeezed his thigh again and then didn't let go after.

Then Brody said, quietly, "Wow."

"Told you, he was a good one," Ramsey agreed.

"Knew I liked you," Dean added in his own understated way.

"Wait a second," Nate said, finally beginning to catch up. "Was that a *test*?"

But Brody just shrugged, a glimmer of a smile on his face.

"You're going to have to forgive these two," Dean said to Nate. "They're both too smart and know it, and sometimes they just can't help it."

Brody scoffed. "Not true. I could've helped it, but I had to know."

"And what were you going to do about if you were right?"

"Not if I was right," Brody said to Ramsey, "if I was *wrong*."

That seemed to take most of the wind out of Ramsey's sails. "Oh."

"Exactly," Brody retorted fondly. "*Oh*."

"After this, we want to see your bar," Dean said.

"We can arrange that," Ramsey said.

"You told *them*," Nate complained, but he wasn't really mad. He wasn't going to date a guy like Ramsey and expect to know all his secrets. As long as he got *some* of them—as long as it was him who Ramsey was coming home to at night, he didn't mind any of Ramsey's chess-mastering. It was kind of hot, in fact.

He'd bet too that he wasn't the only football player at the table who found a big brain attractive, considering that Brody was about to graduate from medical school.

Ramsey just shrugged, a bit of a self-conscious smile on his face. "Yeah, I did. Sorry."

"Just giving you shit, babe," Nate said and felt the warmth inside him grow at the exact same rate as Ramsey's smile spread across his face.

Like Ramsey liked Nate calling him *babe* as much as Nate liked doing it.

Their appetizers came, and Brody and Ramsey started chatting about guys they'd known in college. Mutual friends. Other guys who'd been on the Evergreens hockey team. Nate listened, enjoying learning more about Ramsey, not even from things that he said, but things that Brody volunteered.

"And Ell and Mal are still getting along?"

"Fucking blissful," Ramsey complained. "They couldn't be happier. Except that they moved Ell up to another line for a bit, and you know how they feel about that."

"They're gonna have to learn to play with other guys."

"I know," Ramsey said with a reluctant sigh. "But they're just ridiculously happy just being on the same team."

Brody chuckled. "Remember when we were half-convinced they'd kill each other?"

"Their teammates might still wish that," Ramsey joked.

Dean turned to Nate then and asked in a low voice, "So, tell me how it is dating a guy who could run a small country?"

Even if Ramsey hadn't been able to hear him, Nate would've answered the exact same way.

"Fucking amazing, actually? Some guys get boyfriends who are good at a few things, right? I get one who's killer on the ice, smarter than everyone he's ever met combined, and so hot people literally turn and look at him as he walks down the street." Nate paused. "It's win-win-win."

Dean tilted his head, considering this. "Some guys might be intimidated."

"Some guys have small dicks too."

Dean barked out a laugh. "Brody said he thought we'd get along and I thought he was full of shit, but I should know better, now, than to underestimate his gut instincts."

"Let me guess, you get it."

"Brody could've done anything he wanted. The Hurricanes were wild for him to come play for them. He graduated two years ago, but they still reach out periodically. Willing to place him with their AHL affiliate if he decided med school wasn't for him. Even offered to trade him to a team in California, if that was a sticking point. He could've gone pro but he wants to use that ridiculous brain to help people instead. And *he* wants to be with *me*." Dean shook his head. "What's there to be upset about?"

Nate had a feeling that was a long speech for Dean Scott, and that was confirmed when Brody leaned over, nudging him with a shoulder and tilting his head up towards his boyfriend. "I guess you *do* like him. Said more than three words to the guy." He turned to Nate. "That's unusual, by the way."

"Not surprised," Ramsey said, sipping his drink. "Nate's the best. Easy to talk to."

By halfway through the meal, Nate was actually almost a little disappointed that Dean and Brody lived out in California. And a glass and a half of red wine in, he didn't bother holding that opinion in. Or the opinion that Dean should leave California and come to Toronto. Play for the Thunder. Anchor the other side of Dean's line.

But when he suggested that, Dean just laughed. "And leave behind my three hundred plus days of sunshine for *Toronto*? Fuck no, dude. I'm honored, but no." His face turned sly then. "But maybe I could tempt *you*," he said.

It might have been tempting once, but not anymore. "Not as long as Ramsey plays for Buffalo," he said.

Ramsey looked surprised by this, but he shouldn't be. They hadn't talked about it, but surely, he knew how serious Nate was. Nate knew how serious Ramsey was, even if he never said it out loud. It was evident and obvious in every secret he'd held close to his chest that he volunteered to Nate, now. In the way they kissed. In the way every night and every morning, even in sleep, Ramsey's arm always seemed to reach for him, unconscious and instinctual.

Even if he'd been in relationships before, Nate would still believe that this was serious, but the truth was, Ramsey hadn't been. He'd never done this before. He'd never *wanted* to do this before.

"Serious," Brody teased, but Ramsey didn't argue. Didn't look displeased, just still slightly astonished, like Nate had said something he hadn't anticipated.

Nate wanted to ask him about it but then his phone buzzed in his pocket. It was set to *do not disturb*, except for his favorites list. And there was only one guy on the favorites list that Nate would be tempted to pick up for right now—the other was sitting next to him.

"I gotta grab this," he said apologetically, pushing away from the table.

He glanced at Ramsey, who just nodded. There was no way he didn't know who it was. Ducking out of the private dining room to an empty hallway that led to the bathrooms, Nate picked up the call.

Jordan was breathless and laughing when Nate said, "You okay, bud?"

He thought he could hear a false note in the laughter, but it was impossible to tell for sure, not with all the background noise wherever Jordan was.

Though if he was being honest, he already knew where Jordan was.

The only question was which strip club he'd ended up in, and which one Nate was going to have to head to, ducking out of this dinner he was very much enjoying.

"I'm fucking fine, dude. Don't worry about me. I'm worrying about you. Getting all stuffy and settled."

Nate rolled his eyes. Last night with Ramsey in his jersey and in his bed, he hadn't exactly felt stuffy.

"I'm good," Nate said. Wincing, he added, "Are you sure you're good?"

"Oh my God, Big Dog, I'm fucking fine. It happens." The fake note was back, and this time Nate was ninety-nine-point-nine percent sure he heard it. "Stop angsting about it and get your ass over here. Party with me."

"What are we celebrating?" Nate asked, putting off answering for now. He didn't want to go to a strip club and hang out with Jordan. It would no doubt be another kind of situation like it had been *last* time Jordan had hit the fake panic button and dragged both Nate and Ramsey away from their date.

Nate really didn't want to do it again. Not like this, with a couple he was actually enjoying hanging out with.

"Celebrating being alive, baby!" Jordan whooped loudly. "It's lit down here. I'll text you the address."

"Jordo—" But he didn't get the rest of the word out, even, before the line went dead.

No chance to tell Jordan he wasn't going to show up.

Immediately his phone buzzed, before he even made it back to the table. Jordan had only sent him a pin drop. And then a whole string of incomprehensible emojis.

Nate grimaced and decided *fuck it*. Jordan was fine. How much trouble could he get into at a strip club called the Pussy Palace?

Worst-case scenario, he'd get drunk and belligerent and they'd kick him out and he'd slink back to his apartment and wake up with the hangover from hell tomorrow morning.

He texted back: **wish I could bud, but I'm a little busy right now.**

"Everything okay?" Ramsey asked when he sat back down to finish his dinner.

"Jordan," he murmured under his breath, "but I took care of it."

He wanted to feel as sure as he sounded, but he wasn't. His phone buzzed once, then twice, but he didn't pull it out of his pocket until the waiter was clearing their empty plates and he heard a third buzz.

**Are you fucking serious?**

Then, **I guess you fucking are, dude. Guess the cock's really that good.**

And third, just: **big dog**

The whole string would've been much easier to dismiss if he hadn't sent the third message, long after the first two.

There was something about that last message. A plea, unspoken.

Nate drummed his fingers on the table, and a second later, Ramsey's hand gripped his thigh, squeezing it tightly.

Without Ramsey asking, Nate knew what he wanted and tilted the phone screen so Ramsey could read it too.

He was pretty sure Ramsey wanted him to see his concern. Otherwise, he'd have hidden it, and Nate would be left in the dark.

It made him feel warm and *seen*, to be deliberately included like this. But then a fourth text came through.

**shit big dog**

Concern superseded the warmth, immediately.

He felt terrible that he was going to have to bail and leave before they'd totally finished their date.

Maybe he could meet up with the three of them at Vault later, after he'd checked in with Jordan.

But before he could open up his mouth to make his apologies to Brody and Dean, Ramsey spoke up. "Sorry, guys," he said regretfully, "but Nate and I are gonna have to take off."

"What?" Nate asked in disbelief. "You're not—"

"I'm coming with you," Ramsey said in a voice that brooked no disagreements. He turned to Brody and Dean. Brody was smirking.

"Can't even keep it in your pants for a whole dinner?" Brody teased.

Ramsey rolled his eyes. "No. Nate's got a player in trouble, and well, I'm not letting him deal with it alone."

Nate had known he and Ramsey were heading towards that package deal sort of relationship—the *Nate-and-Ramsey* type—but he hadn't expected Ramsey to embrace it so quickly or so completely. Apparently Brody hadn't either, because he looked happy but also straight-up *shocked*.

"Shit," Dean said eloquently. He turned to Brody. "I hate it when you're right."

"No, you don't," Brody said smugly.

"What is it he's right about?" Nate asked, because he desperately wanted to know. Wanted to know, *is it the same thing I'm thinking too?*

But Ramsey was already tossing bills onto the table and hooking his fingers around Nate's forearm, tugging him towards the doorway.

"Get a car," he told Nate.

# CHAPTER 18

He barely had time to say goodbye to Dean and Brody before Ramsey was dragging him outside. "Uber's eight minutes still," he said to Ramsey, who was trying to hide it but Nate was fairly certain he was vibrating with tension anyway. And considering Ramsey's normal behavior, that fact had his own anxiety spiking considerably.

"I'll try to grab a cab," Ramsey said. He finished typing on his phone and slid it into his pocket. "I added Dean and Brody to the VIP list at Vault. They can go have some drinks on me, and possibly debauch the library."

"Still pissed you wouldn't tell me who already did that," Nate complained.

Easier to focus on the secret Ramsey seemed determined to keep rather on what trouble Jordan was no doubt in.

"What did he say to you?" Ramsey shot him a look and stalked over to the curb, eyes scanning the traffic.

"What do you mean? You read the texts."

"Yeah, I did," Ramsey said, a little impatiently, "but I didn't talk to him, not like you did."

"He didn't seem upset, he just seemed . . ." Nate paused, hesitating. "Actually, I'm pretty sure he *was* upset, and didn't want me to know it."

"He wouldn't."

Ramsey didn't sound like he was guessing. He sounded like he *knew*.

"How do you know—"

Flagging down a cab, Ramsey interrupted him. "Cancel the Uber."

Nate wasn't annoyed but he *was* confused as Ramsey shoved him into the back of the cab, Ramsey sliding in next to him, giving the driver the address and to Nate's shock, promising a huge additional tip if he could get them there fast and a bunch more money if the cab would wait for them at the club.

After he finished canceling the Uber, sure that his rating was going to plummet after this, Nate turned to Ramsey. "I'm worried about him, for sure, but you're . . ." Nate gestured towards where Ramsey was nearly vibrating against the seat.

Ramsey looked over at him, blue eyes full of concern. "Spent a lot of time around guys like Jordan," he said in a clipped voice.

But Nate still wasn't following. "Hockey players get into trouble a lot?" He hadn't heard that, but then, it wasn't like he'd paid a lot of attention to hockey players before meeting Ramsey.

Before falling in love with Ramsey.

Ramsey just shook his head. "No. Plenty of other foster kids, though. Hate authority, through and through. And don't tell me you don't notice how tense he gets whenever Sterling talks at him."

For a second, Nate wanted to correct him. But no, Sterling did speak *at* Jordan, not *to* him.

"Why am I the exception?"

"You don't treat him like an idiot who's going to fuck up."

Nate *did* have to correct that misinterpretation. "He *is* an idiot who's going to fuck up, though."

"Yeah, but you don't treat him like it's inevitable," Ramsey said impatiently. "It's different. I know it doesn't feel all that different to you, but it is. And it's made a difference to Jordan. Enough that when the shit hit the fan, you're the one he reached out to."

Nate couldn't help the way his own shoulders tensed. "How do you know that happened?"

"It's obvious," Ramsey said with a helpless shrug. "You saw it too. He didn't bluster. He didn't beg. He just texted your name, *twice.*"

Ramsey wasn't wrong. That was exactly what had tipped Nate off to the possibility something could be seriously wrong.

"You got any cash on you?" Ramsey asked next.

"Couple hundred bucks, probably." Nate didn't pull his wallet out and check, but he was pretty sure. "And I can sign anything anyone wants." He always carried a sharpie in his pocket, next to his wallet.

Ramsey gave him a sharp nod of approval. "Good."

"You think we're gonna need it?"

"I don't know what we're going to need, but I'd rather know what our resources are ahead of time. I'm not a Leaf, but I'm still a hockey player and we're in Canada. Might have some pull too."

"Plus you're you," Nate said, grateful, not even for the first time, that this was true.

"Yeah?" Ramsey glanced over and there was an uncertainty in his eyes that Nate didn't like. As if somehow Nate might not *like* that Ramsey was Ramsey.

And that was complete bullshit.

"To be clear, I'm so fucking grateful you're you," Nate said, reaching over and squeezing Ramsey's knee. Nate could feel the heat of him through his slacks.

Ramsey's face softened. "It doesn't bother you?"

"The opposite, actually."

Nate didn't have any more time to expound on that theme because before he could, they pulled up at the curb at the Pussy Palace.

Nate grimaced at the name—at least the Wild Leopard had a *theme*—as they got out of the cab.

Ramsey handed the driver a wad of cash, and for a half a second, Nate considered telling Ramsey that he'd pay him back, since Jordan was *his* problem. But the single swift look Ramsey shot him made it clear that he better not offer.

And it occurred to him that maybe Ramsey had already accepted that Jordan *wasn't* just Nate's problem anymore.

They'd become a team, a partnership, and as they walked up to the entrance it felt like it.

It was quiet outside, which was a relief. No cops yet.

But on top of the unfortunate name, Nate could immediately tell that this establishment was not as classy as the Wild Leopard. It was in a dodgier neighborhood, down a darker side street, and the outside brick edifice had the remnants of graffiti that had been half-heartedly scrubbed off.

The bouncer at the front door looked them up and down and Nate had been clocked many times in his years as an NFL player, but never this obviously. He'd also never been sized up and priced out quite like this before.

As he approached the guy, he was painfully aware of the Rolex on his wrist. He didn't look back and see if Ramsey had tucked his diamond-encrusted chain into his sweater, but Ramsey wasn't a rookie at this. The guy could take care of himself—and if he couldn't, he'd be the kind of person Nate would want to have his back in a fight.

Speaking of fights though, the bouncer looked like he'd fight dirty, with a knife to the ribs, or surreptitiously slipping on a pair of brass knuckles.

"Yo," the guy said flatly. "You here for Atkinson?"

Well, they hadn't been exactly slipping under the radar.

"Yeah," Nate said.

"This way," the bouncer said, and as they followed him through the dark doorway, Nate was tempted to ask what was going on, to get some kind of clue what they were walking into. But before he could, Ramsey reached out and took his hand, squeezing it once. Saying, Nate was pretty sure, *not yet*. He was becoming more and more fluent in Ramsey, but then after, Ramsey still didn't let go.

Ramsey either didn't care that they'd get clocked or maybe it was more he cared how much of a united front they presented.

Apprehension bloomed at the base of Nate's stomach as the bouncer led them deeper into the club, past the bar, past the worn-looking stages with their cheap strip lighting and the dancers on the chipped brass poles.

Even though Nate checked every guy they passed, none of them were Jordan.

Ramsey's grip tightened on his. Nate could *feel* his anxiety, even as he presented a cool, collected front, his expression a smooth mask that gave nothing away.

They finally reached an unmarked door, and he knocked twice, and it opened a crack and then opened wider after whoever was behind it recognized one or more of them.

"Here," the bouncer said, and gestured them inside.

It was a small room, cramped with the three guys already inside.

Jordan was in the center, sitting on the single chair, and he was pale under the dangling fluorescent light.

One of the men was dressed like the bouncer, in all black, but he had a utility belt on, webbed and official looking, and there was not just a gun on it, but at least one knife, if not two. From the flat expression on his face and the dead-eyed stare he swung their direction, Nate would bet he knew how to use both of them.

He'd been worried about the bouncer, but this guy was a whole other problem.

The second guy was dressed flashier. Still all in black, but in a suit, with a shiny, oil slick black vest under his jacket, his black shirt open at the collar, and the gold chain he wore at his throat was twisted and thick.

Glinting with diamonds the same way Ramsey's chain did. But he wasn't hiding it like Nate knew Ramsey was hiding his.

There was a pea-sized green stone on his pinky too, and the guy wore not just gold and diamonds and emeralds but power like a cloak over his shoulders.

"Wow, look who's gracing my establishment," the guy in charge said. "Not just another football player, but Nate Bishop, in the flesh. And not just football players, but a hockey player too." He paused, an ugly kind of amusement glittering in his dark eyes, "'Course not sure if you can call yourself a hockey player if you're not really playing."

Nate felt his temper flare, but Ramsey squeezed once, hard. *Don't react,* he said without opening his mouth.

"You've got us at a disadvantage," Ramsey said. If Nate hadn't learned the little tiny tics that always gave Ramsey's true feelings away, he would've guessed that he wasn't upset at all.

But in actuality, Nate knew just how deeply pissed off that comment had made him.

"We're not what's important," the guy said arrogantly.

"You're right." Ramsey's concession was smooth and easy. "You want to tell us why we're here? What happened with Jordan?"

Nate watched as Jordan opened his mouth like he was going to say something and then he snapped it shut again when the man's hand landed heavily on Jordan's shoulder.

What an absolute dick. If it wouldn't get them into even more trouble, Nate wouldn't have hesitated before rearranging the guy's conceited, self-important face.

"No, by all means, tell them how you were harassing some of my best patrons," the asshole said.

Jordan hesitated, fear blooming into his eyes as he furtively glanced over to where the armed man stood, expression impassive, arms crossed over his broad chest.

Normally, Nate wouldn't worry about the three of them physically taking a few guys on. They could all take a hit and dish it out right back. Even Ramsey—once embarrassingly Nate had watched a YouTube compilation of his best hits. He didn't always attack physically on the ice, but when he did? He could handle himself.

But none of them were holding their own against a gun and a knife. Nevermind whatever weapons weren't visible.

"No, really," the asshole insisted. "Tell them."

Jordan's chin jutted out stubbornly. "Your best fucking customer was harassing one of the girls. She doesn't deserve that."

Something cold and horrified settled at the base of Nate's stomach. He'd assumed that Jordan was here, locked up in this room, because he'd done something shitty.

But that wasn't it at all.

"He paid for it." There was a chilling note of acceptance in the asshole's voice. Like that was all that was required to take advantage of anyone. For enough cash to cross the table.

Ramsey's hand gripped his tighter. His knuckles were probably turning white, and the asshole would have noticed if he was paying attention. But he was toying with Jordan still. Having dismissed Ramsey as a too-pretty injured hockey player.

"Doesn't matter," Nate said, finding his voice. "Sounds like Jordan was doing the right thing. And you have no reason to hold him here. Come on, let's go."

But the asshole's grip on Jordan's shoulder tightened, *his* knuckles going white.

"Enough with the bullshit. What do you want?" Ramsey asked it bluntly.

Blunter than Nate would've.

But the asshole only shrugged. "He pissed off one of my best customers. Not sure he'll be coming back. Not anytime soon."

"Punched his teeth out," Jordan muttered.

Nate glanced down and sure enough, there was crusted blood on one of Jordan's hands, and he'd missed it from the way Jordan had been pressing his hand wound-first into his jeans. Like he hadn't wanted Nate to know he'd gotten fucked up.

Nate *was* pissed. He was pissed that this had happened at all, and that was one hundred percent Jordan's fault for coming here in the first place, but it sounded like he'd actually redeemed himself in the end.

Done the right thing, in the middle of a bunch of wrong ones.

"What do you want?" Ramsey repeated. "Clearly it's not the cops and an assault charge."

The asshole snorted.

"Exactly," Ramsey continued evenly, completely in control.

"It's not in anyone's best interest to get the cops involved," the asshole asserted.

Ramsey rolled his eyes. "No, but we *will*."

Jordan made a distressed noise. Cops would mean official records, would mean sanctions by the team, maybe even sanctions by the NFL.

Nobody wanted that, obviously, but at the same time, Nate understood exactly why Ramsey was making it clear that wasn't off the table.

If they didn't want to concede all their negotiating power, they had to be willing to blow this up. Even if it meant injuring Jordan in the ensuing blast.

"Come on, you don't want that," the asshole insisted smarmily.

"Nobody wants that," Ramsey agreed. "So tell me what you *do* want."

The guy's gaze flicked over to Nate's wrist.

The watch was an antique, one he'd bought with his first NFL money. He knew some guys who had dozens, often encrusted with diamonds. Nate's was the only one he owned, and while it *was* valuable, it held more sentimental than monetary value.

Nate would part with it in a second if it meant they could take Jordan out of here, all of them getting away safe and sound.

He'd give so much more, to ensure Ramsey was okay, even if he was intimately familiar with how capable Ramsey was of taking care of himself.

"The watch. Cash too. Whatever you got on you." He paused. "And that diamond chain you wear."

Not even a flutter of emotion crossed Ramsey's face, even as Nate did his best to bury the fury that lanced through his middle, sour and bitter.

"Sure," Ramsey said and let go of Nate's hand, only so he could reach up to pull the chain out from underneath his sweater. "Hockey fan?" he asked casually as he coiled it, diamonds winking, into his palm. But he didn't hand it over. Not yet. Not even when Nate pulled off the watch, Jordan looking distressed as he did it.

The asshole smirked at Ramsey's question. "You're sort of hard to miss."

Ramsey shrugged, like he had nothing to do with that. And it suddenly occurred to Nate that he didn't. That he'd had to learn to live with that face and that body and that brain. And he'd done it by shining himself up as bright and hard as the diamonds in his hand.

No question, Nate had loved him before that, but he loved him even more after the thought crossed his mind. Ramsey had never shrunk from any of it or from the pressure. He'd let everything make him even more beautiful, inside and out.

"Anything else?" Ramsey asked, eyebrow rising.

Nate never wanted to let him go. All he could hope was that Ramsey would be interested in having the most devoted knight, tucked away in his pocket. Half a step behind him, palm nestled in the small of his back.

"Cash," the asshole said succinctly.

They both pulled out their wallets. Thirty seconds later, there were a few thousand dollars in rolled bills in Ramsey's hand, next to his diamonds and Nate's watch.

But Ramsey still didn't hand it over.

Like he was waiting for the other shoe to drop still.

It wasn't like Nate had forgotten about the gun and the knife and the man wielding them, but they'd been less pressing, until suddenly the asshole made a gesture.

Then Nate's heart was in his throat as the bodyguard strode over to Jordan, gun coming out.

A flicker of distress rippled over Ramsey's face.

Nate had a feeling he knew how deep it went, for Ramsey to show it at all, for it to make it past his mask of calm indifference.

The gun was leveled at Jordan's head, pressed into the spot right above his ear, and Nate wondered how fast he could move. If he could move fast enough, push his muscles quick enough and far enough, to reach Jordan and knock the gun away.

The asshole prowled closer to Jordan. Leaned in, met his terrified eyes. Nate felt the same terror echoed in his own organs. Felt them liquifying with it.

"You fucked with my business tonight."

Jordan swallowed hard. Nodded, the barest movement.

"People don't do that and get away with it," he continued.

Sterling had put Nate in charge of watching out for him, and he'd selfishly let Jordan do whatever tonight.

He hadn't watched out for him at all, and something horrifying could happen as a result.

"You're not gonna get away with it," the asshole said, putting his hand over the bodyguard's, digging the metal ring of the barrel harder into Jordan's scalp.

Ramsey laughed.

The asshole straightened.

Met his eyes.

Nate had been afraid before, but it was nothing like the fear cascading through him now as Ramsey faced the guy with a gun fearlessly. *Laughing*.

"You're not going to kill an NFL player, with an NHL and another NFL player watching. You're just trying to fucking scare him. And guess what? He's shitting himself in his pants, so congratulations, you succeeded."

The asshole smirked. "Yeah?"

"Yeah," Ramsey said. "So take our shit and just let us go, man. He's terrified. He's going to have nightmares about this for the rest of his fucking life."

Jordan nodded fervently.

He probably would, but if they got him out of this, intact, Nate had a feeling that he'd take the trade-off. At the very least he wouldn't ever be this stupid again.

The asshole paused for one more moment. A moment that felt like it dragged out forever, but probably actually lasted only a second.

Then he gave a nod.

The bodyguard dropped the gun and strode over to the door, opened it. Ramsey dropped everything into the asshole's palms, Nate grabbed Jordan's arm, yanking him up and they were out of there.

Jordan seemed out of it as they dragged him through the club and into the cab. He was mumbling under his breath.

Nate couldn't quite make it out until they were all piled into the back seat of the car. He was half-expecting Ramsey to take the front seat, but he only slid in the other side.

"Where to?" the driver asked, eyes wide.

Nate wondered if Ramsey was going to demand he sign an NDA for this whole evening, but then he hadn't been in that small, closed-off room with them. He was only witnessing the aftermath.

"I want to go home." Jordan surprised him by speaking up. His voice didn't sound exactly steady, but it was steady enough. He slumped back against the seat, fingers drumming on his knee.

Nate rattled off the address, then turned to him.

But before he could ask what the fuck he'd been thinking, Jordan just crumpled like a piece of paper. "Shit." He exhaled hard. "I shouldn't—we shouldn't—"

Nate decided the lecture could wait for another day. Maybe Jordan wouldn't even need it. He was hoping that this whole shitshow was the wake-up call Jordan needed to get his life together.

"You did good," he only said, patting Jordan on the leg.

Jordan looked shocked. "What?"

"Don't get me wrong, you shouldn't have been in a place that fucking sketchy, *but* it seems like you actually did something good while you were there."

"He was roughing her up a bit," Jordan mumbled. "I stopped him. When he wouldn't listen, yeah, I fucking punched him."

"Good," Ramsey said approvingly from Jordan's other side. Around the man between them, Nate met Ramsey's eyes.

God, they'd made it out of there. Not without a cost, but the cost wasn't nearly as high as he'd been afraid he'd be paying.

"What else?" Ramsey asked.

"Gave her some money. Told her to get out. I think . . .I think she did. And then they grabbed me. I only had a second to send you that text." Jordan sighed. "I know I'm a fuck-up—"

"You're not—"

But Jordan wouldn't let him, interrupting him right back. "No, I am. I fucked up. I . . .I'll be better. During games. And other times too."

Nate didn't know what to say to him. He wanted to believe it, and Jordan's words were everything he'd hoped he might embrace if they made it out of there. But he also knew it wasn't that easy. Jordan was going to have to put the work in.

"You're not a bad dude," Ramsey said, "you'll get there."

"And *shit*, Big Dog, your watch and your chain." Jordan sounded genuinely remorseful. "I'll . . .I'll take care of you, guys. I promise."

"Don't worry about that right now," Ramsey said soothingly.

He seemed unbothered by it.

Nate was a *little* more bothered, but he was also just plain fucking grateful that nothing worse had gone down.

"Okay." Gratitude obvious in his tone, even with the single word. Jordan breathed out, unsteady.

He was going to be okay. They were all going to be okay.

And Nate let himself take a deep breath.

They'd been in the cab for almost five minutes before Jordan started to shake.

"You're gonna be okay," Nate told him firmly. They'd put him between them on the bench seat and it was a tight squeeze, but Ramsey had slid in too instead of taking the front seat because *he* hadn't wanted to be too far away either.

Jordan's teeth chattered and he trembled. "Yeah, yeah," he muttered, but his voice wasn't steady. Not even remotely.

Ramsey pressed his thigh harder against Jordan's and hoped that the added pressure would prevent worst-case scenario from happening.

Not Jordan shaking out of his skin, but *Ramsey*.

He squeezed his hand into a fist, and even despite the way his fingernails curled sharply into his palm, he could feel the tremble on the surface, all of his nerves vibrating with tension.

He'd been through so much shit in his life, so many times he should have lost it like this, but he never had. His foster dad had always told him, approvingly, he had ice in his veins, and for so long Ramsey had believed that was true.

He was super fucking good at removing himself emotionally from basically any situation. That skill had never failed him, not through thick and definitely not through thin. He'd navigated half a dozen foster homes in childhood, most of which had been shitty, at best. He'd kept his composure bailing multiple teammates out over the years. He'd faced down guns before and knives before. Once, he'd gone toe to toe with a guy, his notorious fucking temper and a baseball bat.

He'd even survived the bullshit concussion situation, sanity basically intact.

But *this* scenario, a scenario in which Ramsey had felt he'd had at least ninety-seven percent control over, was apparently the one that was going to remind him that he was still human and could feel things.

A lot of fucking things, apparently.

Ramsey would also have to be a whole lot stupider to not realize exactly why that was.

Sure, it hadn't been Nate being threatened, but he'd been directly involved, and the worst-case scenario hadn't needed to happen for Ramsey to know exactly how terribly Nate would've reacted.

He was personally responsible for Atkinson, and he'd *take* it personally if anything had gone sideways.

But just because Ramsey *knew* why didn't mean he had to like it.

Actually, he really fucking hated it.

The cab pulled up to Atkinson's building. Nate turned to him. "Give me five? Then we can head back to my place?"

Ramsey nodded. He'd cleaned out his regular cash for the cab driver already, giving the emergency stash he kept on him at all times to the guy at the strip club, and it had been enough he probably wasn't going to protest that they were going to idle here for a few minutes before making one final stop.

Eight minutes later, the cab door opened again, and Nate slid in.

Ramsey gave the driver Nate's address and they pulled out in the late night Toronto traffic.

"He's okay. Still shaky," Nate said, before Ramsey could ask. "I was going to make him some hot tea. Load it up with sugar or honey, but of course he didn't have any tea in the place So instead I made him a protein shake with lots of frozen fruit. Poured him into the shower. I offered to stay, but he brushed me off."

Ramsey had already known that Jordan wouldn't want Nate to stay. Wouldn't want his mentor and his idol to witness him falling apart.

"He's got to lick his wounds, so let him do that. He'll come out of it better than when he went in."

Nate still looked worried, so Ramsey put a hand on his knee. Squeezed.

He was still shaking inside. Worried, a little, that he might go back to shaking on the *outside*. Then Nate would see and then he might know.

Ramsey had never shied away from any truths, no matter how uncomfortable, but his mind skittered away from what exactly Nate might know, even as his heart said, *yes, this one*.

Nate was quiet on the drive to his place, and Ramsey met his quiet, unsure what to say, and afraid he might say too much.

Not something he'd ever worried about.

But with Nate it was like he was figuring out how to be a person for the first time. He'd thought earlier that he hated it. But that wasn't really true. He didn't like feeling out of control or out of his depth, but he didn't dislike the feelings.

How could he, when they filled him with so much unexpected warmth and sweetness?

They were halfway up the elevator ride to Nate's condo when he finally turned to him. "Thanks for coming with me tonight. You were . . ." Nate trailed off. Ramsey let him lean more fully into him. Hoping that the way Nate wanted to finish the sentence was something like *helpful* or *necessary* and not *controlling* or *cold-blooded*.

He could be, yes, and Ramsey had always seen it as a positive. But he didn't want *Nate* to see him that way.

He wanted Nate to see the man inside.

"Yeah?" Ramsey said.

"God, I didn't know what to do. And you handled him. You're . . .well, you gotta know. You're fucking amazing." Nate glanced sideways at him after he typed in his door code. "You do know that, right?"

"Yes," Ramsey said, because what else was there to say? There'd always been something that had set him apart from anyone else. Made the distance between him and others feel insurmountable, but he didn't want that between him and Nate.

He'd *never* wanted that between him and Nate.

"You were so fucking cool about it." Nate led them into the kitchen, shaking his head as he went. Ramsey had never regretted his exceptionally good poker face as much as he did right now. "Like you had him in your hand and he didn't even know it. So fucking locked in."

It was a compliment. Ramsey knew it was.

Why was his whole body rebelling against it?

"No," he said lowly, stopping in front of the kitchen island.

Nate glanced over him, a quick little thing as he perused the fridge.

"No, I wasn't locked in. I mean, I *was*, but..." Ramsey didn't want to admit it. It felt like dredging something unwilling, fighting the whole fucking way, out of his sternum. "But I was fucking terrified."

As soon as he admitted it, he started to shake again.

It wasn't normal. It wasn't okay.

But he was doing it anyway.

Couldn't stop it, even if he'd wanted to, and it turned out he didn't really want to.

Nate's eyes widened and a second later, he was at Ramsey's side, wrapping his arms, firm and strong, around him. And Ramsey just shook, endlessly.

"You're okay," Nate soothed in a soft voice, murmuring the words into Ramsey's neck, just under his ear.

He believed them. And he didn't.

But whether they were true or not, Nate needed to understand.

Ramsey pulled back, looking him straight in the eye. He was still shaking, fine little tremors rolling over his skin. "I've never lost it this way. Never. Not once. I . . ." He shook his head, like he could clear it.

Like he could dislodge the confession Nate needed to hear out of it. But the words were stuck inside him.

Nate's hands cupped his cheeks, and his eyes were so fucking warm. "It's really okay," he promised.

But it wasn't. Not if Ramsey couldn't be stronger than this stupid, irrational fear of being *really* seen.

Because it was obvious that Nate really saw him. Saw all the disparate parts behind the smooth walls, and maybe he didn't like all of them, but he *appreciated* all of them.

Nobody else had, ever. Not Wes. Not Brody. Not his foster dad. Certainly never anyone he'd ever slept with.

"I was fucking terrified, okay?" The words came out again, even harsher than he'd intended, but maybe that was the only way Ramsey could figure out how to get them out.

But even then, Nate's gaze was soft. Understanding. "Me too."

Ramsey wrenched himself out of Nate's embrace. "No, no, *no*," he insisted as he began to pace back and forth.

"No?" Nate still sounded amused. Not upset. Like he knew he just had to wait Ramsey and his inevitable meltdown out. That wasn't that crazy. What was *actually* crazy was that Ramsey was having a meltdown at all.

"*No*," Ramsey repeated again. "I'm not ever like this. Not ever. I've dealt with so much shit and I was never afraid. Not once. But I was today. You . . .you're *different*."

Nate smiled, soft and sure. "Yeah?"

Ramsey didn't want to be, but he couldn't help it, filled with an intoxicating mix of exasperation and affection.

Ramsey shot him a look. "You *know* you're different,"

No. Not just affection. *Love.*

Distantly, he'd known what that feeling, pressing inevitably against his breastbone, was. But he hadn't wanted to admit it, even to himself.

"I was hoping," Nate said. It was impossible to miss that look in his eyes.

Ramsey realized, belatedly, that he'd never worried about Nate returning his feelings. He'd only worried *he* wouldn't be able to square with them.

But he'd done it. Well, okay, he was *doing* it. Or he was fucking *trying*.

"You make me feel . . ." *Unhinged, fond, enamored, like myself for the first time* ever.

Nate caught him by the arm and stroked up it, reeling him in. "You know you've always done that to me," he admitted in a soft voice. "Always. It was why I was such an ass. You wouldn't stay in the box I put you in."

Ramsey tilted his chin back. Found a well of determination. The same well that had seen him through so many shitty circumstances. "Because I wanted to be in the box with you."

"God." Nate threaded his fingers through Ramsey's hair and tugged him down into a kiss. It was hot, because he'd never *not* want Nathaniel, but it was more than that too. Sweet and soft and inevitable.

Full of love, Ramsey realized.

Nate pulled back and murmured against his lips. "You know I love you, right? That's what that is."

Ramsey nodded, wordless.

Nate tucked him into his chest. He'd never let anyone else bother about keeping him safe, only cared about how safe he could keep himself. That wasn't going to change, not in any significant way, but once in awhile, if he needed it, Ramsey knew Nate would.

Knew that he'd never even need to ask.

"I do love you," he whispered into Nate's chest.

He wasn't sure if Nate heard him until his embrace tightened just a little more.

It was funny because it wasn't anything that special, and yet it was extraordinary too.

# CHAPTER 19

For Nate, it was amazing how everything changed after the incident with Jordan.

Everything and nothing, at the same time.

He and Ramsey had gone to bed together, like it was any other night, and Ramsey had touched him the same as he had so many other times.

It made Nate wonder how long they'd both felt this way, unsure how to breach that last bit of distance between them.

But regardless, they woke up the next morning, and their routine was the same.

Breakfast. Shower. Ramsey went to the rink and Nate went to the practice facility to work out. Insisted on Jordan joining him, and while he seemed quieter, more subdued than normal, he seemed relatively okay in the aftermath.

Jordan made noise again about replacing the watch and Ramsey's chain, but Nate brushed him off. The watch wasn't *that* valuable, in the scheme of things, something he could fairly easily replace if he chose to, and as for the chain, Nate was intending to take care of that himself.

After working out and showering, he offered to grab lunch with Jordan, but Jordan just huffed with exasperation. "Don't fucking hover, man. I'm okay."

Nate got it. Jordan had fucked up and was still, as Ramsey had put it, licking his wounds.

"Alright, alright," he said and instead grabbed takeout sushi on the way home, hoping that Ramsey would be back from the rink and they could eat together. If not, it would keep in the fridge until he was.

When he walked in, sure enough Ramsey was there, on the phone.

"Yeah," Ramsey said as he paced back and forth in the living room. "Yeah, I know the Leafs want a d-man. They'll be interested. Only question is what are the Wolves going to give up for me."

Nate, in the process of unloading the food from the bags in the kitchen, froze.

Ramsey continued. "I don't care. I just need you to get it done. The deal's there. I can't stay in Buffalo, no matter how much they want me to. Yeah. For personal reasons." He paused. "No, I'm not going into why. With you or with them. Just . . .yeah. I'm not leaving Toronto."

Nate unfroze. Strode into the living room.

Ramsey didn't look surprised to see him, just tilted his head and gave him a look like, *I'll be done in a minute.*

But Ramsey couldn't be done in a minute. Nate needed to talk to him first. Needed to tell him that he didn't have to do this, not unless he wanted to.

He certainly didn't need to do this for *Nate.*

Nate approached, fingers closing around his forearm and Ramsey gave him another look. Nate was sure it was subtitled, *what did I just tell you?*

"I need to talk to you," Nate murmured under his breath despite Ramsey warning him off.

A third look. *You're not stupid; so why are you acting stupid?*

Nate wasn't acting stupid though. He was being a hell of a lot smarter than Ramsey was being right now—though he certainly wasn't going to be dumb enough to phrase it that way.

"I mean it," Nate said insistently.

Ramsey sighed. Pulled the phone away from his ear. "What?" he hissed.

"Don't do this without talking to me first."

"What—"

"I mean it," Nate said.

He loved Ramsey—that didn't mean he wanted him to give up the team that had never given up on *him*, just to make their relationship work.

"Hey Barty, can I call you back?" A pause. Ramsey huffed in annoyance. "I know. I *know*, but you know that personal reason? Yeah. They just got home, and they're insisting. I'll call you back in five."

It wasn't going to take five minutes for Nate to say what he needed to. But maybe it *would* take five minutes for Ramsey to believe it was true.

Frankly, it was probably going to take more like five months, but Nate was willing to put in the work. When he'd fallen in love with Ramsey, he'd done so with eyes wide open. He wasn't always going to be easy, but Nate was going to choose him every time, no matter what.

Ramsey lowered the phone finally. "What?" he sniped, sounding annoyed. Maybe justifiably. "Barty doesn't have all the time in the world, and he's got to—"

"I know what you want him to do," Nate interrupted. "And what I wanted to tell you—what I *needed* to tell you is that he doesn't have to."

Ramsey's jaw dropped a little. "You realize I don't *live* here, right? You're smart. Of course you know that."

Nate waited for him to work through it. Ramsey was maybe the smartest person Nate had ever met, and still it took a beat longer than he was expecting.

"What, you *want* to do long-distance?" Ramsey shook his head, like he was disagreeing with his own conclusion. "Why would you want that—" He broke off. "Fuck, you do want to do that."

Nate looked him straight in the eyes. They were wide and so blue. Nate wanted to get lost in them, but he couldn't. Not yet anyway. He needed Ramsey to believe this first.

"It's a lot of overlap sure, but the distance isn't that crazy, especially if I get a place closer to the border. And while your season goes through what, April? I'm done, best possible scenario, in early February. And you don't start up in earnest until late September."

Ramsey stared at him like he'd just grown a second head.

"We're both intelligent people with a lot of resources," Nate continued.

"You can say rich," Ramsey interrupted him wryly.

"Okay, we're both smart and we're both rich. We can do this for October through February."

"The Leafs *want* a better d-man, though," Ramsey said.

"And you want to stay with Buffalo," Nate said. "When I told you I loved you, I didn't mean I only loved you if you were in Toronto. I meant that I love you, no matter what."

"But—"

"Do you trust me?" Nate asked.

Ramsey shot him a look. "I thought a foundational part of your argument was that you were intelligent—that we're *both* intelligent."

"It is."

"Then don't ask me if I trust you. You *know* I trust you. You know I've never, that I've never even *wanted* to be with someone before. Just you." Ramsey rolled his eyes, probably at himself.

"I know. And you trust me," Nate said patiently. This was going about as he'd expected it would. Maybe a little better, even.

Ramsey nodded, and it seemed like he was on the brink of agreeing. So maybe a *lot* better.

"Is it always going to be easy? I don't think so, but you're worth it, to me."

Ramsey raised an eyebrow. "Just like that? I'm worth probably a longer commute for you. I'm worth dealing with long-distance bullshit. You know we play a lot more than one game a week."

Maybe he didn't want to believe it was true, but Nate was going to make sure of it.

"I know," Nate said steadily.

Ramsey laughed, hysterical around the edges. "Shit. I don't—" He broke off, rubbing his face. "I didn't even *imagine* this was an option."

God, Nate loved him so much. Even when he, the smartest person he knew, was being stupid.

"Guess you aren't that brilliant after all," Nate teased.

Ramsey squawked in outrage, but that sound dissolved easily into relieved laughter. "God, you're right of course. I don't want to play for Toronto. I love Mal and Elliott, but I don't want to play here. I want to play for the team that . . ." He took a deep breath. "The one that wants me. The one that never gave up on me, even though it would've been easier to do it. But then you know that. You knew it the whole time." Ramsey laughed again, unsteadily.

"I did," Nate said. He leaned in, cupping the side of Ramsey's beloved face. It was nice, of course, that it looked like *that*, but it wasn't necessary. It was only necessary it be attached to the man Ramsey was. "I've known for awhile that you were it for me. In the scheme of things, this isn't even the most difficult obstacle we've overcome."

Ramsey smiled at him. A small private amused smile. The kind that Nate had begun to realize he saved just for him. "That was probably my entire self believing wholeheartedly I'd never want anyone. Or *need* anyone."

"Probably," Nate conceded.

"You know me, probably better than anyone else, so you'll get what a big deal this is but . . ." Ramsey laughed again, lighter and carefree now. "But, *God*, I was so fucking wrong."

"I know," Nate said and leaned in, sealing the end of their debate with a kiss.

A second later, Ramsey pulled back. "Wait," he said, "before you do *that* thing with your tongue in my mouth, I gotta call Barty back. Tell him to forget the whole thing."

"How long has it been?" Nate wondered.

"How long has *what* been?"

"Since you hung up with your agent." Nate was pretty sure it had been less than five minutes but he was still curious.

"Like a couple of minutes?" When Nate didn't respond, Ramsey rolled his eyes and checked his phone. "Four and some change. That good?"

"It's fucking amazing," Nate said and leaned in, kissing him again, long and lush.

"Wait, *wait*." Ramsey pulled back an inch. "Did you *bet* you could make me change my mind in under five minutes?"

Nate considered the question. "Is it betting if you're betting with yourself?"

Ramsey stared at him, and for a single moment, Nate wasn't sure what reaction he was seeing. Then Ramsey melted, sinking into him, mouth hot and sure on his. "God," Ramsey murmured against his mouth, "you're so fucking perfect for me."

He reached down, digging his fingers into Nate's waist and pulling him in the direction of the bedroom. "Sex *now*."

Nate laughed. "What about Barty?"

Ramsey typed out a quick message, flashed the screen towards Nate—who barely caught the words **forget it, I was stupid, don't trade me**—and then he tossed his phone onto the couch before pulling Nate against him.

"That's all you wanted to say?" Nate said in disbelief.

"Covered the important points, yeah," Ramsey said and then he was kissing Nate again, and it was so good, so right, it was hard to keep his wits about him.

But then, maybe keeping his wits about him was overrated.

Maybe what they both needed was to get lost in each other for awhile.

"Should I be flattered that you didn't send him a whole three point plan?"

"Baby," Ramsey drawled, "do you *want* me thinking about a three point plan now?"

The answer was unequivocally no, so it just made sense for Nate to kiss him quiet and then turn the tables, him dragging Ramsey towards the bedroom.

A shaft of weak mid-afternoon sunlight cut across the room as Nate pushed him onto the bed and crawled over him. Ramsey groaned deep as Nate blanketed his body, their mouths moving together hot and wet and sure.

Ramsey's hands were in his hair, then digging into his shoulders. Reaching down and pulling his sweatshirt and then his T-shirt off. Palms hot on Nate's bare skin as he arched up, rubbing his cock against Nate's.

Nate felt breathless and needy, already. Every time they slept together it was better than the last. Ramsey was an addiction he'd never get out from under his skin, a burning craving he was looking forward to spending his life gorging on.

"Can't get enough of you," Nate murmured, kissing Ramsey's neck and then pulling back so he could wrangle Ramsey's shirt off.

For a second he rocked back onto his heels, taking in the incomparable view in front of him. Blond curls spreading out like a halo, blue eyes shining up at him, full of awe and affection and lust. Pale skin, rippling with muscle, still vaguely tinged with the sun of a faraway summer.

Nate trailed his fingertips down his chest, then lower, tucking them underneath the waistband of his sweatpants, pulling them down the rest of the way. Ramsey's cock was straining against his dark blue briefs, and the Nate watched every tiny shift of Ramsey's expression as he cupped it, smoothing his palm down its length.

Ramsey's teeth dug into his plush bottom lip, already slightly swollen and wet from Nate's mouth.

"Want you," Ramsey said, the words escaping him, soft and true.

Nate knew Ramsey meant every word. He also knew what else his words meant, the *other* word that replaced *want* in Ramsey's head. He heard it just as good as if he'd said it.

Words were fine and good, but they were nothing compared to the way Ramsey was looking at him now, love shining in his eyes.

He was always beautiful but he was most beautiful when he was looking at Nate this way, his heart written into every line of his face.

"Love you too," Nate said, leaning down to tug Ramsey's briefs down. He caught just a glimpse of Ramsey's face and how it broke open, every bit of his feelings laid bare, before he tucked his head down and sucked the head of Ramsey's cock into his mouth.

Ramsey's whole body jerked, and his hands found Nate's hair, digging into his scalp. "God, yes, *please*," he cried out above Nate.

And what else was Nate supposed to do but give him everything he wanted? Lavish the kind of pleasure on Ramsey that he deserved? He slid his tongue down the underside and then took more into his mouth, savoring the taste and the weight of him.

His own cock throbbed as he built up a good rhythm but it was easier than he'd thought to forget about his own desire and focus on Ramsey's.

So easy to lose himself until Ramsey was clutching his head, every muscle clenching and he was groaning deep as he came down Nate's throat.

Nate raised his head and took in the incomparable view laid out before him—Ramsey melting into the mattress, bliss painted across his features, blue eyes soft and languorous and full of love.

"Come here," Ramsey murmured and Nate didn't need another invitation.

He shoved his sweatpants down and groaned as he got a hand around his dick, aching and as hard as he'd ever been in his life.

As he straddled Ramsey's waist, his hand tucked itself around Nate's and around Nate's straining dick.

"God," Nate groaned. Just his touch felt good, but Ramsey's? And them moving together? On a whole other level.

Once when he was drunk, Deacon had told him that when you fell in love, even the simplest handjob could feel life and mind altering. He got it now.

Ramsey's other hand dug into his hip like he could press all five fingerprints into his skin and *claim* him forever, and that was all it took to send him over the edge. Nate shuddered as he watched stripes of come land on Ramsey's chest.

Marking him right back.

They'd belonged to each other before this, but it felt like *more*.

Not just the sex, but that they'd *acknowledged* the owning of it, now.

"Damn," Ramsey said as Nate gazed down at him for one more second, saving this view for every time they were apart. Of course if he had any say in it, he'd get a lot more views just like this.

Then he collapsed gently onto Ramsey's body, cradling his face with a palm.

Ramsey sighed, a happy exhale of a sound. "I'm not moving."

"Didn't ask you to," Nate murmured into his shoulder. He pressed a kiss in. Wanted to see that on his skin too. Not to prove to anyone else who Ramsey belonged to, but so *he* could see it.

"Good," Ramsey said smugly. He hesitated. "Eventually, though. 'Cause Barty's gonna freak out and I'm gonna have to deal with it."

"I thought you said that text was enough. No three point plan necessary?"

"Oh, it's *not*, but let's just say it's not like me to skip it."

Nate had known it. Had also known what Ramsey throwing all his normal chess-mastering to the wind meant.

Tucked that knowledge soft and sweet against his heart.

"You gonna tell me you let it go for me?" Nate teased.

Ramsey rolled his eyes, but he looked pleased and happy and in love, and that was all Nate had ever wanted. "Are you gonna be insufferable if I say yes?"

"Pleased, yeah? Insufferable, no." Nate leaned in and kissed him. "I'm gonna go take a shower. Come join me whenever you're done with Barty."

Sure enough, when Ramsey retrieved and checked his phone, there were three successive texts from Barty under his initial text.

**????**

**how do I know this is even you?**

**doesn't sound like you. the new you?**

*The new you*, Ramsey thought as he stared at the screen.

How to tell Barty that this wasn't a *new* him, but instead the *real* him. The person he'd long buried behind the walls that had made up the foundations of his self for so long that for a minute he *had* actually wondered if what everyone was seeing *was* new.

But no. The guy who'd emerged with the advent of Nate into his life wasn't new at all, but old.

He dialed Barty's number, hoping that in the last half an hour he hadn't magically gotten busy—or *busier*.

He detoured into the kitchen to grab a bottle of water and to talk to his agent, *again*.

"Oh, so now you can talk to me," Barty snarked into Ramsey's ear as he leaned against the counter.

"Sorry," Ramsey said unapologetically. "We had to re-renegotiate and that took . . .time." Less than five minutes, actually, but Barty didn't need to know the detailed breakdown between the negotiation and the sex they'd needed to have after about it.

"Sure," Barty said, a knowing edge to his voice. "You going to tell me about this personal problem anytime soon?"

"There's not much to tell," Ramsey said lightly, even though that wasn't true at all.

"Please," Barty insisted. "You were sure you wanted me to trade you to the Leafs—which was fucking crazy, by the way. Sure, I could've done it—"

"Only because I laid it out for you on a silver platter," Ramsey reminded him. Barty was a good agent, but Ramsey was better, and Ramsey wasn't going to let him get ahead of himself.

"Well, it doesn't matter now, right?" Barty retorted.

For a second, Ramsey almost told him to do it again. He didn't *want* to figure out how to do long-distance. It was going to suck, sometimes. Maybe even a lot of the time. But then, he thought of how willing Nate was to do it, selflessly, just so Ramsey could stay with *his* team.

Instead, he said, "No, no, it doesn't."

"And you're okay with staying in Buffalo," Barty clarified.

Ramsey took a breath, let it out. He'd never imagined himself in a relationship of any kind, nevermind a partially long-distance relationship with not just another professional athlete, but a *football player.*

"Yes," Ramsey said.

"And you're not going to change your mind."

Ramsey rolled his eyes. "You forget who you're talking to, Barty. I'm not gonna fucking change my mind."

"Hey, you already changed your mind," Barty reminded him.

"I . . ." He hadn't, actually. Because he'd never wanted to make the decision in the first place. He'd only been thinking of how best he could fiercely protect this miraculous situation he'd found himself in. And maybe, just a little, he'd been acting defensively, remembering Wes and Marcus, and how that had ended.

"Actually, no, I didn't change my mind," Ramsey corrected. "I just needed a reminder of what I already knew was true."

Barty was quiet for a moment. It was unlike Barty, so Ramsey should've expected what he said next, but even Barty could surprise him once in awhile. "Like the sound of your personal problem. Though, if I'm being honest, it doesn't sound much like a problem but a solution."

Ramsey froze. Because it was true. In so many ways—in *every* way that mattered—Nate was the key to his lock.

"Yeah, uh. Yeah. That's true."

"Good," Barty said. "Let me know when you want to talk more about it."

"How do you know—"

"You will," Barty said firmly.

Ramsey had initially hired Barty because he *couldn't* negotiate for himself, and Barty had seemed like the best possible option. Creative but not too creative that he'd ignore Ramsey's clear directives.

But maybe he'd been underestimating Barty this whole time.

"I will," Ramsey agreed.

Barty chuckled under his breath. "Go talk to your personal problem, okay?"

He didn't need to be told twice. Hanging up, Ramsey tossed his phone onto the couch to go join Nate in the shower.

The next morning, it was still early when Ramsey let himself into Wes' apartment. He needed more clothes and to deal with some emails on his laptop.

He'd assumed Wes would be there, but he hadn't expected Wes to be sitting on one of the barstools, giving him the eye as he walked in.

"Hey, Dad," Ramsey teased lightly, hoping it might alleviate the incoming lecture. "Yes, I had a great time. Yes, I was safe. I promise."

Wes rolled his eyes. "I had breakfast with Brody and Dean yesterday."

"Yeah, they told me that they were going to." Ramsey set his overnight bag down on the couch.

Wes shot him a look. "You're really serious about him."

Ramsey supposed that now was as good of a time as any to have this conversation. Maybe he could've put it off, but there was no point in doing that.

"Yeah. We're figuring out how to do this long-distance thing," he said.

The moment the words entered Wes' consciousness, he shut down. Whole face went pale and blank.

"That's a—"

"No, it's not," Ramsey said steadily, before Wes could add *mistake* to the end of his sentence. "You think so because you blame the distance on fucking up your relationship with Marcus."

Wes' face went from bleached, like a bone, to bright red. "That's not . . .*no*. And it *did*."

Ramsey had never wanted to say any of this to Wes. Had gone out of his way to *not* say it, but maybe that had been doing both of them a disservice.

Still, he kept his voice soft and gentle, even though he knew the words would land like body blows. "No, it wasn't the distance. It was that you picked football over Marcus, over and over again, and now you're still on the sideline. Maybe that's on you. Maybe it's not. He never got it, why you had to do it, and that was on him. This is a hard life, for anyone, and it's not anyone's fault that it didn't work out between you two. You know what *is* your fault?"

"I'm not sure I want to know," Wes said bitterly. He'd turned away now, probably to try to hide the pain in his eyes, but Ramsey didn't need to see it to know it was there.

"Not calling him and telling him that you regret it," Ramsey said.

Wes didn't say anything for so long that Ramsey actually thought that maybe he'd fucked it up. That maybe it *wasn't* inevitable, and he should've never said it.

"You promised—" Wes finally said, but Ramsey wasn't going to let that stand.

"And I did keep that promise," Ramsey said, approaching Wes with a careful hand between his stiff, tense shoulder blades. "I kept it as long as I could. But this is ridiculous, Wes. You love him. He loves you. Don't let this stupid argument come between you."

Ramsey wasn't surprised, but he was disappointed when Wes shrugged him off with an aggravated movement. "Just because you're happy and in love now doesn't mean you know *anything* about it. And yeah, I *am* thrilled that you are. It's about time. But you're taking a risk."

"I know," Ramsey said. "That's what love is. Taking a risk. Hoping it pays off."

He never had wanted to before, but Nate made every terrifying possibility worth it. Every deliriously happy moment was the payoff for that risk-taking.

Wes' shoulders slumped, and Ramsey wasn't surprised at all when he folded into Ramsey's arms. He'd even known he'd need to catch him, and he did.

For a long time they didn't say anything, just held each other.

"Feels like everything's changing. You're going back to Buffalo. I'm . . .I don't know what I'm doing," Wes finally said, his words muffled in Ramsey's shoulder.

"Yeah, you do. You do know," Ramsey said. "You play quarterback for the Toronto Thunder."

"No, I . . .I don't. I really don't."

"Yeah, you do. You're there, in case anything happens to Aidan. It might, and when or if it does, you're going to be ready."

Wes was quiet a beat longer. "I don't want to text him. I don't want to call him. I love him but I don't want to do either of those things."

Ramsey couldn't force him to reach out to Marcus. That much was something he'd had to come to terms with before. "Okay," he said easily, but he already knew he wasn't going to stop trying.

Or that deep down, Wes wouldn't stop wanting to.

# CHAPTER 20

"I can't believe we're running errands on a holiday," Ramsey complained, glancing out the window of Nate's car. He'd had *plans* this morning. Sleeping in, for sure, tucked up close and warm against his big boyfriend's body, after he'd gotten home at ass o'clock from playing Dallas on Thanksgiving.

But Nate just chuckled. "It's not a holiday, it's the day *after* Thanksgiving, which isn't a holiday in America, and reminder, babe, Thanksgiving isn't even a holiday here."

"Stupid," Ramsey muttered.

"I promised you I'd make it worth your while," Nate said persuasively. "Remember?"

"I'm holding you to that," Ramsey said.

The truth was, he was grumbling, but the last week had been so good. He was hitting all his benchmarks that the Wolves wanted to see from him on the ice, his conditioning progressing well, and in a few days, he'd head back to Buffalo.

"Did you talk to Wes?"

"You mean, when we get to Aidan and Levi's, is he going to be weird and not talk to me? We . . .yeah. We've been texting some. Or I've been texting at him. It's not bad. We're not fighting. He's just not happy with me."

"You're a good friend," Nate said, glancing over and meeting Ramsey's eyes. He reached out and took his hand, squeezing it firmly. "You could've said nothing."

"Yeah, and continue watching him be miserable?" Though it wasn't like Wes was *not* miserable now.

He was, and it was the only persistent problem that Ramsey couldn't seem to fix. *Yet*, anyway.

Ramsey looked back out the window. They'd been driving for at least thirty minutes at this point, far out of the city. "Where are we even going? What even *is* this errand?"

"You'll see," Nate promised.

When Nate had dragged an unwilling Ramsey out of bed, shoved a large coffee in his hand and put him in the car, Ramsey hadn't really asked questions.

Not like him, sure, but Ramsey was trying this new thing where he let Nate call some of the shots. And so far, it was a good time. Usually a *great* time. Though admittedly all of those times had been sex-related, so of course they'd been awesome.

Maybe this was still sex-related, though Ramsey was pretty sure it wasn't.

Finally, Nate pulled off the freeway, taking them through a bedroom community. Ramsey found his curiosity significantly piqued, staring out the window as the car turned into a section of townhouses.

"What's this?" Ramsey asked, unable to help himself from asking again.

But Nate only shrugged and got out of the car. "Come on," he said, beckoning with a hand that he then tucked into Ramsey's as he followed.

The builds were new and modern. Ramsey could hear the sounds of construction far down the block. There was a sold sign stuck into the lawn on the townhouse Nate led him to.

Ramsey had wondered before this, but now seeing the sign, he was pretty sure he knew. Especially when Nate let go of his hand so he could pull out his phone and look up the door code in his email.

Nate pushed the door open and gestured Ramsey inside. Ramsey walked in, gaze flickering over the surprisingly cozy interior, despite the modern fixtures and clean lines.

The foyer led into an open floor combo of living room slash kitchen.

"There's three bedrooms upstairs, including the owner's suite," Nate said steadily, watching Ramsey as Ramsey took in the pale green cabinets and the quartz countertops. It was empty, no furniture at all yet, but the interiors still felt homey, like it was just waiting for them to fill it up not just with things, but with a *life*.

It was everything that his big condo in downtown Buffalo wasn't.

"You got this for us." Ramsey didn't ask, just stated, because it was obvious. Closer, then, to both of them. Not close, necessarily, but *closer*. A central place they could live, at least part of those five months.

"Yeah," Nate said with a nod.

"A further commute for you," Ramsey observed.

Nate's lips quirked up. "Also further for you. We don't have to *always*—I'm going to keep my place and you should keep yours too—but I thought it would be good to have somewhere central for when we're both playing. A place we could live, to make it a little easier."

Ramsey's hands tightened on the edge of the counter he'd been resting them on. Nate had done all this, without being prompted, and had not only done it, he'd done it well and with flair. This wasn't just some blank apartment they'd crash in sometimes. Nate had bought this to be a *home* for them. Not their only home, maybe, but a home nonetheless.

"Still going to be hard," Ramsey said, the words escaping out of him before he could snatch them back. What was he *doing?* He wasn't trying to convince Nate not to do this, that he didn't want to. He *wanted* Nate to want this, with him. Even if it *was* hard.

But then, Ramsey didn't think he could do any of this, even for a short time, and not have it work out. If he put his heart into Nate's hands, Nate was going to need to hold it forever.

Telling him he loved him was a huge step, no question, but this was more than just words. This was *action*. This was working every day to make it work. If Ramsey made that kind of commitment, he'd never want to go back from it.

Ramsey raised his eyes to Nate's.

His gaze was warm and brown. So fucking steady. Loving. Trustworthy.

Like he knew just what Ramsey was questioning. Like he knew how hard this was for him.

And, Ramsey realized with a bolt of recognition, he *did*.

"You're something else, you know that?" Ramsey said.

If a trace of smugness joined the other emotions on Nate's face, Ramsey supposed he couldn't blame him for it. "I think sometimes you forget that you're not the *only* one who can make a good plan and execute it."

Ramsey thought about saying that he *didn't* forget—it was instead that nobody had ever met him plan for plan, action for action, before. Nobody except Nate.

Instead, he said, "I won't forget anymore." Because now he'd *know* that part of Nate's love—just like Ramsey's—contained this element. That he could expect it, that he could *rely* on it.

For a long moment, they didn't say anything, just looked at each other. Ramsey felt like his heart was in his throat.

"So, what do you think?" Nate asked.

It was a ridiculous question.

Nate knew how good he was. Knew intrinsically how perfect he was for Ramsey. It was why he'd been so pissed when Ramsey had run, and Ramsey couldn't even blame him for that.

"I think . . ." Ramsey huffed out a breath. He wanted to be annoyed. He wanted to push all this away, but that was only the fear talking, and he didn't even want to listen to it anymore. It was easier than anything he'd ever done to dismiss it. "I think it's going to be good. Living here, with you."

"Yeah?" The smugness wasn't only in his eyes now, it was in his smile, but Ramsey couldn't even be mad about it, because he was *right*.

"You did better than I could," Ramsey admitted. It had been a little scary calling off Barty and the trade possibility to the Leafs, because on the other side had been this enormous gaping unknown. He'd never been in a relationship before. He hadn't even known what *that* looked like, nevermind a relationship like the one he'd be building with Nate.

But Nate had known that, had taken his hand, and had said, *here, let me show you*.

Turned out it didn't just have form and shape, but all the possibilities spinning out, beginning to fill in the space, they were *beautiful*.

Ramsey pushed off the counter and tucked himself into Nate's embrace. "I'm gonna remember that," Nate murmured into the top of his head. "How about alongside, *you were right*."

Ramsey choked out a laugh, suddenly, unexpectedly emotional. "What about *I love you?*"

Pulling back, Nate cupped a palm around Ramsey's cheek. "Always."

Ramsey leaned in, ready to kiss his boyfriend—the guy he was going to be building this new life with—but Nate suddenly jerked away.

"Shit, I almost forgot," he said and dug into his pocket, bringing out a small velvet pouch. "I got this for you. For well . . .because of what happened to the other one."

Ramsey would deny it until the end of time, but his fingers were trembling as he opened it up and tipped the contents out onto his hand.

He'd known it wasn't a ring, and he was glad—not because he wasn't interested in that kind of commitment, but because, *God*, maybe he *would* be interested in that kind of commitment—and it would have been insane to get engaged before they'd even lived a part of this life they were going to build together.

A long chain coiled up on his palm, twinkling under the kitchen lights. Ramsey swallowed hard. "You replaced it."

"Jordan kept making noise that he was going to, but . . ." Nate shrugged, cheeks flushing. "But I'm enough of a caveman that I don't want to see another guy buy you jewelry. Not something like this. Something you'll wear every day."

"It's beautiful." It was. No question.

And Ramsey knew, also, without a single doubt, that every diamond sparkling on the chain was real.

Unlike the one he'd given up, easy as breathing, to save Jordan's skin.

He should've told Nate, long ago probably, but there were some things that were so ingrained, that he'd held close to his chest for so long, that he didn't know how to admit them. He'd worried too, that Nate would think that somehow his whole persona was like the necklace—a fake front that couldn't be trusted.

But Nate wouldn't think that now. Ramsey knew that. Ramsey *trusted* him to never think that.

"So, funny story," Ramsey said, "I got that chain a long time ago. In the OHL, before I went to Portland. And well, I didn't have a lot of money back then. Not like now."

Comprehension was dawning on Nate's face, and it shouldn't have been funny, but it kind of was.

"It wasn't real," Ramsey finally admitted. "They weren't real diamonds."

Nate didn't look mad though, he just looked amused. "And you gave it to that guy and he had no idea that they were what, cubic zirconia?"

"Lab grown I think, actually?" Ramsey laughed, now, feeling the looseness of letting his last secret go. Nobody else had to know. But *Nate* knew, and that meant something.

Actually, it meant *everything*.

"Well," Nate said softly, reaching out and squeezing the hand that held the chain, "I'm glad you gave it away, then. So I could replace it."

"You didn't have to—"

"I know, but I'm so fucking happy I did. Because you're . . ." He huffed, like he was still a little embarrassed at the sentimentality he was exposing. But Ramsey loved it. "You deserve the real thing. You *are* the real thing."

Ramsey had to kiss him about that. Long and sweet and a promise, for the future.

When they finally broke apart, Ramsey fumbling with suddenly thick fingers at the clasp, Nate stopped him, touch soft on his arm.

"There's a . . .uh . . . an engraving too." Nate rubbed the back of his neck, still flushed pink. "Your number, on the clasp."

Ramsey found it immediately, thumb rubbing over the numbers. They were incised deep into the metal, and Ramsey liked that he could feel them so clearly. This was who he was. An intrinsic part of him, and Nate had always seen that.

"I was going to put my number, right alongside yours, but that felt presumptuous."

He couldn't help it anymore. Ramsey laughed out loud, the sound startled out of him. "That was presumptuous? You bought us a house. Picked it out and everything."

Nate shrugged, blush creeping down from his cheeks to his neck. "The necklace is yours. It was yours before I ever showed up. It's for you. I didn't want to shove myself in where I didn't belong."

The thing was, Ramsey had begun to realize that Nate *did* belong. To him, anyway.

"What if I make space first?" Ramsey questioned.

Because he *did* want Nate around his neck, forever. The two of them, intertwined every single day for the rest of their lives.

Nate smiled down at him. "Well, it's a good thing I left room for it, then."

And Ramsey had known, had kind of *always* known, in fact, that Nate was perfect for him, but he'd never imagined that his jagged pieces would fit so well with someone else, but there was no question that they did.

"That's perfect. *You're* perfect," Ramsey said and kissed him.

# EPILOGUE

"Is this the kind of shit we're gonna be doing now?" Jordan asked as they sat in the stands, waiting for the game to start.

Nate still thought it was pretty weird that hockey players not only played multiple games a week, but also played on weeknights as a matter of course, not just once or twice a year.

But even if it was weird, Nate was still grateful because it meant that he'd been able to drive down to Buffalo tonight and watch Ramsey make his season debut for the Wolves.

"You don't like it?" Nate asked. He knew Jordan didn't watch hockey. Of course, *he* hadn't watched hockey before Ramsey had come into his life.

When he'd told Jordan this morning that he was going to the game tonight, to Nate's surprise, Jordan had invited himself along.

"Hockey's decent, I guess, but Ramsey . . .*well,* he kinda rules, you know?" Jordan said, a telltale flush on his cheeks that told Nate that his boyfriend had won over another fan for life.

He couldn't even be annoyed about it, because Ramsey *was* amazing, and he deserved everybody adoring him the way Nate adored him.

"Yeah, he does," Nate agreed dryly.

Jordan flushed even brighter red. "It's not . . .he's just . . .well, *you* know."

Oh, did he ever. He just reached over and patted Jordan on his knee, putting him out of his misery. "I get it."

Jordan laughed self-consciously. "Of course you do. I just didn't think I *did*, but that new therapist Aidan hooked me up with? We've been talking about why I wanted to spend all that time in strip clubs, with women, and I guess." He shrugged. "It wasn't about the women at all. More like, what was I *supposed* to like? What was I *supposed* to do?"

"That's good work, Jordo," Nate said supportively. "You're gonna figure your shit out, I know it."

Next to him, Jordan relaxed a fraction. "Yeah. Yeah. I think so."

"Just don't figure it out with my boyfriend, okay?" Nate chuckled dryly. Not that he imagined Ramsey would ever do that, or that even Jordan would. It was just a crush, and an understandable one, because Ramsey shone even brighter than the diamonds he always wore.

"Oh God," Jordan said, covering his eyes and groaning. "Is it that obvious?"

Nate just laughed. "Yeah, but it's cute too."

On cue, the lights dimmed, bass pounded and the Wolves streamed onto the ice.

Ramsey had told him he liked to head up the back of the line, and sure enough, Nate spotted him immediately, the *43* unmistakable on the back of his jersey.

But then, Nate would've known him even without his name and number.

"You nervous at all?" Jordan asked him as warmups continued and he found himself growing silent, tracking every one of Ramsey's movements with his eyes. He *seemed* fine. He'd cleared every protocol. He was *ready*. More than ready, if he was going to believe his boyfriend.

When Nate had expressed even the barest hint of concern that he was rushing back, that he was taking things too fast, and that maybe he should have gone to a rehab assignment in the AHL, Ramsey had shot him a very firm look and told him that he wasn't going to be babied. Not by someone who went out and tackled people for a living.

Nate had shut up then, because Ramsey was right.

They both took risks with their jobs, every single day. But no matter what happened, they'd be coming home to each other.

"No," Nate said, though he still was, a little. He'd shake it off, though, same as Ramsey would shake off the last of the rust when he skated his first shift.

"Yeah, okay," Jordan said wryly, and yeah, okay, maybe he hadn't been *that* subtle about it.

"That why you wanted to come with me tonight?" Nate asked. "Worried about me?"

Jordan looked like he wanted to crawl under the seat, but he still kept his chin up and answered, which Nate gave him a lot of credit for. It was hard to become a better version of yourself. "Wanna be a good friend, like you guys were to me. I was . . .I wasn't a good teammate *or* a good friend. And you were to me. *So.* Trying to change that."

He looked embarrassed still, like talking about his feelings meant he was less of a man or less of a football player, but Nate hoped if he spent more time around their group and also more time in therapy, he'd realize that emotional IQ didn't make him any less.

"I'm sure your therapist told you this but intention is everything, man. And you're getting your head screwed on right."

Jordan's smile was small but real.

"Yeah. She did. But really, you're not worried about Ramsey, though? He's got this. He's worked so hard. He's ready."

Nate did not roll his eyes at Jordan's enthusiasm for Ramsey, but he felt a fondness surge at it, anyway. "No. You're right. He's got this."

And it turned out that he did.

There wasn't even rust to shake off. Ramsey took his first shift the way he did everything in life—he embraced it fully, Nate watching with his heart in his throat as he vaulted over the boards, immediately taking the puck away and leading his team into their offensive zone.

When he got the main assist on the game-winning goal, Nate might've shouted himself a little hoarse. He didn't miss how Ramsey turned in his direction as he headed towards the locker room, sending him a huge smile.

"See?" Jordan said, turning to him. "Told you he had this."

"You wanna come down to the locker room with me?" Nate asked.

But Jordan shook his head. "Nah, Big Dog. He doesn't want to see me. He just wants to see you."

"You sure?" Nate said, standing up and slipping his phone into his pocket. He may or may not have sent Ramsey a whole string of texts during the game. Ramsey's had gotten better over the last two months, and he hoped that his were going to be same.

"Yeah," Jordan said, nodding. "I'll meet you in the main concourse."

Ramsey was heading off on a road trip tonight, leaving right after the game, which did kind of suck, but Nate told himself that this was what he'd signed up for. What he wanted. And he still wanted it. More than ever.

"Alright. I won't be long," Nate said, tapping him on the shoulder.

As he took the tunnels down to the locker room, he scrolled through the texts he'd sent—and he was pretty sure none of them would be *that* embarrassing.

Maybe he wouldn't ever be an expert at the game, but he could watch it and understand it pretty well.

Enough to know, for sure, that Ramsey had played great. The score sheet said so, of course, but that was one of Ramsey's pet peeves—everyone judging players, *especially* defensemen—against what the score sheet showed.

"Even plus minus is bullshit," Ramsey had claimed with a dramatic eye roll. "It doesn't say anything about how *you* played, more like your line mates played."

Still, Nate was pleased to see Ramsey's plus minus had been a plus two. He'd be able to tease him about being smug about a statistic he claimed didn't even matter.

The security guard at the locker room door clocked him immediately from the handful of times he'd been here with Ramsey after he'd rejoined the team. "Bishop," he said, giving him a nod.

"Thanks," Nate said as he pulled the door open for him.

It was like every other locker room he'd ever been in, but not, at the same time.

The music was blaring, and guys were shucking off equipment, tossing it into various bins in the center of the room.

Ramsey was on the far side, head bent down, blond curls sweaty and disheveled as he untied his skates.

One of Ramsey's teammates yelled his name, and he glanced up.

Their eyes met across the room. So much like they had, the first night they'd met, and just like then, it was like they recognized each other. Some part of Nate reaching out and seeing a part of Ramsey that he just *knew*.

As good as it had been then, though, it was so much fucking better now. Now, he knew Ramsey, in and out, knew all the extraordinary bits he tucked away, all the secrets that nobody else knew. At one time they'd all belonged to Ramsey. Nate wasn't stupid enough to think they belonged to *him* now, but he did believe, without a single doubt, that Ramsey shared them willingly.

He chucked his second skate off and a moment later, he was across the room, and without a single shred of hesitation, was in Nate's arms. Kissing him. Laughing with him, unguarded in a way that Nate would've never dreamed of, six months ago.

"You fucking sap," Ramsey teased as he pulled back, blue eyes shining. "You texted me the *whole* game."

"Couldn't stop myself," Nate said, and truly that was representative of a *lot* of things with Ramsey. He'd worried about that, once upon a time, but now he just embraced it. Knew that no matter what, Ramsey would have his back. And his side. And *definitely* his front.

"Love that," Ramsey said, his smile going a bit shy. "Love *you*. You wanna meet my teammates?"

Nate's hand slipped down from his waist to his hand. Squeezed it. "I'm all yours," he said.

-

The fourth and final book of this season of the Toronto Thunder is coming in June! Preorder Lane and Trevor's stepbrother, bi-awakening romance here.

-

Don't miss the bonus scene – where Ramsey returns Nate's romantic gesture with one of his own.

-

The second half of the Toronto Thunders series will be coming out starting in early 2027. Characters you can expect to see in books five through eight include: Wes, Mo, Jordan, and Shane (Cam's dad!). Many more details to come! To not miss a single reveal, sign up for my newsletter here.

INTERESTED IN READING MORE OF
BETH'S BOOKS?


CHECK OUT A FULL LIST OF TILES
BY SCANNING THE QR CODE
OR VISITING HER WEBSITE

WWW.BETHBOLDEN.COM/BOOKLIST

WANT TO FOLLOW BETH?

MAKE SURE YOU NEVER
MISS A RELEASE?

SCAN THE QR CODE BELOW
OR VISIT HER WEBSITE
FOR A SOCIAL MEDIA LIST,
NEWSLETTER SIGNUP,
AND SO MUCH MORE!

WWW.BETHBOLDEN.COM/ABOUT